DEATH CALLED
TO THE BAR

Other titles in the series

DEATH CALLED TO THE BAR

A Murder Mystery featuring
Lord Francis Powerscourt

DAVID DICKINSON

CARROLL & GRAF PUBLISHERS
New York

Carroll & Graf Publishers
An imprint of Avalon Publishing Group, Inc.
245 W. 17th Street
11th Floor
New York
NY 10011-5300
www.carrollandgraf.com

First Carroll & Graf edition 2005

First published in the UK by Constable,
an imprint of Constable & Robinson Ltd 2005

ISBN-13: 978-0-78671-696-8
ISBN-10: 0-7867-1696-7

Printed and bound in the EU

For Gay and Charlie

1

There was a tremendous crash right up against the wall. One carriage, maybe two, had turned on its side and fallen to the ground. Horses were screaming in pain as they too were pulled down by the harness to street level. Then came the swearing. Lord Francis Powerscourt did not think it would be possible for one man's voice to penetrate through the thick walls of Chelsea Old Church, but it was. The words the coachman was speaking were not suitable for any morning of the week, let alone a morning of such importance in the Powerscourt family calendar. And here was worse. A different voice, presumably that of the other coachman, rang out in the midday air in language that was if anything even riper than the cursing of the first fellow. Powerscourt realized that he would not be able to give precise meanings to many of these words. They were new to him. He looked down at his two children, hoping they would not ask him what the words meant afterwards. He looked round at the congregation and saw one or two of the men smiling quietly to themselves and one or two of the maiden aunts covering their ears with their hands, scandalized expressions on their faces. The fog had claimed another victim, one more road accident to add to all the others earlier that day. All morning it had swirled round London, filling in the gaps between the people and the buildings, enveloping them in its clammy embrace. There had been accidents like the one outside the church all over the capital. In the West End the omnibuses had given up the unequal struggle and waited in their depots for the air to clear. On the Thames and in the docks the captains steered their boats very slowly, making frequent use of their hooters and sirens to warn oncoming traffic of their passage. The noises echoed round the city like trumpet notes, reports and instructions to soldiers in battles fought far away.

Still the shouting went on. The canon of the church, who had at first been overwhelmed by the racket outside his walls, suddenly inserted another hymn into the service.

'Hymn three hundred and sixty-five,' he said in his loudest voice, sending a meaningful glance to his organist to take note of the change in plan. 'The Old Hundredth. All people that on earth do dwell.' There were five verses of that, the canon thought to himself; with any luck the noise outside would have finished by the end.

'The Lord ye know is God indeed,
Without our aid he did us make. . .'

Lord Francis Powerscourt was an investigator. He had made his reputation in Army Intelligence in India and consolidated it by solving a number of murders in England. He was a little short of six feet tall with unruly black curls and bright blue eyes that inspected the world with detachment and irony.

Powerscourt turned round for another surreptitious inspection of the congregation. He had already conducted his own audit of those present. Anything less than fifty of his wife Lady Lucy's relations on parade and her family would regard the event as a catastrophic failure. Seventy-five might be regarded as a break-even point, a pretty poor show really, but not a total disgrace to the family name. Score a century and the event could be described in future histories of Lady Lucy's tribe as a modest success. A hundred and thirty-one, which was Powerscourt's estimate of the turn-out today, would be a matter for mild congratulation. A hundred and fifty, mind you, would have been better. The hymn was drawing to a close.

'From men and from the angel host
Be praise and glory evermore.'

It was with something of a shock that Powerscourt realized as the canon was leading them back past the congregation towards the font near the entrance to the church that his numbers were wrong. Not a hundred and thirty-one at all, but a hundred and thirty-three. He had momentarily forgotten why they had all braved the fog this February morning. For they were all there for the christening of the two newest additions to the tribe, the twins, his twins, the latest and

2

youngest members of the Powerscourt family. Lady Lucy had given birth before Christmas, and, as Powerscourt said to himself, if her own children, however tiny, weren't to be counted as members of the tribe, then who the hell was?

Just over a mile away, the fog, distributing its favours equally across various sectors of the city, had nearly made Queen's Inn disappear. It was right on the River Thames between Westminster and the City of London – both as rich in legal pickings over the centuries as they were now – and the water seemed to give the swirling white-grey mist an extra depth. A determined student of architecture might have been able to discern a handsome set of eighteenth-century buildings with tall sash windows, and, presumably, grass growing in the courtyards, though any such growth would have been hard to spot unless you were virtually on top of it.

Queen's Inn was the smallest and youngest of London's Inns of Court, training ground and stomping ground for the city's barristers and High Court judges and Masters of the Rolls. It did not have the fabulous history of the Inner and Middle Temple with Knights Templar adorning their pedigree way back in the mists of legal history. Nor did it have the splendour of the Temple Gardens, frequently celebrated in verse, truly one of the most delightful places in London on a summer's day with the grass and the flowers running down to the Thames. Queen's could almost match the austere elegance of Lincoln's Inn's New Square or the gardens of Gray's Inn. It did not claim superiority over the other four Inns. It just claimed to be slightly different. Slightly more worldly, with close links to some of the richer and grander colleges of Oxford and Cambridge. Slightly richer than the others through a complicated system of internal finance. Slightly more likely to tolerate eccentrics, Queen's people would say, proud of the strange dress and sometimes stranger methods of transport adopted by some of its more flamboyant barristers.

And on this day Queen's Inn was preparing for a feast. A feast in memory of one of its more distinguished sons, one Theophilus Grattan Whitelock, one-time bencher, or senior member, of Queen's a man twice passed over for the post of Lord Chancellor, a distinguished judge who sentenced so many people to be transported to the colonies that the cynics said he should have a ship on the route named after him. HMS *Whitelock*, direct to Botany Bay. He had been

3

born, the man Whitelock, on this day, 28th February, so he missed a leap year birthday by a single day. The feast he endowed in his memory took place on this day, irrespective of which day of the week the 28th happened to fall on. Whitelock had consulted three expert legal draftsmen before finalizing the clause which stipulated that if, at any point in the future, carping clergymen or interfering bishops should prevent his feast taking place on the Sabbath, then the bequest would be cancelled in perpetuity. So generous was the bequest and so splendid the food and wine the Inn was able to provide that the members of Queen's Inn would have defied the Archbishop of Canterbury or the Cardinal Archbishop of Westminster, or both, if they dared to protest.

Even as early as midday the preparations were well under way. Queen's had been blessed for many years with a Senior Steward known to all and sundry as Joseph. Few, if any, knew his surname. Some of the younger students claimed Joseph himself had forgotten it. But he had a genius for efficient organization and over the years had developed a remarkable system of alliances and understandings with some of London's finest grocers and butchers and wine merchants so that he could always command the best at very modest prices. Cynics, and what community of lawyers does not have a good supply of those, claimed that the whole edifice was based on back-handers and would, one day, collapse to general disgrace and a long prison sentence for Joseph. Or, the most cynical would add at this point, transportation for him in memory of Theophilus Grattan Whitelock. One more for Botany Bay. Direct.

Where on earth did this lot come from, Joseph said to himself, as he inspected his waiters for the day in the Great Hall. The Inn's normal complement was insufficient for the numbers and complexity of the feast. Recruitment of these worthies was not his responsibility, but that of the Head Porter, a man with whom Joseph did not share the most cordial of relations. Desperately he tried to remember how he might have offended the Head Porter. It came to him in a flash. Three nights before there had been a drinks party for the benchers, an elaborate occasion graced with some of the finest wines of the Queen's cellars. Custom and practice dictated that two or three bottles from this occasion should have found their way to the Head Porter's cupboard. Joseph had genuinely forgotten. So here was the Head Porter's revenge. Four boys who looked as though they were sixteen or so, an age which found it, as Joseph knew only too well, extraordinarily difficult to stand still for more than two minutes at

4

a time. Four old men, hovering, Joseph thought, somewhere between sixty and seventy. They might have been waiting at table long before the Congress of Berlin, but they would need regular and repeated trips to the lavatories to see them through the evening. One of the old men, Joseph noticed to his horror, seemed to be nodding off on his feet, asleep where he stood. If he could do that in the middle of the day, what in God's name, would the greybeard be like in the closing stages of the feast way after ten or even eleven o'clock in the evening? Comatose in the buttery? Passed out, maybe even passed on, in the pantry?

Good generals know how much depends on their relations with their troops. Joseph would have liked to shout at this ludicrous collection of humanity but he knew it wouldn't work. Charm, kindness, that's what's needed here, he said to himself, I've only got to keep them on their toes for ten hours or so.

'Good morning, gentlemen,' Joseph addressed his little army, his perfect teeth gleaming at the heart of his smile. 'Tell me this, have you all waited at table for a feast like this one before?'

There was a general chorus of affirmatives.

'You,' said Joseph, pointing dramatically to his eldest recruit, 'you are serving vegetables that accompany the main course. Which side do you serve from?'

A pair of sleepy eyes gazed at Joseph, as if reproaching him for daring to ask such a question. 'The left, sir.'

'Excellent,' said Joseph, flashing a smile at Metheselah, 'and you, young sir,' he pointed to a youth with huge sad eyes and curly hair, 'which wine would we serve with the fish course, Chablis or Châteauneuf-du-Pape?'

'Chablis, sir,' said the youth, and for a brief second his eyes looked happy before returning to sad.

'Very good,' said Joseph. 'I can see we are all going to get along fine. If you suddenly find that you have forgotten something about the distinguished art of waiting, just ask me and I will tell you the answer. Now, let me tell you the programme for the rest of the afternoon. All around you you can see these canteens of cutlery, with two large cloths and a bottle of polish beside them. That is the first task for you, to polish these knives and forks and spoons until you could shave in them. Then we will do the same for the glasses, the two wine glasses and the glass for the liqueur or port. Then we lay the table, under my supervision. Then we all have a rest before the final briefing after supper. Let us show honour today and this evening to the memory of Theophilus Whitelock, gentlemen. He may not have mentioned us waiters in his bequest, but without us it could not be fulfilled.'

There were nine of them gathered round the font, the cold water very calm inside the marble. The boy twin had two godfathers, Powerscourt's particular friend and companion in arms, Johnny Fitzgerald, and his brother-in-law, William Burke the financier. Burke had recently astonished the family by pulling off the roof of his enormous villa in Antibes and adding a further two storeys to the property. Powerscourt had inquired if he intended accommodating the entire family under this roof at the same time. Powerscourt's eldest sister was godmother to the male and various members of Lady Lucy's tribe did duty for the girl. The canon held his prayer book well away from his face as he read the Exhortation, as if he was losing his sight.

'Doubt ye not, therefore, but earnestly believe that Christ will likewise favourably receive these present infants; that he will embrace them with the arms of his mercy; that he will give unto them the blessing of eternal life, and make them partakers of his everlasting kingdom.'

Powerscourt looked down at the tiny bundle in his arms. The little boy was fast asleep with a blond curl lying on the top of his head. His elder brother and sister had been most eager to attend this part of the service and had been bitterly disappointed when told it was impossible. In vain had they said they had every right to be there. Olivia, the younger child, had pointed out that she already had more practice in holding the two babies than her father and that she would, obviously, be closer to the ground to catch her infant brother or sister if their father or the vicar dropped them. Thomas, the elder, had announced that it was sure to bring bad luck on all of them if he and his sister were not allowed to attend the christening. Lady Lucy had to resort to bribery to buy them off in the end.

Now the canon was conducting the interrogation of the godparents.

'Do you, in the name of these children, renounce the devil and all his works, the vain pomp and glory of the world, with all covetous desires of the same, and the carnal desires of the flesh, so that you will not follow nor be led by them?'

There was a general murmuring of 'I renounce them all.' Powerscourt thought Johnny Fitzgerald and William Burke were not too emphatic on that one. Burke was not an avaricious fellow but he did make his living out of the covetous desires for money of his fellow men. Powerscourt felt Lucy's foot tapping lightly on his shin. She nodded to the pew behind him which had been empty as they came down the aisle. Kneeling happily on it, their faces wreathed in smiles, Thomas and Olivia had left their place to find the closest spot to the action they could find. Powerscourt grinned at them and made a further inspection of his infant.

Then the preliminaries were over. Very gently the canon leant over and took Powerscourt's bundle from him. Powerscourt felt a sudden, irrational spurt of alarm when he remembered how far away the prayer book had been. Would Olivia's worst fears be recognized as the canon dropped his charge on the hard floor? Looking slowly round the assembled godparents the canon said, 'Name this child.'

'Christopher John Wingfield Powerscourt,' they chorused. Very gently and very slowly the canon dipped the head into the font. A mighty wail of protest followed. Powerscourt wondered if the child would be able to make more noise later in life than the two coachmen outside.

'Christopher John Wingfield Powerscourt, I baptize thee in the name of the Father and the Son and the Holy Ghost.'

The wailing bundle was handed back to the earthly father. Then it was the turn of the other twin. Elizabeth Juliet Macleod was added to the Powerscourt family in total silence. Powerscourt could hear Olivia whispering to Thomas that girls were much braver than boys as her sister hadn't made a single squawk during the ordeal.

Six weeks or so after the end of one of Powerscourt's cases the year before, a dramatic and dangerous affair in a West Country cathedral, he had taken Lady Lucy to St Petersburg. It was there, in their beautiful hotel bedroom overlooking the Nevsky Prospekt, that Lucy believed the twins had been conceived. She was absolutely certain of it. Johnny Fitzgerald had suggested calling them Nicholas and Alexandra after the Tsar and his wife but Powerscourt had demurred, pointing out that at some point in the future Britain might be at war with Russia and two children wandering about the country lumbered with the Christian names of the Russian royal house might not be a good idea.

By the end of the first course of the Whitelock Feast Joseph, the steward of Queen's Inn, was reasonably pleased with the evening so far. The Hall looked magnificent. The candles were glittering in their places on the tables and the walls. The portraits of the great lawyers of the past looked down on their successors. Along the bulk of the great room were trestle tables of oak, supposed to be as old as the foundation itself. On the raised area at the north end was the High Table reserved for the benchers of the Inn. On the walls behind them two full-length Gainsboroughs of previous Lord Chancellors, sombre and forbidding in their dark robes, presided over the proceedings. And above them hung one of the treasures of the Inn, Rubens' *The Judgement of Paris*, where a bucolic-looking Paris, son of the King of Troy, held up a ruddy apple in front of three scantily clad goddesses. So popular was this painting with the citizens of the capital, its great appeal possibly residing in the nakedness of the ladies, that the Hall was opened to the public once a week during term-time so the pilgrims could pay tribute in person. American visitors sometimes expressed surprise that it was not a courtroom scene they were seeing, with learned friends appearing before some frosty judge, but they seemed to recover quite quickly. A plaque beneath it announced that the painting was paid for by the generosity of past and current benchers and benefactors.

The first course had been a terrine, a rather intricate terrine principally composed of glazed cured salmon and Beaufort cheese. That had been easy for Joseph's motley army of waiters to serve. The more active service of bringing the plates with the food already in place from the kitchen to the Hall was shared between his regular forces and the young auxiliaries. Joseph had been more impressed by the old than the young. They shuffled about their tasks very slowly but they didn't speak too loudly or nearly drop the plates like the young.

It was the soup that really worried Joseph. It was one of the new chef's special favourites which he claimed to have devised for the members of the Imperial Family in St Petersburg, Borscht Romanov, a beetroot-based broth laced with herbs and a Russian vodka whose name even the chef could not pronounce and lashings of sour cream. Joseph watched with dread as his waiters began the long march with a soup bowl in each hand from the kitchens, over a wet floor, into the Hall and onwards for what was, at its longest, a journey of over a hundred and fifty yards. One hundred and sixty-two guests, eighty-one voyages of the Borscht Romanov. One man tripped in the kitchen and had to be removed from duty altogether as he had pink stains right down his shirt front. Two of Joseph's young men had watched the regular waiters and imitated them, gliding rather than walking with the elbows tucked in tight to the body. The other two held the bowls too far away and were in permanent danger of tipping forward.

Disaster struck the feast shortly after eight thirty, but it didn't come from the waiters. Just as Joseph was congratulating himself on the safe arrival of the soup, he glanced up towards High Table. The benchers were arranged in order of seniority, radiating outwards on either side of the Treasurer in the centre, the top official of the Inn. At the edge, in the most junior position, sat one Alexander McKendrick Dauntsey, KC, right in front of one of Gainsborough's Lord Chancellors. Dauntsey, to Joseph's experienced eye, looked like a man who might have been drinking heavily before the feast. He was perspiring freely and his face was turning grey rather than white. Joseph watched as he took three mouthfuls of his soup, and then, very suddenly, and very violently, pitched forward on to the table, his bowl of soup tipping forward in a pink stream across the white tablecloth and on to the floor. There was a crack as Dauntsey's face hit the wood and a trickle of blood ran from his chin to join the beetroot broth, Borscht Sanguinaire rather than Borscht Romanov. The mixture of blood and borscht continued to drip slowly on to the floor, a pinkish red that looked like watered blood. After a couple of minutes the Hall had fallen completely quiet, only for the silence to be broken by the Treasurer in what seemed to be a very loud voice.

'He's drunk. Bloody fool! Leave him there. He'll come round in a moment. Carry on.'

Two of Joseph's waiters were on hand with mops and cloths to clear up the mess. Joseph indicated with pouring signals that all the glasses were to be topped up to help restore the mood. Soon the noise levels were back to normal and the soup was being cleared away. As the feast progressed through roast venison with juniper, tiramisu with dark and white chocolate sauce, accompanied by Châteauneuf-du-Pape, Domaine du Vieux Télégraphe, Joseph became increasingly worried about Dauntsey. He made no move of any kind. Everybody else in the Hall was growing redder or pinker by the hour. Dauntsey's face had turned a sort of chalky white. Nobody took any notice of him at all, as though collapsed drunks or worse were a regular feature of the Whitelock Feast. Joseph knew how much store the Treasurer set by tradition, how he would hate to disturb the glittering occasion. This particular feast after all, the finest one in the Queen's Inn calendar, was his favourite.

Yet Joseph too had as much loyalty to the Inn as the Treasurer or anybody else present. Perhaps it was because he had come to London from Italy looking for work over thirty years before and had found a job as a temporary waiter at the Inn. Now, of course, he was a permanent fixture, who had watched many of the silks progress from nervous lisping students to giants of the Old Bailey and the Royal Courts of Justice. He knew how damaging it could be to the Inn's reputation if word flew round the gossip-ridden world of London's barristers that the people of Queen's had been eating reindeer and drinking some of the finest burgundy in the capital while one of their number had collapsed into his soup and been left to rot by his peers as they carried on with their feast. Joseph knew that if he consulted the Treasurer, then the other benchers would all have to give their views. That was what it was like working in a place full of lawyers. Every last one of them had to have their say. Invisible judges and imaginary juries were ever present in the deliberations of Queen's Inn. Nothing could have been guaranteed to destroy the atmosphere faster. But, Joseph reasoned, if Dauntsey was simply removed, as if he were an empty dish of potatoes or vegetables, so to speak, it would attract much less attention. It was only that Dauntsey was considerably larger than the Inn's best serving dishes. Joseph took the four strongest men in his command into a little alcove between the Hall and the kitchens.

'Listen very carefully,' he said. 'We're going to move Mr Dauntsey. He's the gentleman who has fallen into his soup at the top table. I want to stick to the usual channels we've been using this evening. So I want you two,' he pointed to two of his regulars, 'to go up behind the top table, as if you were going to serve the benchers, and I want you two,' he nodded to a couple of his young recruits for the evening here, 'to go round the back of the right-hand bench, as you have been doing all evening, and reach Mr Dauntsey that way. Don't rush but don't stop until you have got him into the library. I shall hold the door at the back of the benchers' table open for you. Good luck.'

Joseph led his pincer movement up the Hall. He suspected that his waiters were more or less invisible to the barristers by now. Benchers, for some strange reason, sit on chairs at the Whitelock Feast. It was stipulated in the original bequest. Joseph's plan was that they should simply lift the chair and Dauntsey all in one movement and take him out. It went without a hitch. Nobody asked what they were doing. Nobody challenged them at all. The

Treasurer, in charge at his top table, did not even look sideways as his colleague was swiftly and silently removed. It was as if the waters had closed over a sinking ship. The surface of the ocean returned to normal.

It was only when they had dumped their passenger on a sofa in the library that one of the young men bent down to listen to the KC's breathing. He looked very pale as he stood up.

'Mr Joseph, sir,' he stammered, 'I think the gentleman's dead.'

'Nonsense,' said one of the regular waiters, 'he can't be dead.'

'He bloody well is,' said the young man, 'you see if you can hear him breathing. Look at the colour of him, for God's sake. It's a bloody corpse that we've just carried in, God help us all.'

Joseph bent down and listened for a breath. There was nothing. Joseph had coped with many crises in his time, drunken students, penniless barristers, people who refused to pay their bills, organizing lunch for a temperamental Balkan prince who was rumoured to shoot the staff if the food didn't agree with him, but not death. Not death on the 28th of February on a day still afflicted with fog, not death at a feast, not death served with borscht and sour cream and the unpronounceable Russian vodka. He knew he should return to his post.

'Johnston,' he chose one of his regulars who knew his way about, 'would you please go to the Head Porter and tell him what has happened. He's served in the military so he may know more than we do as to whether Mr Dauntsey is alive or not. Tell him we think we need a doctor, and if he agrees, then could he please send you to fetch one. Tell him that I don't propose to tell the Treasurer anything yet but that I would welcome his advice.'

Johnston ran off towards the porter's lodge. Tragedy seemed to have brought about a temporary truce in relations between the steward's office and the porter's lodge. Back to the Hall went Joseph and his colleagues. It was time to serve the cheese.

Dr James Chamberlain was in the endgame of a chess match with his brother when the summons came. The timing, perhaps, was good for him. His King was trapped in a corner, he had only a castle and a solitary pawn left under his command. The enemy forces bearing down on him consisted of a Queen, a castle and a knight with an ample draft of pawns if they were required. The doctor reckoned he had only a few moves left before defeat, a loss that would put his brother in the lead by sixty-eight to fifty-nine in this marathon match that had now lasted over two years.

'Sorry to deny you your victory.' He smiled at his brother John and departed into the night for Queen's Inn and the recumbent person of Alexander Dauntsey.

Roland Haydon, the Head Porter, solemnly escorted the doctor to the library. It took him less than a minute to give his diagnosis.

'Mr Dauntsey is dead, I'm afraid. The Treasurer will have to be informed at once. And the next of kin, of course. Do you know who his regular doctor was, Haydon?'

'I'm afraid I do not, sir. Mr Dauntsey had chambers here, of course, but his home was in Kent. Maybe his regular doctor was down there, sir.'

The doctor bent down again and looked very closely at Dauntsey's face. He was still looking at it when Barton Somerville, the Treasurer, was shown in, protesting loudly that Dauntsey couldn't possibly be dead, why, he had seen him only a couple of hours before.

'Are you sure, Dr Chamberlain? I think he just had a bit too much to drink, that's all. He'll be much better in the morning, what?'

Dr Chamberlain looked at his watch. He didn't care for a late evening spent disputing a death with a collection of drunken lawyers.

'I'm afraid there can be absolutely no doubt about it, Mr Somerville.' The doctor was not to know it, but Barton Somerville had a special weakness for being addressed as Treasurer, rather than by his name. He had even circulated a note on the subject to his colleagues on taking up his office. 'Mr Dauntsey here has been dead for a couple of hours, I should say.'

Dimly Somerville recalled his own words when the dead man had collapsed. 'He's drunk. Bloody fool! Leave him there. He'll come round in a moment. Carry on.' He thought it unnecessary to mention this to the doctor. He wondered if medical attention then might have saved his life. He wondered briefly if he was liable to a charge of some kind, manslaughter maybe? Criminal negligence? But he thought not.

'There is not much more we can do this evening, Mr Somerville. I suggest you take the poor gentleman to his own rooms and put him on the bed for now. I think you should tell the next of kin. Was there a wife and children down there in Kent?'

The Treasurer nodded sadly. 'Wife, no children.'

'Well, a wire, or a phone call if they are connected. I shall come back in the morning. I shall inform the coroner. And I shall have to bring the police as well.'

'The police? Why do we need the police, for heaven's sake? We're lawyers here, not criminals.'

'It is routine procedure, Mr Somerville, that's all. We have to decide if the death was due to natural causes or not. There may have to be a post-mortem before the inquest.'

'You don't think there was anything unnatural about Dauntsey's death, do you?' said the Treasurer, consumed with anxiety about his own behaviour.

The doctor had decided that he did not care for Mr Barton Somerville. And he thought the man was hiding something, probably about the circumstances of the death.

'It's far too early to say whether your colleague died from natural causes or not,' he said. 'From my brief inspection of the man I shouldn't be at all surprised if there was something unnatural about it, but I could not be sure.'

2

'Poison,' said the pathologist, peering sadly at the human organs that had once been Alexander Dauntsey on the slab in front of him.

'Are you sure?' said the policeman, waiting respectfully some distance away, twirling his hat in his hands.

'Yes, I am,' replied the pathologist, 'but quite what sort of poison it was or how fast it acts upon the human body, I do not yet know. I shall have to send this lot away for further analysis.'

The two men, their faces pale in the antiseptic colours of the mortuary, were very different. James Willoughby, the pathologist, was old and bald and bent. He had only two more years to go before he retired to the little cottage he had already bought in Norfolk. Chief Inspector Jack Beecham had many many years to go before his retirement. He was tall and slim with light curly hair and he looked even younger than his thirty-two years. His superiors in the Metropolitan Police suspected from the start that Dauntsey had been murdered – the doctor had alerted them – and had assigned one of their most intelligent detectives to the case.

Forty minutes later Beecham was shown into the Treasurer's quarters in Queen's Inn. They were on the first floor in Fortune Court, in a glorious room nearly forty feet long, looking out over the Thames with high ceilings and old prints of London adorning the walls. Here you could have seen one of the earliest extant prints of the Temple Church and fine watercolours of the Queen's Inn and its gardens. Barton Somerville was seated at an enormous desk, with a couple of briefs lying at the corner.

'Good morning, constable,' he said, looking with some disdain at the policeman. 'What can I do for you?'

Jack Beecham was well used to people making the wrong

14

assumptions about him. 'I stopped being a constable some years ago, sir,' he said cheerfully. 'I'm Detective Chief Inspector Beecham now. I'm in charge of the case of the late Mr Dauntsey, sir.'

'In charge, are you?' said Somerville incredulously. 'Are you the most senior person they've got?'

'Yes, sir,' said Beecham, trying to remain polite, 'I am. And I'm here to tell you that we believe, or rather the pathologist believes, that we are dealing with a case of murder here.'

With difficulty Somerville resisted the temptation to ask how old the pathologist was. Fifteen? Twenty-one? 'Are you sure it was murder? Are you saying he was poisoned? Do you yet know what sort of poison it was?'

The policeman was beginning to grasp just how difficult this investigation could turn out to be. These lawyers were used to cross-examining policemen in the witness box, trying to undermine their evidence and their credibility. They would not appreciate it when the boot was on the other foot.

'I am not at liberty, sir, to say how the murder was carried out at this stage.'

'Heavens above, young man,' Barton Somerville banged his fist on the table and raised his voice to nearly a shout, 'I am the Treasurer of this Inn. Surely I have the right to know how one of my own benchers died? Surely I have the right to ask for that?'

The policeman had had enough for now. It was time, Jack Beecham thought, for a little salvo back just to let this pompous and self-important man know that he could look after himself.

'The position remains as I outlined it earlier, sir,' he said. Then he paused and looked Somerville straight between the eyes. 'I will tell you more when I can, sir. But for now, I'm afraid, you are a suspect in this case, just like all the other members of your Inn. At the moment I don't see how anybody can expect preferential treatment. And now, with your permission, sir, I and my team would like to begin questioning the people in Mr Dauntsey's chambers and on his staircase.'

With that the policeman picked up his hat and strode from the room. Barton Somerville stared after him in fury. He composed a sulphurous letter of complaint to the Commissioner of Metropolitan Police and had it sent round by one of the porters. He demanded the removal of Detective Chief Inspector Beecham at once. If his request was not granted, he went on, he would be forced to request his barristers to offer the police the minimum co-operation necessary to comply with the law. And, he concluded, he was going to take steps to ensure that the Inn was in a position to conduct its own investigation which would, he felt sure, be more likely to succeed than any inquiry conducted by the infant or cadet branch of the Metropolitan Police. After that he walked north to Gray's Inn to confer with a man he knew who had some expertise about London's private investigators.

Shortly after six thirty that evening a tall man in a very beautiful suit knocked on the front door of the Powerscourt house in Markham Square in Chelsea. Inside he found chaos. There were packing cases everywhere, all along the hallway, in the dining room, stacked high at the bottom of the stairs. Upstairs further noises of departure could be heard, trunks or suitcases being dragged along the floor, small children shouting, a bath being run. The reason for all this confusion and excitement had to do with the two people who knew least about it – the twins. Powerscourt and Lady Lucy had decided that they needed more room with the extra nurses and probably the need for extra bathrooms and bedrooms. It might have looked as if they were moving house but the move was only temporary. Powerscourt had solved the problem of space by buying the house next door, which had come on the market after the sudden and unexpected death of its owner. The family was going to Manchester Square in Marylebone while various alterations were made, alterations which were likely to make more dust than would be good for the twins.

'Powerscourt!' said the man in the beautiful suit, as he saw a rather harassed owner descending the stairs with a small green valise in his hand.

'Pugh, by God! Charles Augustus Pugh!' said Powerscourt, sprinting down the stairs to shake his friend by the hand. In an earlier case involving art fraud an innocent man had been put on trial for his life. Powerscourt and Pugh, with the assistance of some splendid forgeries displayed in court, and the forger himself, had secured his acquittal. Ever since, they had kept in touch with lunches and the occasional dinner at the Pughs' beautiful house by the river.

'I see your crimes have finally caught up with you, Powerscourt,' said Pugh, waving a hand at the packing cases and surrounding confusion. 'Leaving the country before the law comes knocking at the door? I could offer my services free, you know, if they try to deport you.'

'If moving to Marylebone constitutes leaving the country, my friend, then we are indeed in flight. But come upstairs, the drawing room is still free of all this paraphernalia.'

'I'm sure you must be very busy, I could come back another day, or in the morning if that would be convenient. I don't want to get in the way.'

'You're never in the way, Charles, certainly not in a suit as elegant as that.'

As Pugh seated himself on the sofa, Powerscourt organized the drinks and wondered, not for the first time, what the judges and juries made of the Pugh clothes. Would the juries be jealous of a man who could afford such expensive clothes? Would the judges wish that they had such a fine figure to show off the tailors' best? One thing was certain. Both judges and juries would remember Charles Augustus Pugh. Maybe that was the point of it all.

'Had a visitor this afternoon,' Pugh began, 'man by the name of Somerville, Barton Somerville. Can't say I care for the fellow very much. He's the Treasurer – Head Boy, if you like – at Queen's Inn. They had a dramatic death there the other day. Man dropped dead into his soup in the middle of a feast.'

'What sort of soup?' said Powerscourt flippantly.

'Borscht. Beetroot variety, laced with some potent Russian vodka. Possibly laced with something else too, some sort of poison. Post-mortem says Dauntsey – that's the name of the corpse – was poisoned. The point is this, Powerscourt. Somerville has fallen out with the police in a spectacular fashion. Policeman in charge of the inquiry far too young for Somerville, he must want some greybeard with a limp who's about to shuffle off. Anyway, letter of complaint has sped off to the Commissioner and the case is barely a day old. It has to be said, mind you, that Somerville could fall out with the angels inside half an hour of arriving in heaven. Anyway, he comes to see me to ask about you, Francis. Was it true that you were the most accomplished private investigator in London? Were you discreet? Would you respect the privacy and the private lives of his members? And so on. Naturally enough I gave you a very good write-up, Francis. You would have been proud of me.'

With that Charles Augustus Pugh flicked a speck of dust that had had the impertinence to land on the cuff of his jacket to the floor. 'I shall of course be expecting my normal slice of the fee. You could charge for this one in the way we barristers do, Francis, a charge of five hundred guineas for retainers and refreshers at fifty guineas a day. I could do with some new shirts.'

'Did this Somerville inquire about my age, Charles? You can never be too careful.'

'Must have been the only thing he didn't mention,' said Pugh, 'but it's a pound to a penny you're going to get invited into their lair tomorrow and asked to take the case on.'

'I suppose it's one way to get out of the chores of moving,' said Powerscourt ruefully. 'Whole business bores me to tears and the truth is I'm completely useless at it. Lucy knows by instinct where everything ought to go while I wander round like the proverbial lost sheep. But tell me, Charles, you know this world, what is your opinion of Queen's Inn?'

'Queen's?' said Pugh thoughtfully and he stared at the fireplace, temporarily lost for words. 'The surface things are easy. Smallest Inn of Court. Youngest too, only about a hundred and forty years old. Founded in 1761 as a tribute to George the Third's new bride, his Queen a brood mare called Charlotte of Mecklenburg-Strelitz who produced fifteen children for him. Situated right next to the Middle Temple on the river. They think they're special, those people in Queen's, they're arrogant to a man, all of them. I think the best way I can put it, Francis, is that they're like a fashionable cavalry regiment that isn't quite as special or as fashionable as it thinks it is.'

Powerscourt, who had known many cavalry regiments, fashionable and unfashionable, in his time in the Army, smiled. 'And what of the dead man? Did you say his name was Dauntsey?'

'Alexander Dauntsey, he was. About our sort of age, been a KC for about six years, I think, recently elected a bencher – sort of senior prefect – of his Inn. Unusual sort of barrister, he was. On his day he was quite brilliant. He did all sorts of cases, criminal, divorce, Chancery, he could handle the lot. When he was on form he could have got Jack the Ripper off. On a bad day, he was simply hopeless. It made the instructing solicitors rather nervous as they were never sure which Dauntsey they were going to get.'

'Did he have any vices you heard about?' asked Powerscourt. 'Women, gambling, expensive clothes?'

Charles Augustus Pugh laughed. 'There were always whispers about Dauntsey and the women. Nothing you could get your teeth into, but then there never is unless people are foolish enough to land themselves in the divorce courts.'

'Married?' said Powerscourt.

'Yes, he was, very beautiful woman he married too. That was another thing about Dauntsey. He had this enormous house in the country, in Kent I think, hundreds of rooms, ancient deer park with hundreds of bloody deer roaming all over the place. Wonderful art collection.' Pugh paused and smiled to himself briefly. 'Man told me last year that all his relatives thought Dauntsey was mad. He was taking down the Van Dycks and the Rubens and replacing them with those French Impressionist people, water lilies in the garden, strange wiggly lines pretending to be fields or mountains, you know the sort of thing.'

'I'm not sure I like the sound of this case very much,' said Powerscourt thoughtfully. 'I don't mean the man's taste in pictures, he can put whatever he likes on his own walls. It's the thought of all those people who think they're in the fashionable cavalry regiment. I've had enough of those to last me a lifetime. If you were me, Charles, would you take it on? I don't have to.'

'I think,' Pugh replied, 'that it is entirely a matter for yourself. But think about it. If you hadn't become involved in that art forgery case a couple of years ago, Horace Aloysius Buckley, an innocent man, on trial for murder at the Central Criminal Court, would have been hanged by the neck until he was dead.'

There was one small corner, with room for four chairs, left fit for human rather than packing case habitation in the Powerscourt dining room. There was one day left before the removals men came to take them to their temporary home in Manchester Square. As they took their breakfast Lady Lucy looked like a general on the eve of a great engagement. Powerscourt was turning an envelope over and over in his hand. It was a very expensive envelope, the stationery equivalent of one of Charles Augustus Pugh's shirts. He wasn't going to open it yet. He had told Lady Lucy about Pugh's visit and his news the night before.

'For heaven's sake, Francis,' she said, irritated perhaps that while she was being so decisive about the move, the man of the house couldn't even make up his mind whether to open an envelope or not, 'there isn't a bomb in there. It's not going to explode.'

'Sorry, Lucy, sorry,' said Powerscourt, 'it's just that I know what's inside.' With a grimace rather like somebody plunging into a cold bath, he opened his envelope and peered sadly at its contents. 'Pretty pompous,' he said and handed it over to his wife.

'"Dear Lord Powerscourt,"' Lady Lucy read it aloud, '"I write as the Treasurer of Queen's Inn. On 28th February at an Inn feast, Mr Alexander Dauntsey KC, one of our benchers, dropped dead. The post-mortem produced evidence that he had been murdered. I am not satisfied with the personnel, the methods or the attitude of the officers of the Metropolitan Police assigned to investigate this matter. I have written to the Commissioner to convey my most serious reservations. I understand that you are one of the most distinguished private investigators in London and I am writing to ask if you would be able to come and discuss the necessary measures with us. If so, I would be grateful if you could call on me at my chambers at noon today."'

Lady Lucy put the letter back in its envelope. 'I don't think he's very taken with the police, Francis, what do you think?'

'No, he's not. What am I to do, Lucy? I don't want to take this on. I don't like the sound of all these lawyers. And it couldn't have come at a worse time, with the move and everything.'

Privately Lucy thought it couldn't have come at a better time. She was certain she would sort out the move much more quickly and efficiently without Francis hanging around and getting in the way. She thought the case came from providence but she wasn't going to say so.

'You know my views, Francis.' However bad the circumstances, however dangerous the situation, Lady Lucy Powerscourt had never suggested that Francis and Johnny Fitzgerald should abandon an investigation. 'Somebody has killed Mr Dauntsey. That person may kill more people unless you go and find them. Don't worry about the move.' She leant over and covered his hand with her smaller one. 'We'll manage somehow.'

The mood was subdued in the Dauntsey chambers after his death. The young men stopped skylarking on the stairs and having paper fights in the library. The seniors looked grave and conversed with each other in hushed tones about the particular kind of poison that had disposed of their colleague. At the very top of the chambers there was one person who mourned him particularly. Sarah Henderson was their stenographer, secretary and mascot. She was twenty years old, tall and slim with a shock of red hair and bright green eyes. She repulsed all the advances of the Queen's males of whatever age with the same apologetic tone, as if she was greatly flattered to be invited to the theatre, the opera, lunch, dinner, the ballet, but her mind was on other things. The one crucial fact installed in her and all her fellow students at the secretarial college she had attended in Finsbury was that emotional entanglements with people at work were to be avoided like the plague. Nothing, not even bad spelling or mistakes in dictation or arriving at work improperly dressed, was likely to cause such complication or such unhappiness. The lecturer who had warned them of these terrible perils was herself a spinster of over fifty. There was much speculation among the girls that some such error might have wrecked her life, a long affair with a married man who refused to leave his wife perhaps, a lover who ran away and deserted her at the advanced age of twenty-eight.

Sarah had been very fond of Dauntsey. She adored the sound of his voice, quite light, not one to dominate a courtroom by sheer power of delivery, but it had great variety. It danced, she used to say, as she leant back in his chair, feet caressing the desk, and dictated the course of an opening or closing speech. Unlike many of his colleagues, he seemed to find dictating the most natural thing in the world. Sarah knew that he always had one eye on the movement of her pencil, waiting till it stopped before he carried on. He had charm, lots of charm, Sarah thought, remembering how polite he always was and how he took the time and trouble to inquire after her sick mother.

Had Dauntsey or any of the other barristers known how central a role Queen's Inn in general or their chambers in particular played in Mrs Bertha Henderson's life they would have been astonished. Every evening Sarah had worked there she was quizzed on the day's events when she went home. It wasn't intrusive, the questioning, it wasn't rude but it was persistent. Her mother was almost bedridden with arthritis in her early fifties and could only just get around their small house in Acton. She also suffered from a rare form of cancer which meant she might only have two or three years left to live. Queen's Inn had become an alternative world, a world she could escape to in her imagination during the daytime when the external world of London's shops and buses and traffic and movement was closed to her. She could have told you, Mrs Henderson, what prints were on the wall of every room on her daughter's staircase. She could have told you what cases the various gentlemen were currently engaged on. Sarah would bring law journals home so her mother could read about her heroes in print. By now, her

21

daughter suspected, she could have carried out a perfectly respectable prosecution or defence in a simple case in the county court. Queen's had become for her a serial story like the ones they published in such quantities in the women's magazines she read so avidly.

Mrs Henderson had said to Sarah that she would have liked to attend Dauntsey's funeral. But, she went on, she had had a trial run the day after his death was announced to see if she could walk to the end of their road. Just over halfway down, only fifty yards from her house, she reported, her legs simply gave out and a kind stranger had had to help her back to the sanctuary of her home. Could Sarah, therefore, be extra vigilant in reporting the proceedings? Sarah had smiled and promised a detailed account whenever the funeral might be.

Sarah was working on a secret treat for her mother in the springtime. There was only one snag in the scheme. It involved a wheelchair, and wheelchairs, even the mention of wheelchairs, brought her mother to rage and despair. Sarah always wanted to cry when this happened. She felt so sorry for her mother. Wheelchairs, Sarah knew, spelt the end in her mother's mind, the end of activity, the end of choice, the start of dependence, the start of the long, maybe short, decline into the final immobility. But if the wheelchair enabled her mother to be whisked round Queen's Inn, to see the various courts and the rooms where the lawyers who now peopled her imagination actually lived, what a delight that would be. With luck they could make the short journey to the Inner and Middle Temple and her mother could rest in the beauty of Temple Gardens and watch the majesty of the law stalk past her en route to the Central Criminal Court. What a day that would be! Sarah had one brother and one sister, both older, both living away from home. To her great irritation the brother approved the scheme, the sister did not, leaving Sarah no wiser than before. But she thought about it all the time, something to bring joy to her mother's heart before it was too late.

Barton Somerville was flanked by two other benchers of Queen's Inn when Powerscourt was shown into his room. On the left sat Barrington Percival KC, a specialist in commercial law, a thin little man with a thin face and a tiny beard. On the right was Gabriel Cadogan, KC, a specialist in criminal law, a huge bear of a man with an enormous beard and a booming voice.

'Thank you for coming to see us, Lord Powerscourt,' Barton Somerville began. 'We thought we'd like to have a little discussion before we proceed further. We don't want to rush things, do we? I presume you know why you are here?'

Powerscourt nodded. Even after less than a minute he was beginning to have some sympathy with the policeman. He was being made to feel as if he was applying for a junior position in somebody's chambers and that he would be extraordinarily lucky to be taken on. Most people inquired about his past cases and came to him with recommendations from previous clients. His first sponsor, Lord Rosebery, was a former Foreign Secretary and Prime Minister for God's sake. His reputation had been enough for the minders of the Prince of Wales, apparently, but not for the benchers of Queen's Inn.

'What do you think of the police, Lord Powerscourt? The Metropolitan Police, I mean.' Cadogan sounded as though he could do duty as a foghorn at weekends if he wanted alternative employment. His voice echoed on even after he had stopped speaking.

'I think very highly of them, sir,' said Powerscourt, determined not to let down the people who had assisted him so nobly down the years. 'I understand there has been some unfortunate misunderstanding between them and yourselves in this matter, but I am sure that can be patched up.'

Powerscourt, advocate of friendship with all men, smiled at the trio. They stared at him. 'It may be that the age of the Chief Inspector is an issue,' he went on. 'I do not believe it should be so. I have heard only the highest reports of his abilities. And surely, gentlemen, there must be times when a shooting star will cross the Bar, some young man of such brilliance that he immediately rises to the top by sheer ability.'

Barton Somerville snorted. 'Haven't seen one of those for years, not in my Inn at any rate.' Something told Powerscourt that brilliant young men might not be very welcome in Queen's Inn.

'Tell us this, Lord Powerscourt,' Barrington Percival's thin voice sounded insubstantial after Cadogan's, 'why should we co-operate with the police at all? If they were that successful, people wouldn't employ investigators like yourselves. You'd all be out of a job. But you're not.'

'I have always worked with the police most carefully in all the cases I have been involved with,' said Powerscourt. 'They have always been most useful. To take but a few examples of their uses, they have extensive records. They can tell, in a way I could not, if people have criminal records. They have resources of manpower which I could only dream of. I have one close friend who works with me and one gentleman from Scotland I sometimes send for. That is the extent of my manpower. The police have thousands of officers all over the country. They can be very useful when you need them.'

The boom was back. Gabriel Cadogan was cross-examining now. 'So tell us what your plan of campaign would be if, and I emphasize the word if, we hired you to investigate this murder, Lord Powerscourt. How would you solve it?'

Powerscourt was beginning to feel really irritated. He wondered if the murderer might have enough poison left to return and polish off this troublesome threesome. He rather hoped he had. He just managed to smile. 'I have no idea,' he said. 'Until I start, no idea at all.'

'Surely you must have some general principles you adhere to?' Cadogan was now clutching the lapel of his jacket. The jury, Powerscourt thought, were right behind him. 'I find it hard to believe that an investigator of your experience does not have some scheme he adheres to.' Once more the boom lived on, hurtling across the room to perish in the velvet curtains.

'No,' said Powerscourt. The three benchers looked at each other. Even the delights of this interview had not prepared Powerscourt for what was to come.

'Perhaps,' said Somerville, 'you'd like to wait outside for a few minutes. We'll call you when we're ready for you.'

Powerscourt was incandescent as he made his way to the outer office. Outside the wind whipped across the grass and the gravel. Further away tiny wavelets were beating helplessly against the side of the Thames. The seagulls were out in force, complaining about something as usual. Five minutes passed, then ten. Groups of people, three or four at a time, were making their way out of the Inn for lunch in one of the neighbouring restaurants. Fifteen minutes gone. Powerscourt seriously considered walking out. Almost twenty had passed before Gabriel Cadogan opened the door and boomed at Powerscourt to return. His anger had ebbed in the outer room. Now he felt it returning.

'Thank you for waiting,' said Barton Somerville with the air of a man who couldn't care less how long anybody had waited. 'I am pleased to be able to tell you that by a majority verdict we have decided to appoint you as investigator to this matter.'

So one of these bastards doesn't want me, Powerscourt said to himself. To hell with him. To hell with them all. There was a pause. Powerscourt said nothing.

'Have you got nothing to say, men? Don't you want to know about your terms of employment? The manner in which you would be expected to conduct yourself?'

Powerscourt rose to his feet and looked down coldly on the three lawyers. 'I think you are labouring under a misapprehension, gentlemen. I'm sure it must be rare in your world. But let me remind you of a few things. I did not apply for this position. You invited me to come here this morning. I came. It is not for you to appoint me to a position I did not apply for. I have urgent business to attend to. I shall consider your offer with family and friends this evening. I shall let you know of my decision in the morning. And, I fear that, like yours, it may be a majority verdict. Good day to you.'

Johnny Fitzgerald had left a message for Powerscourt at Markham Square while he was away. It said that he had returned from his bird watching and would call on them in the evening. He would bring his own packing case to sit on. Birds and bird watching had become a major, if not the principal, interest in Johnny's life. All his days he had been interested in them, once endangering his and Powerscourt's life in the Punjab when he had refused to take evasive action because some exotic Indian vulture was passing overhead. Now he followed them everywhere, not just in Great Britain but across Europe as well. Birds migrating, birds nesting, yellow-flanked and yellow-nosed, red-vented and blue-cheeked, black-headed, black-faced and black-crowned, crested honey and double-crested, spotted, striped, great spotted, lesser whistling, Johnny loved them all. Powerscourt had accompanied him for part of a day the year before, rising in the dark to stride out to a position on the edge of a marsh near the sea in Norfolk. There were plenty of birds but Powerscourt did not feel the appeal. Johnny could never explain it. He liked to see them fly and soar and swoop, he would say. He liked knowing where they had come from and where they were going. He liked watching the young ones taking their first experimental flights under the watchful eye of their parents. But he could never transmit the secret of the appeal, if there was one, any more than some lovers of classical music could explain their devotion. Lady Lucy wondered if it all had to do with Johnny being single. He had simply adopted an enormous airborne family with wings, she would say, to compensate for the lack of a two-footed one rooted to the earth.

It was the patience Powerscourt admired most. Johnny seemed to pass into a world on the other side of time, lying there for hours and hours with never a pang of hunger. And sometimes he would talk of the exotic birds he wanted to see one day, a list as romantic as those of the train fanatics who wish to visit the last station on the remotest train lines in the world, somewhere out in the remote snows of Siberia or the mountains of the Hindu Kush. The short-toed eagle, he would murmur, the king eider, the spectacled eider. Then the birds would become more exotic yet. Johnny would enthuse about masked and brown boobies, about Chinese pond herons and goliath herons or the semi-collared sometimes double-spurred francolin, the magnificent frigate bird, the black-winged pratincole. Some might be able to recite the names of the major English football clubs. Johnny could respond with yet more species on his journey of discovery. Some day, he promised, he would be able to tick them all off his list, sapsuckers, shelducks, shrike, snowcocks, stonechats, silverbills, smews, scaups, shikras and shovelers, sanderlings and shearwaters, siskins and sprossers.

'It's like a rather bad public school,' Powerscourt said to Johnny and Lady Lucy in the early evening in Markham Square, 'one where they concentrate on the games because they haven't got any good teachers, and they beat the boys too much. This man Barton Somerville is the headmaster, and those other two are his housemasters. Like schoolmasters everywhere they can't bear not being in control.'

Powerscourt had explained his lunchtime encounter with the benchers of Queen's Inn. In his heart he knew, and he knew the other two knew, what he was going to do, but he wanted to hear what they had to say.

'It's almost as though they have something to hide,' he went on. 'There was an obsession with control. The policeman, Chief Inspector Beecham, mentioned it to me this afternoon. He noticed it as well.'

'Do you think they know who killed Mr Dauntsey?' asked Lady Lucy. 'And that they're worried you would find out the truth?'

'I don't know,' said Powerscourt.

'Institutions can go very strange when they've got something to hide,' said Johnny Fitzgerald, scratching his head as he spoke. 'Do you remember that terrible case in India, Francis, where half the regiment were carrying on with the Colonel's wife and everybody knew except the Colonel? Very strange atmosphere there.'

'Even stranger,' said Powerscourt, 'when the Colonel found out what was going on and began shooting the officers one by one. Regimental Sergeant Major, only sane man in the place, put it down to the heat.'

'God bless my soul,' said Lady Lucy, who had always believed that the main danger in the sub-continent came from rebellious or ambitious native warlords rather than fellow officers of the regiment. 'Are you going to take the case, Francis? That's what we all want to hear.'

'Do you think I should, Lucy? Even with these dreadful people?'

'You know my views.' Lady Lucy looked steadily at her husband. 'However dreadful they are, you must do it. You may save some lives. We don't want any more people collapsing into their soup.'

'Johnny?' said Powerscourt, turning to his friend.

'Well, Francis, I don't know a lot about this case yet. No doubt if you accept you will write them a most ferocious note, sounding like the Lord Chancellor himself, outlining your terms of reference and reserving the way you conduct the investigation to yourself. I can think of three reasons for taking it on.' Lady Lucy was hugging herself secretly. Surely an investigation like this couldn't be very dangerous. She would have felt differently if it was. But she felt sure that Francis would be out of her way and the move could be accomplished in peace and efficiency.

'The first one, I think, is rather childish,' Johnny Fitzgerald went on, 'but at some point in our inquiries I am sure there will be an opportunity to pay back those bastards – forgive me, Lucy – for the way they treated you. Petty maybe but valid nonetheless. And the second is to do with our reputation. Think of it. We have conducted investigations into the secrets of the Royal Family, into the machinations of the City of London, into the world of fine art and fraudsters and into the strange intrigues of a Church of England cathedral. Now we could add the law to our list of successes – if we succeed, that is.'

Johnny Fitzgerald paused for a moment

'And the third reason, Johnny?' asked Powerscourt, feeling rather important suddenly as their investigations were rolled out one after the other.

'The third reason,' said Johnny Fitzgerald, 'is the most important of all. A man told me years ago, I can't remember where, that if you want to drink the finest wine in London, you have to go to the Grosvenor Club, or to any one of the Inns of Court. Any one of them, Francis. Bloody great cellars they all have under those pretty buildings. A chap might get very thirsty wandering around and talking to counsel, don't you think?'

Powerscourt laughed. 'I'm afraid I don't think you will be anywhere near the Strand or the Inner Temple for a while, Johnny,' he said. 'You see, even after that dreadful meeting I knew I couldn't live with myself if I didn't take it on. So when I had calmed down I had a long chat with the clerk who looks after Dauntsey's chambers. He drew up a list of his major cases over the last seven years, concentrating on the criminal trials. The clerk was concerned with the case of a man called Howard, Winston Howard, who'd been on trial for armed robbery at the Old Bailey. Dauntsey defended him on the instructions of the solicitors, firm called Hooper. The solicitors implied to the robber Howard that Dauntsey would get him off. And he was innocent, it would seem, of this particular bit of armed robbery. Done lots of it before and not been caught, too smart for that. But Dauntsey didn't get him off. Howard went down, apparently absolutely livid about the injustice. He swore he'd get even with the fools who'd sent him down.'

'This is all very interesting, Francis,' said Johnny Fitzgerald, 'but what has it to do with me?'

'I'm just coming to that,' said Powerscourt. 'I think you should go and see this solicitor, Mr Brendan Hooper, of Hooper Hardie and Slope, 146 Whitechapel High Street. You see, Howard came out of Pentonville ten days ago.'

'Pentonville,' Johnny Fitzgerald muttered to himself, 'Whitechapel, where the Ripper plied his ghastly trade. Why do I get all the best locations?'

'According to what Hooper told Dauntsey's clerk, Howard was even angrier on coming out than when he went in. Hooper's had to move house for the time being. He's under police protection. Dauntsey, of course, isn't here at all. Dauntsey's dead.'

3

Over the next two days Powerscourt went through an intensive course in the professional life of Alexander Dauntsey. He made appointments to see everybody in his chambers and one or two more besides. He became a familiar figure to the porters as he flitted in and out of Queen's Inn, shuffling the new information in his mind. From the Head of Chambers, a charming bencher called Maxwell Kirk, he learnt principally about Dauntsey as a member of chambers. 'You've been in the Army, Lord Powerscourt, I can tell from the way you walk. Well, you know how some fellows fit very naturally into the military life, and some don't. They never seem to get the hang of it at all. Killed first in battle, the ones that don't fit in, I noticed. Nobody else prepared to put themselves out for them. Well, Dauntsey was one of those who fitted in. He belonged here as if he'd been born to it. I invited him to join us here seven years ago and I've never regretted it for a second.'

'What was he like as a lawyer?' Powerscourt asked, suspecting that he would not be told the whole truth. There was a slight pause as if Kirk wasn't sure how much to give away.

'I'm going to use a rather strange analogy, if I may, Lord Powerscourt. When I was at school I was very keen on cricket, still am when I can find the time. We had a chap there in the year above me called Morrison. On his day you would have said he was bound to play for England. He had beautiful style – a cover drive direct from heaven – he could cope with any kind of bowling, he could bat on any kind of wicket. People said he was bound to take the field for England later on. Only thing was, he was erratic, poor chap. Some days he could hardly hit the ball and certainly couldn't score any runs. It was strange, very strange. Dauntsey was a bit like that.

Brilliant some of the time, absolutely brilliant, solicitors queuing up to instruct him, triumphs in court. Next day listless, just about able to get the words out, hopeless. Instructing solicitors tearing their hair out. Clerk to chambers in despair. It didn't happen very often, mind you, maybe once in ten or twelve outings before the judges, but significant none the less.'

'Did this mean that his income went down?' asked Powerscourt. 'Fewer people prepared to employ him?'

'I suppose it did,' said Maxwell Kirk slowly, staring out of his window as if Dauntsey's ghost might be hovering above the Thames. 'I suppose he never made as much money as he could have done. But some of the solicitors were very loyal. They kept coming back.'

'Was it possible,' said Powerscourt, suspecting that Kirk would not know enough about Dauntsey's private life to answer his question, 'to work out why he lost his talent, as it were? Did it happen when he was depressed? Had he been drinking too much beforehand, anything like that?'

'You're not the first person to wonder about that. Our clerk here, the chap before the present one, used to make a note of Dauntsey's moods every day. And, of course, he had records of Dauntsey's cases and when he had his off days. Our clerk had his very own system of notation. C was cheerful. H was happy. VH was very happy. N was neutral, meant he couldn't decide one way or the other. S was sad, B was black and VB was very black. He kept this going for a whole year. Then on New Year's Eve, so he told me, God knows what his family must have made of this, he tried to match up the two lots of information. He could find absolutely no correlation between the two. He could be very black for three days in a row but very brilliant in court. He could be very happy first thing in the morning and completely tongue-tied at the Old Bailey in the afternoon. It was extraordinary.'

'Did he,' Powerscourt always kept this question till the end, 'have any problems with money or women?'

'If he did,' Kirk replied, 'he wouldn't be telling me, unless he was in desperate trouble. I don't believe he was in any money trouble. That place he had in Kent cost a lot to keep up, but in a good year he was making a very fine living here. As for the women, I simply don't know. I should have said that he was a man who lived his life in tight little compartments, if you know what I mean. Right hand barely aware what the left hand was doing. He could have been involved with women – I think they found him attractive – but as to facts I haven't a clue.'

As he wandered down the stairs Powerscourt wondered if Kirk would have told him anything about Dauntsey's affairs with women if he had known about them. 'Actually, Lord Powerscourt, he was a most frightful womanizer, he went through them at the rate of one every three months. . .' No, he couldn't imagine Kirk saying that. In fact Powerscourt couldn't think of anyone he had talked to so far who would have told him if Dauntsey was having affairs. They closed ranks, these lawyers, and only told the world what they felt the world should hear. Truth was rationed in the lawyers' chambers; it was potentially too dangerous to be let loose.

Of the great battle with Porchester Newton, however, he was told a great deal. The benchers in Queen's Inn were elected, he learned, and at the last vacancy a month or so before Dauntsey's death there had been a fierce struggle between the two men. The benchers, in effect, were the governing body of the Inn. Like the other Inns of Court Queen's demanded a substantial payment from new benchers. But unlike the others Queen's also demanded that every bencher remember the Inn in his will, though the precise percentage of the total estate was not known. This double collection made the little Inn one of the richest places in London, with almost all the money earmarked for scholarships and bursaries for students from humble backgrounds. The largest Inns of Court had forty or even fifty benchers on their books. Queen's had only eight. And Powerscourt heard whispers even on his first day about the bitter fight that had preceded Dauntsey's election as bencher. These affairs, he was told, are not conducted like Parliamentary contests. There are no slates of candidates, no formal speeches. But aspirant benchers give sherry parties so they can shake the hands of voters they might not have met. Discreet dinner parties are held to win over the waverers. Supporters of the rival candidates whisper about the deficiencies of their opponents into the ears of all those who will listen, and there are many who will listen. Right up to the end it seemed as though Dauntsey's great rival Porchester Newton was going to win. Nobody was prepared to say what rumour Dauntsey's people had spread in the last twenty-four hours before the voting, but it worked. The ballot was secret but it was widely known that Dauntsey had a comfortable victory. Newton had not spoken to him since. Newton, Powerscourt realized, would make a formidable enemy. He was the opposite of Dauntsey in almost every way.

Dauntsey had a soaring imagination which enabled him on occasion to see motives that were apparent to nobody else. Newton was a solid performer, plodding through his cases with little sparkle. Dauntsey was quick, mercurial. Newton was slow, stolid, some even ventured that he was stupid. Powerscourt's only doubt about Newton as a possible murderer was the murder weapon. Certainly there was motive. Some of the insults traded during the vicious election campaign would have produced a duel in Temple Gardens in years gone by. Powerscourt wasn't sure he could see Newton as a poisoner until he heard that he had worked in India in his youth. You could learn enough about poisons there, as Powerscourt well knew, to last you a lifetime.

Then there was Edward, the slim silent young man who did most of Dauntsey's devilling, researching and preparing cases and submissions to the legal authorities. Edward did have a surname, but nobody except Edward seemed able to remember what it was. Everybody wondered why he had joined the profession of barrister for he had one overwhelming defect for his chosen calling, a defect that should have told him that, of all professions, this was the last one he should aspire to. Edward watchers, and there were plenty of people fascinated by him, said it was like a man who fainted at the sight of blood trying to become a surgeon or an atheist signing up for the priesthood, although the cynics pointed out that this might be an ideal quality for a career in the modern Church of England and that the atheist would probably end up a bishop at the least, if not Archbishop of Canterbury. Edward was painfully, incurably, woefully shy. The porters referred to him behind his back as Edward the Silent. He could manage to get through whole days without speaking. He could attend case conferences and not say a word. At dinners in Hall he would nod unhappily to his neighbours. Once, when he had really picked up his courage and asked his neighbour to pass the potatoes, a huge cheer had gone up from the company and Edward had fled the Hall, almost weeping with embarrassment. But according to the clerk, Dauntsey said that Edward was the finest deviller he had ever come across, that he had a very sophisticated understanding of the workings of the law in general and of judges in particular. He kept a form book on judges, the clerk told Powerscourt, so he could know how their particular temperaments might be affected by the new cases in front of them and the demeanour of the barristers arguing them.

Powerscourt planned his assault on Edward's silence like a military operation. For a start he decided to remove Edward from his normal routine and transport him a mile or so across town to the drawing room in Manchester Square for afternoon tea. Lady Lucy, fresh and sustained by a triumph over packing cases and disorder, was on parade to inquire about Edward's family. Olivia had been pressed into service, instructed to do whatever she could to make the young man feel at home. Even one of the twins was paraded through the drawing room to be admired. It was almost impossible, even in England, Powerscourt felt, for babies to be put on display without those present feeling they had to pass a comment, whether on their looks or their intelligence or their resemblance to more senior members of their families. The twin did not speak but Edward did on this occasion, observing that the infant looked very intelligent.

When the tea campaign was complete, Edward having displayed a considerable appetite for muffins, the family departed, leaving Powerscourt and the young man alone. 'Thank you so much for coming, Edward. I'd be very grateful if we could have a conversation, in confidence of course, about Mr Dauntsey,' Powerscourt began. 'I wonder if you could tell me about his last case.'

There was a pause. For a second Powerscourt wondered if his entire strategy had failed, if the reasonable amount of speech Edward had managed during tea was now going to be replaced with silence once again. Then he was relieved. Perhaps Edward had been collecting his thoughts. Maybe the muffins had done their work.

'Last case, murder, sir. At the Old Bailey. Eight days. Mr Justice Fairfax.' Powerscourt thought Edward seemed to have a bias against verbs.

'Mr Dauntsey appearing for the prosecution, sir. Quite rare these last years. More often retained for the defence. Very horrible case, sir. Young woman battered to death on a beach in Great Yarmouth. Former lover seen in the town on the day of the murder. Former lover had grudge against the victim. Defence admitted the man was in the town but denied that he killed her, sir.'

Verbs, Powerscourt noted, were beginning to make an appearance.

'That judge didn't like Mr Dauntsey for some reason, sir. He had quite a difficult time of it. But he won in the end. Jury out for only twenty minutes. Judge puts his black cap on and the defendant is probably gone by now, sir.'

'Was Mr Dauntsey pleased with the verdict, Edward?'

'Oddly enough, no, he wasn't, sir. I think he thought the man was innocent. He never said anything to me but something about his manner gave me that impression, sir. I could be wrong.'

'What was the defendant's name, Edward? Can you remember where he came from?'

'Moorhouse, sir. James Henry Moorhouse, 15 Hornsey Lane, London.'

Powerscourt wondered briefly if Edward knew the shoe and hat size as well.

'Large family up there in Hornsey Lane, Edward?'

There was a brief pause as if some piece of machinery in Edward's brain had got stuck. Then it clicked into place.

'Four elder brothers, two younger sisters, sir.'

'Thank you. And what about the next case, Edward?' asked Powerscourt. 'Not another murder, I hope?'

'No, sir, the next case would have been a huge one, sir. Mr Dauntsey was going to be Number Two for the prosecution, sir, with Mr Stewart, another one of our benchers, leading. They used to work together a lot in the old days, sir. It's a fraud trial, sir. You remember that man called Puncknowle, Lord Powerscourt? He started up a whole lot of companies and the public subscribed by the tens of thousands. Companies paid good dividends, close on ten per cent most years, so more people subscribed. Only problem was the companies lost money and the dividends of the old ones were paid for by the new investors in the new companies. That's why Puncknowle had so many companies, sir, he needed the new money to pay the dividends on the old ones.'

'Didn't he run away to America, this fellow, and have to be brought home again?'

'He did, sir,' said Edward, 'and this is one of the most complicated cases I've ever seen. The opening speeches are going to last all day or even longer, sir.'

'Tell me, Edward, you must have known Mr Dauntsey as well as anybody in the months before he died, devilling for him in these complicated cases. Was there anything unusual in him? Did anything change after he became a bencher, for example?'

Edward looked at Powerscourt carefully. Normal speech seemed to have been returned. Powerscourt felt sure Lady Lucy would put the transformation down to feminine company and the ease and security that came from being in a proper home rather than cooped up with a whole lot of men all the time. Edward took his time before he answered.

'All the other gentlemen have asked me that, sir. Mr Somerville, Mr Cadogan, Mr Kirk, that police inspector. I didn't tell them anything at all.'

There was another pause. 'It was after his election as a bencher, sir. Something changed after that. Not immediately but two, maybe three weeks or so later, I should say, sir. Mr Dauntsey was very cross about something. I never knew what it was. One afternoon I came into his room when he wasn't expecting me. I think he assumed I was in the library. He was studying some figures on a pad in front of him. He looked at me. Mr Dauntsey, sir, almost in despair. "It's not right, Edward," he said, "it's just not right." He sort of stared at the wall for a moment or two, sir, and then he put away his pad. He never referred to it again, whatever it was, not to me anyway, sir.'

Powerscourt saw Edward out into the evening air of Manchester Square. Lady Lucy came to say goodbye and to tell Edward he could come to tea whenever he liked, he would be most welcome. As Edward passed the Wallace Collection on his way home, lights blazing from the upper floors, Powerscourt wished he had asked just one more question. He should have sought information on any extramarital females in Mr Dauntsey's life. He felt sure Edward would have had their names and addresses.

But for Edward afternoon tea had been an epiphany, a revelation. He tried to remember the last time he had been able to speak so freely and knew it was a long long time ago. Now perhaps he would be able to do what he most wanted to do in the world, speak to Sarah Henderson. Sarah had many admirers in Queen's Inn and the Maxwell Kirk chambers, but few as devoted as Edward. He knew the softer tread of her shoes on the staircase as she went up to her attic quarters, he would watch her swinging walk as she made her way across the courts. Three times he had made up his mind to speak to her, three times he had promised himself that this time he would not fail. But he did. Until today he had been bound to fail. But now, with the confidence engendered by Powerscourt tea and Powerscourt muffins, now he would try once more.

Mrs Bertha Henderson had been in a state of growing excitement all afternoon. She managed, with great difficulty and considerable pain, to make a small cake. The effort involved in beating the mixture to the proper consistency exhausted her. As the cheap clock on her little mantelpiece moved on towards early evening she consulted it more and more often. Half past four. Quarter to five. Mrs Henderson was doing mental arithmetic in her head. Ten minutes to the station in Kent, forty-five minutes or so to Victoria, half an hour, maybe less, to their own little station in Acton, five minutes' walk and Sarah would be home. Five o'clock passed and half past. Mrs Henderson was torn now between excitement and worry. Had anything happened to the trains? Had there been some delay at Victoria, always notorious for inefficiency at peak hours? Had anything happened to Sarah? For today was the day of Mr Dauntsey's funeral and her Sarah, along with all the members of his chambers and the benchers of the Inn, had gone down to see him off. And, in Mrs Henderson's excited imagination, not only would she hear the details of that poor Mr Dauntsey's funeral and burial, but she should receive some intelligence about the treasures of Calne, the fabulous house where the Dauntseys had lived since time immemorial. Mrs Henderson had looked the family up once in the Dictionary of National Biography in the big reference library in Hammersmith but there were so many entries for so many different branches of the family that she had given up, overwhelmed by the available knowledge. One or two Lord Chancellors, back in the seventeenth century, she remembered, a Dauntsey who became a key figure at the Restoration Court of Charles the Second, a libertine involved in the foundation of the Hellfire Club.

From her vantage point in the window Mrs Henderson could see the local residents making their way home. It was ten to six before she finally caught sight of Sarah, wearing her new black coat and hat, looking rather tired, Mrs Henderson thought, as she let herself in and sat down by the fire.

'I'll just put the kettle on,' Mrs Henderson sang, as she made her way to the kitchen. 'I've made a cake. I'll bring it in with the tea. It's only a little cake.'

'You shouldn't have bothered,' said Sarah, wondering how much effort must have gone into that fairly simple domestic activity. She felt that her mother might be disappointed with her tales of the day. She suspected that her mother had been building up her hopes for days, looking forward to tales of magnificent drawing rooms and ornate long galleries, with possibly – Sarah felt her mother was perfectly capable of this – some young scion of the Dauntsey clan, of remarkable beauty and even more remarkable wealth, on hand to fall in love with her daughter and carry her off to marriage and glory, a sort of Kentish equivalent of Mr Darcy, as Sarah had put it to herself on the train.

'Well then,' said her mother, setting the tray with the tea and cake on the table between them in front of the fire, 'how was your day, my dear?'

Sarah took a large gulp of her tea. 'It was all rather tiring, mama,' she began. 'Just before midday the carriages came to take us to the station. Mr Kirk, he's the Head of Chambers as you know, had arranged all that.'

'I hope you didn't have to pay for that, dear,' said Mrs Henderson, concerned lest her daughter's inadequate wages should be frittered away on the cost of carriages.

'No, no, Mr Kirk saw to all of that, mama.'

'Who did you sit next to?' said her mother eagerly. It was this hunger for every detail that Sarah found irritating, dearly though she loved her mother.

'I sat next to Mr Kirk, actually,' said Sarah, helping herself to a slice of cake.

'Next to the Head of Chambers himself,' said Mrs Henderson proudly. 'Remind me, dear, is he married, Mr Kirk?'

'He is, mother, he has four children and he is very old, he must be nearly fifty.' That, Sarah felt, should put paid to that particular fantasy.

'And the train?' her mother pressed on. 'Had Queen's Inn organized a special train to take you all down?' Mrs Henderson had heard of special trains. She herself had never had the privilege of travelling in one. Now, perhaps, her daughter could remedy the situation. That would be a good piece of information to pass on to Mrs Wiggins next door, always boasting of the progress her son was making in the Metropolitan Railway. As far as Mrs Henderson knew, he sold tickets at Baker Street station.

'No special, mama,' said Sarah with a smile. She knew the way her mother's mind worked but there was one piece of news which, while not having the knock-out punch of a special, did have a certain weight of its own. 'But Mr Kirk had reserved three first class carriages.'

'Three first class carriages,' Mrs Henderson repeated, awe and wonder in her tones. 'Three.'

'I was still talking to Mr Kirk, mama, about this big fraud case that's coming up soon. There's a great deal of work I've got to do over the next few days. In fact I talked to him all the way to Calne.'

'Do they have a station of their own, the Dauntseys?' asked Mrs Henderson hopefully. The Dauntseys of Calne, she said to herself. How well it sounded. And her own daughter, borne there in splendour from Victoria station in a first class railway carriage, conversing with the Head of Chambers himself.

'I think they used to, mama. Somebody told me that they owned a lot of the land used to build the railway. But the station is only ten minutes' walk from the house.'

'You didn't all have to walk on a day like this, Sarah? There was a terrible wind up here at any rate. It could have wrecked people's hair.'

'But you wouldn't have been able to enjoy the park, mama,' said Sarah with a smile, 'it starts very near the station. Thousands and thousands of acres of it. And deer, lovely little deer, trotting all over it. I was told there are hundreds and hundreds of them. They've been there for hundreds of years.'

Mrs Henderson smiled quietly to herself. Thousands of acres and hundreds of deer should be able to flatten anything the Metropolitan Railway and Mrs Wiggins might have to offer.

'And what was the house like, Sarah? Big, was it?' Sarah suspected her mother imagined a building three or four times the size of Buckingham Palace.

'Well, we didn't see a great deal of it, mama. It's enormous. They say there's a room for every day of the year and a staircase for every month.'

Mrs Henderson was overwhelmed by this news. Three hundred and sixty-five rooms? It was scarcely credible. She wondered what they did in the leap years. Perhaps they had a room with open double doors in the middle. In leap years they would just have to close the doors to add on the extra room. But she mustn't divert herself. More intelligence was coming from Sarah.

'We went across two great courtyards, mama, one called Brick Court, I think, and the other one Reservoir Court.'

Funny, Mrs Henderson found herself thinking, there was Mr Dauntsey leaving all these courts at his home to go and work in a whole lot of different ones in London.

'Just inside Reservoir Court there is the Great Hall, mama. That's where Mr Dauntsey's coffin was until just before the service when the pall bearers came to take him away. It's a huge room, with great portraits of previous Dauntseys all over the walls and dark oak panelling everywhere. It's where the servants used to eat in the seventeenth century when most of the house was built. They had an enormous oak table in there, about the length of our road I would say, where they all used to sit.'

'How many pall bearers, Sarah?' asked Mrs Henderson, leaning forward now in her chair, her eyes bright with curiosity.

'Six, mama. Two gentlemen from chambers, two from the estate and two members of the family. So all parts of Mr Dauntsey's life were there. They walked very slowly, mama. I remember thinking the coffin must have been heavy because Mr Dauntsey himself can't have weighed very much. They went out across the two courts and turned right at the main entrance to reach the family chapel. Then there was the most extraordinary thing, I've never seen anything like it.'

Sarah paused. Mrs Henderson looked expectant. Sarah looked slightly embarrassed as she went on. 'It was the deer, mama. It was as if they knew what was going on. A whole lot of them, I don't know, thirty or forty maybe, came and stood very still about twenty yards from the funeral cortège. As if they were paying their last respects. One of the young barristers said afterwards that he'd never seen a man go to his funeral service with an honour guard of his own four-legged friends.'

'Did they stay like that for the service?' asked Mrs Henderson. 'Were they still there when you all came out again?'

Sarah laughed. 'No, they weren't that patient. I looked round just before we went into the service and they were all trotting off. Maybe they thought they had done their duty.'

'And the service, Sarah? What was that like?'

Sarah was beginning to realize how the victims of the Inquisition must have felt as their interrogators kept on and on with their questions. She helped herself to a large slice of Protestant cake.

'All the usual stuff about I am the Resurrection and the Life,' said Sarah with the world-weary resignation of a twenty-year-old attending her second funeral. 'Mr Kirk read one lesson. Mr Dauntsey's brother did another. The vicar preached a sermon about how impossible it was to understand God's purpose. One of the young barristers in the pew behind me was whispering to his friend that it was equally impossible to understand the purpose of the vicar.'

Mrs Henderson shook her head at the flippancy of the young.

'They buried him next to his father,' Sarah carried on. 'Nearly at the top of the hill. You could see most of the estate and the house and the deer and the cricket pitch, a lovely place to end up in, I thought.'

'Was the church full, Sarah? Fifty mourners? A hundred, would you have said?'

'More than that, mama, some people had to wait outside the church, it was so packed. Hundred and fifty, maybe more. That young policeman came, which I thought was nice of him. And that man Lord Powerscourt the benchers brought in to investigate Mr Dauntsey's death. He was there.'

'And the widow, Sarah? Was she very upset?

'She looked very beautiful, mama, Mrs Dauntsey. Black suited her. And she had a black veil made of very fine lace, maybe it was a mantilla, which made her look rather mysterious.'

'I'm not sure people should look mysterious at funerals. I was taught they should look sad.'

'I was never very close to her, mama. There was one odd thing just when they were lowering the body into the grave. You know how they have four ropes or runners round the thing before they lower it into the ground? Well, Mr Dauntsey's coffin sort of slipped. It looked for a second as if it might flip right over and fall in upside down. The bearers had a terrible time, almost wrestling with it. There was a sort of collective gasp from the congregation, everybody holding their breath for a moment. Then it was under control again. Just think, mama, how awful it would have been if Mr Dauntsey's coffin had fallen in the wrong way round or the wrong way up.'

Mrs Henderson looked into the fire. 'You could say, could you not, that the whole thing was a parable, a metaphor for Mr Dauntsey's life. He ended up the wrong way round, the wrong way up, slumped into his soup bowl at that feast. You're not meant to end up murdered, not in this bright new century of ours.'

4

There was another note from Johnny Fitzgerald waiting for Powerscourt when he returned from the Dauntsey funeral in Kent. Peace, Powerscourt learned, had returned to the troubled East London borough of Whitechapel where Johnny had been sent to check out Winston Howard, the man unsuccessfully defended by Dauntsey at his trial for armed robbery some years before and recently released from prison. Reports from the East End had indicated that the ex-convict might bear a grudge against his legal team for his lengthy incarceration within the unfriendly walls of Pentonville.

Johnny Fitzgerald claimed to have won prizes for his handwriting at school. Powerscourt had no reason to doubt it. But he wondered if decades of consumption of Pomerol and Meursault, of Chablis and Chardonnay, of Bordeaux and Beaujolais and Muscadet and Armagnac and the other treasures of Johnny's wine merchants might not have had an impact, the hand grown shakier with the passing years, some letters and words virtually indistinguishable. Then there were all those hours peering at birds through those heavy German binoculars Johnny was so proud of. That must damage your wrists. The Fitzgerald script was becoming more and more indistinct as it staggered its way down the page and over to the other side. There had, Johnny reported, been an obstacle, was it, in Whitechapel. No, it couldn't be obstacle, it was miracle. Surely not. Miracle in Whitechapel? Powerscourt read on. There was, at the present time, a major crusade being conducted in the crime-ridden borough by the Salvation Army, ever vigilant for the propagation of the gospel and the salvation of souls. At one of these torch-lit rallies, Powerscourt read, the star turn of the preaching department of the

41

Salvation Army, God's equivalent to W.G. Grace in Johnny's phrase, had reaped a mighty harvest of souls. The sinners of Whitechapel had formed long queues to confess their sins and be borne into the bosom of the Lord. And among those carried into this spacious resting place, Powerscourt learnt to his astonishment, was none other than Winston Howard, former burglar, armed robber and vicious inhabitant of His Majesty's prisons. So great was the conversion that Howard had taken to proselytizing in the unlikely quarter of Whitechapel High Street. Johnny himself, the note went on, had been accosted by the prodigal only the day before and could only effect escape from the speeches of conversion by the purchase of four copies of the Salvation Army newsletter. It was therefore unlikely, in Johnny's view, that Howard would be contemplating violence against any of God's creatures, or not for a while at any rate, as long as the Salvation Army had him in their clutches.

The last paragraph was the most difficult to read. Even Lady Lucy, a veteran and expert in decoding Johnny's messages, was stumped. He was going to watch some birds for a day. Wigeon? Pigeon? Redwing? It was hard to tell. These creatures were expected to come, or was it go, at this time of year over the mudflats of . . . Essex? Sussex? Wessex? Powerscourt doubted if Johnny would be going there. The problems with the decoding became less serious once the last sentence had been deciphered. Johnny would not want Francis to think he was being abandoned. He would be back in London the day after tomorrow. But of one thing he could be sure. Whoever had killed Dauntsey, it was not Winston Howard.

The following morning a bizarre meeting was taking place in the Powerscourt dining room in Manchester Square. All the chairs, except three at the top end, had been taken away from the table and placed against the wall. Stretching round the table were a series of cardboard labels, roughly inscribed with a thick black pen, with the legends nine to ten, ten to eleven, eleven to twelve and so on all the way round the clock to seven to eight. And standing behind the three chairs were Powerscourt, Detective Chief Inspector Jack Beecham and his detective sergeant, an absurdly young-looking man called Richard Gibson whose uniform was slightly too big for him. Looking at Sergeant Gibson, Powerscourt wondered if his mother thought he hadn't finished growing yet. And piled up on the table in front of the trio was an enormous heap of paper, the typed records of the detectives' interviews with the inhabitants of Queen's Inn, and the two black notebooks where Powerscourt kept his own records of his interviews. And, to complete the display, several pairs of scissors.

Chief Inspector Beecham set out the rules. 'We're most grateful to you, Lord Powerscourt, for inviting us here. What we want to do is to sort all this lot out in terms of time of day.' He pointed to the small mountain of paper. 'We have here the records of all the people we have talked to in the Inn. Sergeant Gibson, despite his tender years, is an expert not only in the shorthand but in the typing department. The training school of the Metropolitan Police believe his is the fastest hand they have ever seen, faster than all those young ladies you see going off to adorn the offices of the City of London. Now, the procedure is quite clear. If the transcript mentions a time between eight and nine then it goes over there.' The Chief Inspector pointed to the relevant cardboard label. Powerscourt noticed that the nails were bitten down to the quick. Perhaps the detective was very highly strung.

'And if,' he continued, 'the interviewee saw him twice at different times of day, then we just cut the paper at the relevant point and move the new section to the later time. I don't think it should take us very long.'

Gradually the piles of paper began to decrease. And all three of them found it easier to talk as they entered their material under the relevant time. A ghostly history of Dauntsey's last hours began to emerge, a plainchant between two policemen and an investigator that followed a man to his death.

'Eight thirty or just afterwards. Dauntsey seen by the porter coming into the Inn.' This in a solemn voice from the Chief Inspector.

'Eight forty, clerk of chambers reports exchanging Good Mornings as he enters his chambers.' This from the sergeant in a nervous voice.

'Eight forty-five, meeting with Edward in his room about forthcoming fraud case.' Powerscourt, wondering how much effort it cost Edward to pass on the information.

'Ten fifteen, meeting with clerk about forthcoming cases.' The Chief Inspector again.

'Ten forty-five, leaves his chambers. Meeting in chambers of Woodford Stewart about forthcoming fraud case.'

'Twelve thirty, leaves Inn with Stewart, lunches in the Garrick, returns shortly after two.'

The piles were growing around their cardboard sentries, Powerscourt noticed. But the bulk of the replies were still on the table in front of him. He presumed that the feast, with the largest number of lawyers present, must also have contained the largest number of sightings. The paper round continued. Powerscourt paid particular attention when it reached five o'clock. The doctors were still not sure what time the poison must have been administered but the earliest possible hour was five o'clock.

'Ten past five,' said the sergeant. Dauntsey had been in the library since four thirty-five, looking up some precedent for the fraud case. 'Dauntsey back in his own chambers. Has tea with Edward during further meeting about fraud case. Edward leaves Dauntsey still wearing normal clothes at five forty-five.'

'Six o'clock, Dauntsey leaves his rooms in evening clothes to attend pre-feast drinks party in the Treasurer's chambers in Fountain Court.' The Chief Inspector added his paper to the pile and shuffled it into a neat package.

'Two of these reports, sir.' the sergeant held two pieces of paper aloft as if they were suspects. 'Unknown person spotted on staircase of Dauntsey's rooms shortly after five forty-five. Another witness saw the person shortly after six o'clock. Described as of average height, slim, with light brown hair, late twenties or early thirties. Smiled, but did not speak to our witnesses, sir.'

'Who the devil do you think it was, Powerscourt?' said the Chief Inspector. 'Not normal for total strangers to be wandering about an Inn of Court that time of day, is it?'

'A murderer?' said Powerscourt quietly. 'A murderer of average height with light brown hair, come to drop something into Dauntsey's tea or his gin or his sherry if he had started to drink at this time? I don't suppose there are any reports of him entering Dauntsey's room, sergeant?'

'No, sir, there aren't. There's nothing between Edward leaving and Scott, the man in the chambers above, seeing him set off for Barton Somerville's rooms a couple of minutes after six.'

The sergeant had been scrabbling around in the papers left on the table. 'I hadn't connected this person with the mysterious visitor, sir, but here we go. The porter at the gate reported somebody leaving the Inn at about ten past six. If you weren't a very quick walker, that's about the time it would take you to get to the lodge from Dauntsey's rooms, sir. The porter said goodnight and the man nodded but didn't speak, sir. Wonder why he never opened his mouth, sir?'

'Foreigner perhaps?' murmured the Chief Inspector. 'Strong regional accent?'

'Sore throat?' said Powerscourt flippantly. 'Dumb visitor? Both pretty unlikely.'

'You don't suppose. sir,' said the sergeant, 'that the visitor might have had something to do with the feast? Something to do with the catering arrangements?'

'If he had,' said the Chief Inspector firmly, sounding as though he had a pretty poor view of this particular theory, 'he'd have gone to the kitchens or the Hall, not to a barrister's room.'

'Client of Dauntsey's? Any mention by the clerk of our mysterious visitor?'

'No, sir, there isn't,' said the sergeant.

They continued the distribution of the papers, an enormous pile in the seven to eight section when the guests at the feast turned into witnesses to a murder.

'There we are, sir,' said the Chief Inspector at half past eleven. 'Sergeant Gibson will type up an hour-by-hour version for us all. I'll make sure you get a copy first thing in the morning.'

Powerscourt had ordered coffee and biscuits as a reward for finishing the job.

'Gentlemen,' he said, 'that is an excellent morning's work. But there is one area where I know I have not been able to talk to the relevant people, and that is the steward and his waiters who served the food and drink. The steward has been ill, I understand, and without him there is little point in speaking to the waiters half of whom, I think, were brought in from outside.'

'That is correct, Lord Powerscourt,' said the Chief Inspector, 'but the steward will be back in the next few days. Would you like to join us when we speak to him?'

'Very much so,' said Powerscourt, 'but I would venture a further suggestion. We need to talk to the steward and the waiters in the Hall itself. We need to put them back in exactly the roles they had at the feast. There is a catering committee here in the Inn and I spoke to its senior member yesterday about the way things are handled at the feast. And,' Powerscourt paused for a sip of his coffee, 'from what he told me, it would have been extraordinarily difficult, if not impossible, to poison Mr Dauntsey at the feast.'

Powerscourt strode up and down the table, putting the chairs back in position and signalling to the sergeant to move the timetable documents somewhere else. From a large press to the side, he brought out a pair of glasses and a couple of soup bowls.

'Let us pretend, gentlemen, that my dining room is the Hall of Queen's Inn. This dining table,' Powerscourt pointed dramatically to his right, 'is the High Table at the top of the room where the benchers and their guests were sitting. Down there, at right angles to us up here, are three other long trestle tables housing the rest of the barristers.' Powerscourt waved airily at the imaginary area below him. 'Now, Chief Inspector, if you would, if we place you here at the very end of our High Table you could be Mr Dauntsey. Sergeant, would you like to be a waiter, or Mr Dauntsey's neighbour?'

The sergeant grinned. 'Don't think I'd like to be next to Mr Dauntsey when he goes off, sir. Might be a suspect. Think I'll have to be a waiter.'

Powerscourt managed to lay a primitive place setting for the Chief Inspector, mat, two sets of knife and fork, a couple of spoons, a cheese knife. He thrust two soup bowls into the sergeant's hands.

'The important thing,' said Powerscourt, 'about the service at the feast, gentlemen, according to my man, is that it is served from two ends.' He took the sergeant down to the bottom of the room, at the opposite end to the dining table. 'The food comes from down here. The kitchens are on the far side of that wall with a passage between them and the Hall. Don't come to serve the soup until I say so, sergeant.' Powerscourt strode back to the other end of the room and grinned at Jack Beecham. 'But the drink,' Powerscourt had found a couple of empty bottles at the back of his cupboard and carried them, one in each hand, to the door into the dining room, 'the drink comes from the opposite end, what they called the buttery in my college in Cambridge. The white wine will have been kept cool and opened as late as possible. It will, my man informs me, have been served in its original bottles. The red would have been decanted and placed in those elegant French containers the benchers are so proud of. But, alas, we are not concerned with the red here, for Dauntsey was dead before it came on the scene. The bottles will have been lined up on a great bench on the far side of the two Gainsboroughs here on the Inn walls, gentlemen. The only people allowed in there would have been the waiters. Anybody else would have been suspected of wanting to steal some of the Inn's finest wine and kicked out. If you were a murderous waiter, you could pop your poison into a bottle at a special place, but you could not be sure that somebody else would not pick it up first and kill the wrong person. I am just going to pop out and return as a wine waiter complete with bottle.'

The Chief Inspector smiled. The sergeant waited patiently, his two soup plates filled with imaginary scup. Powerscourt looked quickly up his hall. It was empty. He returned with the bottle in his right hand.

'Right, gentlemen, let us suppose I am the murderous waiter. I have managed to pop the poison into this bottle in the few seconds it takes to pass from the buttery into the top of the Hall here. But the gentlemen are drinking at different speeds. Maybe Mr Dauntsey's glass is still full, refilled by one of my colleagues. Let us further suppose that I have come back with just one glassful in my bottle. Mr Dauntsey doesn't want any of it. But two places away the Treasurer himself beckons you over He likes this Meursault very much. He would like some more. He would like some more this minute. Do you kill the wrong man?'

The Chief Inspector looked in horror at Powerscourt. 'My God, Powerscourt, you don't suppose that it happened as you describe? Only Dauntsey was the wrong man. Some other bencher was meant to be murdered.'

Powerscourt paused. 'I think not. I don't know why. If I could complete the demonstration, I think the same problem applies to the soup. The soup is served at the top end of the kitchen. There is a parade of four to six waiters bringing it up in relays.' Powerscourt waved at his very own waiter to come forward. 'Suppose you have somehow managed to drop the poison into one of your soup plates, gentlemen. Hidden up your sleeve perhaps and released by some secret and ingenious mechanism. You have no idea if Mr Dauntsey has been served his borscht or not. If he has, what do you do? You can't very well turn round and take your deadly cargo back to the kitchens. Everyone will think you are a bit mad and somebody may send the soup out again to kill some other innocent barrister. It's all very risky, poisoning at the feast.'

'If you're right, Lord Powerscourt,' said the Chief Inspector, 'the poison must have been administered earlier. Either in his rooms, or at the Treasurer's drinks party.'

'I think we need to wait,' replied Powerscourt, 'until we get hold of the steward and all his waiters at the same time in the Hall and hear what they've got to say.' Powerscourt began putting the soup plates back in their cupboard when another thought struck him.

'Chief Inspector, sergeant, I've had a mad idea. You know how people never notice anything when murders are being committed because they don't know a crime is going on?'

The two policemen nodded. 'Why don't we restage the feast? The whole lot, food, drink, everything. These people can certainly afford it. We hire an actor to play Dauntsey. Immediately afterwards we interview every single person there about what they remember, in case there's anything that's just come back to them.'

'Wouldn't that give the murderer the idea that we think the man was poisoned at the feast?' said the Chief Inspector.

'That might be very useful to us, Chief Inspector,' said Powerscourt with a broad smile. 'It might draw attention away from the fact that we think he was murdered somewhere else.'

A fine rain was falling on Calne Park a day later as Powerscourt made his way towards the great house. A couple of deer examined him carefully on his passage as if he had no right to be there. But his invitation was in his pocket, a polite letter from Dauntsey's widow inviting him to tea this afternoon. She directed him not to the entrance through the main gate and on to the back of Reservoir Court where the mourners had foregathered for the funeral the week before, but to a small green door almost directly opposite the main entrance. Here a young footman showed him to a small drawing room where a great fire was burning vigorously.

Powerscourt felt disappointed, even slightly cheated. For Calne was one of those English houses that people associated with grandeur, with vast drawing rooms adorned with mighty chandeliers, the walls hung with full-length Old Masters, French furniture sitting decorously on the polished oak floorboards, or great galleries hung with Flemish tapestries, their ceilings decorated with elaborate plasterwork. But the room here was small, with a cheap carpet on the floor and reproductions rather than Raphaels on the walls. Mrs Elizabeth Dauntsey was dressed in a widow's black, a long black skirt and an elegant black blouse. She was tall with very fair skin and light brown eyes.

'I expect you're thinking you've come to the wrong place, Lord Powerscourt,' she said, rising from her chair to shake his hand. 'Most people do. I shall explain later.' Powerscourt thought she was one of the most striking women he had ever seen. Maybe Dauntsey had been a connoisseur of feminine beauty.

'I look forward to the explanation,' Powerscourt sat in a chair opposite her on the other side of the fire, 'and can I say how grateful I am to you for seeing me so soon after your tragic bereavement.'

'Think nothing of it,' said Elizabeth Dauntsey. 'You said in your letter, Lord Powerscourt, that you thought I might be able to help you in some way. Please tell me what it is.'

Powerscourt paused for a moment. 'As I said, Mrs Dauntsey, I have been asked by the benchers of Queen's Inn to investigate the circumstances of your husband's death.'

'Do you find the benchers easy to deal with?' Elizabeth Dauntsey was very quick with her interruption. 'Some people find them rather difficult,' she went on.

This was not, Powerscourt felt, the conversational tone one would expect from a lady whose husband had been murdered so recently. Levity rather than grief seemed to be the order of the day. Maybe Elizabeth Dauntsey was one of those unfortunate people who always speak their mind. Maybe the rules for widows had changed now they were free of the long shadow of Victoria's forty years of mourning.

'The benchers?' Powerscourt smiled at his hostess. 'Well, let me say that I have found easier people to deal with.' Most murderers of his acquaintance, he might have said, were easier to deal with than Barton Somerville and his colleagues. 'But my purpose here at Calne is not with the benchers, Mrs Dauntsey. There are two reasons behind my visit. The first is mundane – would you mind if I talked to your family solicitor? It is sometimes helpful.'

'Not at all, Lord Powerscourt. The man you want is Matthew Plunkett of Plunkett Marlowe and Plunkett in Bedford Square. He's already been to see me. I shall drop him a line telling him to expect you and to help you in your inquiries.'

'Thank you so much,' said Powerscourt, wondering how old this Matthew Plunkett would prove to be. 'I have found,' he went on, looking carefully at Elizabeth Dauntsey, 'in all my investigations that the more I know about the deceased,' deceased was a more neutral word than victim, less upsetting than murdered man, he thought, 'the easier it becomes to work out why he perished in the way he did. I have only one side of your late husband, the professional aspect. You don't need me to tell you that lawyers are economical with the truth. They are very cautious with their words. Some of them measure out their version of the truth as though it were some tiny amount of a very expensive medicine being poured on to a rather small spoon. I need a broader picture of Mr Dauntsey, madam, and I am sure you can provide it.'

Elizabeth Dauntsey looked sad for the first time in their conversation. This time her voice was very soft and had no hint of raillery.

'Tell me what impression you have formed so far, Lord Powerscourt, and I will do what I can to fill in the gaps.'

Powerscourt paused and looked at Mrs Dauntsey very closely for some time. 'Mercurial,' he said. 'That, I think, is how some of his colleagues would have summed him up. A man of very great gifts, an advocate who could be brilliant, absolutely brilliant in court, a man who could dazzle juries and judges with his eloquence. But the brilliance had another side. Brilliance often does. On the bad days your husband lost all his gifts. It was as if he mislaid them or he never had them. In court on the black times he was hopeless. Of course, there were far more good days than bad ones, but it may have meant that he never rose quite as high, his fees and refreshers were never quite as great as those of some of his distinguished but less gifted contemporaries.'

Powerscourt looked at Elizabeth Dauntsey again to see if she was bearing up. She was.

'I think he was a kind man, your husband. I think he was popular with his colleagues. I think people in his Inn liked him. But I also sense, though nobody ever said this, that he was a private man, that there were areas of himself that were closed off.'

Elizabeth Dauntsey smiled again. 'How strange that you should have said that Alex had areas of himself that were closed off, Lord Powerscourt. Most of his house here is closed off, certainly all the grand bits, they have been for years. But that's not relevant. I think what you say about Alex is fair, very fair. He could be mercurial at home too, you know. We had what he called his black days sometimes when he could hardly speak to me.'

She leaned forward and put her head in her hands. Powerscourt thought she was more beautiful than ever.

'And he was a private man in some ways.' Elizabeth Dauntsey was speaking quietly, as if fearful of waking the dead. 'Even after ten years of marriage there were times when I felt shut out, that he'd gone off somewhere else. Alex believed in God, which is becoming rare these days. He was very kind to the servants. He was a great believer in the Liberal Party even though he had always loathed Gladstone. He was a passionate devotee and player of cricket. One of his ancestors was turned back at the Dover boat, you know, at the time of the French Revolution. He was taking a team to play a match in Paris. Can you imagine, Lord Powerscourt, spin bowling in the Tuileries or the Bois de Boulogne while severed heads were dropping to the ground from the guillotine?'

She paused for a moment, then carried on. 'And Alex was very fond of children.'

Suddenly Powerscourt knew from the tone of her voice that Elizabeth and Alexander Dauntsey had never had any children, that this loss might have blighted their marriage. He could not begin to imagine the depths of pain and despair it might mean for both man and woman, this desperate longing to have what your friends and neighbours were blessed with but you were not, a different but no less painful form of bereavement.

She looked at Powerscourt with tears in her eyes. Powerscourt knew he must speak now, he must steer her away into different ground or she might collapse and his interview would be at an end. But she battled on.

'We never had any children, Lord Powerscourt. That was very hard for both of us. I think Alex would rather Calne was inherited by a son of his than pass to one of his nephews, but it doesn't matter now, it doesn't matter at all.'

'Was your husband a sportsman, Mrs Dauntsey? Fond of hunting and fishing, that sort of thing?'

Powerscourt had no idea why he asked that question, maybe he was trying to move away from children as fast as possible.

'No, he wasn't.' The tears had been vanquished. 'He often quoted that line of Oscar Wilde about the English country gentleman galloping after a fox being the unspeakable in full pursuit of the uneatable. He was very fond of Italy, Alex, not the well-known places except for Venice which he adored, but the medium-sized cities with great histories, Cremona and Urbino and Ferrara and Parma, places like that.'

'I'm sure you won't be surprised to hear, Mrs Dauntsey, that there are fantastic rumours about your husband's interest in art circulating round the courts of Queen's Inn. The stories grow more fantastical in the telling.'

'Tell me the most outrageous,' she said, smiling at the investigator. Powerscourt felt rather weak.

He smiled back. 'The most outrageous, which I must have heard about five or six times, was that, in a fit of modernity, Mr Dauntsey had thrown all the Old Masters into the cellars and replaced them with modern works by the French artists known as Impressionists. It was furthermore alleged – I'm beginning to sound like a lawyer myself, Mrs Dauntsey, – that he was intending to strip out the ancient oak panelling and replace it with contemporary wallpaper by Edward Morris and the Arts and Crafts movement.'

Elizabeth Dauntsey smiled a beautiful smile. She rubbed her hands together in delight.

'Excellent, Lord Powerscourt, I do like that. The truth, however, is more prosaic. Some of the Old Masters were indeed taken down, but that was on advice from a very earnest young man from the National Gallery who said the air was too damp for them and they should be stored elsewhere. I believe we still pay a large amount of annual rent for their storage at a London gallery. The panelling was taken down because it had some rare form of woodworm and had to be repaired. How prosaic the truth is.'

Tea appeared, on a very expensive-looking silver tray.

'Cake, Lord Powerscourt?' asked Elizabeth Dauntsey, elegant hands offering him plate and chocolate cake at the same time. 'There's something else I think you ought to be aware of, and I don't quite know how it would fit in, or what use it would be. But you wouldn't understand Alex without it. It has to do with being brought up in this house, living in it all your life, being baptized and buried in it. It must be like growing up in Chatsworth or Blenheim. You're surrounded by so much history and so much beauty and so many precious things that you simply don't notice them after a while. They become part of you. Perhaps you become part of them too. Perhaps somewhere in the air there's the spirit of Dauntseys past and Dauntseys present waiting to welcome Dauntseys future. Alex loved this house with a very deep love. Even when we were on holiday somewhere he liked a lot, the Italian lakes maybe, or a Venetian palazzo, he'd be thinking of Calne. Maybe he compared all those fine houses and their treasures with what he had at home. I don't have any doubt which he preferred. There was always a smile on Alex's face when he came back up that drive past the deer even if he'd only left the place in the morning. Can you understand that, Lord Powerscourt? Were you brought up somewhere special?'

Powerscourt nodded. 'I certainly can understand it.' He thought of his parents' house, the dances until dawn in the great drawing room in the summer, the ornate steps down to the great fountain, the ever-changing reflections in the lake with the water lilies, the blue-green of the Wicklow Mountains in the background, the riders in their scarlet coats leaving for the hunt from the Powerscourt front door on crisp winter mornings. He thought of the funerals and the burials of his parents and how the entire family had to flee their grief and escape to the colder world of London after their parents died. 'I was brought up in the country in Ireland,' he went on, 'not anything as grand as Calne, but Irish country houses have charms of their own, as you know.'

'Forgive me, Lord Powerscourt,' said Elizabeth Dauntsey, 'look at the time. It's beginning to get dark. I'm sure you would like to see the house, everybody always does. The really grand bits aren't in use at all, the family haven't lived in them except for special occasions for decades. But I'm sure Marshall, our butler, could show you round. He doesn't say much but he does know the way. Some people went off to tour the place on their own last year and got terribly lost. It was hours before they were found. Please come back and say goodbye when you've finished.'

Powerscourt was to tell Lady Lucy later that evening that it had been one of the stranger experiences of his life. Some of the state rooms of Calne had the shutters drawn or the curtains pulled so there was little light there in the first place. In others the grime of ages had accumulated on the windows, forming a thick film, now laced with enormous cobwebs and malevolent spiders. Marshall had a lantern which threw extraordinary shadows on the walls, baroque reflections from enormous marble mantelpieces that seemed to touch the ceiling, fleeting shafts of light on nymph and shepherd on the tapestries that lined the walls. The sound of their boots on the oak floors was muffled by a protective layer of threadbare and faded carpet. Marshall himself was a giant of a man casting giant shadows on floors and ceiling as they went. They passed long galleries two lined with pictures and one with elaborate tapestries. A dining room that seemed to have walls of pale blue had an enormous ghostly dining table, far longer than a cricket pitch. They passed through shadowy bedrooms with vast beds, four-posters that looked as if they could accommodate entire families at a time. Marshall hurried them through dressing rooms and retiring rooms and sitting rooms and studies. The lantern swung across an entire wall of books in the vast library, surprising a full-length Restoration Dauntsey at the far end and a pair of rats in the skirting board. Vast pieces of furniture, draped in dust sheets, loomed in front of them, like ocean liners in a fog. Everywhere they could sense other Dauntseys watching their progress, full-length Dauntseys in robes of state, miniature Dauntseys in Jacobean lockets, Dauntsey wives in green and blue and scarlet peering out of the frames at a future they never saw. Sometimes they would hear the scuttling of tiny feet as the mice or the rats retreated from the invaders to regroup on a higher floor. When the lantern swung upwards the ornate plaster patterns on the ceilings assumed grotesque shapes, racing down the room to vanish in the darkness. They passed statues nude and statues clothed, ancient statues, Roman statues, some that might have been sold as Greek but were made in Florence or Bologna. The heads of innumerable deer and stags stared down at them from on high as they passed. They sped through an enormous kitchen where the brass saucepans on the wall gleamed and glittered for a brief second of glory as the lantern went by. In some places the air was musty, as if the tapestries and the pictures on the walls had only each other for company. Some of the clocks still worked, sounding out the quarter hours as the lantern sped on and the chimes echoed round the great empty rooms of Calne.

'I take it, sir, that you don't wish to see the cellars on this occasion?' Marshall spoke for the first time as they descended yet another oak staircase, dust sheets on the ornate banisters, rough matting on the floor. Powerscourt had a sudden nightmare vision of Goliath-sized shadows flitting across abandoned wine racks, of discarded pieces of furniture, sharp at the edges, lying in wait for the unwary, of cobwebs and spiders brushing across his face, of dirt and grime and smell and squalor.

'You are quite right, Marshall,' said Powerscourt, now deposited outside Elizabeth Dauntsey's doorway once again. 'Thank you very much.'

Powerscourt thanked Mrs Dauntsey profusely for her time and her insights into her husband. She thanked him for his visit and said she hoped he would feel free to come again if he thought she could help. But it was the handshake Powerscourt remembered most vividly as he set off back towards the station. It had been cold, her hand, and the grip firm, but it seemed to him, or was it just his imagination, that the grip meant more than it seemed to say. Quite what that might be, he did not know. But he did feel that at some point in the future it might be necessary, if not vital, to return to Calne and shake Mrs Dauntsey by the hand once again. Most of all, he fretted about the children that were not there.

5

I wonder if she'll come, Edward said to himself. He checked his watch again. She was ten minutes late already. Edward had placed himself at the top of the drive that led into the Wallace Collection, a famous collection of paintings, armour and furniture in Manchester Square. He had sent Sarah Henderson a note the day before asking her to join him here at three o'clock on the Saturday afternoon. She had dropped in to see him on her way home and said she would be delighted. Powerscourt, who had appointed himself to a position of unofficial godfather to the attachment and the meeting, had insisted that the pair should come to tea at his house in Number 8 Manchester Square. He had, he told Edward, recently purchased a typewriting machine and would be grateful for an expert opinion on the instrument.

Sarah had not intended to be late. Perhaps her mother had planned it. For just as Sarah was about to set off for the distant quarters of Marylebone and the Wallace Collection, her mother suddenly announced that she had run out of one set of pills. It would be all right, she said, if Sarah got them on Monday, but then she might be in agony for the rest of the weekend. Maybe, maybe, Sarah could find the time to pop down to the chemist's and collect the medicine this afternoon. Surely her other engagement couldn't take precedence over her mother's health. Fuming quietly under her breath, cursing her brother and sister for having escaped the drudgery and the intensity of their Acton home, Sarah walked as fast as she could to the chemist, but it was fifteen minutes there and fifteen minutes home again. When she got back her mother calmly informed her that she was now so late it was hardly worthwhile going. Nobody would wait that long. Sarah might as well stop at home and read to her mother from one of the weekly magazines. Sarah smiled sweetly, said she would see her mother later and fled to the smoky embrace of the District Line.

Some people might have wondered how Sarah reconciled her earlier resolve to have nothing to do with her colleagues at work with an afternoon tryst with a young man, even if he seldom spoke. That had not proved too difficult. For a start, she told herself, most of the men she had been warned against on her secretarial course were older. They were married. They had families. Edward fitted into none of those categories. Anyway, she thought, Edward was perfectly harmless. Everybody knew that.

It was only after about fifteen minutes delay that Edward began to grow seriously worried. I'll go at twenty past, he said to himself. Twenty past came and went and Edward was still there. There were vague rumours, nothing substantiated, nothing Edward would ever have allowed any of the men he devilled for to take into court, but rumours nonetheless that Sarah's mother was ill and liable to be difficult. Half past came and half past went. Edward was reluctant to abandon the afternoon because he had arrived two hours early. He had spent them learning about the story of the collection and about the most famous of the pictures. He had astonished himself by asking one of the curators two questions about one of the Fragonards. And on his afternoon vigil, he could console himself with surreptitious glances at the Powerscourt house and wonder about what was going on inside. He hoped he might meet the other twin this time, but then he wondered if he, an outsider, would be able to tell the two of them apart.

'Edward, I'm so sorry.' Sarah was out of breath and put a hand briefly on Edward's arm as if to slow herself down. 'I'm so glad you waited.' All the way there on the trains Sarah had been wondering if Edward would write her little notes, as he had with the invitation, or would he actually speak? He spoke.

'Take a seat,' he said, escorting her to a wooden bench just outside the house. 'We'll go in when you're ready.'

Sarah wanted to say Well Done. Nine consecutive words from Edward in Queen's Inn would be a day's portion, if not a week's. Now it was tumbling out.

'Have you been here before, Edward? Can you tell me about the place?'

Sarah watched as Edward collected his thoughts. She wondered if he had realized how much conversation might be involved on this sort of afternoon. Or had he thought they would peer at the pictures in silence?

'Named after Sir Richard Wallace. Illegitimate son of fourth Duke of Hertford.' Edward had reverted to staccato prose once again. 'All Hertfords collected pictures and things. Wallace died. Left everything to wife. Wife lived here for last seven years of life. Famous for smoking black cheroots. On her death left all to the nation. Pictures and stuff, not cheroots. Now here for ever.'

Sarah wondered about the black cheroots. Where had Edward found that out, she wondered? Once a deviller, she recalled, always a deviller. You could root out facts about art galleries as easily as you could those about court cases.

'Shall we go in? You'd better lead the way, Edward.'

Edward wondered if Sarah had been to this sort of establishment before. He was constantly amazed by the number of people who didn't even know where the National Gallery was. He had planned a route round some of the more dramatic pictures, the ones that should interest a newcomer. The armour he had resolved to ignore, and the furniture he would leave to the end. Edward was bored to tears by armoires and escritoires and secretaires and writing tables and garderobes and commodes and wardrobes. He led them rapidly across the hall and into the Housekeeper's Room.

'This one,' he whispered, 'very bloody, but very dramatic. Painter French Romantic, name of Delacroix. Called *The Execution of Doge Marin Falier.*'

The painting showed the interior courtyard or loggia of a great Venetian palace. White marble stairs led up to a higher level. Lining the stairs and crowded round a figure at the top were noblemen some dressed in rich costumes. A beautifully dressed Moor with an orange headband stared into the courtyard below, as if he were expecting trouble. At the top a Venetian senator held aloft a bloody sword. At the bottom of the steps, a few feet from the supercilious Moor, the headless body of the former Doge Marin Falier lay flat on the ground.

'What's going on, Edward? Why did this poor man have his head chopped off?'

'Falier Doge of Venice. Meant to be constitutional ruler like our King Edward. Power very limited. Falier wanted to smash the constitution and make himself tyrant. Nobles found out. Nobles cut his head off. Byron wrote poem about it. Byron fond of blood and gore. Painter probably knew poem. Painter also fond of blood and gore, probably fonder even than Byron.'

Sarah looked closely at Edward who was perspiring lightly from all this conversation. She hoped it wasn't going to make him ill.

'Going somewhere bit more peaceful now. Still Venice.' Edward led the way into the small drawing room where a pair of unusually large Canalettos looked across the Basin of St Mark from opposite directions. One showed the view from the mouth of the Giudecca Canal with the Customs House on the left out to Palladio's Church of San Giorgio Maggiore. The companion piece looked out from the steps of San Giorgio back to the mouth of the Giudecca Canal. The water was pale green, the sky a light blue with fluffy clouds. Small groups of Venetians discussed their business on the quays. Gondolas carried cloaked men and bales of cargo across the bay. A couple of sailing boats lurked at the edges of the picture. The great Venetian symbols, the Doge's Palace and the huge baroque dome of Santa Maria della Salute, reminded the viewer of the topography of the city. In both paintings there was an air of great calm as if Venice were at peace with itself and the world, as if these scenes had existed for hundreds of years past and would go on for hundreds of years into the future.

Again that hand briefly on Edward's arm. 'It's so beautiful,' said Sarah. 'I would so much like to go to Venice, wouldn't you, Edward?'

Edward nodded. 'English on Grand Tour bought Canalettos,' he said, 'like photographs on your holiday. Only in colour. Time for some froth and fluff now.'

So far, Edward hoped, Sarah had not realized how deliberate their itinerary was. Edward was taking them to the places where he had done his homework. If Sarah had wanted to stop in front of the Greuzes or the Watteaus, Edward would have been lost for words. As it was he was heading straight for Fragonard.

'*The Swing*,' he said quietly. 'Frenchman. Eighteenth-century. Name of Fragonard.'

In a dreamy forest of varying shades of green an attractive girl rode on a swing, dressed in layers of pink silk. Behind her, in the shade, an elderly gentleman in a dark green suit controlled the strings of the swing. Convention dictated that he was her husband. And on the far side of the girl, who was hiding him from sight of her husband, stood a handsome young lover in a pale green suit with a flower in his buttonhole, his hand stretched out towards the girl. One of her feet was much higher than the other on the swing, giving a view of her legs, and her slipper had fallen off her foot and was flying upwards through the air.

'Edward!' said Sarah, giggling to herself. 'Just look where that young man's looking! You're very naughty showing me this one, nearly as naughty as that girl in the picture. Haven't you anything more decent to show me?'

Edward smiled at her. 'All right, Sarah. Not naughty, these ones. But fantastic all the same.'

Edward took her to the first-floor landing where the world of François Boucher awaited them. This was a world where the laws of gravity and reality, of time and space, had been suspended, a world where naked gods rode chariots across the sky and semi-naked goddesses scattered pink roses among the clouds. Clothes were the exception in these fabulous landscapes although some scanty shifts were included from time to time so the artist could show off his brushwork. There were putti everywhere, plump little cherubs rolling back clouds or performing arabesques in the sky or gambolling playfully on the surface of the sea. Almost everything was subordinate to the naked female figure. A judgement of Paris was constructed in such a way as to give three different perspectives on the female form, groups of nude women frolicked on the waves, a glorious naked Venus caressed her husband Vulcan, god of fire and armourer of the gods. These were the wilder mythological poems of the wilder mythological poets translated on to canvas in shades of pale blue and pink and diaphanous green, a world of rococo and make believe and fantasy.

'My goodness me,' said Sarah, 'how absolutely wonderful. I wouldn't tell my mother this, Edward, but I like them, I really do. I think they're marvellous. Are there any more?'

Edward smiled. 'Not here. Probably in National Gallery. Nothing else as exotic as Boucher here.'

Sarah lingered in front of the rising and the setting of the sun.

'Boucher had important patron, Madame de Pompadour, official mistress of Louis the something or other,' Edward whispered. 'Kept wolf from door later on by designing tapestries for royal tapestry factory.'

'Where now, Edward?'

He led them halfway down the Great Gallery on the first floor, past a couple of sombre Van Dycks, a gorgeous full-length Gainsborough, and a sumptuous Rubens landscape. He stopped in front of a young man with a turned-up moustache, an elegant black hat and very fashionable clothes. Even back in the seventeenth century painters were keen to show how versatile their brushwork could be. This young man had a beautifully depicted ruff with a dark grey kerchief hanging from it, and a very intricate white cuff on a richly embroidered jacket. A faint smile played across his lips as if he were thinking of a secret or a joke that only he and the painter knew. It all looked totally spontaneous as if the young man had walked in and parked himself on Franz Hals's canvas the afternoon before.

'That's the Laughing Cavalier,' said Sarah knowledgeably. 'Everybody knows him from the advertisements. Isn't he by Franz somebody or other?'

'Good,' said Edward solemnly. 'But work originally called *Portrait of a Young Man*. Franz Hals. Dutchman. Early sixteen hundreds.'

'But why,' asked Sarah, 'do we call The chap The Laughing Cavalier?'

'Painting up for sale,' said Edward, now firmly back in cryptic mode, 'forty or fifty years ago. Nobody paid much attention. Nobody heard much of Hals chap. Fourth Marquess of Hertford takes a fancy to it. So does a Rothschild. Big battle in the auction rooms. Sells for six times its asking price. Newspapers drawn to battle between a Marquess and a Rothschild, supposed to be as rich as Croesus. Laughing Cavalier makes better copy than *Portrait of a Young Man*. Not good title. Look carefully.'

Sarah inspected the gentleman on the wall carefully. 'I'm afraid I can't see what you mean,' she said, frowning slightly at Edward.

'Look again,' he replied. 'He's not laughing, he's smiling. And look at his clothes. No indication he's a cavalier at all. Just the name stuck.'

Sarah looked round the gallery. The place was going to close in ten minutes' time and they were the last people there apart from a solitary curator lost in his own thoughts in the far corner.

'Last picture, Sarah. Another portrait. Different story.' Edward led her ten yards away from the Laughing Cavalier and stopped in front of another young man. He had a head ringed with dark brown curls and a dull red beret on top. His face was pale and handsome. He was looking slightly to the left of the painter. The young man wore a dark brown robe with a gold chain. Some people thought they detected a hint of a smile on his red lips. Others felt he had more serious matters on his mind.

'Titus,' said Edward gravely, moving back a few yards to get a different view. 'Titus Rembrandt. Terribly sad story. Titus's mother dead. Rembrandt married again. Rembrandt declared bankrupt the year before. Rembrandt not able to sell any pictures. The Dutch people in Amsterdam didn't care for them, didn't commission any. God in heaven. It's as if the English abandoned Shakespeare. Under the rules of the guild, Titus and the second Mrs Rembrandt had to administer the production of his etchings and the sale of his paintings. It's terrible.'

Sarah noticed that Edward was speaking in perfect sentences now and that he was more animated than she had ever seen him.

'There's worse,' he said. 'Much worse. The second Mrs Rembrandt died. Then Titus died. This Titus here, the boy in the painting, died before his father. Rembrandt had to bury his own son.' Sarah thought there might be a tear in the corner of his eye now as he recounted the various disasters that befell the great painter.

'When Rembrandt died, one of the finest painters who ever lived, all he left were some old clothes and his painting equipment. How very sad! So if anybody ever says to you, Sarah, that the Dutch produced some great painters, that is perfectly true. They also turned their back on the greatest.'

Ten minutes later Edward and Sarah were eating their first muffins in the Powerscourt drawing room. Olivia was there, and Thomas, and both twins, fast asleep. Listening to all these young voices, Olivia asking Sarah what it was like working in an Inn, Thomas discussing football teams with Edward, who had an encyclopedic knowledge of all of them, Powerscourt found it hard to believe that he earned his living investigating violent death and that his latest victim had been poisoned as he tucked into his beetroot soup. After tea they all trooped off to inspect the new typewriter. Sarah pronounced it an excellent model and astonished the children by typing perfectly coherent sentences as she looked over her shoulder. Olivia made her do it again with her eyes closed. Touch typing, Sarah explained, meant that you knew where all the keys were automatically so you didn't have to look down to find the letter you wanted. Both Thomas and Olivia thought it was a form of witchcraft or magic. Powerscourt wondered how long it would take to learn. He suspected that the young policeman had already mastered it.

'I want to ask your advice, Lucy,' he said when Edward and Sarah had gone and their own children had departed to the upper floors.

'Of course, Francis. Whatever you want.'

'I've been thinking about the Dauntseys and their lack of children.

61

I have no idea if it has anything to do with this investigation. Can you tell me what it would mean to Elizabeth Dauntsey, knowing you couldn't have children?'

Lady Lucy looked at a child's picture book left lying on the sofa.

'I'm sure you know as well as I do, Francis,' said Lady Lucy. 'I think it must have been absolutely frightful. I presume she didn't go into any details of what the doctors told them. I presume they have no idea who is at fault, although fault is the wrong word completely and I take it back.' She bent down to pick up a diminutive teddy bear, bought for one of the twins, sitting upright against a side table.

'Guilt,' she went on. 'I think you'd blame yourself for not being able to have children. I think you'd feel incomplete without them, that you hadn't fulfilled your duty by being a mother. Every time you went out into the streets and saw all kinds of people, people with less money than you, people with less taste than you, people uglier than you, people stupider than you, carrying their children about or holding their hands as they learn to walk or watching them run about in the park, why, it would nearly break your heart. When you went to stay with people you would have to watch others getting their children up in the morning or reading them bedtime stories at night, it would be awful, just awful. You don't think we've got too many, Francis, do you?'

'Too many what, Lucy?' said Powerscourt who had been thinking of Elizabeth Dauntsey going through Lucy's litany of misery.

'Too many children.'

'No,' said Powerscourt firmly. 'Four isn't very many between us. Two each. Lots of people have more than that, ten twelve, fifteen, imagine fifteen of them, Lucy, you could scarcely remember all their names. But tell me, is there anything a woman in such a predicament might try?'

'I don't understand, Francis,' said Lucy, looking confused.

'Might she try to get pregnant by a different man?'

'And pass the child off as her husband's?' Lady Lucy looked as though she found the conversation distasteful. 'Well, she might, I'm sure that's been done often enough in the past. Risky though, if the husband finds out. Or I've heard of people who go abroad for nine months or a year and come back with a child they say is theirs. It may be adopted, or the husband may have paid some other woman to have his child and then they pass it off as theirs. At least half the genes will be right that way.'

Powerscourt remembered what Elizabeth Dauntsey had said about her husband's love of Calne, his feeling for its past and its future. A man with that sense of historical continuity would find the lack of heirs more distressing than most.

'It must have been pretty frightful for Dauntsey too,' Powerscourt said. 'That place meant so much to him, that sense of it belonging to Dauntseys past, Dauntseys present and Dauntseys future. Only there might not be any future, or a different future peopled by relations, your own flesh and blood of course, but not your own issue.'

Lady Lucy smiled at him. 'I always think issue is such a dreadful word, Francis. It's a lawyer's word, beginning halfway down the first page of some dreary document about inheritance or something.'

'Sorry,' said Powerscourt. He was struck once more by the image of Elizabeth Dauntsey in her slim elegance gliding through the deserted drawing rooms and empty galleries of Calne, hoping maybe to find inspiration in the portraits of the ancestors who lined the walls. 'Dauntsey could have had an illegitimate child with some other woman,' he continued, 'somebody he could maybe adopt or make his heir later on. That chap whose widow left the Wallace Collection to the nation, he was illegitimate, but he was still able to inherit the lot. I don't think, forgive me, that he'd want to breed from any old stock. I can't see Alexander Dauntsey hoping to produce his heir with some common female who was prepared to bear his child for money.' Powerscourt paused and looked closely at the teddy bear. Already it was beginning to show signs of wear and tear, from the twins or Olivia. The fur on one arm had almost disappeared as if some strange disease had struck. One eye was slightly out of position, giving the bear a rather sinister aspect as if it was looking in two directions at once.

'I can't very well advertise in the newspapers, Lucy, can I? Would anybody involved with the late Alexander Dauntsey, especially in a child-bearing capacity, please get in touch with Francis Powerscourt, of Manchester Square?'

Lady Lucy shook her head. She knew what was coming. In a number of his previous investigations Lady Lucy had activated for her husband the vast tribe of her relations to report on particular individuals, whether they had fallen out with their wives or husbands, whether they were having affairs, who had been jilted in love. Powerscourt attributed the success of the venture to one important difference between the sexes. Women, he believed, were more curious than men. Women liked gossip more than men. What else were institutions like hairdressers' and ladies' luncheon clubs for, in heaven's name. Women were more interested in human relationships, their rise, their decline and fall, their occasional recoveries. Women, in his view – and he did not condemn them for these characteristics – were able to talk, gossip, if you will, about a particular topic or person or relationship for hours longer than their male counterparts. The final proof of his theory, in Powerscourt's view, had been given to him by one of London's leading booksellers, who informed him that women outnumbered men by a factor of four to one in the purchase of the novels of Miss Jane Austen.

'Do you think, Lucy, that you could rouse the team? Bring them out of retirement or wherever they've been to report on Elizabeth and Alexander Dauntsey? Not a clarion call, not a drumbeat, just a whisper, it all needs to be very quiet. I don't suppose any of your relations live anywhere near Calne, Lucy?'

Lady Lucy blushed slightly. 'I'm afraid, Francis, that I have a second cousin twice removed who lives on the other side of Maidstone. Her husband is very rich, something in the City, I think. I'm sure they move in the same circles as the Dauntseys.'

'Put the word out, please,' said Powerscourt, rising to his feet and holding his wife by the hands. 'What do you say to dinner out, Lucy? It's all those young people we had here earlier on this afternoon. I'm feeling quite reinvigorated.'

Powerscourt and Chief Inspector Beecham were greeted by a bizarre sight when they went to meet Joseph the steward in the Hall on the Tuesday morning after Edward and Sarah's tea in Manchester Square. The top half of the tables were roughly laid out with knife, fork and spoon. Each place had its own wine glass. And circulating round this phantom feast were the waiters who had served at the real one. It was, Powerscourt thought, like looking at the three ages of man. The old boys were back, swaying slightly as they carried round their dishes of imaginary vegetables, the veteran nearest Powerscourt with a face that looked like a parchment map. The regular staff of the Inn, middle-aged mostly, looked as if they served imaginary guests every day of their lives. The young men, two of whom did not look to be properly awake yet, were carrying bowls full of imaginary soup, or filling glasses with water Joseph had put in empty wine bottles. Powerscourt thought the prospect of it being turned into wine were slim.

'I thought this would get them into the swing of things,' said Joseph cheerfully, emptying a couple of wine glasses into a bucket. 'I've told them all to be ready to answer questions in a few minutes.'

Chief Inspector Beecham had gone to Dauntsey's place and sat down in it, looking carefully at the passing waiters.

'Gather round!' said Joseph and a macabre circle assembled round the place of the poisoned bencher. 'Lord Powerscourt!' He introduced him like a major-domo.

'Thank you all very much for coming in today,' he began. 'I know it can't have been easy for you. Now, do any of you remember anything about the feast? About Mr Dauntsey's death?'

There was a certain amount of shuffling and then one of the regular waiters spoke up. 'We've talked about this a lot, my lord, on the night itself and earlier this morning. We don't see how the poor gentleman could have been poisoned at the feast. They started with that terrine. We took the plates up to the High Table and nobody could have known which one was going to Mr Dauntsey, no one at all. Then there was the soup, my lord. How are you meant to put a drop of poison into a bowl of soup when you're carrying two at a time? It's not possible. Same with the wine, you don't know whose glass you're going to refill when you collect a fresh bottle from the wine room. If you wanted to kill the whole lot of them' – Powerscourt suspected this might be the preferred option for this particular waiter from the vehemence with which he said it – 'that would be easier. The cook slips the poison into the soup and off you go. Or you add something special to half a dozen bottles of wine and finish them off like that. But one person, no, not possible.'

The waiter stared at them rather defiantly, as if he thought they would contest his findings. They did not.

'First class,' said Chief Inspector Beecham. 'We agree with every word of that.'

It is a rare, almost impossible event for an investigator like Lord Francis Powerscourt to come face to face with the man whose death he is investigating, for the living, as it were, to meet the dead. But it was happening now, the day after the phantom feast in the Hall. Edward had been the midwife to the meeting.

'New benchers,' he said cryptically to Powerscourt, 'always have portrait done. Hangs in Hall or library.' Now Edward mentioned it, Powerscourt remembered seeing some of these portraits displayed in prominent positions. He recalled, in particular, the two full-length Gainsboroughs of previous benchers behind Alexander Dauntsey in the Hall on the night of the feast. 'Painter man wants to see somebody from Inn. Check he's got the details right.'

Powerscourt and Edward were walking along the Mall that runs from Hammersmith Bridge along the river in the direction of Chiswick. Some of the houses were recent but there were also some fine eighteenth-century specimens looking out over the Thames. Number 35, The Terrace, Powerscourt learned, was where their painter lived, a man by the name of Stone, Nathaniel Stone.

'Who the hell are you? What the devil do you want? Why can't you leave me alone?' This violent reaction to Edward ringing the bell came from a small red-bearded man with angry eyes, wearing a painter's apron now stained with all the colours of the rainbow and a few more besides.

'My name is Powerscourt,' said Powerscourt in his most authoritative voice, 'and this is my friend Edward. We have come from Queen's Inn about the portrait of Mr Dauntsey. As you probably know, Mr Dauntsey is dead but the Inn still wants his portrait.'

'Why couldn't you say so?' The red-bearded man sounded as though he was going to continue in the same vein. 'You'd better come in. Thought you'd come about a bill. You look like you might have come about a bill. Had a lot of trouble lately with that bloody bill.'

He led them upstairs to a great drawing room that looked out over the river, back to Hammersmith Bridge on the left, and across the water to the fields of Barnes on the other side. A large easel, Powerscourt noticed, contained a full-length portrait of a society beauty, almost finished, he suspected, except for some elaborate lacework on the cuffs.

The little man glowered at the portrait. 'She's been driving me mad all day, that woman.' He walked right up to the canvas and stared moodily at where the lace should have been. 'Progress, that's what they keep telling us, progress. Bloody electricity coming in to light everything up. Bloody motor cars coming along to run us all over.' Nathaniel Stone picked up a brush and began prodding uncertainly at his canvas. 'Bloody telephones coming in so your creditors can harass you in your own home without ever leaving their bloody offices. Bloody cameras – all right, I know they've been around for a long time – but they're getting better and better all the time. Won't be any bloody portraits left for us painters at all, some bloody monkey with an expensive camera will take our trade away.'

The little man paused and peered at those elusive cuffs once more. Powerscourt was about to speak but he wasn't quick enough.

'Progress? What progress?' Nathaniel Stone spat bitterly into his fire. A sudden hiss flared up, matching the temper of the owner. He pointed back to his easel. 'Four hundred years ago, three hundred years ago, any fool with a brush could have painted that cuff. Last year I could have done it. The year before I could have done it. When I was twenty-one years old I could have done it with my eyes closed. Now I can't do it at all. I'm not progressing. I'm not progressing at all. I'm going bloody backwards.'

Powerscourt wasn't sure how much this bravura display was genuine and how much was for effect. 'Mr Stone,' he said firmly, 'you underestimate yourself, you really do. The reputation of Mr Nathaniel Stone in London's artistic circles would not be what it is today if you were a man going backwards.' Powerscourt would have had to admit that his knowledge of the Stone reputation was small, if not non-existent, but wounded artistic egos must be salved somehow. 'I am sure it is the bill that is responsible,' he went on. 'Bills have a habit of being extremely disagreeable. They put a man off his stroke or his brush. They occupy the brain so it cannot issue proper instructions.'

Out of the corner of his eye Powerscourt saw Edward making discreet signs at him. Edward's right thumb was moving rhythmically down into the palm of his left hand. The gesture was repeated over and over again. What on earth was Edward trying to tell him? Powerscourt saw that Nathaniel Stone was limbering up for another broadside of oaths. Suddenly he got the message. Edward was counting banknotes.

'However, Mr Stone,' he continued, 'if it would help with the disagreeable bill, we could make a preliminary payment on Mr Dauntsey's portrait.' Powerscourt began rummaging about in his wallet. 'Should we say thirty pounds, Mr Stone? Perhaps that would help?'

Stone looked at the notes greedily, like a man who finds the oasis after long days wandering in the desert. Powerscourt wondered what happened to the money. The man must be well paid and his portraits were excellent. Perhaps there was a Mrs Stone and a battalion of little Stones to feed. Maybe there was more than one Mrs Stone.

The painter stuffed the notes into his back pocket. They didn't seem to have improved his temper very much. He swore violently as he lifted the society lady off her easel. 'Bloody cuffs,' he said bitterly, 'bloody lace, why didn't I make the bloody woman wear those very long gloves? Even I can manage gloves these days.' He began heaving the painting towards the door. 'Be back in a minute. Bringing your Mr Dauntsey for you to have a look at.'

Powerscourt and Edward smiled to each other. Then there was a great bang from next door. 'My God,' they heard Stone say, 'the Hungarian Ambassador! In his Robes of State! With that damned Transylvanian fur! He was meant to be finished three months ago!' Then a thin scraping sound as if something was being pulled across the floor. 'Christ!' There was real pain in the voice now. 'The bloody Bishop of Rochester! Four months late and I never got that bishop's crook right!'

The back room seemed to be a treasure house of unfinished masterpieces. Maybe he was like Leonardo, Powerscourt reflected. The man seemed to be constitutionally incapable of finishing a picture.

'No, please God, no.' Stone's voice had turned into a high-pitched wail now. 'The Cabinet Minister's wife! That's so far back I can't remember the woman's name!'

A loud crash followed as if a group of paintings had all fallen forward on to the floor. 'Where's that bloody lawyer gone? Who's this? Oh, my God, it's the Great Conductor! I should never have tried him with that baton, it was never going to work. And who are you, for heaven's sake?' Again they heard the scraping sound as if a canvas was being pulled along the floor. 'You're not, my God, you're not. You can't be. You can. You are. You damned well are. In Christ's name, you are the bloody Governor of the Bank of England, due for delivery, it says here on the back, eight months ago.'

There was another loud bang. Powerscourt was to say afterwards that it was yet another canvas falling over. Edward maintained that Nathaniel Stone had kicked the wall very hard. The complaints went on.

'You're not a damned lawyer, you're the Editor of The Times, for God's sake. When were you due to be delivered? Six weeks ago. They might forgive me that. And you? Are you Dauntsey? No, you are not. You are some miserable banking person, meant to be handed over last October. Oh my God!'

Powerscourt suddenly remembered that his sister had commissioned a portrait of her husband, the distinguished banker William Burke, but he had no recollection of seeing it on the Burke walls. Perhaps it was still here. Perhaps he could ask the little man about it. Another wail came from next door.

'How could I! One of the very few people I've painted I really liked! You wouldn't expect me to like the bloody King's Private Secretary, but I did. And he's still here! Five months late! All because of that monocle! I should never have tried it! And here's some bloody General with huge moustaches. Who the hell are you? I don't bloody know. Here's Dauntsey. Thank God for that.'

Muttering under his breath, Stone returned and placed Dauntsey on the easel. Edward was astonished. 'Brilliant, Mr Stone,' he said, 'absolutely brilliant. It's a perfect likeness. I can't tell you how lifelike it is.'

Nathaniel Stone had painted Dauntsey in some great room with a grey wall, a pillar behind him and wooden boards at his feet. He was wearing a light grey suit with a cream shirt. The red bencher's robes sat comfortably on his shoulders. Powerscourt saw that he had light brown hair, thinning slightly at the temples, a high forehead, a Roman nose and eyes of light blue. In his left hand he was holding a number of briefs, the fingers long and slender. His expression was serious but there was a very faint hint of a smile. Surely this was a man, Powerscourt thought, you could imagine walking the great park with its deer at Calne or playing cricket on his very own pitch in the hot and dreamy days of summer. Above all, he reflected, Stone had made him impressive. a man to be reckoned with. Powerscourt thought he would have liked him if he had met him alive.

'Tell me, Mr Stone,' said Powerscourt. 'what did you make of Mr Dauntsey? Did you like him? You must have spent a fair amount of time with him at the sittings.'

'It's a very strange thing,' said Stone, shaking his head. 'how people behave when they're sitting for a portrait. It can take up to ten hours, five two-hour sessions, if things aren't going well. Some of them tell you their life story, they really do. I had a man last year, peer of the realm, no less, and he spent the entire ten hours complaining about his wife. You'd think he might take a break now and then, but no, on and on he went. Last month I had a woman who complained about her daughter all the time. Envy possibly. But Mr Dauntsey was different. He didn't treat me as his father confessor. He was very polite, very considerate, asking if he was sitting the right way. Quite unusual, that, he treated me as an equal, not some hired hand.'

'Did he mention Queen's Inn at all?' asked Powerscourt.

Stone looked at the Dauntsey in oil in front of him. 'I don't think he did,' he said, scratching his head. 'Hold on, he did say one thing, but I didn't pay much attention to it at the time. It was something about very strange things going on there. He didn't say any more than that.'

'He didn't give any detail about the strange goings on?'

The painter thought for a moment. 'No, he didn't,' he said finally, 'he said it quite quietly, almost as if he was talking to himself.'

'Anyway, it's a very fine painting. You must be very pleased with it, Mr Stone,' said Powerscourt tactfully.

There was a sort of low muttering from the man in the apron. 'Fools they send me! Fools! Blind people despatched to look at pictures, my pictures! God help us all!'

Stone subsided into a battered chair to the left of his easel and glowered at them. Powerscourt suddenly realized what the trouble might be. The man might be a perfectionist. Plenty of people of his acquaintance wanted things, their clothes, their lawns, their horses, their women, to be as near perfect as possible, but knew that they were never going to reach one hundred per cent success. But a few, an unlucky few, were destined to be dissatisfied with anything less than perfection. One of Lady Lucy's elderly relations was so obsessed with the perfection of tidiness in her home, as Lady Lucy called it, that she practically had a fit if you moved an ashtray two inches to the left. And for a painter it might be much worse. A section of Transylvanian fur, a conductor's baton, a courtier's monocle might reduce a man to despair. Powerscourt felt rather sorry for Nathaniel Stone.

'It's the bloody shoes, for God's sake.' Stone was speaking quietly now as if the long encounter with the unfinished works had exhausted him. Powerscourt and Edward peered closely at the shoes. Black. Leather. Highly polished. Expensive. New. There didn't seem to be anything wrong with them at all.

'Can't you see, Pursecourt or whatever your name is, that the shoes are all wrong?'

Powerscourt couldn't see it at all. Stone leapt out of his chair. Some of the earlier vigour and all of the earlier bad temper seemed to be returning.

'A child of three, for God's sake, could tell you that the light in the painting is coming from the right of the sitter. There's even a

70

bloody great shadow behind him so the morons of Queen's Inn could tell where it was coming from if they put their minds to it.' Now he pointed dramatically at the two shoes. 'The direction of the light means that the left-hand shoe should be in the light and the right-hand one in shadow. And what have I done, fool that I am? They're the other way round, for Christ's sake. I've tried three times to fix it and everything just gets worse.'

'Mr Stone,' said Powerscourt firmly, 'I have absolutely no doubt that the benchers and the barristers of Queen's Inn will be happy with your splendid painting just as it is.' Little bit of pomposity might not go amiss, Powerscourt said to himself. 'I go further. Speaking on their behalf, and as your patron as it were on this occasion, I forbid you to attempt to change the shoes. I shall arrange the transport of the painting from here to the Inn tomorrow and the completion of the payment of your fee. And soon there will be another commission. As I said when we arrived, Alexander Dauntsey is dead. A new bencher will be chosen to replace him after a decent interval. A new portrait will be required. I cannot speak for my colleagues but I am sure it is more than likely you will be asked to carry out the work.'

The mention of death seemed to subdue Nathaniel Stone. 'How did he die?' he asked very quietly. 'He was here in this room only two weeks ago.'

'He was murdered,' said Powerscourt, rising to take his leave.

The red-headed man saw them out, down his creaking stairs. Even as the door closed behind them they could hear him muttering, 'Murdered, murdered, murdered,' over and over again.

'Wish we could have seen them,' said Edward, walking briskly beside the Thames on their way back to the underground railway.

'Seen what?' said Powerscourt, trying to populate Calne with various versions of Dauntsey, Dauntsey taking his dinner in the great dining room, Dauntsey walking through his estate, Dauntsey relaxing at his billiard table or looking at his paintings after supper.

'Those other paintings,' said Edward. 'The Hungarian Ambassador. The Private Secretary. The Governor of the Bank of England. I bet they were all very good. Like our Mr Dauntsey.'

But as they reached Queen's Inn, they could tell that something was wrong. Groups of porters were inspecting every staircase. Powerscourt thought he could see Chief Inspector Beecham and a couple of his men on the roof. The Head Porter told them what had happened in the middle of the great court.

71

'It's Mr Woodford Stewart, sir. He's disappeared. We know he meant to leave early today, sir. He mentioned it to two people in his chambers and to his clerk. He meant to leave by two at the latest. It's now five o'clock. He's not at home, sir. We spoke to his wife by the telephone. His coat and his papers that he would take away with him are still here, sir.'

'When was he last seen?' asked Powerscourt, as two of Beecham's policemen slipped into the staircase behind him and marched up the stairs.

'Midday, sir. Said he was going to a meeting. Didn't say who with. That's five hours he's been gone. There's plenty round here say he's the next in line.'

'Next in line for what?' asked Powerscourt, wondering if this was some strange legal term he did not know.

'Next in line after Mr Dauntsey, sir. Next in line for murder.'

6

Edward set off at great speed across the grass. He sprinted up the stairs and burst into Sarah Henderson's room without even bothering to knock. She held up a hand motioning him to silence. She was working at top speed, her fingers racing over the keys of her typewriter, the left hand slamming the carriage across when she came to the end of a line. Her eyes were darting down to a shorthand notebook by her left side. Edward admired the straightness of her back on her chair, the red sheen on her hair, the white hands with their long fingers he longed to hold in his own. From the small window he could see more policemen marching in and out of the staircases, Chief Inspector Beecham and the Head Porter conferring over a large sheet of paper that might have been a map of the Inn with all the staircases marked. At last she was finished.

'Sarah,' said Edward, 'are you all right?'

She smiled at him. 'Of course I'm all right, Edward, why should I not be all right? And, yes, I have heard about Mr Stewart going missing. Have they found him yet? There seem to be more policemen every time I look. Perhaps they're breeding in the library.'

'They haven't found him,' said Edward. 'It's my belief that he's not in Queen's Inn at all.' Since their trip to the Wallace Collection Edward seemed able to converse with Sarah in perfectly normal sentences.

'Do they think he's dead?' Sarah asked the question in the same tone she might have asked a guest if he took sugar in his tea.

'Some people do. There's a whole lot of rumours about him already. Did you know him, Sarah?'

'I took a very short piece of dictation for him once when his own girls were away,' said Sarah, 'so I couldn't really say I knew him at all. That's why I can't get very excited about it. I was so upset about Mr Dauntsey. I thought I would never get over it. He had such a lovely voice, you see.'

Edward peered out of the little window on the top floor. 'There's even more of them now, Sarah – police, I mean. They must be very worried.'

'They always come too late,' said Sarah, as if she had been covering crime cases for years, 'so they make up for it with the numbers.'

'Are you finished now, Sarah? Finished for the day, I mean?'

'Yes, I am. Why do you ask?'

Edward looked shy for a moment. Sarah wondered for a second if his new confidence was going to desert him. 'I would like to escort you to the underground, Sarah. I don't like to think of you going there alone with a murderer on the loose somewhere.'

Sarah quite liked the thought of being escorted by Edward though she would have preferred a more romantic destination than the Tube. A masked ball at some elegant house in the country? A tea dance at one of London's great hotels? She consoled herself with the thought that the Temple at least was one of the finer names on the underground system. You wouldn't want to be escorted to Colliers Wood or Shadwell, she thought.

'It's hardly any distance from here to the Tube, Edward,' she said kindly, 'and there seem to be enough policemen to look after the Crown Jewels. But if you would like to, I should be happy to be escorted.'

Fifteen minutes later Edward was back in Queen's Inn. Sarah had refused all offers of his accompanying her back home to Acton. She sat down next to a barrister she knew from the Inner Temple and Edward felt fairly sure that she would not be violated before she found her way home. The police were still crawling all over the Inn. Barton Somerville himself was glowering down at them from the steps into the library as if they were particularly repulsive aliens, recently landed from a distant and disagreeable planet beyond the Milky Way. Powerscourt he could not find anywhere. None of the policemen, not even Chief Inspector Beecham, knew where he was. Edward found him at last, sitting at the desk that had been Dauntsey's, rummaging through the papers in the drawers.

'Edward,' said Powerscourt, smiling at the young man, 'have you been seeing Sarah to the Tube?'

'I have,' Edward replied, wondering how the devil Powerscourt had worked that out, 'but I have something to tell you which may be important, I'm just not sure.'

'Fire ahead, Edward,' said Powerscourt, 'take your time.'

'Yes, sir,' said Edward, looking closely at a print behind Powerscourt's head of an eighteenth-century cricket match taking place at Calne. One of the batsmen looked remarkably like the oil painting he and Powerscourt had seen only that afternoon.

'It's to do with the link between Mr Stewart and Mr Dauntsey, sir,' he began. 'They've always been close and in the past they've always conducted a lot of cases together.'

Edward paused. There, just behind the distant outfielder in the print, a couple of deer were standing to attention, watching the action carefully. 'There's another case they were going to do, Lord Powerscourt, sir. It was huge. A fraud case, involving the man Jeremiah Puncknowle.'

'Were they prosecuting or defending?'

'They were for the prosecution, sir, with splendid fees and very lavish refreshers indeed, some of the biggest I have seen. I was going to devil for them, sir, I have done a load of work already and was going to make it full time tomorrow.'

'Forgive me, Edward, are you suggesting that the defendant Puncknowle may have had something to do with these deaths?'

'I don't know what I am suggesting, sir. I only know that this case is now scheduled for the end of next week. There's been a delay. Before that it was to have started in two days' time.'

'And if both the prosecuting lawyers were removed from the scene, Edward, would the Crown apply for an adjournment while they briefed some more?'

'They would, sir, but it would be up to the judge to decide.'

'Have you formed any opinion about the character of this Jeremiah person? Would he have ordered up a couple of murders?'

'I couldn't say, sir. I could tell you a great deal about his companies but not very much about his character. You don't get a lot of that looking at balance sheets.'

'Edward,' said Powerscourt, rising to his feet and looking at his watch, 'I hope to be able to give you some sort of answer tomorrow. I am going to call on my brother-in-law.'

'Is he an expert in character, Lord Powerscourt, sir? Is he that sort of man?'

'He may be, Edward, come to think of it he probably is. But he is a great financier, now one of the greatest in the City of London. He will be able to tell me all the stuff about our Mr Puncknowle that never appeared in the papers.'

Powerscourt departed towards his sister's latest house. They moved their London house so often now that he and Lucy had once actually turned up for dinner at a fashionable address that the Burkes had vacated a month before. Edward had brief conversations with the policemen before they left. There was still no sign of Mr Woodford Stewart, and his wife reported that he had not turned up at home. Tomorrow they would broaden the search into the Inner and Middle Temples. Maybe, the Chief Inspector confided to his sergeant, they would have to send divers in to search the bloody river.

'You're not here on a social call, Francis, I can tell.' Powerscourt's middle sister Mary Burke kissed him warmly on both cheeks. 'Before I pack you off to William, how is Lucy? How are the children? And those gorgeous twins?'

'All very well indeed,' said Powerscourt, smiling at his sister. 'All well here?'

'We're fine,' said Mary. 'William's in his study, one floor up. I forget you haven't been in this house before.'

'I'm sure I can find the way.' Powerscourt departed, taking the stairs two at a time. He found his brother-in-law shrouded in cigar smoke and surrounded by figures. On the desk in front of him was an enormous ledger with numbers chasing each other up and down various columns. Surrounding the mighty tome were a series of smaller volumes in a variety of colours, muted colours it would have to be said, garish colours not being available in the kind of stationer's shop in the City patronized by the likes of William Burke.

'Delighted to see you, Francis, delighted.' Burke had risen from his chair and was shaking Powerscourt vigorously by the hand. He had assisted Powerscourt in a number of his inquiries and had proved a most valuable companion in arms. Powerscourt always said you could pick his brother-in-law out in a crowd of five hundred by the cut of his suit. There were many in the City who prided themselves on wearing the latest fashions. William Burke went in the opposite direction. Johnny Fitzgerald maintained that he bought two or three suits every autumn and then left them in the shop for twenty years. Powerscourt objected to this theory on the grounds that a man could not be sure he would keep exactly the same shape over a period as long as twenty years. His theory was that William Burke had a very old tailor indeed, a man who kept detailed records of all the fashions going back to Disraeli's time or even earlier. Powerscourt imagined that Burke would be measured in the normal way. On his way out, this Nestor of the tailoring world would ask, 'Which year, sir?' and Burke would reply, '1882, please.' In appearance, apart from his suits, Burke was perfectly normal, normal height, not fat and not slim, an ordinary sort of face with an ordinary sort of nose and rather sharp grey eyes. You could see thousands and thousands of people looking exactly like him climbing on and off the buses or the trains for the City every working day. Looking at the face, Johnny Fitzgerald once memorably remarked, you would not imagine its owner's facility for mental arithmetic would be so great that he could multiply one hundred and forty-eight by seventeen in his head while walking down the street without having to pause and without contracting a headache. Burke had taken ten pounds off Johnny in a wager many years ago by performing this feat while walking down Threadneedle Street in the rain.

Certainly this evening's suit, though of excellent cloth, was not one likely to be worn by the Beau Brummells of the capital's dress elite like Charles Augustus Pugh.

Powerscourt waved a hand at the multicoloured concentration of ledgers and financial fire power in front of his brother-in-law.

'Selling up, William?' he asked cheerfully. 'Preparing to flee before the bailiffs come round?'

William Burke laughed. 'Annual audit, Francis. Once a year I make myself go through all the family accounts, see how we're doing. Are we better off than last year, that sort of thing. Can Mary buy a new pair of shoes, you know? We make all our big companies do it, don't see why we shouldn't do it at home.'

'And are all the coloured books for different kinds of investment? And the huge tome the master document, the Book of Numbers as it were, for the whole lot?'

'They said you'd been consorting with lawyers, Francis. They seem to have sharpened your wits. Red for property – I've got a couple of other houses in London as well as the place in the country.' Powerscourt recalled that the place in the country stood on the banks of the Thames not far from Goring and had twenty-seven bedrooms and fourteen bathrooms. Not to mention the huge palace on the sea front at Antibes. 'Blue for stocks, green for bonds, maroon for savings accounts, it's all fairly simple. But you haven't come here to talk about annual balance sheets, Francis, you've come to talk about something else.'

Powerscourt smiled. 'I want to know about a man called Jeremiah Puncknowle,' he said.

William Burke moved to the sofa in front of his fireplace. He looked closely at his brother-in-law. 'Could you be a bit more specific, Francis?' he said. 'Puncknowle as businessman, Puncknowle as family man, Puncknowle as friend of the deserving poor? It's pronounced Punnel by the way, like punnet only with an l at the end.'

Powerscourt had always put his cards on the table with William Burke. 'Right, William. This is how it goes, or might go. Friend Puncknowle is about to go on trial, sometime in the next ten days at the latest. The two main prosecuting counsel both come from Queen's Inn. One of them, man by the name of Dauntsey, was murdered almost two weeks ago. He was poisoned and fell face forwards into a bowl of soup at a feast. The benchers, governing body of the Inn, have asked me to investigate his death. Now the other lawyer, fellow by the name of Woodford Stewart, has disappeared. The Crown will either have to proceed with the case and give new counsel virtually no time to prepare what is a very complicated case, or they will have to ask for an adjournment which they may or may not get, depending on the judge. So, you might think, what a coincidence. Just as this massive fraudster is about to go on trial, the lawyers going to attack him are dead or disappear. And, if you were of a suspicious mind, William, you would want to warn the new lawyers to mind their step as they cross Chancery Lane or set out for the Old Bailey. I want to know if this Puncknowle is capable of ordering up a murderer or two. But before that I want to know what sort of fraudster he was. And before that, though why you should have this information I do not know, I want to know if he is in jail or out on bail.'

William Burke closed his eyes briefly. He put the fingers of his two hands together and opened them out into a kind of fan or steeple. 'He's not in jail,' he began, 'though there are many in the City who were astounded when he was given bail. The policeman in charge of the investigation insisted on the Bank of England itself confirming for him that the relevant sum had been posted. And it was an enormous figure, some men claimed to know it was half a million pounds.'

'How did this crook persuade a judge to give him bail in the first place? Surely they would have wanted him kept under lock and key until he appeared in court?'

William Burke laughed. 'It was a fearsome combination, Francis. Clever lawyers and clever doctors. God knows how much they were paid. They told the judge that Puncknowle was perfectly willing to appear in court, but that he had a heart condition. This condition made it highly likely that he would not survive a period as a guest of His Majesty. Many of the other inmates after all would have been defrauded by our friend Jeremiah and might not take too kindly to finding him in their midst. They might wish to take physical revenge for their financial suffering.'

'Why couldn't they put him in solitary? Leave him alone for the duration?'

'Simple minds, Francis, simple minds might think along those lines. There was a further ramification to the heart condition, you see. Claustrophobia, from which our Jeremiah suffered acutely, would be brought on by solitary confinement. There could well be a fatal attack in a couple of days at most. And then what would the great British public and the great British newspapers say of the authorities who had, in their intransigence, kept Puncknowle out of the dock and denied the British investor the chance to see some reparations made for his suffering and his losses?'

'Surely to God there must have been some place the prison authorities could have put him?'

'I'm sure there was,' said Burke cheerfully. His fingers were still arching up towards his fireplace. 'But they had hit on a master-stroke, Puncknowle's people. They had discovered, or one of the doctors giving evidence on his behalf had discovered – large sums changing hands, no doubt – that the judge suffered from precisely the same heart condition that Puncknowle was supposed to have. So the judge could imagine only too well what his reaction would have been to a bout of solitary. It would have killed him for sure. So he gave the fellow bail.'

Powerscourt laughed. William Burke looked quite pleased with himself. He sent an enormous puff from his cigar directly into his chimney.

'And the frauds, William? How did they work?'

Once again Burke paused. This time he looked carefully at his ledgers as if checking they had not been infected by the Puncknowle virus of financial irregularity. He knew his brother-in-law was

79

perfectly capable of grasping financial facts, unlike, to his enormous and eternal regret, his wife and his three sons.

'Very simple really, to begin with, I suppose. Most fraudsters should stick to their original trick. It's when they become too elaborate that the house falls down.'

'So where,' asked Powerscourt, 'did he start, this Jeremiah Puncknowle?'

'He started in the West Country, Francis. I don't know if you were aware of it but there's a whole host of tiny dissenting religious communities down there, Muggletonians, Shelmerstonians, Babbacombians, Yalbertonians, hundreds and hundreds of them, all only too happy to knock you down if you disagree with their version of the Book of Revelations or the precise order of the re-awakening of the saints on Judgement Day.'

'Did they think that God had some sort of enormous batting order for Peter and Paul and Sebastian and all the rest of the saints when they'd be called to the wicket for the first innings of the new world?' As a small boy Powerscourt had always been worried about how Sebastian would be able to rise from the dead when his turn came with all those arrows in him. Surely, he had thought, Sebastian might get up, but he would just as surely fall down again.

'I'm not acquainted with the finer points of Muggletonian theology, Francis, but the point, for our purposes, was this. The man Puncknowle set up a building society aimed at these religious brethren. It was very successful. The idea of helping their fellow men even if you disagreed violently with their religion appealed to these West Country characters. The society was a success. It was straight. It is still going to this day, the only honest business ever founded by Jeremiah Puncknowle. It did give him one important idea. Some of the pastors helped set up the building society, they sat on its board, they advertised its products.'

'So did he move in for wholesale corruption of the clergy?' Powerscourt asked with a grin.

'Not quite,' said William Burke, 'but they say that he was surprised by two things in his West Country venture. One was how useful the clergy could be if they were on your side. And the other is as old as the hills in terms of money but people are always forgetting it. If you're floating public companies you can aim for a lot of money from fairly few people or institutions or a small amount of money from a great many people. Puncknowle chose the latter. He toured the country promoting his schemes. They say he followed the routes of Wesley himself, the founder of Methodism. He employed dissenting ministers as a clerical collar sales force and paid them generous commissions. And he raised money in millions for his building societies. Their prospectuses were a wonderful combination of piety and greed. There was the noble purpose of helping those of lowly means to save safely, so that eventually they could purchase their own dwellings, humble maybe, but no less glorious in the sight of the Lord. There were the donations to charity and good works – precise figures never specified – but that section was usually penned by some leading dissenter. Once they even got an evangelical Church of England dean to write it but they say he got into trouble with his bishop. And then there were the earthly rewards, never oversold, normally placed quite discreetly in the prospectuses, but eight per cent is eight per cent if you're a railwayman or a Rothschild. I don't think you or I would have wanted to invest, Francis. My own broker swore he'd have been able to sell a bucketload of the shares to the late Queen, Victoria well amused by the piety and the good works and the eight per cent to pay for her grandchildren's extravagance.'

'So what went wrong, Edward? Our Jeremiah must have had millions rolling in.'

'It's the normal story,' said William Burke. 'Caveat emptor, as the poet said. Let the buyer beware. Only trouble was most of these investors didn't know much about caveating and even less about the traps awaiting the emptors. If you can get two and a half per cent interest on government stock anybody who comes along offering you eight per cent is virtually certain to be a crook. But these poor little dissenters didn't know anything about that. Their pastors could go on about the difference between the gospels of Matthew and Luke for hours at a time but they had no knowledge at all of interest rate differentials. And while the Bible is full of crooks and shysters all over the shop, the pastors wouldn't recognize one if he walked up to them and shook them by the hand. Which, of course, is precisely what Jeremiah Puncknowle did. One of his critics in later years claimed that Puncknowle had shaken hands with over three thousand men of the cloth. The building societies did their stuff, houses got built, all that sort of thing, but they were never going to produce eight per cent return. So there was another company floated, the subscribers to the second unwittingly paying out the dividends of the first. And a third, whose investors paid out the dividends of the second. It became like one of those card tricks where the conman has the cards spinning faster and faster. Soon there was nearly a football team of these companies. Then they moved into banking and property and building, the whole golden wheel spinning faster and faster. Then the people at the top got too greedy. They began selling properties between one company and another and then selling them on to a third so they could make off with the notional profits that appeared in the accounts. That's what brought them down – property companies with too many debts and virtually no assets. Whole house of cards had taken about twelve years to set up. It fell down in three days flat.'

Powerscourt had often urged his brother-in-law to take up his pen and write short and amusing sketches of financial behaviour for the magazines. He was sure they would be very successful and make his brother-in-law even richer than he already was. But William Burke always declined.

'Tell me, William, was there ever any hint of violence about our friend Puncknowle? Any whispers about people being beaten up or disappearing?'

'You're wondering about those two lawyers, of course. I don't think there was. I've never heard of any such thing but I can't be sure. Tell you what, I'll speak to a couple of fellows tomorrow and let you know. On the face of it, it's highly improbable, nothing more likely to put those kind of investors off than the chairman's thugs beating people up. It would be very different if we were talking about South African diamond shares ten or fifteen years ago, but we're not.'

'I'm much obliged to you for the information,' said Powerscourt as he prepared to take his leave.

'I've only one other titbit for you about that trial, Francis,' said William Burke, inspecting the last few inches of his cigar rather sadly. ' I don't know if you're aware of it, but the people in the City don't have a very high opinion of the people from the Temples and the Inns when it comes to big fraud cases. The money men think the lawyers can't read balance sheets, finance may be something other people may want to dirty their hands with but it's way beneath counsel with their wigs and their gowns and their seventeenth-century libraries. But that chap Dauntsey rated very highly with the men of Mammon. The odds against a conviction went up drama-tically when he toppled forward into his borscht. I don't know how this other fellow is rated but I suspect the odds will get longer still. Would you like me to take a flutter on your behalf, Francis? Just a little flutter, five or ten pounds?'

Powerscourt laughed. 'I don't think I could do that William. I don't think it would be ethical to bet against my current employers, however unpleasant they may be.'

Try as she might, Sarah Henderson could not see how she could disguise from her mother her unease at what was happening in Queen's Inn. For she was more concerned, much more concerned than she had told Edward, about the events of the afternoon. She felt sure Mr Stewart was dead. You just had to look at the policemen, or at Lord Powerscourt, to realize that. And now, here she was, clearing away the tea things, her mother about to start the evening interrogation across the fire. Sarah wondered about a headache and going to bed early, but that would only postpone matters. She wished she could have stayed with Edward all evening and not had to come home to her sick mother.

'I think I'd like a cup of hot chocolate, Sarah dear, when you're through in there.'

'Any cake, mama?' said Sarah, playing for time. There were still a couple of slices left of the Victoria sponge baked in honour of Mr Dauntsey's funeral.

'No thank you, dear, the chocolate will do me fine. I only bought it today in the grocer's. Mrs Wiggins was in there, telling me for the third time how well that son of hers was doing in the Metropolitan Railway. I was able to tell her you'd been to Mr Dauntsey's funeral in a first class carriage and had conversed on the way with the Head of Chambers. She left quite soon after that, Mrs Wiggins.'

Even in the confined quarters of the little kitchen Sarah could appreciate the glory in her mother's victory, the forces of darkness or the Metropolitan Railway in the person of Mrs Wiggins routed and forced to flee from the field.

Sarah knew she was looking anxious as she went to sit on the opposite side of the fire. She wondered if she could tell her mother about Edward as a means of avoiding telling her about Mr Stewart, though quite what she would actually say about Edward she had no idea. Her mother had, she felt, been fairly unmoved about the death of Alexander Dauntsey, even though she, Sarah, had been so very upset.

'Something went wrong at chambers today, dear, didn't it? Mrs Henderson took a preliminary sip of her chocolate. 'I can tell.' Privately Mrs Henderson suspected that Sarah was not very accomplished as a shorthand typist. As a child she had been clumsy, awkward with her hands, often dropping things. Her mother could not imagine how she would be able to keep up to the exacting standards of an Inn of Court. In fact, she could not have been more wrong: the twenty-year-old Sarah was a very different character from the child Sarah and knew very well how highly her work was valued.

'It's Mr Stewart, Mr Woodford Stewart, mama. He's disappeared.'

In spite of all the months of conversations about the Inn the name of Stewart had not yet been entered into Mrs Henderson's filing system.

'Mr Stewart? Is he one of the porters?'

'No, mama, he's a KC in a different chambers from mine. He is or was a great friend of Mr Dauntsey. They were going to work together on that big fraud case I've been telling you about.'

'Mr Bunkerpole? I read about him today in the paper.'

'Pucknowle, mama, pronounced Punnel, like funnel on a ship.'

'I don't need lessons in pronunciation from my own daughter, thank you very much, Sarah.' Mrs Henderson paused to take a large mouthful of her chocolate. 'So what do they think has happened to this Mr Stewart? Has he run off with somebody?' Mrs Henderson's paper and her magazines contained regular features about wicked men running off with people who were not their wives and causing great unhappiness. Less than a year ago she had given Sarah a long lecture on the Dangers of Being Run Away With by Wicked Men which Sarah had completely ignored.

'There's no sign of any running away, mother. That's all nonsense. People think he may have been murdered, like Mr Dauntsey.'

The minute she said it, Sarah regretted it. She was only trying to take out a pathetic revenge for the pronunciation remark, this over her mother who was ill and in pain all the time and might not be around much longer. Surely now her mother would be worried.

'He might well have run away with somebody, Sarah. People like that always take very good care to keep it secret. That's probably why nobody knows where he is. He'll turn up sooner or later, maybe travelling in the South of France under a false name, mark my words.'

For some reason that Sarah had never understood, the wicked runners away always seemed to end up in her mother's version in the South of France. The place seemed to carry spectacular undertones of villainy, a Mediterranean equivalent of Sodom and

Gomorrah, in her mind. But she doubted it would have much appeal for Mr Woodford Stewart, whose holidays, she had overheard somebody telling one of the policemen that very afternoon, were usually spent in the Highlands where he could pursue his twin delights of walking the hills and playing golf. But she knew how difficult it would be to shake her mother's belief in the running away theory. She tried

'I don't think any of the policemen or Lord Powerscourt think he's run away, mother. They think he's disappeared or he's dead.'

'This Lord Burrscourt, Sarah. Is he a friend of the Punchbowl man?'

Sarah was gripped by a moment of panic and a moment of total recall. She was back in the doctor's surgery with Dr Carr, old and white-haired now, the man who had looked after her father so well in his last, fatal illness. Dr Carr was talking to Sarah and her mother, his voice weary now after forty years of dealing with the sickness of London's poor, a dead look in his eyes. He had almost finished describing the likely course of her mother's illness, when he told them that in a few cases, not many at all in his experience, the mind began to deteriorate, not into senile decay as the doctors called it, but the memory began to fail, particularly about what had happened very recently. Sarah looked closely at her mother before she spoke. The last drop of chocolate was being drained with great enjoyment. She prayed that her mother was tired today, maybe the pain had dulled her wits.

'Lord Powerscourt, mama, is the man the benchers brought in to investigate Mr Dauntsey's death. I shouldn't think he knows Mr Puncknowle at all. Edward says that Lord Powerscourt once solved a murder mystery for the Royal Family.'

'What sort of age is this Lord Powerscourt?'

Sarah smiled at the transparency of her mother's behaviour. 'He's in his early forties, I think. His wife's just had twins. Edward and I saw them last Saturday. They're very sweet – the twins, I mean.'

'Your father's sister had twins long ago. Bad lot, both of them. Your father used to say how unfair it was. One bad one might just be bad luck, but two bad, it was terrible. Nearly killed the parents.'

Sarah wanted to ask what form this wickedness had taken. Had they, perhaps, ended up in the been-run-away with category? But there was a tightened look about her mother's lips which hinted that the topic was now closed. Suddenly Sarah decided to float her idea of a treat to her mother. She felt so sorry for her, so frail, growing less and less able to cope all the time.

'I've been thinking, mama, about a treat for you when the weather gets better.'

'A treat, my dear? I don't think people get treats at my time of life and in my condition.'

'Listen carefully, mama. It would involve putting you in a wheelchair some of the time, but we could say you'd twisted your ankle. People wouldn't have to think you weren't very mobile. Anyway we'd get you down to Queen's Inn and we could wheel you round the courts and you could meet lots of these barristers we've talked about so often. With any luck we could get you invited to lunch in the Hall, as a guest of one of the barristers. Wouldn't that be wonderful?'

Mrs Henderson looked rather frightened all of a sudden. Sarah suddenly remembered that they had hardly had time to talk about the disappearance of Mr Stewart so at least her mother wouldn't worry about that.

'I'll have to think about that, Sarah. It's very kind of you to suggest it, very kind indeed. I'm not sure I feel strong enough for it now, let alone in a couple of months' time. And I've got nothing to wear.'

'Just think about it, mama, you don't have to decide now.'

Later that night, after Sarah had helped her mother up the stairs and into bed, she decided that she needed some assistance in the planning of this escapade. Tomorrow, she decided, she would talk to Edward.

Lord Francis Powerscourt had evolved a new routine all of his own in his new house in Manchester Square. After breakfast he would go and see the twins, sometimes talking to them or reciting poetry if they seemed to be awake, and then he would cross to the Wallace Collection for a ten-minute visit. Usually he would go and look at some of the paintings in the Great Gallery on the first floor where the Gainsboroughs and the Van Dycks held sway, but today he was looking at the hardware of death on the ground floor. Just round the corner, on this very floor, he thought, there were some exquisite pieces of craftsmanship, a French musical clock that could play thirteen different tunes including a Gallic equivalent of 'Baa Baa Black Sheep', an astronomical clock, again from France, where you could find the time in hours, minutes and seconds, solar time as on a sundial in hours and minutes, the sign of the zodiac, the day, the date of the week, the time at any place in the northern hemisphere, the age of the moon and its current phase, and the position of the sun in the sky or the moon if it was night. But here, right in front of Powerscourt, resting innocently inside their glass cases, lay a couple of daggers from India and a tulwar, previously owned by the Tipu Sultan, which could have ripped a man's innards out or cut his throat so that he would die inside a minute, pausing only to reflect, as the light faded fast from his eyes, on the exquisite carvings on the sword blade and the diamonds and gold inset into the pommel. Upstairs Watteau's musicians danced out their private version of a pastoral heaven. Downstairs lurked long swords from Germany with very sharp edges, thin rapiers from Italy intended to cut and thrust their way into their victims, a curved Sikh sword that could cut a person in two, an Arabian shamshir with a walrus ivory grip which would leave terrible wounds. Above, Gainsborough's Perdita, one-time mistress of the Prince Regent, gazed enigmatically down the Long Gallery. Down below stood suits of armour, rich men's attempts to counter the stabs and the slashes and the thrusts, armour for men, armour even for horses, armour that grew so heavy that most warriors discarded it, armour designed to replicate the fashions of the day so that the Elizabethan Lord Buckhurst, in his armour with its peascod doublet with a point at the waist and an extravagantly puffed trunk hose reaching from waist to middle thigh, could probably have clanked into court at Greenwich or Westminster without anybody paying much attention. Upstairs gods danced across the sky and various versions of Heaven, mythical and Christian and metaphorical, were on display. Down here – Powerscourt looked suspiciously at a deadly Italian falchion, a broad sword tapered to a vicious point at the end – was a stockpile of weapons that could send a man to heaven or hell in less than ten seconds.

He wondered, as he made his way out towards Bedford Square and Queen's Inn, what had happened to Woodford Stewart. Had he too been poisoned? Or had the murderer turned to an easier and older means of death, a mighty blow from a steel sword, a thrust through the throat with a scimitar, a fatal stab with a dagger or kris?

The reception area for Plunkett Marlowe and Plunkett was pretty standard stuff, Powerscourt thought, as he surveyed the comfortable but fading chairs, the anonymous carpet, the prints of hunting and other rural pursuits on the walls. It was as though heaven for the solicitor breed was to be found somewhere in the hunting territory of Hampshire or Gloucestershire. The barristers, he thought, would prefer something more confrontational, perhaps some secret county with cock fighting and bear baiting. But Mr Plunkett, the younger Mr Plunkett as he had been referred to by the receptionist, was certainly a surprise. He was young for a start, very young. Powerscourt thought he could not have been out of university very long. He wondered, indeed, if the young man had started shaving yet as his cheeks were as smooth as silk. He positively bounded across the room to greet Powerscourt warmly.

'Lord Powerscourt, welcome. Matthew Plunkett. What an honour to meet you in person! Come with me!'

With that the young man led his visitor at breakneck speed up two flights of stairs, along a corridor, past a small library and into Mr Plunkett the younger's spacious office, decorated with prints of London. At least this one wants to stay where he is, Powerscourt said to himself, rather than escape to the Elysian Fields of horn and fox.

'Now then, please take a seat across my desk, Lord Powerscourt, and we can get down to business.'

Powerscourt thought this was the youngest solicitor he had ever seen . Normally they were middle-aged or elderly citizens. Perhaps the younger ones were sent away to practise elsewhere until they came of age, hidden away in the attics until sometime beyond their fortieth birthdays.

'Mrs Dauntsey has given me full discretion in what I tell you about the will,' he said cheerfully, smiling at Powerscourt. 'In some ways it's a simple document, but it does have one fascinating oddity.' He collected a group of papers together on his desk but Powerscourt noticed that he did not refer to them once as he gave his description of Dauntsey's last will and testament.

'The estate itself, the house, the land, the paintings and so on are all covered by the family trust. I believe that this document was started at about the same time Moses was found among the bulrushes in Egypt. It covers every possible eventuality and it stipulates, quite simply, that in this case of an owner dying with no children, the estate should pass to the eldest brother, if there is one, in this case Nicholas Dauntsey, currently thought to be resident in Manitoba and expected back to claim his little kingdom in the next month or so.'

Matthew Plunkett paused to inspect a tattered seagull that had taken up temporary residence on his window sill.

'Mrs Dauntsey, of course, is well provided for, with accommo-
dation inside the house if that should suit, or in one of the decent
houses on the fringes of the estate There is ample financial provision, as we lawyers like to say. There are a number of small
bequests to staff or local institutions like the cricket club. And then
we come to the mystery bequest.'

Matthew Plunkett was enjoying this. He leaned forward and
addressed Powerscourt directly.

'After the ten pounds here, and the five pounds there, Lord
Powerscourt, we have the spectacular sum of twenty thousand
pounds left to one F.L. Maxfield. Maxfield the mystery man we call
him here now, my lord.'

'You can't find him?' said Powerscourt.

'Correct. Now you know as well as I do that solicitors have to
spend a lot of time tracing people in cases like this. Plunkett
Marlowe and Plunkett is also a founder member of a specialist firm
devoted to finding persons like this Maxfield. We can't find him.
They can't find him. We've tried Mr Dauntsey's old school, his
Cambridge college, his regiment in the Army, every single chambers
he's ever served in We can't find a birth certificate but they do get
mislaid sometimes or he might have been born abroad. We can't,
you won't be surprised to hear, find any evidence of marriage or
even death which would make our lives easier.'

'Are you sure it's a man? Might this be a Miss Maxfield or a Mrs
Maxfield, an old flame from days gone by?'

'We've talked about that a lot, Lord Powerscourt. My view is this.
Mr Dauntsey was a lawyer, trained to be precise in his use of
language. If the Maxfield was a woman, he would have put Miss or
Mrs in the document, I'm sure of it.'

Busloads of Maxfields, Maxfields old, Maxfields young, Maxfields
rich, Maxfields poor, floated past Powerscourt's brain and disappeared.

'When did he make this will, Mr Plunkett? Was it the first one or
an updated version of a will that had existed before? And did he
make it here, with one of you gentlemen present?'

'My goodness me, Lord Powerscourt, you do ask a lot of
questions. To take them in order, he made the will three years ago
and we think he wrote it in his chambers. It was the latest in a series
of wills the trustees encouraged him to make ever since his twenty-
first birthday. That, I fear, is rather the kind of thing the trustees go
in for.'

89

Powerscourt smiled. The young man was not completely indoc-
trinated with the solicitor's mindset, or not yet at any rate.

'He'd been in to talk to my uncle, the one they call Killer Plunkett,
the day before he wrote this will. This latest one, dated 1899, was
the first appearance of the wretched Maxfield.'

Powerscourt wondered what this perfectly law-abiding Plunkett
had done to earn the nickname Killer. 'So whoever Maxfield is or
was,' he said, 'his association with Dauntsey must have been
complete, so to speak, three years ago. I mean, whatever the reason
for giving him the money, it was all there then. Do you know, Mr
Plunkett, if Dauntsey told his beneficiary about his plans? Did
Maxfield, not to put too fine a point on it, know that he would get
twenty thousand pounds if Dauntsey fell into his borscht?'

'I'm afraid he did,' Matthew Plunkett grimaced slightly, 'or rather
he said he was going to. He told Killer he was going to write to
Maxfield and give him the good news.'

'Did he indeed?' said Powerscourt, realizing that another name
had to be added to his list of suspects. 'But, of course, he didn't leave
a copy of the letter which would have had an address on it, did he?'

'No, he didn't,' Matthew Plunkett replied. 'That would have made
life far too easy for everybody. Mind you, to be fair to Mr Dauntsey,
I don't think he was the kind of man who would have wanted to
cause trouble after he had gone. Not like some I could mention.'

Matthew Plunkett sounded as if he had many lifetimes' experience
of obstreperous corpses and troublemaking cadavers.

'Never mind,' said Powerscourt, 'I think I can be of some assistance in your quest, Mr Plunkett. Dauntsey's death is the subject of
a police investigation. This Maxfield person is obviously suspect.
Therefore, we can ask the police to look for him too. They have
enormous resources at their disposal. If anybody in Britain can find
him, they can.'

Matthew Plunkett smiled. 'I cannot tell you, Lord Powerscourt,
how pleased I am to hear that. Will you please come and report any
progress to us here? And I'm so glad we are no longer alone in our
search. Surely we should know who and where he is within a week
or two.'

Making his way down the stairs, past a couple of stags that looked
as though they might be enjoying their last day on earth,
Powerscourt wasn't so sure.

7

Robert Woodford Stewart went missing on Wednesday afternoon. They didn't find his body until the Monday morning. It was discovered under a pile of masonry rubble, covered with a black tarpaulin, at the side of the Temple Church, the chapel and spiritual home of the Inner and Middle Temples, next to Queen's Inn. Restoration work was being carried cut in the nave, and when another wheelbarrow of rubble was carried out to the pile outside the church, Stewart's body was found at the top of it.

'Shot,' said Chief Inspector Beecham to Powerscourt later that morning. 'Shot twice in the chest. First one enough to kill him, I would have thought. Maybe the murderer wanted to make sure.'

'I don't suppose you have any idea yet as to when he was killed, Chief Inspector?' asked Powerscourt.

'Not yet, my lord. We should know later in the day.'

There was a knock on the door of Dauntsey's old room where Powerscourt had established a temporary command post and a porter brought an envelope addressed to him.

'Damn,' said Powerscourt, reading the note very quickly. 'I've got to go and see that bloody man Somerville. I notice you're not included in the invitation, Chief Inspector. Does that mean that he doesn't know you're here, or that he doesn't want to see you?'

Beecham laughed. 'He doesn't want to see me ever again. He tried to get me moved off the case, you know. Letters to the Commissioner. One or two of the people here who are judges, they all made representations.'

'What did the Commissioner say?' said Powerscourt, curious to see how Somerville had been beaten off.

'He said that he had no intention of telling the judiciary which

91

judges should preside over their various trials and he would be obliged if they would leave him the same freedom in appointing detectives to murder cases.'

'One thing before I go, Chief Inspector,' said Powerscourt. 'Was Stewart a big man, heavy, difficult to lift, would you say?'

'No, he was slight, fairly easy to pick up and carry about the place if you'll forgive my language. There's just one thing that worries me about these murders, Lord Powerscourt.'

Powerscourt stayed where he was. Somerville could wait. 'What's that?'

'Well . . .' The Chief Inspector spoke slowly, as if he wasn't sure of his facts. 'Murder Number One, poison in the beetroot. Murder Number Two, shot through the chest. If it was the same man, why did he not use the same technique? Most murderers do. And there's a theory, although I'm not sure I believe it, that poison is likely to be a woman's choice of murder weapon, and guns a man's.'

'You don't think, Chief Inspector,' Powerscourt was on his feet now and heading for the door, 'that there are two separate killers at work here?'

'I just don't know. Do you think it's one killer or two?'

'One,' said Powerscourt with more certainty than he actually possessed. 'The chances of two killers operating in one small community like this must be very very small. I should be most surprised if there were two murderers at work here.'

Barton Somerville was not at his enormous desk when Powerscourt arrived in his chambers on the first floor of Fountain Court. Powerscourt had been delighted to hear that his practice at the Bar was not doing well, that his self-importance and pomposity now annoyed some of the judges so much that the instructing solicitors were deserting him, fearful that their clients would lose their cases because of their barrister's bombast.

'Morning, Powerscourt.' He dragged himself away from his tall window with the perfect sashes and withdrew to the fortified position that was his desk. 'What do you have to report?'

Powerscourt felt he had been summoned to his housemaster in a dispute over late arrival of homework, previous negotiations over its delivery having broken down.

'Before I bring you up to date, may I inquire if you have heard about Mr Stewart?'

'Woodford Stewart or Lawrence Stewart? We have two. I'm surprised you haven't noticed that in the time you've been here.'

'Mr Woodford Stewart. He's been shot dead. His body was found by the Temple Church this morning. We won't know any more, time of death and so on, until the doctors have had a look at him.'

Barton Somerville stared at Powerscourt for what seemed over a minute. 'I hold you personally responsible for this latest death, Powerscourt. If you'd been doing your job properly, the murderer would have been unmasked by now and locked up. As it is, he's still wandering around picking off his victims. And might I remind you, in this Inn and particularly in these rooms, you call me Treasurer. Now, what do you have to report?'

Powerscourt stared at the ceiling. He had an intense dislike of telling his clients anything at all while an investigation was in progress. So often his final conclusions were the direct opposite of what he had suspected at the beginning. And Somerville was certainly a suspect, though why the Treasurer of an Inn like Queen's should want to go about killing off his own members Powerscourt, for the moment, could not imagine. But if Dauntsey had not been poisoned at the feast, that left only two locations where the crime could have been committed, either in his own chambers, or at the drinks party before the feast, given here in this very room by none other than Somerville himself.

'I don't think it would be helpful for me to say anything at this stage,' he said finally.

'I beg your pardon?' boomed Somerville, his face growing red with fury. 'Do you dare refuse to tell me what you have found out so far, I who brought you into this matter in the first place! It is monstrous!'

'I don't think it is monstrous, actually,' said Powerscourt as reasonably as he could, and more determined than ever not to give anything away. 'You see, in my experience, whatever people like myself think at this stage of the investigation is usually wrong. As things develop, our opinion changes.'

'I presume,' Somerville interrupted him quickly, possibly thinking he was back in court, 'that by things developing, you mean more members of my Inn being killed off by your incompetence.'

Powerscourt shrugged his shoulders, well aware that a policy of total calm would infuriate the Treasurer even more. 'I'm sorry I can't help you at this stage. When I have something definite to report I shall let you know.' Powerscourt suddenly felt rather sorry for the pompous and unpleasant Somerville. If his practice was drying up, so must be his income. And if his income was drying up, the expenses of his position, which Powerscourt suspected must be considerable, must be growing harder to bear. And now these two murders, which would almost certainly be the permanent mark of his period in office. Somerville's Treasurership, people would say in years to come, wasn't that when those dreadful murders happened?

'Powerscourt, Powerscourt,' the voice was calmer now, 'you had gone on a journey in your mind just now and seemed almost incapable of speech. I just hope you understand my position here.' Somerville had removed his thick spectacles and was polishing them on a bright blue handkerchief. Maybe tentative peace overtures were being launched. 'Every day I am asked for the latest news of Dauntsey's murder. After this morning I shall be asked for news of two murders. It is difficult for me to say I know nothing at all. After all, the barristers say to me, we are employing this man Powerscourt to find out the truth. Why, they imply, have you nothing to tell us? Can you understand?'

Powerscourt nodded. An uneasy truce seemed to have broken out over the battlefield, though Powerscourt suspected it would soon be broken by skirmishes elsewhere. 'Of course I understand. I will do what I can.'

Five minutes later he was at the side of the Temple Church where the body of Woodford Stewart had been found. One of Beecham's sergeants, a man who looked old enough to be the Chief Inspector's father, if not his grandfather, greeted him solemnly.

'He wasn't killed here, the poor man,' he said slowly. 'There's marks where his body was dragged along the ground. We couldn't work out what they were at first, these marks, until one of the constables remembered pulling a colleague out of a fight in Stoke Newington. Looks like he may have come from a room somewhere in the Inner Temple, or even from Queen's itself, my lord. Frightful business.'

Powerscourt was surprised that the sergeant was still capable of such sympathy for the dead. Most of the Metropolitan policemen he had known had formed a thick carapace against terrible sights by the time they were thirty, if not before. It was as if that was the only way they could cope with the bloody remains of London's citizens, wounded in gang fights in the East End, London's suicides pulled out of the River Thames or lying in bloody fragments behind the wheels of the Tube trains, London's murdered dead who might turn up anywhere from Whitechapel to the Temple Church in the Strand.

Edward had begun to feel that the power of words had been replaced in his brain by the power of numbers. He had been working late for the past two days on the accounts of Jeremiah Puncknowle's companies. All he could see in his mind this morning were these numbers forming and re-forming in front of him in strings and sequences and series, looping round each other, breeding somewhere in the basement of his brain and resurfacing again, numbers infinite, numbers serial, numbers prime, numbers eternal, numbers to do with money raised from flotation, numbers to do with money handed out in commission, numbers to do with money paid out in dividends, numbers to do with the difference between the first number and the second and third combined, numbers to do with the size and extent of the vanishing numbers, the ones that disappeared from the published accounts and must have ended up in the clutches of Jeremiah Puncknowle. But now he had had enough. He might, he felt, turn into an equation if he carried on or be carried out gibbering madly about prospectuses and interim reports. Only one thing had kept him sane in the midst of his mathematical Stations of the Cross. He was going to ask Sarah for another assignation. The destination had only occurred to him when he saw a poster that morning on the walls of Temple underground station.

He climbed up past the first and second floors, where the voice of a senior could be heard tearing strips off some young deviller who had failed to carry out his work properly, and up to the attic floor that was Sarah's kingdom. He heard the sound of the keys, two typewriters, he thought, so Sarah's friend must be there too today. The sound was music to Edward's ears, like a gang of woodpeckers attacking a whole row of trees at the same time.

Sarah's companion, a small mousy girl called Winifred, fled once Edward put in his appearance to renew their stocks of typing paper in the stationery shop across the road.

Edward stood looking at Sarah, who was wearing a cream blouse today with a blue scarf and those long red tresses trailing down her back.

'Edward,' Sarah said with her finest smile, 'how very nice to see you. You don't look very well this morning.'

Edward opened his mouth to speak but no sound came forth. Damn, he said to himself, damn, damn damn. Just when I thought I was over all that business with Sarah. He wished Lord Powerscourt was there, or even better, that he and Sarah were taking tea in Manchester Square once more.

Sarah was thinking very fast. If she took Edward by the hand, she was sure he would speak normally. But then Winifred might come back and find them in a compromising position. Winifred was so light on her feet she was the only person in chambers you couldn't hear coming up the stairs.

'How is Lord Powerscourt?' she said instead, trying to bring him back to happier times. 'Do you think we will be invited to tea there again? Any news of the twins?'

One of those cues must have worked. Sarah watched the lines of strain on Edward's face relax. She wondered, not for the first time, what had caused his speech problem. Sometimes her mother read her extracts from the newspapers about people being struck dumb by some personal or professional catastrophe. Edward seemed far too young to have gone through anything like that.

'Twins well,' said Edward, his face going red with the effort. 'Lord Powerscourt is well too.' He beamed at Sarah as if he had just climbed a mountain. Perhaps he had. 'Accounts. Puncknowle accounts. Head of Chambers said to keep going even though Mr Stewart dead. My head is spinning.'

Sarah had noticed before that once one verb appeared, others were sure to follow. Maybe Edward's problem had to do with verbs rather than words in general.

'Want to make a suggestion, Sarah,' Edward carried on bravely. This after all was the reason for his mission.

'And what might that be?' asked Sarah, looking at Edward in her most flirtatious manner. His eyes, she thought suddenly, his eyes were a wonderful sort of soft brown colour and looked as if they might melt if their owner was maltreated.

'Oxford,' said Edward in his most authoritative tone. 'Let's go to Oxford for the day on Saturday.' Then he nearly spoilt it all by adding, 'There's a special offer on the train. From Paddington.'

Sarah had never been to Oxford. She didn't think Edward had either. She had a sketchy picture in her mind of ancient colleges, of a river running through the city, of great libraries, of hundreds and hundreds of young men lying about on the lawns, or draping themselves across punts and rowing boats with straw hats on.

'Why, Edward,' she said, 'that would be lovely. Would you like me to bring lunch? Isn't there a river up there where we could have a picnic?'

'I believe there is,' said Edward hesitantly. 'I've not been there before, Sarah. One of the young silks is going to brief me, a man I did a lot of work for last month. He went to Magdalen College. He says that's the best. It's by the river. And it's got a deer park.'

'Just like Calne,' said Sarah sadly, thinking of Dauntsey's funeral.

'Will your mother be all right?' asked Edward anxiously.

Sarah had long suspected that Edward must have or have had a close relation who was not well. Otherwise he wouldn't understand how important these questions were

'As long as it's not a surprise,' said Sarah. 'I'll tell her this evening.' Just then they caught the faint mouse-like tread of Winifred's return. Edward made his way back downstairs. Sarah continued with her typing. It was nobody else's business after all if they were going to Oxford for the day on Saturday with a special offer on the train.

Johnny Fitzgerald's stockinged feet were draped elegantly on the Powerscourt dining table. His right hand was holding a glass of crystal clear Sancerre, his left a bundle of papers filled with drawings that might have been birds. To his left, Lady Lucy was drinking tea, as was Powerscourt on the opposite side of the table. At the far end, sleeping peacefully in their Moses baskets, were the twins. Lady Lucy believed they should see a bit of family life from time to time and she knew how much her husband loved looking at them or talking way above their heads with poetry or whatever was passing through his mind.

'It'll make my fortune, I'm certain of it,' said Johnny Fitzgerald, waving his papers vigorously at his friends. 'I'm astonished nobody's thought of it before.'

'What's the plan, Johnny?' said Powerscourt.

'Please forgive me, Lady Lucy, if I repeat some of what I told you just now.' Johnny took an appreciative gulp of his Sancerre 'It all started the other morning, Francis. I woke up very early and I couldn't get back to sleep so I went for a walk. I don't know if you've been to Kensington Gardens at five o'clock in the morning, but the noise is fantastic. It's the birds.'

Johnny doesn't need to catch trains to obscure railway stations in the countryside any more, Powerscourt thought to himself. He can just take a stroll in the middle of London.

'Some of them are singing,' Johnny went on, 'some of them are squawking, some of them are belting out bits out of forgotten operas, some of them seem to know some special hymns of their own, some are just saying this is my pitch, why don't you bugger off, you other birds, some are screaming and some are twittering, some are chirping away to themselves and some seem to be saying "Pink, pink." All this within two hundred yards of the Round Pond.'

Johnny paused and looked down at his papers. The old Johnny, Lady Lucy found herself thinking, would have taken another quaff of his wine at this point, a suitable moment for refreshment, but no. This Johnny carried on without a drop passing his lips.

'Only thing is, Francis,' Johnny went on, 'I didn't have a clue who these bloody birds were. In the dark, I mean. Couldn't bloody well see. They could have been the black-browed albatross or the short-toed eagle for all I damned well knew. So I went to this Natural History Museum place in South Kensington – fascinating place, full of stuffed birds and things, you should take the big children there, they'd love it – and they sent me to an old chap who lives out Acton way, who knows the sound of almost every bloody bird in England. Used to be a sailor and he's nearly blind, but I took him out to Hyde Park yesterday at five fifteen in the morning and this is what we've produced.' He waved his papers at them enthusiastically. Powerscourt saw that they were full of rough descriptions of birds followed by rather precise descriptions of their sounds.

'I've got great plans, Francis.' At last Johnny Fitzgerald yielded to temptation and took a considerable pull of his wine. He eyed the bottle carefully as if trying to gauge how many glasses there were left in it. Powerscourt wondered if he would, unusually, restrict himself to a single bottle.

'Do you remember that little chap we had working with us in Indian Intelligence, Francis? Fellow by the name of Cooper, Charlie Cooper, who did all the maps and could draw you a snake or a vulture right down to the last nail in its talon? Well, he works for a publisher now, illustrating books and magazines, and he's said he'll do all the birds for me, so you see them in their proper habitat, not just stuffed in a glass cage with no branches to cling on to. It's going to be a book describing all these different creatures and the sounds they make. Lady Lucy, what do you think of that?'

Lady Lucy smiled. She was pleased Johnny had found something other than the vintages of France to occupy his spare time, but she doubted if he would meet many eligible females on his dawn patrol up and down Rotten Row in the hours before daybreak. 'I think that's tremendous, Johnny,' she said. 'Maybe you could put it in the newspapers in sections first, like the novelists used to do.'

'Serialize it?' said Johnny. 'That would be good, we could all get paid twice. Mind you there's me, and there's the sailor man and there's Charlie Cooper all of us to get paid. Still, we can try. I give you a toast, doesn't matter if it's drunk in Sancerre or Darjeeling, let us drink to *The Birds of London.*'

'*The Birds of London,*' Francis and Lucy chorused in unison. There was a faint moan from the far end of the table. A twin was stirring in its sleep. They all fell silent for a moment.

'Johnny,' said Powerscourt, 'I think that's a tremendous scheme. But I hope it isn't going to drag you away from detection completely. I would be lost without you. And I have something I want you to do.'

'Rest assured, my friend,' said Johnny Fitzgerald with a grin, 'that I shall not desert you in your investigations. The birds may have to wait, the birds on occasion may have flown, but the solving of the crime will take priority.'

With that he finished his glass, refilled it, and looked expectantly at Powerscourt, who was looking for something in his trouser pocket.

'You know about the first murder in Queen's Inn, Johnny, the man Dauntsey.'

'The fellow who fell into his soup?'

'Precisely so,' said Powerscourt. 'There's been a second murder, another barrister in Queen's called Stewart. The two of them were going to prosecute that fraudster Jeremiah Puncknowle. Just days before the case is due to start, they're both in their graves. Convenient for Mr Puncknowle, very convenient. William Burke didn't think our Jeremiah would go in for violence, not good for the Low Church image, but he sent me this note today.'

Powerscourt handed Burke's message over to Johnny Fitzgerald.

Good to see you last week. As I said, Puncknowle had no reputation for violence. But he had a colleague who came with him to London from the north. Name of Bradstock, Linton Bradstock. Distinguishable by enormous black beard and very stout cane, carried at all times. If you didn't keep up your mortgage payments or meet your interest bills on time, you might receive a visit from Bradstock or his friends. Broken legs commonplace, broken arms likewise, in one or two cases people said to have disappeared completely. Also on trial for fraud with Puncknowle. Take very great care, Francis. Love to the family, William.

Johnny handed the note back to his friend. 'So you would like me to exchange a blackbird for a Bradstock, Francis? I presume you want to know if he or any of his colleagues, who may, of course, not be on trial for fraud, have been knocking off barristers down there in the Strand. You don't have any idea where he lives, our blackbeard friend, do you?'

Powerscourt pulled another piece of paper from his breast pocket. 'Very short note from William an hour or so ago. Big mansion in Belgrave Square, he says, Number 25. Place full of Bradstock's thugs.'

Johnny Fitzgerald took an absent-minded sip of his Sancerre. 'Think I'll approach this in a roundabout sort of way, Francis. Don't fancy knocking on the front door and asking if anybody here murdered a couple of barristers recently. Might not be good for the prospects of *The Birds of London*, if you follow me. I'll try to see if there's any gossip in the criminal circles, there usually is if a job that size has been pulled off.'

'There's more news, Francis.' Lady Lucy had been sitting quietly through the male conversation, waiting for her moment. She was looking very serious. With the late afternoon sun shining on her hair Powerscourt thought she looked very beautiful. He was so proud of her.

'You remember you asked me to make some discreet inquiries about the Dauntseys?' she went on, totally unaware of her husband's reflections about hair and late afternoon sun.

'Of course, Lucy,' said Powerscourt, wondering what sort of reply she had received.

'Well, it's only a whisper,' she went on. 'Maybe a whisper is too strong. My informant said it was like a very distant bell you can just hear ringing a long way off.'

'And what was the rumour, Lucy?'

'It had to do with Dauntsey's brother. The elder one. The rumour said that Mrs Dauntsey had been very close to him, that they had gone on holiday together or short weekends away quite a lot.'

'How long ago was this meant to be?' asked Powerscourt, running a hand through his hair.

'Two years ago, something like that.'

'And who was your informant?'

'A second cousin who lives quite close to Calne and has dined there many times. I would regard her as a reliable witness.'

'So,' Powerscourt was whispering as if he didn't want his

thoughts to reach the purer minds of the twins. 'Think of it. Here you are, Alexander Dauntsey and your beautiful wife. You have been trying to have children for years and have failed. For Alexander, one of the cores of his being is his house. His people have lived in it for centuries. His descendants must carry on that tradition. But he cannot have any descendants. Or perhaps his wife cannot have any. They simply do not know. Let's suppose they are going to try this route first. Dauntsey makes the suggestion to his wife. My brother instead of me. I can imagine her, oddly enough, agreeing to it out of her love for him. He suggests it to his brother, less difficult with such a beautiful woman. But still no children. The adulterous experiment failed. I wonder what happened next. Was the brother married?'

Powerscourt had a sudden vision of a vengeful wife, realizing that the blame lay with the husband rather than the wife, organizing a mysterious visitor to Queen's Inn, a poison phial concealed about his person.

'He wasn't married, the brother. But there's one thing,' Lady Lucy was looking at Johnny's pieces of papers as she spoke, 'that makes me think it might be true.'

'What's that, Lucy?' asked Johnny Fitzgerald.

'The elder brother,' she too spoke very quietly, 'he's gone away. They think he's gone to some remote part of Canada, but nobody knows for certain where he is. They think he may be in Manitoba.'

'That's where the Dauntsey lawyers think he is, Lucy. Manitoba.'

'Do you want me to see if I can find him, Francis?' asked Johnny Fitzgerald, 'I've always wanted to go to Canada. Wine has to be imported but the birds are said to be wonderful.'

Powerscourt smiled. 'Not yet, Johnny. We've got enough to do here for now. Lucy, do you have further inquiries you can make, the younger brother perhaps, or any male cousins who might have taken part in the same experiment, if there was one?'

'I discovered some new relations only yesterday, Francis, I'm sorry to say. But they too live not far from Calne.'

Johnny Fitzgerald was gathering up his papers. 'I've just had a thought,' he said, looking up at his friends. 'After *The Birds of London* I wondered about *The Birds of East Anglia*, *The Birds of the West*, *The Birds of Wales*, that sort of thing. But there's not many people living in those places. It was thinking of Canada and their French connections that did it. Not only a bird book, but a wine book as well. Two for the price of one. *The Birds of Bordeaux*, Lucy. *The Birds of*

Burgundy, Francis. We could probably do some of them by describing the birds that live in the actual vineyards that produce the Meursault or the Gevrey Chambertin. Wouldn't that be grand?'

They both laughed. 'Excellent, Johnny,' said Lady Lucy. 'You'll be famous in France as well, maybe.'

Johnny Fitzgerald looked serious all of a sudden. 'Tell me, Francis,' he said, 'what are you going to be doing in the next few days in case any of these fraudsters and murderers want to kill you too and I need to tell them your whereabouts?'

Powerscourt suspected Johnny had a different motive for his question. After their last adventure at a West Country cathedral and a vicious attempt on Powerscourt's life, Lucy had taken great care, unobtrusive care, of course, to make sure Johnny was never far away from her Francis.

'I have two journeys in mind, Johnny, for you to tell your assassin friends about. I shall be going to Calne to renew my acquaintance with Mrs Dauntsey, although how I turn the conversation to where I want it to go, I have no idea. Of mutual embarrassment there could be no end. But before that I am going to visit one of the most extraordinary houses in Britain. It is in England, but it is French, it has telephones and a telegraph, it has furniture that used to belong to Marie Antoinette, it has more Sèvres porcelain than anywhere else in England.'

'Where on earth is this domestic heaven?' asked Lady Lucy.

'It is in the Chiltern Hills, my love. It was designed to the wish or the whim of a man who was then thought to be the richest man in Britain. Typically he called his vast pile simply Paradise. The man is Jeremiah Puncknowle and the house is his fantasy and his folly.'

Johnny and Lucy left the Powerscourt dining room, chattering happily about *The Birds of London*. Powerscourt himself wandered slowly to the top of the table and looked down at the sleeping twins. One had a tiny fist resting on a pink cheek. The other was virtually invisible beneath the covers. He began whispering to them. You would have to have been very close indeed to realize that he was telling them the words of the Lord's Prayer.

8

I have just entered the gates of Paradise, Powerscourt said to himself as his cab rattled past a couple of mock Tudor gateways that marked the entrance to Jeremiah Pucknowle's estate. My appointment, confirmed yesterday, is for eleven o'clock.

They were up in the hills, nearly as high as the Chilterns reached, just past the little town of Wendover. The cabbie, a cheerful young man in his early twenties, had offered to point out some of the interesting features of the Pucknowle establishment as they went along. His commentary and directions usually led to very generous tips.

'Prepare to look left after the next bend, sir,' he called out, stooping down to adjust a piece of harness. Up till this point the road ran between tall trees of birch and oak, then suddenly Powerscourt saw a great rectangle of green, with a small square in the middle enclosed by thick posts with rope between them. And at the far end a large building in red brick, with wide windows looking out over the grass and balconies for spectators to view the action. Even as they went by, Powerscourt saw a couple of men painting the doors. Two flags were flying from the flagpole, the Union Jack and a strange white flag with a couple of rampant lions. He knew he had seen the building before. He remembered the last time he had been there, with William Burke and a colleague of his from the City. For this was a perfect reproduction of the pavilion at Lord's Cricket Ground, home to the County of Middlesex and the headquarters of the Marylebone Cricket Club, the most famous of its kind in the world. As far as Powerscourt could tell, it was a perfect replica.

'Lord's pavilion,' said the cabbie happily, 'complete with Long Room and paintings of ancient cricketers and an honours board where they put your name up if you score a hundred or take five wickets in an international.'

'God bless my soul,' said Powerscourt. 'Did they go down and make detailed drawings of the building?'

'Nothing as complicated as that, sir. Mr Puncknowle just bought the plans off the architect who did the original one down there in London.'

'I see,' said Powerscourt, wondering if perfect replicas of Buckingham Palace or St Paul's Cathedral were about to appear round the next bend. The road was climbing steeply now but Powerscourt thought there must be a flat area of land, a small plateau at the top.

'They say Mr Puncknowle took his holidays in France one year, sir, and came back determined to have one of them château things of his own. Must have cost a heap of money, they even built a special railway to bring the stones up to the bottom of the hill.'

'How did they get them to the top?' asked Powerscourt.

'They had a French architect, and a French landscape designer, so they brought in teams of those Percheron mares, sir. Amazing what they could do.'

Even when you knew what was coming, the vista as you rounded the last corner was astonishing. There was a large area of Italian garden with gravel paths criss-crossing it. The cab, Powerscourt noticed, had slowed almost to walking pace so that visitors could be impressed. And there it was, the Bath stone gleaming in the sunlight, a building that could not have come from anywhere other than France with its mansard roofs, its turrets and pinnacles, its dormers and chimneys and ornamental bits of fantasy dotted all around it. Close your eyes, Powerscourt thought, and you could hear, faint but unmistakable in the clear Chiltern air, the sound of the Marseillaise.

Powerscourt asked the cabbie to wait. A sepulchral butler led him into the East Gallery, lined with Italian paintings and a chimney-piece from a post office in Paris. They went past a sumptuous dining room, virually choking on the richest collection of Sèvres tableware Powerscourt had ever seen, and on into a great drawing room looking out over the valley.

Powerscourt's first impression of Jeremiah Puncknowle was that he was a collection of billiard balls. His head, totally bald, with a very small nose and small eyes and hardly any chin, was the white ball. His centre, again perfectly round with a gold watch chain hanging off a round stomach surrounded by a scarlet waistcoat, was the red ball. He was quite short and even his feet seemed to be trying to become round though that might have been the shoes

'Mr Pancknowle,' said Powerscourt, shaking his host by the hand, 'thank you so much for agreeing to see me at such short notice, and let me say that I have rarely been so impressed by a house as I am by your magnificent mansion here.' He bowed stiffly.

'Thank you, Lord Powerscourt, thank you. How very kind of you. Might I inquire as to which part of my house impressed you the most?'

The man likes flattery, Powerscourt thought, and he proceeded to offer it by the bucketful. 'First of all there is the conception, Mr Puncknowle, the astounding idea of bringing a French château to England. So obvious when you think of it, but how daring and original in execution. I have most of my knowledge from a friend but I understand you have here one of the finest collections of French art, tapestry, sculpture, paintings and so on anywhere in the world. How blessed we are, sir, to have such glory in our midst!' I pray to God, Powerscourt said to himself, that nobody I know hears me spouting this frightful tripe.

Jeremiah Puncknowle had still not had enough flattery. He wanted a sweet course, probably followed by cheese.

'Did you see my cricket pitch, Lord Powerscourt? What did you think of that?'

'My dear Mr Puncknowle,' Powerscourt was rubbing his hands together now, 'I thought that was genius, pure genius! The idea of reproducing the Lord's pavilion here, what a wonderful idea! And I fancy your ground is slightly larger than the one at St John's Wood, would I be correct?'

'You would indeed be correct, sir. When I can find the time we're going to build seating all the way round. There'll be more room for spectators here than there is down there in London. Then we can arrange some big matches. W.G. Grace has looked at the wicket and pronounced it excellent.'

Powerscourt wondered how much the Doctor had charged for that. 'Indeed,' he said, 'what excellent news. I look forward to returning here for some great match, Mr Puncknowle.'

Something seemed to have upset the little round man's equilibrium. He left his armchair and began walking – waddling might have been a more appropriate term, Powerscourt thought – along a narrow strip of carpet close to his windows and the spectacular views.

'You see before you a man sadly misused by his time, Lord Powerscourt, sadly misused.' Puncknowle had just passed Powerscourt's position at the edge of the sofa. 'I am sure you are aware of the misfortunes that have been heaped upon my poor head, heaped high indeed.' The little man stretched his arms out as wide as they would go, as if he was about to be raised up on the Cross. 'My enemies have no idea of business. They are merely consumed with their obsession to bring me down.' Puncknowle had turned round now and was coming back down the room towards Powerscourt. He was about to pass under a magnificent full-length portrait by Sir Joshua Reynolds of Colonel St Leger, friend and equerry to George the Third. The Colonel was leaning insouciantly on his horse, looking out into the distance, perhaps, Powerscourt thought, to the race that bore his name. 'Any man of commerce would tell you, Lord Powerscourt, that the affairs of great businesses do not proceed in regular patterns. Trade does not beat regularly like a person's heart. It is irregular. There are good years. There are bad years. Some years the sun shines upon the figures that mark your fortunes in this unhappy world, other years the figures are plunged into shadow.'

Puncknowle stopped now directly opposite Powerscourt's position on the sofa. Outside, two peacocks, confident in their residence in one of the most unusual houses in England, were strutting arrogantly towards the garden.

'But my enemies are wrong, Lord Powerscourt, to say that in the years of the shadow, theft and larceny were taking place, that I, Jeremiah Puncknowle, was robbing the honest citizens who had entrusted their savings to my care. That was not so! That was the trade cycle! Had my enemies not pulled the wool over the eyes of the police, my positions would have been restored, more than restored, when the sun came out again. Which it did, of course,' Jeremiah Puncknowle had gone quieter now, almost speaking to himself, 'only I was not here to profit from it, forced to flee the land of my fathers, and barred from trading on the Exchange.'

Powerscourt wondered if he was going to break down. But anger returned to fire his spirits.

'The police! God help us all, Lord Powerscourt, the police! I am sure,' he cast a crafty look at Powerscourt as he said this, 'that you have had a lot to do with them over the years and they may be perfectly satisfactory in your line of business. But in mine? Hopeless, completely hopeless!' Puncknowle began walking again, his hands now clasped firmly behind his back as he headed off towards a gorgeous Gainsborough of a society beauty. 'One inspector did not know what the word dividend meant. He thought it had something to do with the Football Pools. One man, more senior yet, thought that if a firm made a loss in any given year, somebody, probably me, must have been stealing the amount of the deficit. And yet another, a Chief Inspector would you believe, a Chief Inspector, thought that double entry bookkeeping meant that you wrote up the notes from those little books they're so fond of once, and then you wrote them up again! That's why it was called double entry. Really, Lord Powerscourt, I ask you, what is to be done? I look forward to seeing them in the witness box, I tell you, I really do.'

The little man returned from his forced march and sat down opposite Powerscourt. 'I've got Sir Isaac Redhead as my lead counsel, you know,' he went on, 'and I've got that young silk Charles Augustus Pugh. They say he's a fearsome cross-examiner.'

Puncknowle referred to the pair as if they were leading stars in his favourite football team.

'I know Charles Augustus Pugh, Mr Puncknowle. A tiger in the courtroom!' Powerscourt had long since ceased being surprised at what he thought of as the moral neutrality of the Bar. Even with the little he knew he did not think he could go into court and defend Jeremiah Puncknowle. The man was too obviously a fraudster. Yet here were two highly respectable barristers, happy to take his shilling. Maybe it was more than a shilling. The lawyers, he had decided, were like the rows of cabs you could see outside the great railway termini, they were just waiting for the next fare to come along. Now seemed as good a time as any to raise his own business in Paradise.

'It is of lawyers that I wish to speak to you, Mr Puncknowle, to ask your advice, really.' Powerscourt was at his most emollient.

The white billiard ball bowed slowly to Powerscourt. 'Please continue, Lord Powerscourt. Of course I shall be happy to help.'

'You know only too well, Mr Puncknowle,' Powerscourt purred, 'that you are not alone in your forthcoming trials in the Royal Courts of Justice. There are a number of other characters appearing who do not appear to have any known connection with your companies or indeed with yourself.' God forgive me, thought Powerscourt. If I were a Catholic I would have to go straight to confession after

leaving this house. It was an offence for which his Irish grandmother, now long in her grave, would have told him to go and wash
his mouth out with soap at once. But he was relieved to see that
there was no eruption from the billiard balls. They seemed to be
nodding in agreement. He plunged further in.

'And people say, Mr Puncknowle, though I have no means of
knowing whether this is true or not, that one or two of these
gentlemen – and I could be completely wrong here – are none too
scrupulous in dealing with their opponents.' Privately Powerscourt
was certain that these men were intimately linked with the
Puncknowle activities. He referred to them in his mind as the
enablers, the enforcers and the extractors.

'At present,' Powerscourt went on, 'I have been engaged by the
benchers of Queen's Inn to investigate two murders. The first, fairly
recently, was a man called Dauntsey, poisoned at a feast. The other,
only a few days ago, a man called Woodford Stewart, shot twice in
the chest.'

Jeremiah Puncknowle made suitably sympathetic mutterings.
Powerscourt could not decide whether his host was a consummate
actor or not. For he seemed to be hearing this news for the first time.
Powerscourt felt it hard to believe that a man who took such pride
in Sir Isaac Redhead and Charles Augustus Pugh would not know
of the destruction of their opponents in court.

'The point is this, sir. These two lawyers were the ones chosen by
the Treasury solicitor to prosecute you and your companions. Now
they are both dead. The reason for my visit is to ask you to make
inquiries, discreet inquiries as only you would know how, as to
whether any of your associates, in what we might call an excess of
zeal for their own defence, arranged or organized for these two
barristers to be put out of the way.'

Powerscourt held his breath. But there was no explosion of fury.
Instead, to his astonishment, Jeremiah Puncknowle leant forward
and seized his hand.

'My dear Lord Powerscourt, of course I will make those inquiries
for you. I shall start this very day. You can rest assured of my full
support, my full support.' With that he released his hand and sank
back in his chair. 'What wicked times we live in, Lord Powerscourt.
I have often said that morality simply disappeared from public life
with the death of our late Queen. How can you have proper standards from a sovereign with mistresses, an arbiter of behaviour in
public life who consorts with grocers and money brokers?'

Powerscourt desisted from pointing that kings without mistresses were virtually unheard of. He thought he should retreat while the ground under his feet was still firm.

'Mr Puncknowle, I am so grateful for your assistance. And I look forward to hearing from you in this sad and unhappy affair. Let me say how much I have enjoyed meeting you, and what a wonderful mansion you have built here. It is a masterpiece, sir, a masterpiece.'

Powerscourt was to tell Lady Lucy afterwards that he thought his host literally swelled with pride at this point. The sepulchral butler glided silently across the carpet to escort Powerscourt to the front door. As his cab rolled back down the hill towards the railway station he reflected that there was always a problem in Paradise. There was a serpent. In this case a rather chubby serpent in the person of Jeremiah Puncknowle. Powerscourt shivered slightly as they clattered their way down the hill. For he felt sure that if Puncknowle wanted people out of the way, be they barrister or investigator, he would not hesitate. The serpent would strike.

'Two day returns to Oxford on the special offer, please.' 'Oxford, special offer, day return for two, please.' 'Special offer to Oxford, two for today, please.' 'Two day returns, special offer, Oxford, today please.' Edward had been repeating these formulas and variants on them to himself for nearly two days now. He knew he would have to make his request in a busy ticket office. He imagined a large and tyrannical ticket man, far worse than Barton Somerville and wearing an intimidating uniform, mocking his efforts and laughing at his silence. If he couldn't get the words out, then the people in the queue behind him would grow angry and start to shout at him. Edward had already written the words out in large letters on a piece of paper which he could send over the counter if speech failed him. It was all too irritating.

The day before, Friday, he had achieved, if not a breakthrough, then something very close to it, in his inspection of the accounts relating to Jeremiah Puncknowle's companies. He saw that the figure missing from the amount raised in the flotation of the second company was virtually identical, except for a few pence, to the total amount of the dividend paid out to shareholders of the first company. By declaring just the dividend per share, they avoided giving the total amount of dividend paid out to all the shareholders. That way, they disguised the first of the Puncknowle frauds. But once you knew the dividend per share, all you had to do was to multiply that by the total number of shares issued in the first place. Edward expected to find the pattern repeated all the way down the various flotations. But in the gaps in his calculations, when his brain was reeling with the figures and he needed a break, he would walk round and round New Court repeating his mantra about the train tickets to Oxford.

Now it was Saturday morning and Edward was standing close to the epicentre of his fears, the ticket office at Paddington station. He had conducted a brief reconnaissance and discovered that there were four ticket clerks on duty that day. One kindly old man who looked as though he should have retired years ago. One sharp-faced young man who reminded Edward of a bookie's runner. One middle-aged man with very thick glasses. And finally another middle-aged man who smiled kindly at his clients. Edward was torn between the old gentleman and the smiling one. He looked around for Sarah and checked his watch. The first train on the special offer left at twenty past nine. It was now ten past and they had no tickets. Edward wondered if he should try to buy them without Sarah but knew that if all else failed and she was there she could take over. Then she was beside him, wearing a dark blue skirt and a lemon blouse. She had a raffish little hat on which she had borrowed from a friend down the street. 'Makes you look a bit special, this hat,' her friend had said, 'that should cheer Edward up.' She had a basket on her arm with lunch hidden beneath a pale green cloth. One look at Edward's face told Sarah that there was anxiety about something related to speech, probably the tickets. There was no queue in front of the old gentleman. Edward advanced slowly. He opened his mouth. The words wouldn't come out.

'Take your time, sonny,' the old man said, 'there's no rush.'

Edward tried again. Still no words came out. He began to wonder about the piece of paper in his pocket. The old man smiled. Then Edward felt a soft touch on his hand. It was, he thought, one of the nicest touches his hand had ever had. He opened his mouth once more.

'Two day returns to Oxford on the special offer,' he said, all in one go.

'Enjoy your trip,' said the old gentleman, handing Edward his tickets and his change. He had a grandson the same age. He hoped his grandson would find a girl as pretty as Sarah. 'Platform Four,' he called after them, 'first on the left!'

They managed to find a compartment to themselves. Sarah put her basket on the luggage rack and Edward showed her the guide-book to Oxford he had bought at the station bookstall.

'What's in the basket, Sarah?' asked Edward, full powers of speech now restored.

'Well,' said Sarah rather doubtfully. 'I hope it's going to be all right. There's ham sandwiches and egg sandwiches and tomato sandwiches and apples and some hard cheese and a bottle of lemonade.'

'That's a feast,' said Edward happily and returned to his perusal of the guidebook. Sarah was remembering her evening session with her mother two evenings before when she had told her mama about Edward.

'Who are his parents, Sarah? What are his family like?'

Sarah had confessed that she had no idea about Edward's family at all. She didn't even know where he lived.

'Really, Sarah, you do have to be careful, especially these days. What does he look like, this Edward person?'

Sarah had described him as just under six feet tall, very slim, with brown eyes and curly hair. And then she had made her big mistake although, looking back on it later, she saw that it would have been worse if Edward came round to her house and had trouble speaking to her mother without her knowing about his difficulties.

'He has trouble speaking sometimes, mama,' she had said defensively, 'but he's usually fine with me.'

'What do you mean, he has trouble speaking, Sarah? Is he some sort of defective person? Are you going to Oxford with a deaf mute?'

'No, he's not deaf, mama. He can hear perfectly well. I'm sure he'll get over it.'

'If it's lasted this long, it'll probably go on for ever. He may go to his grave with his mouth open and no sounds coming out. How does he manage in court?'

'He doesn't speak in court, mama.'

'What do you mean, he doesn't speak in court? You're not going to win any cases if the judge and jury don't know what you want to say, are you?'

'I'm sure he will, in time, mama.'

'How does he earn his living if he can't speak and he can't appear in court? What's he doing in a barristers' chambers in the first place, I should like to know. Does he sweep the floors? Put the cat out?'

'He's a deviller, mama, you know, one of those people who prepares the cases for the barristers.'

111

'I don't need you to tell me what a deviller is, thank you, Sarah, I've known about them for a long time. But do you get paid? Or does Edward just get what the lawyers feel like giving him? Is he a sort of charity case, really?'

'No, he is not a charity case, mama. He charges by the hour, like the barristers charge their clients. Some people make a career of it, they never appear in court at all. Edward is one of the best devillers in London, mama. He's doing the work for the Puncknowle fraud case.'

Sarah thought this might have an effect.

'Is he indeed?' said her mother thoughtfully. 'But you can't become attached to a person who doesn't speak most of the time. It's like being one of those actors who never have any lines but just carry spears around in Shakespeare. You can't be serious about him.'

'I'm not serious, mama, Edward is just a friend.'

Her mother muttered something under her breath.

'Perhaps you'd better bring him round here so I can have a look at him.'

'Yes, mama, I'll ask him when we're in Oxford.'

'Why's he taking you to Oxford anyway? Is there some sort of silent zone up there where the dons and the undergraduates aren't allowed to speak?'

'Not as far as I know, mama.'

'Will he be able to speak to me, Sarah? Or will he just sit there, this Edward of yours, opening and closing his mouth like a goldfish? I don't know what I'm going to say to Mrs Wiggins next time I speak to her, I really don't.'

'I'm sure,' said Sarah, trying to be diplomatic, 'that he'll be absolutely fine as long as you're not fierce with him.'

'Fierce, Sarah? Did you say fierce? I wouldn't know how to be fierce for a moment. You've never known me to be fierce, have you?'

'Well,' said Sarah, smiling at her mother, 'maybe stern would do it.'

Her mother snorted and there the matter was laid to rest. And now it was Saturday morning, the sun was shining, their train had just reached Oxford station and Edward was reaching her picnic basket down from the luggage rack. They had decided to go straight to the river and inspect Oxford later. At this time of year Edward was almost certain it would rain at some point in the day. Their route took them into George Street and then right into Cornmarket. At the junction, they stared to their right at the buildings of Balliol,

Trinity and St John's, with the Ashmolean Museum and the Randolph Hotel on their left. On their way down St Aldate's they peeped into Pembroke College. Christ Church on the other side of the road looked too grand for words.

'It's virtually the same as an Inn of Court!' exclaimed Sarah as they came out of Pembroke. 'They've even got people's names on the staircases just like Queen's Inn. Do you know which is the older, Edward?'

Edward looked up a section of his guidebook. 'Pembroke is older than Queen's,' he said finally, 'but I don't know if the oldest Inn in London is older than the oldest Oxford college, which is, according to this guide, University College, founded in 1249. So it's over six hundred and fifty years old, Sarah.'

Sarah thought the boat keeper at Folly Bridge was probably about that age. He seemed to have only two front teeth left and he sat hunched over the desk in his little boat house like an elf or a gnome from a different world.

'Rowing boat or punt?' he croaked. 'If you haven't punted before then I would definitely recommend a rowing boat.'

'Punt, please,' said Edward firmly. Sarah looked closely at him as Methuselah's assistant, a mere youngster in his middle seventies with almost all his teeth, led them down a little wooden jetty that led into the river. He installed Sarah and the picnic basket on the cushions in the middle of the boat and Edward took up his position at the end. With a loud grunt the old man shoved the boat well out into the stream.

A punt is a long thin rectangular vessel with a faint resemblance to a Venetian gondola except the Venetian vessels have tapered ends. At one end of the punt is a covered platform well able to accommodate a man or woman standing up. In Cambridge the punter stands on this platform. The opposite end has a rising series of slats. This is known as the Oxford end. The centre of the boat is equipped with comfortable cushions and is, traditionally, the place for picnics and romance. The means of propulsion is a very long wooden pole with metal spikes at the end which grip the gravel at the bottom of the stream. When the pole is dropped in straight, the punter then pulls on it so the boat proceeds along the river. When the pole has gone from being vertical to an angle of forty-five degrees or so behind the boat, the punter pulls it out and starts again.

Edward was muttering to himself as he stood on the platform at the end of the boat. Stand at right angles to the boat, he was telling himself. Flick the pole up, don't pass it up hand over hand. Let it drop straight down into the river. Don't hand it down into the water, just let it fall. Bend your knees as you pull on the pole. Twist it when you bring it up in case of mud down below. He carried out a couple of decent strokes and steered the punt with the pole until it was proceeding happily along the right-hand side of the river.

'Are you saying your prayers up there, Edward? I didn't know you knew how to punt.'

'I'm trying to remember the instructions of the man who taught me, Sarah,' said Edward, flicking the pole up through his left hand.

'Who was that?'

'Oddly enough, it was Mr Dauntsey,' said Edward. 'We had to go to Cambridge one day last summer and he taught me how to punt then. He was a Cambridge man, Mr Dauntsey, Trinity, I think. It took me half an hour to go from Magdalene to St John's, which is less than a hundred yards, ten minutes to get from John's to Clare, which is a couple of hundred yards, and by the time we passed King's I was getting the hang of it. Mr Dauntsey had very firm views about punting – he said you could never take any work out on the river or it would bring bad luck and you had to be graceful while you were doing it.'

'Well, you're looking pretty graceful to me, Edward,' said Sarah with a smile.

'He showed me some of the tricks people get up to on the unwary.' Edward was grinning happily to himself now. 'There are a lot of bridges along the back of the Cam, Sarah, and a person standing on them is about the same height as the pole of the punt at the top of its throw. Innocent tourists were often caught like this. A couple of people on the bridge would grab hold of the pole. The punt, of course, keeps moving. The man holding the pole has to let go or else he falls in. Most people fall in to great glee among the spectators. Then there's another misfortune that sometimes causes confusion. The pole gets stuck in the mud at the bottom. Again the boat keeps moving. Sometimes, Mr Dauntsey told me, you can see people clinging on to the pole in clear water while the punt carries on.'

Further up the river, by the other bank, they could see a party of two punts, travelling in tandem, with about a dozen people on board. The noise and waving of bottles indicated they had started drinking at an early hour. Edward thought he could hear shouting and see fingers pointing.

'What are those people saying, Sarah?' asked Edward, bending his knees in the approved manner to send their punt skimming along the water. Sarah turned round, and looked slightly alarmed as she faced Edward again.

'I think they're saying "Wrong end!"' she said. 'Then', she looked rather apprehensive at this point, 'I think they're saying "Throw him in!"'

'Are they indeed,' said Edward and his eyes began measuring distances between their two punts and his. 'I'm punting from the Cambridge end, Sarah. In Oxford, for some unknown reason, they do it from the other end.'

They could hear the shouts again now. Sarah's original version was undoubtedly correct. Bottles were being waved in the air. And a ragged cheer broke out every time the punters pressed their craft forward.

Edward, Sarah thought, was not looking at all alarmed. Indeed he seemed to be coaxing extra speed out of the boat, shooting the pole up through his hands and then dropping it down in one continuous movement. Sarah also saw that he was making experimental movements with the pole as if it were a rudder, trying to see how fast he could alter course. Enthusiastic the Oxford-enders might have been, but they were not very good punters. Their boats were travelling quite slowly, much more slowly than Edward and Sarah's vessel.

When the punts were less than a hundred yards apart, Edward changed direction. He shot across the river at an angle of about sixty degrees into clear water.

'Wrong end! Throw him in! Wrong end!' The taunts continued.

At first Sarah had not understood what Edward was trying to do. There was a look of fierce concentration about him. Then she saw that they would intercept the Oxford-enders quite soon unless Edward could stop or alter course. And she didn't see how he could alter course in time at this speed. There was, she thought, going to be a most almighty collision.

'Throw him in! Wrong end!' The jeers went on, but then began to fall silent. For the Oxford men could see this other boat, many hundredweight of it, coming at them like some ancient vessel from Salamis or Actium. They were going to be stove in amidships. Then Edward made a minor adjustment with his pole as rudder. A terrible silence fell over the Oxford craft as they saw their fate hurtling towards them. The two punters, suddenly realizing that they might

115

receive the full force of the other boat, jumped desperately into the water on the far side of their punts. Then Edward dropped his pole to the bottom and heaved ferociously, not on a line parallel with the boat as he had been doing before, but towards himself as hard as he could pull. Just when a crash seemed inevitable, the Cambridge boat turned sharply to the right, at a distance of only a few feet from the other punts, and then shot ahead of them. Edward turned round and shouted, 'Wrong end, anybody?' There was a round of applause from the spectators watching from the bank. Even the vanquished Oxford boats joined in.

'Well done, Edward, that was tremendous,' said Sarah, clapping furiously. 'The Philistines have been routed.'

'I just think,' said Edward, panting slightly from his exertions, 'that I'll put some distance between us in case those fellows turn around and come after us. I don't think they will, and we're faster than they are in any case, but I'd feel happier all the same.'

Sarah gazed at her young man with new respect. Edward the Silent had turned into Edward the Conqueror.

'And there's another thing,' said Powerscourt, who was still trying to decide if Jeremiah Puncknowle was friend or foe, 'I have to go to these solicitors in the next few days about this missing Maxfield person. The one Dauntsey left twenty thousand pounds to in his will.' Powerscourt had told Lady Lucy and Johnny about the missing Maxfield before. 'The police haven't found any trace of him, nothing at all. Chief Inspector Beecham thinks he's probably dead. But they've checked the records at Somerset House, and there's no record of him there either. He seems to have disappeared.'

'Perhaps he's gone abroad,' said Lady Lucy. 'Do you think Alex Dauntsey gave him the money to buy him out of trouble?'

'God knows,' said Powerscourt. 'Just as easy to say he was paying off a blackmailer.'

'What happens if he's locked up?' said Johnny Fitzgerald cheerfully. 'Debtors' prison, lunatic asylum, that sort of place. Have the police checked those out?'

'They have, Johnny,' said Powerscourt with a sigh, 'but what happens if he's joined up to a different form of institution altogether? Suppose some earlier Maxfield has died and left our Maxfield his title. He's not Maxfield any more, he's Lord Kilkenny or something like that. Our Maxfield has now vanished clean away.'

'Wouldn't somebody remember?' asked Lady Lucy.

'Not necessarily,' said Powerscourt with a grin. 'I look forward to seeing the Chief Inspector's face when I ask him to check this one out. He may be very intelligent, our Jack Beecham, but like all policemen he's taken a very heavy dose of loyalty to all the institutions of the state he's called to protect.'

9

Twenty minutes later Edward and Sarah had escaped from the buildings of Oxford altogether. They had passed Magdalen with its tower and its deer park, the punt still flying along at a rapid pace as Edward made sure that the Oxford-enders weren't following them. Now a kind of open country with rather damp-looking fields and suspicious cows was around them. Edward steered the punt carefully into the shade of a weeping willow on the bank and clambered forward to sit opposite Sarah in the main section of the boat.

'Are you hungry, Edward?' asked Sarah, checking that her picnic basket was still there, feeling quite important as the person in charge of the catering.

'Starving,' said Edward happily and he proceeded to devour seven sandwiches in rapid succession, favouring the ham and the tomato over the egg. Sarah, not used to living with young males, was astonished at the amount he put away. When the demolition of the sandwiches had slowed down, she decided to ask her questions. It was so peaceful out here, nobody could mind being asked a few questions about themselves.

'Edward,' she began hesitantly.

'Sarah,' said Edward, polishing an apple on the sleeve of his shirt.

'Can I ask you a great favour?' the girl went on.

'You ask whatever you like, Sarah,' replied Edward, inspecting his freshly polished apple as if it were a diamond of some sort.

'It's just I promised when I said we were coming to Oxford today.'

Edward suspected at once that this must have something to do with Sarah's mother. He waited. Sarah was looking rather helplessly into the water. It was clear here and you could see right to the bottom.

'Will you come and meet my mother, Edward? She's very keen to meet you.'

Edward began eating his apple. 'If you want me to come and meet your mother, of course I will. What sort of person is your mother?'

Sarah wondered if she could buy time by not explaining the likely turn of events to Edward. But she thought that wouldn't be fair.

'She's curious, my mother, Edward, very curious. And I probably shouldn't tell you this, but she's quite ill. The doctors think she may have only a couple of years to live. And she's in quite a lot of pain. As if,' a bitter note crept into Sarah's voice at this point, 'it wasn't bad enough my father having that stroke and dying two years ago. Two years and four months today.'

Edward wondered if he should put an arm round her for comfort.

'My poor Sarah,' he said, laying off his demolition of the apple for the moment, 'I thought from what you said that your mother wasn't very well, but I didn't know about your father. I'm so sorry. Were you close to him?'

Sarah managed a little smile. 'I was the last child, Edward, I was a girl, I was quick when I was little, very quick. I adored him. And I knew he adored me. I suspect, although he would never have said so, that I was his favourite.'

'What did he die of? He can't have been very old.'

'He had a stroke and never recovered. The doctors couldn't do anything about it. He'd been a teacher in the primary school up the road for years and years. It was so sweet, the teachers were so fond of him that they brought the older children to his funeral. All these lovely little children singing those sad hymns, it was so moving.'

Sarah suddenly realized that far from teasing out of Edward the facts of his parentage, she had merely given him her own. But she felt she hadn't given him proper warning of his likely reception.

'My mother, Edward,' Sarah hesitated. Two enormous cows had plodded over to the side of the river and were inspecting them both.

'Are these cows bothering you?' said Edward suddenly, 'We could move on if you like.'

Sarah shook her head. 'Cows don't bother me,' she said. 'Anyway my mother will want to ask you a whole lot of questions about yourself and your parents and where you went to school and what you want to become later on.'

'Will she indeed?' said Edward. Sarah noticed he was growing rather tense. 'Will you be there all the time, Sarah? You won't go off to bake some scones or make the tea or something and leave me at your mother's mercy?'

'Not if you don't want me to, Edward. Do you think you will be able to cope?'

'Do you mean will I be able to speak, Sarah? God knows. I got so worried about ordering those tickets at Paddington this morning, I'd been practising for days. I'll get worried about meeting your mother too.'

'What will you say about your parents, Edward?' Sarah had been dying to ask this question herself for a long time now. She hoped Edward wouldn't mind, not here on the River Cherwell with a couple of cows for company and the spires of Oxford dreaming behind them.

There was a pause. Sarah didn't know if Edward had been struck dumb at the prospect of her mother or if he didn't know what to say. He flung the core of his apple angrily into the field and picked out another one.

'Sorry about that,' he said, moodily. Sarah kept silent. She felt sure that whatever Edward's answer was going to be, assuming one ever came, it would tell her a lot about the nature of his character and, perhaps, about his problems with speaking.

Edward drew his knees up to his chin and wrapped his arms around his legs. Sarah wondered if he was going to meditate.

'My p-p-parents are dead,' he said finally. 'They were killed in an accident along with my elder sister and my little b-b-brother.' There was no attempt to keep the anger out of his voice.

'How did it happen, Edward?' said Sarah. 'I'm so sorry, it's so terrible losing parents.' So very terrible, she realized, that even the thought of it had brought on the stammer which Edward struggled so hard to keep to at bay.

'Train crash,' he said. 'We were all going to Bristol on a train. There was something wrong with the points. The carriages came off the line at about fifty miles an hour and rolled down a slope. I was buried beneath my parents and the remains of the carriage for hours. When the police pulled everyone out of the rubble I was unconscious beneath them. They say I didn't speak for a week after that.'

'My God,' said Sarah, almost wishing she hadn't been told this ghastly news. Perhaps she should ask her mother not to speak to Edward about his parents at all. 'How frightful, Edward, how absolutely frightful. Your poor family, just wiped out in front of you.'

120

Edward began munching on his apple. The cows wandered off to another part of their field. A couple of rowing boats, going quite fast, sped past them on their return journey to Oxford.

'So where do you live now, Edward?' Sarah had a vision of Edward living on his own in some squalid boarding house where the food was terrible and he never tidied his room.

'I live with my grandparents,' he said with a smile. 'They're very good to me. Maybe you should come and meet them, Sarah. I'm sure they'd love to see you.' Even in his sixties Edward knew his grandfather had an eye for a pretty girl. Sarah would enchant him. The thought seemed to cheer him up.

'Right,' he said, 'we'd better think about getting back or we won't have any time to look at Oxford at all.'

Lord Francis Powerscourt was trying to review his knowledge of the Queen's Inn investigation as his train carried him down to Calne and the beautiful Mrs Dauntsey. Murder Number One, her husband, poisoned at a feast, the poison probably administered at a drinks party in the rooms of the Treasurer of the Inn, the unpleasant Barton Somerville. Murder Number Two, Woodford Stewart, shot twice in the chest. Connections between the two? Both were retained for the prosecution in what would be one of the great fraud trials of the decade, that of Jeremiah Puncknowle and his associates. And both were benchers of their Inn of Court, though why that should make them liable to sudden and violent death Powerscourt didn't know. He did know that Woodford Stewart had been elected two months before Dauntsey so they must have been the most junior members of the Inn's governing body. And what of the missing Maxfield? Had he resurfaced to murder Dauntsey for his twenty thousand pounds? Then there was Porchester Newton, Dauntsey's great rival in the election to the bench. He had disappeared shortly after Dauntsey's death but was due to return the following week.

Had he, perhaps, returned in time to shoot Woodford Stewart and dump his body by the Temple Church? Powerscourt could think of lots of reasons why somebody might want to kill Dauntsey and Stewart individually. It was the connection that worried him, assuming the two deaths were linked. Surely it had to be professional, he said to himself, as the train rattled through a tunnel.

He still didn't know what to say to Mrs Dauntsey, how to bring up the very delicate subject he was travelling to Calne to raise.

As his cab rattled past the grey stone walls of the great house, Powerscourt remembered the covered furniture, the sofas under wraps, the floors covered with rough matting, the vast expanse of the great house that most people never saw, a forbidden kingdom for the dust and the shadows and the ghosts of Dauntseys past.

She was waiting for him, Elizabeth Dauntsey, still dressed in black that showed off her creamy skin. She smiled as she offered her hand to him.

'Lord Powerscourt, how very pleasant to see you again. I trust you had a pleasant journey? Would you care for some tea, perhaps?'

'A little later for the tea would be most agreeable, Mrs Dauntsey. My journey was fine. Your park is looking very well with all these early flowers.'

'I think it likes the spring, our park. It always looks good about now. But come, Lord Powerscourt, before you disclose your business, I have something to tell you. I don't know if it is important or not but you did ask in your letter if I could think of anything unusual Alex might have said in the month or so before he died.'

Powerscourt nodded gravely. 'Have you thought of something, Mrs Dauntsey?'

She looked down at her hands briefly. 'There was something, I hope it's not too trivial. It must have been in the weeks after he was elected a bencher, you see, and there was quite a lot that was new to him about all that.'

She paused and looked closely at Powerscourt as if he could help her. He gave her what he hoped was an encouraging smile.

'He said it more than once, I'm certain of that, Lord Powerscourt. He said he was very worried about the accounts.'

'Whose accounts, Mrs Dauntsey? Your own personal accounts? The estate accounts perhaps? Some extra expenditure needed for improvement, maybe? His legal accounts? Or the Inn accounts, which I suppose he now had access to after his election?'

'What a lot of accounts you can rattle off at a moment's notice Lord Powerscourt! Do you think it's because you're a man?'

Powerscourt smiled. 'I think it's because of my brother-in-law. He's a mighty financier in the City of London. When I called on him the other day he was surrounded by records of income and expenditure and ledgers and an enormous volume called the Book of Numbers which contained the secrets of all the other accounts.'

Now it was Mrs Dauntsey's turn to smile. 'It must be very useful having a brother-in-law who's good with money, Lord Powerscourt. Nearly as good as, maybe better than having one who's a doctor. You don't have one who's a medical man, do you?'

Powerscourt did a lightning audit of Lucy's vast tribe of relations. Not one of them, he realized, had entered the medical profession.

'No doctors,' he said, 'one or two naval men, plenty of soldiers, probably enough to form a small regiment. But to return to your husband, Mrs Dauntsey, do you have an idea in your mind of which kind of account he was talking about?'

'I've thought about that a lot,' she said, 'particularly as you were coming to see me today. I don't think it was our personal accounts and I don't think it was to do with the accounts of his chambers. That clerk they had ran those as if it was the Bank of England. That leaves us with the estate and Queen's Inn. I'm honestly not sure which one it would have been, I'm afraid. Alex kept the estate accounts very close to his chest.'

'Can you remember exactly what he said, the words he used, Mrs Dauntsey?'

She frowned. Powerscourt thought she looked even more attractive when she frowned. 'I can't,' she said finally. 'I can't decide if he said unusual, or strange, or worrying. It was something along those lines.'

Powerscourt groaned mentally as he thought of the problem of asking Barton Somerville if he could cast an eye over the Inn accounts. 'I don't suppose,' he said hopefully, 'that he brought any of the Inn accounts down here, to look at them over the weekend, perhaps?'

'I don't think so. I'll have a look in his study and let you know, if that would be helpful. Perhaps we should move on to what you wanted to talk to me about, Lord Powerscourt. Then we could have some tea.'

Powerscourt felt rather nervous all of a sudden. 'The matter is exceedingly delicate, Mrs Dauntsey. It touches on the most delicate and intimate of subjects, one we discussed last time, if you recall, about children and heirs and all sort of thing. If you have any objection, please tell me now.'

Elizabeth Dauntsey did not blush, or look down, or ask to be excused. 'I am sure, Lord Powerscourt, that you would not be raising such a matter if you did not think it might be important.'

'Thank you, Mrs Dauntsey, thank you. Sometimes, I must confess,

I think this area may be of the utmost importance, at others I feel I may be wasting my time.'

Outside the sun had gone in and a fierce wind was whipping through the trees. Rain was now lashing against the windows of the Dauntsey drawing room.

'Perhaps I could put my concern to you in the form of a fairy story, Mrs Dauntsey. I hope you like fairy stories?'

She smiled. 'I have always been most devoted to fairy stories and plays about magic islands like Prospero's in *The Tempest* or Illyria in *Twelfth Night*. Alex and I saw *Twelfth Night* a couple of months ago in Middle Temple Hall. It was the three hundredth anniversary of its first performance in 1602 in the very same building. It was extraordinary. Sorry, Lord Powerscourt, I'm holding you up.'

'I went to that performance too. Perhaps we passed one another, like ships in the night.' Both *The Tempest* and *Twelfth Night*, he remembered, featured shipwrecks. The current fate of Mrs Dauntsey? Certainly she didn't look very like one shipwrecked now, he thought, her beauty shining through the pain of bereavement.

'A long long time ago,' he began, 'when the world was young, there was a small kingdom perched high up in the mountains. These mountains were much higher than any we have in this country. Snow sat on the highest of them for most of the year and only the bravest of the young men climbed to the very top. Their customs were very different from ours. This, after all, was long before the invention of the telegraph or the spinning jenny, the telephone or the motor car, of paved roads and of great steamships. The people of the Mountain Kingdom, for that was how its name translated into English, had never seen the sea. But their land was rich. There were fertile valleys as well as the great summits. Their horses were beautiful and very fast and could race most of the day without being tired. The seasons were beautiful, Mrs Dauntsey. In spring the slopes of the mountains would be covered with flowers. In summer the sun shone but the streams that came down from the hills were always cool. In autumn the trees lost their leaves in a blaze of colour, yellows and gold and black and hectic reds. And in the winter the snow sat on the turrets and the battlements of the Royal Palace until it looked like fairyland.

'The people were ruled over by a King, who was getting old at the beginning of our story, but he had a son, a handsome Prince who would succeed him. As the Prince grew to manhood he looked about him for a beautiful girl he could marry. None of the daughters

124

of the nobles pleased him very much. He began to despair until a wise old man told him about the child of a king two little countries away, who was said to be very beautiful indeed. So our Prince rode off to the Kingdom of the Plain and fell in love with the Princess. Eight months later they were married. Two weeks after that the old King died in his sleep and the Prince and Princess became the King and Queen.'

You'd better get to the point, pretty soon, Powerscourt said to himself or you'll be here all day.

'For the first few years,' Powerscourt went on, 'everything seemed perfect in this highland Garden of Eden. The harvests were good, the people were contented, peace reigned inside and outside the little kingdom. There was only one shadow across perfection. The new King and Queen had no children. Now it was the custom in this land that each new King had to be the son of the previous one. Nephews, younger brothers, distant cousins just wouldn't do. The custom dated back many centuries to a time when civil war had torn the country apart. On that occasion when the old King died, the courtiers tried to put his younger brother on the throne in his place. The nobles would have none of it, declaring him not to be the rightful sovereign and plunging the country into a civil war that lasted fifteen years.

'Time went by, some more years passed and still the King had no heirs. The nobles became restless and began to plot among themselves as nobles always do. The citizens were fearful of the bloodshed that might follow his end. The King went on a journey, accompanied only a by a few faithful followers, to a temple in the mountains where the holy men lived. They listened to his story and told him to travel further on still, up into the high mountains. When he had lived among the snows for ten days, he was to return to the holy place for his answer.

'On his return, the holy men gave the King their message. Now in this kingdom there were no laws about relations between the sexes, only customs. So it was the custom for husband and wife to be faithful, one to the other, but it was not a legal obligation. The Queen, they told the King, must lie with your brother, or any of your cousins, until she be with child. And you also must lie with her so nobody will know that you may not be the father. The peace of the kingdom demands this, they said to the King. For if you have no son and heir of your own blood, what will happen to the kingdom?'

Powerscourt stopped. Elizabeth Dauntsey looked at him carefully.

'Don't tell me the story stops there, Lord Powerscourt,' she said, 'with the King still up there in the mountains.'

'I'm afraid that's where the manuscript runs out, Mrs Dauntsey, I'm truly sorry.'

She rang the bell and ordered tea. 'Well, let me see if I could help you out, Lord Powerscourt, with the story, I mean. I'm not a storyteller like yourself and I could only speak for the Queen, I think, not for any of the other characters.'

She stopped and a faint twinkle came into her eyes. 'How can I put this? I think my contribution to the story, speaking for the Queen of course, is that it is always very important for a wife, especially if she is a Queen and married to a King, to obey her husband at all times.'

Powerscourt laughed. 'How very well you put it, Mrs Dauntsey, and what an important moral to take from the story.' By God, it's true, he said to himself, those faint reports from Lucy's relations must be true. Where does that leave my investigation, he asked himself. His brain was reeling.

'Tea, Lord Powerscourt?' she said as the butler departed once again to the wider realms of Calne. 'You must be thirsty after telling all those stories.' Powerscourt saw that the subject had been closed by the arrival of the Darjeeling. He felt oddly relieved. He wondered briefly which of the characters in *Twelfth Night* Elizabeth Dauntsey might have been. Cesario? Who certainly had been shipwrecked. Probably even in Powerscourt's biased eye, she was too old for that. Olivia perhaps, with her great household and unruly relations? Certainly, he thought, you could hide Sir Toby Belch and Sir Andrew Aguecheek well out of sight in the dusty recesses of Calne. She brought him back from his daydream.

'Tell me, Lord Powerscourt, somebody informed me the other day that you have had additions to your own family. Is it true that you now have twins?'

Edward had punted back to Folly Bridge very slowly. There was no sign of their previous adversaries and no more rude comments about Edward standing at the wrong end. Sarah leant back on the cushions, her hand trailing in the water, and peered at Edward through semi-closed eyes. Eventually the motion of the boat sent her off to sleep. Edward smiled down at his passenger, so innocent as she lay there, her head slightly to one side, her red hair bright on the cushion. Then they had walked through Christ Church, marvelling at the size of Tom Quad. London's Inns of Court could hold their heads up against most Oxford colleges but this quadrangle had no equal near the Strand. Lots of politicians, Edward informed Sarah, had been at Christ Church, Canning and Peel and Gladstone and Lord Salisbury.

'Would you like to have been to Oxford, Edward?' asked Sarah, staring at a group of undergraduates about to go into Hall. She thought Edward would look nice in one of those gowns.

'I don't think so, Sarah. I'm not sure I would fit in. Most of these people are very rich.'

It was only in the train back to Paddington that Sarah raised her fears about Queen's Inn. They were alone in their compartment and Edward was polishing off the remains of the sandwiches and the apples from the picnic.

'How long do you think it will be, Edward,' she said rather sadly, 'before they catch this murderer?'

'Oh dear,' said Edward, 'I hoped a day in Oxford would take your mind off it all. I know it's easy for me to say it, but you mustn't worry. Nobody's going to want to harm you. Lord Powerscourt is one of the best investigators in the country and that policeman is very sharp. I don't think there's anything to worry about.'

'It's not me I'm that worried about so much, Edward,' said Sarah, her eyes large and bright as she looked across at him. 'Who worked very closely with Mr Dauntsey? Who worked closely with Mr Stewart? Who must know a lot of the secrets they knew? Who is the best-informed person in the Inn about that huge fraud case? In every case, Edward, the answer is you. I'm so worried you're next on their list.'

'That's ridiculous, Sarah,' said Edward, secretly touched by the amount of her concern – surely she must care for him, maybe he should hold her hand. 'I'm not going to be on anybody's list. It's absurd. I'm in more danger crossing the road.'

But all of Edward's protests came to nothing. Sarah remained convinced he was in great danger. An offer by Edward to come and meet her mother the following week did something to calm her. He may not like being interrogated by my mother, she thought, but at least he won't get killed.

It was no longer enjoying the pride of place it had occupied at the time of Powerscourt's last visit to his brother-in-law William Burke, but it still took a fairly prominent position. It sat in the centre of the lowest row of bookshelves to the left of Burke's fireplace. It was taller than the others and its black cover gave the Book of Numbers an air of great authority. Powerscourt wondered if the benchers of Queen's Inn had a similar volume, a financial Holy of Holies, the Ark of the Covenant of the Inn's accounts.

'Alexander Dauntsey, William,' Powerscourt began, 'the chap who got poisoned, was apparently very worried about the accounts before he died.'

Burke's reply was the same as Powerscourt's had been down in Calne. 'Which ones, Francis? Estate? Personal? Chambers? Queen's Inn?'

'Exactly the same question that I asked. Two were more or less eliminated, his chambers' because their clerk is so efficient, and the personal ones because they were usually in good health. So that leaves us with the estate and the Inn. Mrs Dauntsey couldn't remember which one it was.'

'Strange how even very intelligent women often get a mental blank about money, Francis. Take your sister, my beloved wife, highly intelligent woman, not the slightest idea about money.'

'Some of them must be good at it, William. Women, I mean. Exceptions that prove the rule. Anyway, the reason I am here is to ask you which of those two you think more likely and what kind of irregularities we might be talking about that would worry a cool and experienced barrister like Dauntsey. The estate accounts or the accounts of the Inn?'

William Burke took a careful sip of his white port. 'This really is guessing in the dark, Francis. But I think it is less likely to do with the estate accounts. They will follow the same sort of pattern year after year. There may be some exceptional event like a bad harvest. But even then they work like a see-saw.'

'See-saw, William?' Powerscourt had a mental image of his daughter going up and down on one. The twins, when their time came, could have an end each.

'Sorry, see-saw in the sense that a bad harvest is bad for the people whose crops fail, but very good for those whose don't because the prices go through the roof. I don't think there have been any natural disasters that could have affected things . You didn't see any sign of natural catastrophe down there in Kent, Francis? Vesuvius-type eruptions? Fire and brimstone consuming the cities of the plain? Death of the firstborn?'

'It all looked fairly peaceful to me. William. Deer running about, spring flowers everywhere, the vast hinterland of that house smothered in dust jackets and sheeting. So, it must be the Inn, or perhaps I should say it is more likely to be the Inn. What could be going on there?'

Burke rose from his chair and wandered over to the window. He looked out into the square below, a couple of pedestrians going home, a lone policeman plodding along the opposite side. He came back and sat on his sofa.

'I can't say I know very much about how an Inn of Court organizes its finances, Francis. They must have somebody, I presume, to arrange the collection of all those rents for the various chambers. I doubt if anything fishy could be going on there. If they pitched the rents too high, presumably the barristers might decamp to Gray's Inn or the Middle Temple.'

Burke paused. 'Let me ask you a question, Francis. Presumably you think this worry about money might have been important. Do you think it might have led to the two deaths? Because if you do think that, then it must have been some enormous financial crime for somebody to have murdered these two fellows.'

Now it was Powerscourt's turn to pause. 'I simply don't know. It might be nothing at all. But just give me a list, if you would, of the kinds of money crimes that could lead to murder.'

'The actual crime might not that be all that huge, Francis. But suppose there was blackmail. Suppose Dauntsey and Stewart were operating some kind of blackmailing ring down there in Queen's. A worm turns. Poisons one and shoots the other. In terms of the big financial crimes, they're almost all related to theft in one form or another, theft from fellow shareholders like Mr Puncknowle, theft from banks, theft from the public by fraud and deception. What makes life so difficult with the Inn, Francis, is that they will all keep silent on you. They may all have been paying Danegeld to some blackmailer or other for years and years but they're not going to tell you about it. Any attempt to get a look at the accounts of individual chambers isn't going to be greeted with birthday cake and balloons, and any attempt to look at the accounts of the Inn itself will be running into a blank wall. "Terribly sorry, Powerscourt," they will say, "Inn is a closed body, under no obligation to show our accounts to anybody, even if we wanted to, which we don't."'

'I'm very grateful, William. You've raised a whole host of possibilities.'

'I'm sure,' said Burke, 'that I haven't got the right one. Let me give you a word of advice. I do not know how many other possible theories you have for the motive for these murders, quite a few, I suspect. But let's suppose it does have to do with the money. Let's suppose that supposition holds good. If you get anywhere near the truth, Francis, you won't live to tell the tale. These people have killed twice already. No reason to doubt they will do it again. I don't mind going to the funerals of very aged and decrepit customers of my bank, but I'm damned if I'm going to go to yours.'

10

A rather sombre council of war took place later that evening in the Powerscourt drawing room in Manchester Square. Johnny Fitzgerald had returned from talking to the fringes of London's underworld about the deaths in Queen's Inn. Lady Lucy had returned from another mission round the outer fringes of her relations for any fresh intelligence of Mr and Mrs Dauntsey. Powerscourt told them first about Mrs Dauntsey and her reaction to the fairy tale. Lady Lucy was fascinated.

'So it must be true, that rumour,' she said, looking intensely at her husband, 'but don't you see what it means, Francis? If the Queen has obeyed her husband and lain with cousins and brothers she's still not pregnant. So what are they, what were they, going to do now? If they cannot get an heir from the Dauntsey blood lying with Dauntsey's wife, then surely the answer is obvious.'

'What is the answer, Lucy?' Johnny Fitzgerald was fiddling with a corkscrew but he hadn't yet opened a bottle.

'Well, there are two possible answers, now I think about it, but I'm sure which one I think is right. Poor Mrs Dauntsey. Either she has to start consorting with people who aren't her husband's relations at all, in which case any heir wouldn't have any Dauntsey blood in them. Or it's time the boot went on the other foot. It's time for Mr Dauntsey to find somebody to bear his child.'

'And if the person was married her husband might not take too kindly to her being used as a sort of brood mare,' said Powerscourt, thinking of Mrs Dauntsey as she poured the tea with that slight smile playing around her eyes.

'He might even think of dropping poison into Dauntsey's drink,' said Johnny Fitzgerald, 'and then have to shoot Woodford Stewart because he'd seen him do it.'

'I think we should slow down a bit,' said Powerscourt, 'or we'll all get carried away. We just need to keep a very close eye on Mr Dauntsey's doings and any new friends he may have been making. What news do you have, Johnny?'

Johnny Fitzgerald still had an unopened bottle of Nuits St Georges in front of him. He was peering closely at the label. 'Lucy, Francis, do you think this St George chap is the same George as the English patron saint? That he had to slay the dragon because the creature was guarding the bloody vineyards? So all he really wanted was some nice burgundy and the fire-breathing creature got in the way? Never mind. I have to tell you, Francis, that I am worried, very worried indeed, about what I have discovered down there in the East End and one or two other places as well.'

'What's that, Johnny?' said Lady Lucy, concerned that the news might affect her husband.

'My purpose in going to talk to all these people was to do with Jeremiah Puncknowle and his co-defendants, as you both know. Was it likely that any of those defendants would have tried to organize the murder of Mr Dauntsey or Mr Stewart, or indeed carried out the deed themselves? From all over London, in the back rooms of public houses, in the stinking alleyways of Shoreditch, in the corners of illegal drinking dens, the answer was always the same. The answer was No. The risk was too great. But,' Johnny paused and looked closely at his friend, 'somebody knew something about the murder of Dauntsey. Maybe it had to do with the poison, I couldn't find out. But there was something else, Francis, something to do with you. Some of these criminals sounded as though they were actually concerned with your health. I don't think there is a contract out on your life, but I think somebody has been making inquiries about who would take the job on, how much it might cost, how it could be arranged. Most of them knew something was going on. One of the villains, delightful man till you remembered he'd served fifteen years for armed robbery with violence, said you ought to leave the country. So what have you been doing with these lawyers, Francis, down there in the Strand with the wigs and the gowns and the daily refreshers, that they're thinking of arranging your murder?'

'Are you serious, Johnny?' Lucy had turned pale and hurried to her husband's side.

'I am deadly serious, Lucy,' said Fitzgerald, leaning forward to open his bottle at last. 'I think Francis should take his gun with him every time he leaves the house.'

'It'll be like being back in South Africa, going round armed. That's twice in one night I've been told to take care of my health,' said Powerscourt bitterly, 'and I still don't have much of an idea who is behind these murders. It reminds me of Easter Week in that case in Compton when the whole cathedral chapter was going to desert the Anglican faith and become Catholic. I was terrified one of the clerics would change their mind and be killed like the other three before them. It may be the same with these bloody lawyers. Ask the wrong question, or more likely ask the right question, and you've signed your death warrant. Well, I don't care what people say, I'm not going to give up now.'

That night Lady Lucy added another prayer to her collection. She prayed that God would save and preserve her Francis, that He would keep him safe from the devices of his enemies, that he might live long as father to his children and husband of his wife.

The main court of Queen's Inn looked like a convocation of ravens to Powerscourt as he crossed it at about nine thirty on Monday morning. Down every stairway they came, sometimes singly, sometimes in pairs, sometimes in threes and fours, ravens in pack formation. Papers were checked, ties adjusted, fragments of dust flicked off gowns that had spent the last few days on a hook at the back of a door, wigs settled firmly in place. Then the convoy set off, arms flapping in their gowns, to the welcoming embrace of the Royal Courts of Justice or the Old Bailey. The whole procession must have taken ten or fifteen minutes, one or two latecomers actually running at full speed across the grass so as to reach their courtroom on time.

Edward was not among them. Edward was a solitary bird this morning, still devilling into the fraud case of Jeremiah Pucknowle, now expected to start later that week.

'Can you spare me half an hour, Edward?' asked Powerscourt respectfully as his young friend sat down with his papers.

'Of course, sir,' said Edward, who would have laid down his life for Powerscourt or his family.

Powerscourt led the way out of the Inn down the Strand and into a quiet corner of the Regent's Hotel, looking over the river. He ordered coffee.

'I apologize for all the secrecy, Edward. I very much need to ask you for some information. But I think it could be very dangerous for both of us if we were overheard in Queen's.'

Edward looked sceptical for a moment.

'Think of it like this, my friend,' said Powerscourt, taking a large gulp of his coffee. 'Suppose it was something to do with money that led to the two deaths. I know for a fact that Dauntsey was very worried about the accounts in the period before he died.' Powerscourt took care not to let slip where his information had come from or that it might have related to accounts other than those of Queen's Inn. 'If the murders are to do with the money, then anybody else found inquiring too closely into the finances may well end up murdered too.'

Edward nodded. 'You're not going to get murdered, are you, Lord Powerscourt? I couldn't bear that, not after the way you and your family have been so kind to me.'

Powerscourt grinned. 'I have absolutely no intention of departing this life and leaving Lucy a widow and the children a life without a father. Why, there's hardly been time so far to get to know the twins properly. Anyway, Edward, I am presuming that the accounts are not available for general inspection by members of the Inn. I believe that there must be some official who supervises the payments of rent for chambers and bills for food and so on, though that person would not necessarily know the true state of the accounts.'

'There's a new Financial Steward who came last year,' said Edward. 'The chap who did the job before, man by the name of Bassett, kept going till he was seventy-five before he stopped. For some reason they all stay for a very long time. There's only been six of them in the Inn's history.'

Six in around a hundred and forty years, Powerscourt said to himself. One every twenty-five years or so.

'But I presume, Edward, that these stewards do not necessarily know the true picture of the accounts. They know all about the bread and butter stuff but not any investments that may have been made, or monies or property that may have been inherited.'

'That's true,' said Edward. 'There have been all kinds of rumours about the wealth of Queen's. At one end of the scale it's the poorest Inn of Court in London, at the other it owns most of Mayfair and half of Oxford Street. But what do you want me to do?'

'Can you get me the names of all the people who have been benchers here and the dates of their death?'

Edward dropped his coffee cup on to the hard floor. The cup shattered into a thousand fragments. The coffee concentrated in one narrow stream and made for the nearby carpet. The whole room looked round and stared at Edward as if he had ruined their morning. 'I'm t-t-t-terribly s-s-sorry.' he stammered to the elderly maid who arrived at remarkable speed to clear up the mess.

Powerscourt, disturbed by Edward's full-blown stuttering, decided to keep talking for a while until calm returned to his mind.

When the maid was out of earshot Powerscourt continued. 'If we have those dates, we can look at the wills in Somerset House or wherever they keep them. The wills won't tell us a great deal, but they will give us an indication of how much may have been left to the Inn, or perhaps to the benchers. Now, they may have invested five per cent of their income from the rents for years and years and made a tidy sum, we just don't know and the wills won't help, but they'll be a start. Do you see my point, Edward?'

Edward nodded. Then it was his turn to grin. He took a deep breath and swallowed hard. 'I was thinking how difficult it was going to be, Lord Powerscourt,' he said. It was all right. He was in control of the words again. Sometimes they were just so elusive, so slippery. 'Then I remembered. There's a little guidebook they give to all prospective members, everybody who's interested in coming here. I think they give it to visitors too, sometimes. It lists all the benchers in the back, and the dates they served. Some places retire people in their late sixties or early seventies. Not here. Once a bencher, you're a bencher for life. It's like the Supreme Court in America.'

'So,' said Powerscourt, suspecting that his job had suddenly become a lot easier, 'can you remember, and please remember too that one particular answer to this question will make me very happy, are the dates given in years only, or do they include the month of the year as well?'

Edward thought for a moment. 'You're in luck, Lord Powerscourt. They must have been very concerned with accuracy. Very proper, I suppose, for the legal profession. You do get the month. And in most cases you get the day of the month as well.'

One hour later Powerscourt was staring at his list of names. There were, he had counted, just over a hundred benchers who had served Queen's Inn since its foundation. Now he was in a basement room in Somerset House where details of all the wills up to 1853 were recorded in enormous dark brown ledgers. Clerks of the Court of Canterbury had entered the main points of each will as they reached

135

them. Historians, necrophiliacs, any of the deranged who wanted this material had to copy the wills they wanted out of the big books. The room was in the shape of a rectangle with a long oak table in the centre. There were enough chairs for about twenty ghouls, Powerscourt saw, though only five were occupied this morning. A little light filtered through from glass skylights set into the ceiling that was the floor of the courtyard outside. The electric lights on the walls gave off a slightly yellowish tinge as if they weren't connected properly to the supply. There was a strange smell, a compound of sweat and dirt and the musty odour that came from so many opened ledgers. Ferocious notices were pinned up everywhere, warning of the dangers of misbehaviour. Writing in the ledgers guaranteed life expulsion from the premises. Spilt ink was almost as serious with a ban of five years. Marking the covers of the ledgers with a penknife or sharp nib would bring a fine of twenty pounds. And, sitting at a high desk at the far end of the room, underneath a fading picture of Queen Victoria on her Jubilee, were the guardians of this Valley of Lost Things, two enormous curators with identical handlebar moustaches, wearing a Prussian-looking uniform of dark blue. They stared relentlessly at their customers with an expression of the deepest suspicion. Powerscourt thought they must be former sergeant majors, ferocious drill at the double in the Somerset House courtyard an extra punishment, perhaps, for the miscreants and defaulters among the ledgers.

Truly, Powerscourt thought, this room with its great brown books and their baleful contents and those dreadful guardians, this is the kingdom of the dead. We, the living who pass through here, are mere wraiths, doomed to wander in the world of shadows outside from the Strand to Aldwych to Holborn trying to forget that our own futures too will one day end up down here or in the sister chamber that holds the wills of later years. Did these rich men – for on the whole, he thought, you would have to be rich to qualify for a place in these ledgers – know that one day, hundreds of years after they were gone, complete strangers would come and inspect their wills, in an act that amounted to posthumous financial rape? Would the same fate happen to Powerscourt in his turn?

The names of former benchers fascinated him. James Herbert Pomeroy, passed away in the 1770s, left twenty pounds to his wife and a house in Lincoln's Inn Fields to Queen's Inn. Edward Madingley Chawleigh, died 1780, left fifty pounds for the maintenance and education of poor students 'that the poor might be afforded the advantages vouchsafed to us by birth'. Was Josiah Sterndale Tarleton, passed away 1785, the father of the Colonel Banastre Tarleton, painted with such verve and panache by Sir Joshua Reynolds? Tarleton had been engaged in the American War of Independence. Powerscourt could see the painting now, the young man in skin-tight white breeches and a green jacket studded with gold buttons, the smoke of a great explosion behind him and gathered around his person the varied accoutrements of war, a pair of horses, for the Colonel was of horse rather than foot, a mobile cannon and what may have been the colours of his company in deep red. Old Mr Tarleton had at least passed on before the disappointment of the loss of the American colonies his son had fought to keep. And then, Powerscourt remembered, this Colonel Banastre Tarleton had been the lover over many years of Perdita, one-time mistress of the Prince of Wales, still hanging on the walls of the Wallace Collection, painted by Gainsborough. Was Robert Fitzpaine Wilberforce, died 1792, the father or the uncle of the man who campaigned so effectively for the abolition of slavery?

By the time he left for the day Powerscourt had entered details of over twenty wills in his thick red notebook, specially purchased for the occasion. After a while he found he was concentrating on transcribing the material as fast as possible with little attention to the content. But he had made, he thought, one significant discovery. Every single bencher so far had left some money or property or investment to Queen's Inn. Powerscourt wondered if leaving money to the Inn in your will was a necessary part of becoming a bencher. He hoped that somewhere in William Burke's vast range of acquaintance in the City of London there was a man who could compute how much two hundred pounds in 1800 was worth today and the likely value of property that seemed to be dotted like stardust round the lawyers' quarters in a radius of three or four miles.

Detective Chief Inspector Beecham was waiting for Powerscourt on his return to the Inn from Somerset House. He was exceedingly angry.

'Bloody man,' he said, slamming the fist of his right hand into the palm of his left, 'the bloody man.'

'Have you been talking to the benchers again, Chief Inspector? You know how that upsets you.'

137

Beecham managed a laugh. 'I have not been talking to any of those benchers. It's the bloody man Newton, Porchester Newton.'

'What about Newton? What's he done to upset you?'

'He's come back, for a start,' said Beecham. 'And any sane person would have to put the wretch very high on his list of suspects. Huge row, as you know, with Dauntsey about that election. Dauntsey wins the election, Newton doesn't, takes himself off in a huff after the wretched feast. He could easily have come back secretly to shoot Woodford Stewart and then disappeared again.'

'Sorry, Chief Inspector,' said Powerscourt, 'I don't follow you. What exactly is the latest problem with Newton?'

'Sorry, my lord,' said Beecham, running his hand through his hair, 'he won't speak.'

'What do you mean, he won't speak? Has he gone dumb or something?'

'He won't speak to me. He won't answer any questions. He refuses to give an indication at all of his whereabouts on the day of the feast or any day since then. He has gone mute in this affair.'

Powerscourt remembered an old judge telling him years before that if you were guilty on a major charge your best course was to say nothing at all. Any information you gave to the police led them somewhere else, then to more questions which brought more discoveries until you were thoroughly trapped.

'That's not very wise of him, surely?' Powerscourt said.

'It's not,' said the Chief Inspector. 'And much bloody good it is going to do him. I'm going to put a team of my men on to his whereabouts since the Dauntsey murder full time. And if they find anything, however small, we'll have him in and lock him up on a charge of obstruction. Maybe a night or two in the cells would restore his powers of speech.'

Powerscourt wondered if he should volunteer to try his own, different, powers of persuasion to induce some speech out of Porchester Newton. But he didn't want to offend the Chief Inspector. Before he had decided, Beecham was already there.

'Why don't you try, my lord? You get on better with those bloody benchers than I do. He might talk to you more easily than to me. After all, I don't care how we get the information.'

Three minutes later Powerscourt was knocking on the door of Newton's rooms on the ground floor of the little Stone Court hidden away at the back of the Inn. Newton was an enormous man, well over six feet tall, going to fat about the face and stomach, florid of complexion and with rather brutal hands that ooked to Powerscourt as though they should have belonged to a butcher rather than a barrister.

'Good afternoon,' Powerscourt began. Nobody could complain if you said good afternoon to them. 'My name is Powerscourt. I have been asked by the benchers to investigate these murders. I wonder if you could spare me the time to answer some questions.' Powerscourt was speaking in what he hoped was his most emollient voice. The reply was loud, virtually shouted.

'No! Get out!'

'Mr Newton, I am, I would humbly remind you, a man of some experience in murder investigations. It is my belief that refusal to answer questions makes people suspicious. It makes people, particularly policemen, think that the refusal is meant to conceal something. From there it is but a short step to the assumption that the person is refusing information about the murder. And from there it is only another short step to the assumption that the person refusing to speak may actually be the murderer. We are fortunate here that we have very intelligent policemen engaged on the case. I have known less intelligent policemen send those refusing to speak to court on the charge of murder because they though silence denoted guilt. On one occasion it only transpired after the man had been sentenced, Mr Newton, that his silence had been to protect a woman. If she had not come forward, with all the shame and obloquy it brought her, the man would have been hanged. I ask you again. Could you spare me some time to answer a few questions?'

The voice was even louder. 'No! Get out!'

Anybody listening might think, Powerscourt reflected, that the fellow doesn't want to talk to me.

'Let me make one last appeal, Mr Newton,' Powerscourt suspected it was hopeless but was resolved on one last attempt. 'Let me remind you of the difficulties your colleagues are facing each and every day these mysteries remain unsolved. There are policemen crawling all over the Inn. I haunt the place, asking uncomfortable questions from time to time. Nobody can be certain there will not be another murder, that they are not going to be the next victim. I am sure that some of the stenographers are contemplating leaving their employment here because of the uncertainty, not knowing if they will be poisoned as they eat their lunch or shot on their way to the underground railway station. I am sure you could help, Mr Newton. If your knowledge would advance the quest for the murderer, then surely it is your duty to talk to us.'

Porchester Newton stood up. Powerscourt saw with some alarm that those butcher's hands were rising to his waist as if preparing to wring something that might have been a pillow case or a human form.

'No! Get out! One more word and I'll throw you out!'

Nobody could say, Powerscourt thought to himself as he made his way to confess his defeat to the Chief Inspector, that Porchester Newton had failed to make himself clear.

'Is my hat straight?' Sarah Henderson asked Edward the day after Powerscourt's unsuccessful jousting with Porchester Newton.

'Your hat is fine, Sarah,' said Edward, thinking that she looked even more attractive in black. They were making the final adjustments to Sarah's clothes in her attic office before proceeding to the memorial service for Alexander Dauntsey in the Temple Church. It was the custom in Queen's Inn for all benchers not buried at the Temple Church to be given a sort of memorial service with addresses by their colleagues there within two months of their death. In less than a week, Sarah had reminded Edward gloomily that morning, they would be doing exactly the same thing for the unfortunate Woodford Stewart.

The church was full, not only with Dauntsey's colleagues from Queen's, but with lawyers from the other Inns of Court, instructing solicitors, two men from the East End he had saved from the gallows who had come to pay their last respects, a couple of men from the City he had played cricket with, and members of various financial institutions he had represented with distinction. There was a sprinkling of women, some wives who had known him closely, some stenographers he had employed like Sarah. The benchers sat in splendid isolation in their allotted rows at the front. Mrs Dauntsey sat alone in the left-hand pew at the front. Porchester Newton was staring bitterly at the benchers from halfway down the nave. Edward and Sarah were squeezed in right at the back with a couple of criminals and a Chancery judge in full regalia who looked as though he might have adjourned his court to attend.

Powerscourt was taking a special interest in the service. He had handed over the sum of five pounds to the Head Porter to be distributed among himself and his colleagues who were shepherding the guests into position in return for information relating to two particular questions. The first he regarded, at best, as a shot in the dark. Suppose Alexander Dauntsey had found a woman, a woman who might bear him a child to inherit the glory and the desolation that was Calne, would she appear at this memorial service? Surely she wouldn't have gone to the funeral in the alien county of Kent. But might she just pop in here, maybe sometime before the service started, for a last encounter with the ghost of Dauntsey? Powerscourt had left instructions with his team that anybody unknown to them was to be asked to give their name and address. If questioned, they were to say it was for insertion in the record of the service that would appear in the respectable newspapers and for Queen's own records. Nobody could refuse such a request, Powerscourt thought, though they might give a false name. Any Mrs Smiths, those regular visitors to the divorce courts, he would regard with extreme suspicion. And his second line of inquiry related to the mysterious visitor to Dauntsey's chambers on the day of the feast. The porter who had seen this person had been told to brief all his colleagues on the appearance of the stranger. Powerscourt had offered a further reward of five pounds if anybody recognized this person again. Powerscourt had protected himself from false sightings by saying that this further instalment of cash would be handed over only when the visitor admitted his earlier trip to Queen's on the day of Dauntsey's death.

The living of the Temple Church was in the gift of the Inner and Middle Temples. The elders of those Inns of Court, concerned that eloquence should be confined to the legal profession and not be displayed by what they regarded as the inferior body of the Church, usually picked somebody with a good speaking voice, audible at the back of the church, who gave very short and very undistinguished sermons. Even on Sundays, after all, lawyers were busy people. The present incumbent, one Wallace Thornaby, was a tall, balding man in his fifties who had learned long ago, at the start of his ministry in the Temples, that it was never a good idea to argue with the lawyers.

As the Reverend Thornaby made his way up the nave behind his choir, Powerscourt saw that it was going to be standing room only in the Round Church at the end. People were going to be packed in there as though they were at a football match. Maybe there would be an overflow congregation outside, close, he suddenly remembered with a shudder, to the spot where the body of the other dead lawyer Woodford Stewart had been found.

The priest began by leading his congregation through the Lord's Prayer and the Collect of the Day. He recited the bare facts of Dauntsey's career and introduced the first speaker, a lawyer from Gray's Inn who had worked on numerous cases with the dead man. Much of this was technical stuff about Chancery and the Queen's Bench Division and the Court of Appeal, and Powerscourt's brain drifted off. Who had killed Alexander Dauntsey? Porchester Newton, in a fit of pique after he lost the election to bencher? Some old criminal whose conviction and imprisonment he had secured? Had he made some startling discoveries about the monies of Queen's Inn? From the little he knew so far Powerscourt doubted that. And what of the mysterious Maxfield, still undiscovered, still with twenty thousand pounds waiting for him in the vaults of Plunkett Marlowe and Plunkett? Did Mrs Dauntsey know more than she was saying? Behind that beautiful and haughty reserve was she hiding some information vital to his inquiry?

With a start he realized that the man from Gray's Inn had departed and the congregation had risen for a hymn. With a guilty grin he saw that even here the legal profession had made their mark.

> Day of dark and doom impending
> David's word with Sibyl's blending
> Heaven and earth in ashes ending!
> O, what fear man's bosom rendeth,
> When from Heaven the Judge descendeth
> On whose sentence all dependeth!

There was more, to Powerscourt's delight, a verse later.

> Lo the book exactly worded
> Wherein all hath been recorded
> Thence shall judgement be awarded.
> When the Judge his seat attaineth,
> And each hidden deed arraigneth
> Nothing unavenged remaineth.

From the Middle Temple and from Queen's, from Gray's Inn even unto Lincoln's Inn Fields, yea, even from the Inner Temple, Powerscourt said to himself as another lawyer climbed into the pulpit to give his contribution, the judges shall come to pronounce not on the living in the dock before them, but on the dead in some celestial court, not on the crimes they may have committed on earth, but on their prospects for a place in Paradise. Maybe they would have new livery, fresh colours and fresh gowns, white possibly, to pass this eternal judgement. Powerscourt only sat up from his reverie when he realized that the man was talking not about the law but about cricket.

'Many of you' – the man was called Fraser and came from the Middle Temple, Edward told Powerscourt afterwards – 'would have said that Dauntsey's heart, the most important thing in his life, was his work here, in Queen's Inn. I do not believe that to be the case. I would suggest the cricket pitch at Calne, or that extraordinary house that is Calne, or something indefinable that you might call the spirit of Calne had better claims on his heart. I am not sure how many of you have seen the vast interior of that house, room after room, hall after hall, gallery after gallery, boarded up, covered in dust sheets, protected from dry rot but very little else, an exquisite interior, probably one of the finest in England, merely holding time at bay and not showing off her glories to the world. Alex Dauntsey dreamed of restoring that house, of bringing it back to what his ancestors had made. His periods of depression were, he told me once, the greatest cross he had to bear for they ensured he would never be consistent and respected enough at the Bar to earn sufficient money for his task.'

Mr Fraser paused and looked carefully at his audience. They were spellbound, even the eldest bencher of Queen's, who was reputed to be ninety-six years old, hanging on his words.

'And if the house was his dream unfulfilled, then the cricket pitch was where some of his dreams came true. Alex never played very well on away matches, he was, as he said to me in the slips once, only happy at home with his own deer watching over him. Even those of you who do not know much about cricket and cricketers will know that the tribe is divided, on the whole, into bowlers and batsmen. Bowlers are more prosaic, they are instruments of speed and cunning and attrition and, occasionally, guile. You do not imagine that bowlers would be poets or composers. Batsmen, on the other hand, can display grace and style and class that can take your breath away. Giorgione would have been a batsman if cricket had ever arrived in Cinquecento Venice. Keats, I am sure, would have been a batsman. He would have played some beautiful strokes and got out for a disappointing but exquisite thirty. Alex was a batsman. I once saw him score a hundred and fifty and then get himself out.

He refused to let the scorer enter his total in his book, insisting his runs be attributed to someone else. 'They were hopeless,' he said to me, 'unworthy opponents.' On another occasion I saw him score twenty-five not out at Calne with the light fading and two of the fastest bowlers I have ever seen racing in to bowl at him like the Charge of the Light Brigade. 'Best innings of my life,' he said to me after that.

'One of my children once asked me, in that disconcerting way that children have, if I thought Gladstone was a great man. I was on my way to court at the time so I just told him Yes. He never asked me about it again. Was Alex a great man? I think that's the wrong question in his case. Greatness was not what he was about. But he was a man of enormous personal charm, a man with a mind that worked like a rapier, the finest companion I ever knew and the best friend I ever had.'

There was complete silence in the church as Mr Fraser returned to his pew. If you listened very carefully, you could hear some of the women crying. Powerscourt wondered if Sarah, so devoted to Dauntsey, was among them. After that there was an anthem from the choir, 'I Know that My Redeemer Liveth' from Handel's *Messiah*. Try as he might, Powerscourt was unable to find any references to judge or jury, earthly or celestial in it. A bencher from Queen's Inn spoke about Dauntsey's contribution there. Powerscourt thought the man must have given the same speech before. Then a final prayer from the vicar and the congregation, with that look of relief people often have when leaving church services, streamed out into the windy sunshine. Powerscourt saw that the porters were being particularly assiduous in their duties. He observed, but did not disturb them, that Sarah was leaning heavily on Edward's arm as if the service was still upsetting her.

Exactly one hour after the last person had departed, Powerscourt presented himself, as stealthily as he could, in the back parlour of the porter's lodge. A fire burned brightly in the tiny grate and a junior porter was despatched to hold the fort while Roland Haydon, the Head Porter, conferred with Powerscourt.

'Please take a seat, sir, and I'll tell you what we found out.' Haydon was a surprisingly youthful Head Porter, just into his thirties, easily the youngest man in that position in any Inn of Court. He had begun his career in the hotel trade and then become a junior porter in Queen's five years before. His quickness and discretion made him a natural choice when his predecessor finally retired at the age of seventy-one, not, he said, because he was getting old, but because he'd always believed in giving youth a chance.

'That's very kind of you,' said Powerscourt, taking his place by the left side of the fire.

'Well, sir, there's two pieces of intelligence, I suppose you could call them. And I'm not sure what to make of either of them. You remember you asked us to look out for any young women who might be scouting round before the service but not actually attending it? Well, we found one of those, about an hour before kick-off, sir, if you'll pardon the expression. Young Matthews spoke to her, he's very good at being polite when he wants to be, is young Matthews. She told him her name was Eve Adams, sir, and she gave her address as Number 7, Eden Street in Finsbury.'

Powerscourt laughed. 'I'm glad to see you agree with me, sir,' said Haydon. 'I told Matthews he'd been sold a pup, a biblical pup from the Book of Genesis, mind you, but still a pup. I had to make him look it up on the street map to show him there was no Eden Street in Finsbury.'

'Well, she showed some spirit, this female, Mr Haydon. What was she like?'

Haydon smiled. 'He's got an eye for the ladies, young Matthews has. I will not repeat the precise words of his description or what he said he would like to do to the young lady, sir. When you decode his statement, she was about thirty years old, well spoken, blonde hair, brown eyes and a shapely figure, sir, that might be the best way to translate the Matthews version.'

'Had he ever seen her before?' asked Powerscourt.

'No, he hadn't, but he very much hopes he'll see her again. Matthews says what she needs is a younger man, sir. He's only nineteen.'

'I'm sure,' Powerscourt said with a smile, 'that he'll keep a good lookout for her. And how about the other piece of news?'

Roland Haydon scratched his head at this point. 'That's more curious still. You'll recall that two of the people who saw the mysterious visitor saw his back only. They didn't get a front view at all. They both of them thought they saw the visitor today around the time of the service, but realized later that they must have been mistaken.'

'Why was that?' asked Powerscourt, sensing that anything that puzzled such a capable man as Haydon must be hard to grasp.

'It's this, sir,' he said. 'They thought Mrs Dauntsey was the visitor seen from the back. Once they realized who it was, they knew they must be mistaken, but it's strange all the same.'

145

Powerscourt looked curious. 'How odd that they should have made the same error,' he said, reaching for his wallet. 'Your men have done splendidly, Mr Haydon, and so have you as officer commanding. May I present you with another five pounds for distribution as you think fit? No, I insist. Just one last thing, Mr Haydon. Could you let me have the address for the previous Financial Steward, Mr Bassett?'

Haydon disappeared into his seat of custom and came back with an ancient ledger. 'Here we are, Number 15, Petley Road, Fulham. Funny thing, Lord Powerscourt, Mr Dauntsey asked me for the address, must have been a week or so before he died. It went right out of my mind.'

Powerscourt was on his way to talk to Edward in New Court when he almost bumped into Chief Inspector Beecham.

'Come, my lord, I have news, but I would rather not impart it here.' He led the way out of the porter's lodge and on to the Embankment. Jack Beecham remained silent until they were well away from Queen's Inn.

'We've got the report from the government analyst, Dr Stevenson, about what was used to poison Mr Dauntsey, my lord. The reason it took so long was that he had been on holiday in France, Dr Stevenson.'

'Well?' said Powserscourt.

'Strychnine, sir, that's what it was. He found 6.39 grains of it in the stomach and its contents. He wasn't taking any chances, our murderer, my lord. It only takes half a grain to kill you.'

'What about the time it was administered? What did Dr Stevenson say about that?'

'You know as well as I do, my lord, what these medical gentlemen are like. He said it could have been as little as fifteen minutes before death, but he doubts that. If pressed he would say about one hour to one hour and a half before the fatal accident.'

'So,' said Powerscourt, 'Dauntsey probably took the fatal dose at that drinks party in the Treasurer's rooms before the feast. He could have taken it in his own rooms just before six o'clock but we do not know if he had any visitors. Do we know, Chief Inspector, if Treasurer Somerville had one of the Inn servants in attendance on his guests, or did he do it all himself?'

'I checked that in our transcripts but half an hour ago, my lord,' said Beecham. 'It seems the servants were all tied up with the preparations of the feast. Either the gentlemen helped themselves or Mr Treasurer Somerville poured the drinks.'

11

And still, Powerscourt thought, irritated now by his inability to solve the mystery, there was Maxfield. Or rather, there wasn't Maxfield. Surely a man couldn't just vanish off the face of the earth and defy the efforts of the police, solicitors, private inquiry agents to find him. One of his junior officers, Jack Beecham had told Powerscourt with a grin, had thought of the House of Lords solution very early on. It had been checked. Maxfield wasn't there. The police had now extended their search to all the mental hospitals and asylums in the North of England, to all persons recruited in the last three years into the armed forces, the Merchant Navy and the coastguard. Johnny Fitzgerald had put forward the theory that Maxfield had joined the French Foreign Legion and would never be seen again.

Powerscourt was walking up and down his drawing room now, wrestling with the problem. Something from his very first meeting with Matthew Plunkett was floating elusively at the edge of his brain. It was something to do with a name. No, it wasn't a name, it was a nickname. Plunkett's uncle answered to the name of Killer Plunkett, that was it. No doubt, in the same way that his own close friends referred to him as Francis, this Plunkett was hailed and greeted as Killer. Did Maxfield have such a name? A name, or rather a nickname, he must have had for so many years that most of his close friends would not have known or had forgotten he was called Maxfield at all? How did that help to find him?

Powerscourt sat down at the little desk by the window where he sometimes wrote his letters. There were two things he felt sure of about Maxfield, even though his mind told him they were completely irrational. One was that he had to do with cricket. The second was that he had been in serious financial trouble, that Dauntsey's money was to bale a friend out of debt, gambling debts perhaps. Even on the Stock Market, he did not think Maxfield could have lost that much money. Perhaps he would check with William Burke. He began writing a series of letters to different parts of the organizations already visited by Plunkett Marlowe and Plunkett. They had written to the bursar of Dauntsey's old school, to the admissions tutor of his Cambridge college, to the adjutant of his regiment in the Army and so on. They had merely inquired about a past member called F.L. Maxfield. Powerscourt wrote to the senior groundsman at the same places, asking after a boy or a young man who had been known throughout his time with them by his nickname. Powerscourt had to admit that he had no idea what the nickname might be, but that the person's real name was F.L. Maxfield. He added that this person was a keen cricketer and had possibly played in the same team as one Alexander Dauntsey. Only at the end of the letter did he mention that Dauntsey had been murdered. He stopped when he had reached five and was about to address his envelopes when he thought of one last shot. He wrote a final letter and popped it in its envelope. It was addressed to the Head Groundsman, Calne, Maidstone, Kent.

It was odd, Sarah Henderson reflected to herself, how the presence of a man changed the atmosphere so considerably. She supposed you would have to count her Edward, as she now mentally referred to him, Edward himself not yet informed of the change of ownership, as a man, though she usually thought of him with his gangling frame and innocent face as a boy. But here he was, sitting in front of the fire in her home at Acton, with her mother on one side and herself on the other. Everything about this evening had been totally unexpected. Sarah had told her mother days before all she had learnt from Edward, about his train crash, about his speech difficulties, about living with his grandparents. She was resigned to a long inquisition. None came. She thought her mother would be her normal crabby self, ever ready with a sharp interjection or a put-down. None came. It was as if Edward brought a change of personality to her mother. And that, in turn, made Sarah feel irritated. Why she should feel irritated because her mother was going out of her way to be pleasant to her young man she did not know. Deep down, she suspected, she might feel – not jealous, that would be too strong, peeved perhaps that somebody else was trying to captivate her Edward. Her mother had developed a deep interest in the forthcoming Pancknowle trial.

'Remind me, Edward,' she said, smiling kindly at the young man, 'when exactly is it coming to court? I know you've told me, but I've forgotten. My memory isn't what it was.'

Playing for the sympathy vote, Sarah said to herself.

'It starts on Thursday, Mrs Henderson,' said Edward.

'And how wicked has Mr Puncknowle been? Is he as wicked as the Ripper or that terrible fraudster Jabez Balfour, Edward?'

She's getting bloodthirsty in her old age, Sarah thought. Suddenly she wondered if she herself was going to end up like this. She rather hoped not.

'Well, he's pretty wicked,' said Edward cheerfully, 'but he didn't actually kill anybody, as far as we know. He's not been charged with murder or anything like that. But he's defrauded a great many people, Mrs Henderson, that's pretty wicked.'

Edward was showing admirable patience, Sarah thought, seeing he had answered all these points at least once before.

'Just tell me again how he defrauded them, Edward. I don't think I quite got the hang of it first time round even though you explained it so beautifully.'

Poor Edward, Sarah thought, having to explain everything three times and then once more for luck.

Edward picked up a teaspoon, one of a number lying on the tea trolley. He winked at Sarah when he was out of the line of sight of her mother. That made her feel better.

'Think of this as Company Number One, Mrs Henderson. Mr Puncknowle asks people to invest, or buy shares in a great company called the Freedom Building Society. Lots of people buy them. But Mr Puncknowle and his friends are greedy. They take lots of the money for themselves rather than using it to help people buy houses. The promise made to the people when they bought the shares was that they would get a dividend, a share of the profits, twice a year. But after all the money he's stolen, Mr Puncknowle doesn't have any money left. So he launches another company, Company Number Two.' Edward picked up another teaspoon. This time he blew Sarah a kiss. 'More people subscribe or buy shares. That new money goes to pay the dividends of the old company. And so on,' said Edward, realizing that Companies Four, Five and Six in the Puncknowle house of cards might be too many for Mrs Henderson to grasp. And there weren't enough teaspoons.

149

'How beautifully you explain it, Edward,' said Mrs Henderson.

Flatterer, thought Sarah. Even Edward may be susceptible to flattery.

'So he really is quite wicked,' said Mrs Henderson, who seemed to get some special satisfaction out of the word wicked. 'How long will he be sent to jail for?'

'He has to be found guilty first,' said Edward with a smile.

He doesn't have to smile at her every time he speaks, Sarah thought to herself, maybe the stuttering would have been better. Then she told herself off. That, she said, was bad. Edward talking properly is a great advance. If he goes on like this he'll be perfectly normal in another six months.

'And will you be in court, Edward? Will you have a ringside seat?'

'Some of the time, I will, Mrs Henderson. I won't have to say anything, though. I'll only be there to give advice to our barristers.'

It was Mrs Henderson's parting shot that was the most astonishing of all. As Sarah was helping her upstairs to bed, she turned in the doorway and said, 'I want you to remember, Edward, that you have two very good friends in this house. I hope you will feel free to come and see us as often as you can.' And with that mother and daughter began the slow ascent of the stairs. Sarah hoped it wouldn't put Edward off, the prospect of further lengthy interrogations every time he came to Acton. Edward was wondering if he could find the courage to kiss Sarah when she came back downstairs.

Lord Francis Powerscourt did not give the impression of having been unduly alarmed by Johnny Fitzgerald's report that there might be a contract on his life. He had, after all, been in danger for much of his adult life, with the Army in India, as Head of Intelligence in the Boer War, in the pursuit and apprehension of various murderers. But this time he did take it seriously. Ever since that day he had revived a practice he had followed religiously in India. There, usually at the end of each day, he had written down his findings for the past twenty-four hours, where he believed the enemy to be, what strength they had, what reinforcements they might expect. In this way, if he was killed, his successor would not be denied the benefit of his knowledge. The Daily Will was how Johnny Fitzgerald used to describe it. Now, in this time of civilian danger, he had first put down a description of the murders and brief records of all his interviews during the case. He entered too his suspicions, the lines of inquiry he wished to pursue over the next few days. He would have entered the name of the murderer if he felt sure of it.

That task completed, and a letter despatched to the Financial Steward Bassett, saying he proposed to call on him the following afternoon, he went to join Lady Lucy in the drawing room in Manchester Square. She was seated at the piano, playing, very softly, 'Jesu Joy of Man's Desiring'. Powerscourt loved to hear her play. She began to stop but he waved her on. He wondered if she was going to sing when Johnny Fitzgerald walked in, clutching a fistful of sheets of paper covered in drawings. Lady Lucy turned round and greeted the two of them. 'Don't stop, Lucy, please,' said Johnny.

> 'If Music be the food of love, play on,
> Give me excess of it that surfeiting
> The appetite may sicken and so die.
> That strain again! It had a dying fall.
> It came o'er my ear like the sweet sound
> That breathes upon a bank of violets . . .'

Johnny had been making melodramatic gestures as he spoke. Lady Lucy smiled at him. Powerscourt had turned pale.

'Just confirm this for me, if you would, Johnny. Those are the opening lines of Shakespeare's *Twelfth Night*?'

'They are indeed,' Fitzgerald replied cheerfully. 'Shouldn't I know that as I played your man Orsino at school. My housemaster thought I should have been Sir Toby Belch and the headmaster said I should I have been Sir Andrew Aguecheek, who's even more of a drunken layabout than Sir Toby. Quite why I should have been identified with the fruits of the god Bacchus at such an early stage I have no idea. The man who did the drama thought I should be Orsino so that's who I played. But look here, Francis, I've brought an early draft of *The Birds of London*.'

Normally this would have been the focus of intense study and excitement, but Powerscourt seemed to have no interest in birds or anything other than his own thoughts. He was pacing up and down his drawing room like Nelson on his quarterdeck, muttering to himself from time to time, shaking his head, pausing to look out of the window into Manchester Square.

At last he stood still by the fireplace. Even then Lady Lucy could tell his mind was still far away. She waited. Johnny looked at his bird drawings. He had known his friend in this sort of mood before, once prowling outside their tent for a full hour and a half one winter's night in India before returning inside to prophesy, correctly as it turned out, that the attack would come from the east, not from the south where everyone expected it.

'Lucy, Johnny,' he said at last, his hand stroking the top of the mantelpiece, 'I'm sorry about that. I've had a most extraordinary idea I'd like to try out on you.'

There was a pause while he collected his thoughts. Outside they could hear a couple of cabs rattling round the square and heading north into Marylebone High Street.

'Let me give you, for your consideration,' Powerscourt began, 'a series of apparently unconnected facts.'

He's going to start numbering points soon, Lady Lucy thought, the index finger of the right hand slamming into the closed fingers of the left.

'Fact Number One,' Powerscourt went on, quite unaware that his wife had perfectly foretold his current actions, 'is that there was seen hanging around the Temple Church before the service, but not attending it, a well-bred and very attractive young woman who gave her name as Eve Adams, living in Eden Street. There is no Eden Street where she said it was and the name is obviously false.

'Fact Number Two is that on the day of Dauntsey's murder, a mysterious visitor was seen in Queen's Inn, including one sighting near his chambers. It is perfectly possible that the mysterious visitor actually went in to see the man and came out again without being seen. He was seen again, leaving the Inn by a porter. The visitor did not speak.

'Fact Number Three, a couple of the porters saw, or thought they saw before they realized they were mistaken, the mysterious visitor again today at the memorial service. The reason they thought they were mistaken was that they saw Mrs Dauntsey's back and when they realized the person was female, not male as on the day of the murder, they repented of their ways.

'Fact Number Four. Early in January this year there was staged at the Middle Temple Hall a three hundredth anniversary production of Shakespeare's *Twelfth Night*. It was first put on in the same hall on the same date in 1602. Among the audience, on her own admission, were Mr and Mrs Dauntsey. *Twelfth Night* has, as its main character, a girl called Viola disguised as a boy called Cesario. To add to the confusion she, or he, had a twin brother. In

Shakespeare's time when no women were allowed on the stage at all, the gender complications with boys who were cast as girls pretending to be boys must have been even more severe.'

Powerscourt paused. 'Do you see it? Surely you must see it,' he said. Lady Lucy and Johnny Fitzgerald both shook their heads.

'It's only a supposition. It could be completely wrong. But suppose we have read the Dauntsey marriage completely wrong. We know – well, we don't know, we suspect that she cannot have his children or children bearing the Dauntsey blood in some admixture or other. Dauntsey decides to leave her. And the person of his choice is none other than the Eve Adams who cannot resist sniffing round the church where her late lover is to have his memorial service. But Mrs Dauntsey knew what was happening and determined to stop it. She decides to take revenge. Remembering the Viola/Cesario person from *Twelfth Night* she dresses in man's clothes, goes to Queen's Inn, pops into her husband's room and poisons him.'

'Good God,' said Lady Lucy.

'What about Woodford Stewart?' asked Johnny.

'Easy. He saw her leaving the Inn so he cannot be left alive. A couple of weeks later she comes back, probably with that giant butler of hers, and shoots Stewart. You can't tell me that somebody who lives in that world of Calne doesn't know how to shoot. She leaves the giant butler to dispose of the body. By that time she's back safely in her own drawing room.'

'Do you believe it, Francis?' said Lady Lucy. 'Do you think it's true? If it is, you've solved the murder.'

'Different question, Francis,' said Johnny Fitzgerald. 'How are you going to find out if it's true or not?'

'That's easy, Johnny,' said Powerscourt. 'Tomorrow morning I'm going to send her a telegram. In three days' time I shall arrive at Calne for tea. Then I shall discover the answer.'

'I shouldn't eat anything while you're there, Francis,' said Johnny Fitzgerald, 'not even the best chocolate cake. And I should watch your back all the way there and the way home.'

Petley Road was a terrace of respectable Victorian houses in Fulham not far from the river and its great warehouses. Schoolteachers, rising bank clerks, those sort of respectable citizens, Powerscourt reckoned, would be the inhabitants here. Mr John Bassett's house was Number 15 and Mr Bassett himself opened the door. He was a small man, with ears that seemed to be pointed, and he sported a well-trimmed goatee beard that gave him the appearance of a troll or other resident of some forbidding German forest. His living room, Powerscourt saw, as he was ushered to the most comfortable chair, was full of painted panoramas of some of the world's remotest places, the Sahara desert, the Arctic or the Antarctic, Powerscourt wasn't sure which, a view of the back of Mount Everest, the vast steppes of Siberia.

'Are you a traveller, Mr Bassett?' Powerscourt asked. He wondered if the whole house was full of these kind of pictures, if you might have to cross the Gobi desert in the bathroom or traverse the sands of Arabia before you could go to sleep.

'I wish I had been,' said the little man. 'I have a constitution fitted to the counting house, not to great liners and the rough conveyance of the wagon train or even to arduous treks on foot. But I like to contemplate these great spaces, as you see. Now, how can I be of assistance to you, Lord Powerscourt?'

'I presume, Mr Bassett, that you have heard about the terrible murders in Queen's Inn?'

John Bassett nodded sadly.

'I have been asked to investigate these murders and I understand that Mr Dauntsey came to see you shortly before he died. Is that so?'

The little man remained silent. Powerscourt wondered briefly if he had been sworn to complete secrecy by his employers. That hardly seemed necessary – why would they want to silence a man who knew all the details of the Inn's plate and how many spoons went missing in an average year?

'I must make a confession, Lord Powerscourt. And please forgive me. It is my age. I shall be seventy-seven next birthday if the Lord spares me that long. Sometimes, I must tell you, I rather wish he would call me home before that. But my memory comes and goes. I do not remember Mr Dauntsey's visit. All I can remember is that he asked a question I could not answer and I had to check with the bencher who looks after the money at the Inn.'

'Can you remember the question, Mr Bassett?' Powerscourt asked gently, wondering if this visit had been a complete waste of time. 'Anything at all?'

The little man's face brightened. 'I've got it, I think. It wasn't anything important, just something about bursaries for poor students.'

Powerscourt felt rather disappointed. He wished suddenly that he had finished off the business of reading the rest of the wills. Edward had volunteered to do it for him, saying that it would be good experience for his legal work. He felt he could not in all decency just stand up and leave now, it would look so rude to leave the man to his remote corners of the globe in less than five minutes.

'Can you tell me, Mr Bassett, exactly what the nature of your work at the Inn entailed?'

John Bassett smiled. 'Seeing as I started there nearly fifty years ago, my lord, and the work didn't change very much, I can do that right proper. Memory's all right going back to the Crimean War. Once up to them Boers it gets a bit hazy.'

He fidgeted about in his chair as if settling himself for some great speech.

'Money goes in, money goes out,' he said as if he had just discovered an eleventh commandment, 'that's the secret. Money comes in, that's money for chambers, cheaper if the gentlemen pay a year at a time, money for food, money for wine. Money goes out, wages for the servants, payments for the food and wine, payments for benchers, payments for the gardeners, payments for painters and decorators. If the in and the out are more less the same, you're fine. If the in is more than the out, even better. Only if the out is a lot more than the in are you in trouble. And I can truthfully say that the out was more than the in only once in my time, my lord, and that was when we had to repaint everything unexpectedly for a visit from Queen Victoria.'

'That's very clear, Mr Bassett,' said Powerscourt, 'and could you tell me what your relationship was with the bencher who looked after the overall financial picture? I believe he's called the Surveyor.'

'That he is, sir. Just two of them I knew in my time. Mr James Knighton, he was the first, sir, and now Mr Obadiah Colebrook, why, he's even older than me, sir, he's eighty if he's a day. Funny how they don't retire at Queen's like they do in them other Inns, but ours not to reason why. I got on fine with both of them, sir, better with Mr Colebrook, I think, definitely better.'

Mr Bassett leaned forward and began speaking in a confidential voice, as if he was betraying the state secrets of Queen's Inn. 'Fact is, my lord, that Mr Knighton, he was a Quaker or one of those strange sects that don't believe in washing or whatever it is, and he didn't touch a drop. Completely teetotal. Mr Colebrook, sir, he was the wine steward as well for part of the time, and he used to invite me to sample the latest stuff the Inn was thinking of buying. "If you like it, Bassett," he used to say, "then the ordinary barristers will like it too." I was never sure whether that was a compliment or not, sir.'

'I'm sure it was a great compliment to your palate, Mr Bassett. One of the best assets a man can have, a fine palate. Now tell me, did Mr Colebrook control a lot of money you never saw? Money from investments, that sort of thing?'

'There was two kinds of accounts, my lord. Both operated on the same principle, money comes in, money goes out. I was Ordinary Accounts, if you follow me, my lord. Mr Colebrook was Special Accounts. I didn't have anything to do with them, sir, nothing at all.'

'You never even managed a peep at them, Mr Bassett? People can get curious sometimes.'

'That was not my place, nor my position,' said the little man indignantly, as if his integrity was being impugned, which perhaps it was. 'I would never have done such a thing.'

'My apologies, Mr Bassett, I never meant to suggest that you might be party to some underhand action,' said Powerscourt. Suddenly he remembered some of the bequests he had noted in his basement. 'Did you have anything to do with bequests for poor scholars like the ones Mr Dauntsey mentioned?'

'That would be Mr Colebrook's line of business, sir.'

'I see,' said Powerscourt. 'And finally, Mr Bassett, was there anything you can remember about the finances of Queen's Inn that might lead to murder, anything at all?'

John Bassett was very quick to answer. 'Nothing, sir, on my honour, nothing at all.'

The following afternoon Edward had promised Powerscourt a treat. For it would be the second day of the Puncknowle trial before Mr Justice Webster in a Court of the Queen's Bench. Maxwell Kirk, head of the Dauntsey chambers, leading for the prosecution, with Edward acting as his junior for this day, was expected to begin his cross-examination of Jeremiah Puncknowle, the first day and a half having being taken up with the opening statements. Early in the morning the queues stretched out from the Royal Courts of Justice way down the Strand, almost as far as Waterloo Bridge, as the British public waited for the chance to see Puncknowle in the dock. He had, after all, cheated so many of them out of their savings. So deep had he penetrated into the lives of the working classes of Britain that four members of the jury empanelled to try him obtained exemption from service on the grounds that they had financial interests in one or other of his companies.

Edward, Powerscourt thought, was looking even younger than usual in his wing collar and ill-fitting wig, as he brought Powerscourt past the afternoon crowds and into the court. He parked him with the instructing solicitors one row behind the gladiatorial seats occupied by Kirk and himself, facing the jury with the judge on their right.

Kirk began in solemn fashion. He had outlined the nature of the prosecution's case the day before. Now he intended to run the general headlines past Puncknowle at the beginning of the cross-examination to try to establish fixed points of suspicion in the minds of the jury. Edward was partly responsible for this strategy. He and Kirk both believed that the technical aspects of accounting practice and revaluation of assets, so crucial to their case, might pass right over the heads of the jury. Better, they had decided, to keep making the more intelligible points over and over again.

Maxwell Kirk was not an emotional barrister. Not for him the histrionics, the dramatic gestures of a thespian advocate like the great Marshall Hall. But after a quarter of an hour it seemed as though something was beginning to go seriously wrong. His voice grew lower. He began to shake slightly. He was sweating profusely. The defence barristers were exchanging notes with their solicitors, Charles Augustus Pugh, shining out as the best-dressed man in the court, if not in London, with an Italian suit in light grey of exquisite cut, and a pale blue silk shirt. Edward turned round and looked in desperation at Powerscourt. The spectators in the public gallery began to mutter to themselves. Was the man drunk? Was he having a stroke or a heart attack before their very eyes? With a loud bang of his gavel Mr Justice Webster brought the uncertainty to an end.

'Silence!' he said, looking sternly at the public gallery. 'This court is adjourned for fifteen minutes. If Mr Kirk is unable to carry on, his junior will continue in his place.'

With that the judge swept away to his room. Two porters helped Maxwell Kirk out of the court into a waiting room at the side. One of them left to find a doctor. The spectators did not want to leave in case they lost their places and had to go to the back of the queue. The prosecution team were looking up something in a battered law book. Edward had turned deathly pale. This was his worst nightmare come true. He was busy talking to the clerk when Powerscourt summoned one of the runners who were lurking around the courts ready to take urgent messages.

'Do you know Mr Kirk's chambers in Queen's Inn?' The young man nodded. 'Run as fast as you can to the top floor. Find a stenographer called Sarah Henderson. Tell her Edward has to speak in court. She must come at once. My name is Powerscourt.' The young man sped off. Powerscourt heard the clerk talking to Edward and the senior solicitor. 'Until we know precisely what has happened to Mr Kirk, Mr Edward has to carry on. We simply cannot ask for an adjournment. It would not be granted. Barristers present in court for one side or the other are supposed to be able to continue if their colleague falls ill or breaks down. If Mr Edward does not continue, then the case will fall by default. Puncknowle will walk free. He cannot be tried on the same charge twice. All of these villains may be free men before the end of the day. And Kirk's chambers will never receive a brief from the Treasury Solicitor again.'

Powerscourt felt that encouragement would work better than threats. At that moment, Edward looked, if anything, more ill than the unfortunate Kirk had done just before the adjournment. Powerscourt checked his watch. There were six minutes to go.

'Edward,' he said, holding the young man firmly by the elbow, 'you wrote most of those questions for Mr Kirk, didn't you?'

'I wrote all of them,' said Edward miserably.

'Well, all you have to do is to say them yourself. You can do it. Think of all the people willing you to success, all the people in your chambers, your grandparents, Lady Lucy and Thomas and Olivia and the twins, they all know you can do it. Think of Sarah – she's on her way. Think of Sarah's mother, wanting you to do well.'

'I've never spoken in court before, Lord Powerscourt, never.'

'Remember this, Edward. There was a time when Napoleon fought his first battle, there was a time when W.G. Grace played his first innings, there was a time when Casanova made his first conquest. Sarah and I will be silently cheering you on when it starts, Edward. You'll be fine, absolutely fine.'

This oration brought some colour back to Edward's cheeks. Powerscourt saw he was digging his nails into the palm of his left hand. There was a rustle in court to announce the return of Mr Justice Webster. Edward took a drink of water and picked up his notes. To his right Powerscourt sensed a hint of perfume and the swish of a skirt as Sarah squeezed in beside him. She coughed discreetly and beamed a smile of intense, passionate devotion into the well of the court. Powerscourt thought that statues of the dead cast in bronze or marble might come back to life for such a smile. Edward turned round and smiled back. Sarah was so nervous she seized Powerscourt's hand and held it as if they were going down together in a sinking ship.

One person had been able to enjoy the confusion and wonder how to turn it to his advantage. Jeremiah Puncknowle, still standing in the dock, felt glad that the sombre and serious figure of Maxwell Kirk had been removed from the scene. He patted his ample stomach and rolled his bright little eyes as he contemplated the callow youth being sent out to question him. How young the fellow seemed! How innocent! How helpless. Jeremiah felt rather like the wolf who has not eaten for some days when he finds a herd of succulent sheep. Powerscourt remembered that Puncknowle had reneged on his promise in Paradise. He had never been in touch about a possible threat to Powerscourt from any of his co-defendants in this case.

Mr Justice Webster glowered at the whisperers at the back of his court. 'The case for the prosecution will resume. Mr Hastings!'

So that was Edward's surname, Powerscourt thought. Hastings, a perfectly respectable name. He wondered if Sarah knew. For a terrible moment he thought Edward was not going to stand up. He seemed to be rooted to his chair. Very slowly, like a tree falling in reverse, he attained the upright position and turned to face the jury. Powerscourt wondered if Edward had dreamt of this moment, a great ordeal in court which would cure him of his stammer for ever. There was a long and terrible pause before he spoke. The judge was staring at him. Puncknowle was smiling at him as if welcoming him into armed combat in some dreadful arena from long ago. The earnest gentlemen of the jury were mesmerized. The clerk had his head in his hands. Powerscourt closed his eyes.

'Gentlemen of the jury,' Edward began, slightly hesitant, but fluent, 'you were hearing before the adjournment about the strange accounting practices of the defendant's companies. Mr P-P-Puncknowle.' He turned to face the dock, struggling through the p's but reaching the other side.

'Objection, my lord,' said Sir Isaac Redhead. 'This youngster has neither the years nor the qualifications to continue this important trial which could result in my client being falsely incarcerated for the rest of his days. The defence submits that the case be dismissed now.'

159

'Mr Hastings?' said the judge.

'I have been published, my lord, as a practising barrister of my Inn as Sir Isaac has of his. I do not believe age has anything to do with it. Mr Edmund F-F-F-Flanagan, my lord, conducted a defence in a murder case at the Old B-Bailey, my lord, in the year 1838, I believe, and he was only twenty-one.'

'Objection overruled. Mr Hastings.'

'Mr P-P-Puncknowle,' Edward began, 'I would like to draw your attention to various documents relating to the first of your p-p-public companies.' There was a rustle as judge, jury and defendant riffled through their papers for the relevant piece. Sarah Henderson wished the letter P could be erased from the English alphabet. Something told Powerscourt that things might be all right if Edward could get through the next ten minutes and into his rhythm.

'P-P-Page three, line seven, sir.' Edward appeared to have decided to avoid using the Puncknowle surname altogether. 'The figure for commission for the disposal of these shares is some thirteen thousand p-p-pounds.' Edward turned his absurdly young-looking face round to address the jury. 'The normal figure for commission in the City for such a figure would be between two and three thousand p-pounds. Why, sir,' he turned back to face Jeremiah Puncknowle, 'was the figure so large?'

Puncknowle smiled avuncularly at Edward. 'I believe you must have been six or seven years old when that company was floated, young man. No doubt your expertize in its figures began at a very early age. The figure was such, sonny, because nobody had tried to sell shares to this class of person before and the intermediaries had to be well rewarded. I don't suppose they were teaching you any financial lessons at school at the time. You were probably still learning to read.'

There was a low muttering from the public gallery. Powerscourt heard Sarah muttering 'Disgraceful' to herself several times. Her hand was still locked in his own. But Edward didn't seem very concerned.

'We shall have to take your word for it, sir, that these monies went to the intermediaries, not to line the pockets of yourself and your colleagues. I come now to an entry on the next page. Halfway down under the heading Property there is an entry of two hundred and fifty thousand pounds credit.' He turned again. 'I would remind you, gentlemen of the jury, that it is this holding which puts the company into profit and enables it to pay its enormous dividend.

Perhaps you could tell the court, sir, what and where these various properties were?'

Jeremiah looked flustered. 'I cannot remember, sonny,' he said finally, 'any more than you can remember what toys you had at the same time when you were seven years old.'

'I would suggest you try again, Mr P-Puncknowle,' said Edward in a calm yet firm voice. 'After all, you have had six or seven years yourself to prepare your defence against these charges.'

There was laughter from the public gallery and a low cheer from Edward's supporters' club, the clerk looking as though the horse lately at the back of the field, once in danger of falling down completely, was now moving cleanly through the other runners and might even be first to the winning post. There was a lowish rumble that might or might not be a throat being cleared from the judge.

This time there was no answer from Puncknowle. Not bad, Powerscourt thought to himself, reducing a figure of this stature to silence at Edward's age. Perhaps they were witnessing a historic moment that would be talked about in hushed tones for years to come, like Shakespeare's first play or Gladstone's maiden speech.

'I put it to you, Mr P-Puncknowle, that it is much better for you to have forgotten the details of those properties. And since you have no recollection of them, I will tell the members of the jury what was going on.' Edward looked down at his notes once more and faced the jury. 'What we have here,' he went on, 'is essentially a conjuring trick. The p-p-property concerned was a group of hotels in London which were initially p-purchased by another of Mr P-Puncknowle's companies, the Barnsley Development Corporation, for forty thousand pounds. Then they were sold on to another company owned by Mr Puncknowle for one hundred and twenty thousand pounds. I should add that no substantial improvements were made to the hotels between the two purchases. Nor were there any improvements made before the final sale to the Puncknowle Property Company for two hundred and fifty thousand pounds. We have been unable to find any traces of payment. The whole exercise was designed to increase the apparent assets of the Puncknowle company to the point where it could appear solvent. Without this sum, which existed only on paper, the company would have been bankrupt.'

Mr Puncknowle was on the verge of losing his temper. 'Stuff and nonsense, sonny! Stuff and nonsense! Fairy stories, that's what he's telling you, members of the jury, he's still of an age when fairy stories are all he can understand.'

Edward had had enough. 'I would remind you, Mr Puncknowle,' – the age difference between the two must have been nearly forty years – 'of the conventions concerning the behaviour of defendants and witnesses towards the barristers appearing before them in court. Any more insults from you and I shall have to ask the judge to arraign you for contempt.'

There was a smattering of applause from the public gallery. Mr Justice Webster glowered fiercely at the spectators and the noise fell away. Jeremiah Puncknowle looked down at his boots. A smile flickered across the normally sphinx–like features of Sir Isaac Redhead. Charles Augustus Pugh slapped his thigh. Sarah squeezed Powerscourt's hand even tighter. Edward looked at his watch. He was extraordinarily tired.

'If I could make a suggestion, my lord,' Edward was addressing Mr Justice Webster directly now, 'the next area of cross-examination has to do with the dividend payments, my lord, a complicated matter, needing considerable exposition. It could take well over an hour. I have no doubt that the jury are perfectly capable of holding half of the matter in their heads overnight, but I would feel I had performed my service to the Crown with more clarity if we could handle the question all together.'

He's saying the jury are too stupid to take it in two halves, Powerscourt said to himself. He felt the pressure of Sarah's hand beginning to abate.

'Sir Isaac, do you have a problem with this suggestion?' said the judge.

'No, my lord, we are in agreement with it.'

And so Mr Justice Webster ended Edward's first day in court as a speaking barrister. Both Sir Isaac and Charles Augustus Pugh congratulated him on his debut. Edward watched in a daze as the spectators and the barristers and the instructing solicitors left the court. Powerscourt hastened off to Queen's Inn to a meeting with Detective Chief Inspector Beecham. Eventually only Edward and Sarah were left.

'Edward,' said Sarah, 'I am so proud of you. You were wonderful.'

Edward's reply was to hold her very tight and kiss her passionately on the lips. He had had enough of words for one afternoon.

In the middle of the embrace Edward heard a door opening. The judge had forgotten some of his papers. Edward and Sarah disengaged themselves as fast as they could. Edward looked anxiously at Mr Justice Webster. He seemed to be staring at Sarah with some interest. Was there some terrible penalty Edward wondered, for being caught kissing your beloved right under the judge's chair in a Court of the Queen's Bench?

'Objection, my lord?' Edward asked in a quizzical voice.

The judge smiled at the two of them. It was, though they did not know it, the smile of a grandfather looking at his favourite granddaughter, rather than the smile of a High Court judge.

'Objection overruled, Edward. Carry on.'

The judge shuffled off back to his quarters. As the door closed behind him they heard the faint echo of a judicial chuckle echoing down the corridors of the Royal Courts of Justice.

12

Spring seemed to have turned back to winter as Powerscourt's cab took him on the short journey from railway station to house at Calne. Sheets of rain were pounding on the vehicle's roof and the wheels were throwing up jets of spray as they raced through the wide puddles that formed on the narrow road. The sky was dark and angry. The deer in the park had become invisible, huddling beneath the trees or trying to take shelter behind one of the great stone walls that enclosed the house and inner estate.

Mrs Dauntsey's enormous butler ushered him into the drawing room. His mistress, still looking radiant in black, was sitting peacefully by the fire reading a novel. Powerscourt felt nervous as the pleasantries were exchanged. This was the third time he had been entertained in this house and, while the nature of his mission was not as delicate this time as it had been on his previous visit, it was still fraught with great potential for embarrassment. What if his theory about the mysterious visitor was wrong? Suddenly what had seemed so certain in Manchester Square seemed vaguer, less likely in this drawing room in Calne.

'Mrs Dauntsey,' he began, 'yet again you have in front of you a man with a delicate subject to discuss. I must ask your forgiveness in advance if my theories turn out to be wrong.'

'Have you come with some more fairy stories, Lord Powerscourt? I did enjoy the last one, most of the time. I was never sure about the end. Endings can be quite difficult in fairy stories, don't you think?'

'They can indeed, Mrs Dauntsey,' Powerscourt smiled at his hostess, 'but I'm afraid there is no fairy story this time.'

'Perhaps there will be a surprise instead, Lord Powerscourt. Please carry on.'

Powerscourt took a deep breath. 'I do not know if you are aware of it, Mrs Dauntsey, but on the day of the feast there was a mysterious visitor to Queen's Inn. Every single member of the institution and everybody who attended the feast was questioned about who or what they had seen by the police.'

Powerscourt suddenly remembered that he had not mentioned his theory about the mysterious visitor to Detective Chief Inspector Beecham. Maybe he was failing in his duty. But he felt that if the police knew Mrs Dauntsey had been in her husband's room a few hours before he died, she would be arrested immediately.

'Little is known about the visitor. The person did not speak. They were seen in the vicinity of your husband's rooms and they were seen again leaving the Inn by one of the porters where they did not say goodnight.'

He looked at her very carefully. There were no signs of nervousness at all. Maybe she was just a very good actress.

'It only occurred to me very recently, Mrs Dauntsey, that the reason the mysterious visitor did not speak was related to gender. To speak would be to betray the fact that the visitor was female, not male. This was Viola turned into Cesario, come not to the Middle Temple Hall on Twelfth Night, but to Queen's Inn on the day of the feast. I put it to you, Mrs Dauntsey, as the barristers say, that you were the mysterious visitor, that you walked into Queen's Inn dressed as a man and that you visited your husband in his rooms. Am I right?'

Mrs Dauntsey remained silent for some moments. Powerscourt though he could see tears forming in her eyes. But she brushed them aside.

'Yes,' she said very quietly, 'it was me.' There was another period of silence.

'Mrs Dauntsey,' Powerscourt said, trying to be as emollient as he could, 'I think it would be best if you told me the truth, all of it. I do not believe you poisoned your husband,' – Are you sure about that, a small inner voice asked him insistently – 'but I think your position is difficult. Had you owned up to being the mysterious visitor, or told us that you went to see your husband on that day, your position would still be problematic, but not as awkward as it is now. You see, the police do not know that you were the mysterious visitor They have very suspicious minds. The fact that you have concealed this information up till now will leave them thinking you have something to hide. They may assume that you were the murderer. Juries have been known to convict on flimsier evidence than that, I assure you.'

Elizabeth Dauntsey rose from her chair and went to stand by the window. Even in her hour of difficulty her back was as straight as a soldier on parade. The rain was still falling, racing down the glass and dropping with a plop on the gravel beneath. One or two deer could be seen in the distance running quite fast from one place of shelter to another.

'I wish I could make up fairy stories like you, Lord Powerscourt. Maybe that would make life easier.'

'Take your time, Mrs Dauntsey, there's no rush.'

She came back to her chair and looked into the fire for a while. 'It all has to do with children,' she said finally, 'with Alex's wish to have descendants for Calne and with my inability to give them to him. I'm sure he wouldn't have married me if he'd known I was barren.'

A small trickle of tears broke through her defences and ran slowly down her cheeks. Powerscourt offered a handkerchief. 'Why do men always have clean handkerchiefs, Lord Powerscourt? It's always been a mystery to me that they're never dirty.' Elizabeth Dauntsey just managed a slight smile.

'We'd reached the end of the road as far as my having children was concerned, Alex and I,' she went on. 'As you know from your last visit, we, or rather I, had tried everything possible to become pregnant. That wasn't going to work. So Alex was going to try and find somebody else.'

This somebody, Powerscourt reflected, had managed to pass completely undetected through the filter of Lucy's relations. This was most irregular. He waited.

'About two months ago . . .' Elizabeth Dauntsey paused and stared into the flames once more. 'I'm sorry, Lord Powerscourt, I haven't told this to anybody before, about two months ago, maybe more, Alex thought he had found somebody. She was a young woman in good health, she was married to a much older man, she had no children of her own and her brother played cricket for Middlesex. I'm sure that last fact must have been an important factor in Alex's calculations.'

For the first time Powerscourt thought he detected a hint of sarcasm, dislike maybe, towards her late husband. He wondered about the different Elizabeth Dauntseys presented to him each time he came, as if she was like one of those Russian dolls with different characters packed inside each other.

'We talked about it a lot,' Elizabeth Dauntsey went on. 'Alex kept me informed about what was going on, not in detail, just the broad picture. And then, the night before he died, Alex and I had the most enormous row.'

Powerscourt dreaded to think what the police might make of that.

'We hardly ever rowed, Lord Powerscourt. And this one went on for a very long time. You see, Alex had arranged to go away for the weekend with this woman. As far as I know, it would have been the first time. They were going as husband and wife to some hotel on the Thames where Alex knew the owner so there wouldn't be any questions asked. Her husband was going to be away at a medical conference.'

'Is he a doctor?' asked Powerscourt.

'Yes, he is. He's a Professor of something or other medical, I can't remember what. That's what the row was about, not about the husband, but about Alex going away with this woman. I knew why Alex was doing it. Part of me approved of it. But the other part of me couldn't bear it. I shouted at him over and over again that he was betraying me, that he would destroy our marriage, that it would break my heart. The worst thing was that he never spoke. He hardly said a word, this man who earned his living by speaking and arguing in the courts of law. When we stopped rowing he went off to sleep in some other part of the house and he left very early the next morning. So if I hadn't gone to see him that afternoon, I would never have seen him alive again. I had to tell him, you see,' her voice began to crack slightly, 'that I still loved him, that he had my blessing for the weekend, that he was to ignore anything I said the night before. I wanted everything right between us. I couldn't bear it when he was angry with me.'

She stared at Powerscourt as if he could make things better

'But why did you go in disguise? You didn't have to do that, surely?' Powerscourt spoke very softly

'You'll think me very silly,' she said, 'but I thought one or two of his work colleagues must have known about the other woman had probably met her. Once anybody in that place knew anything the gossip went round the entire Inn faster than a Derby winner. They would all have known that the two of them were going away for the weekend. You know how men like to speculate about successes with women. I couldn't face the embarrassment. I couldn't have borne it. So I adapted some of Alex's old clothes and went as a man. Even then I was terrified somebody might speak to me. I was completely exhausted when I got back here.'

Powerscourt wondered yet again if Elizabeth Dauntsey was a tragic figure or a murderer. He couldn't tell.

'Did you meet anybody when you were in your husband's chambers? Anybody at all?'

'Not a soul,' replied Elizabeth Dauntsey.

'Was he drinking anything while you were with him? It must have been about a quarter to six.' Powerscourt could see, very faintly in his mind, the shadow of the gallows.

'He was drinking Châteauneuf-du-Pape,' Elizabeth Dauntsey had gone pale, 'the stuff they were going to have later at the feast.' Only Alex Dauntsey never got that far, Powerscourt said to himself, the strychnine got to him first. The poison concealed, perhaps, behind the strong taste of the red wine.

'And did you put a drop of poison in his drink when you were there, Mrs Dauntsey?'

There was a slight pause, whether through guilt or insult Powerscourt could not decide.

'I did not.' He couldn't decide if she was telling the truth. He thought she probably was.

Now it was Powerscourt's turn to walk to the window. A jury, he thought, could well convict on what he had heard this afternoon. The rain had stopped. Spring sunshine was beginning to dry the park out. The deer had abandoned their hiding places and were gambolling about on the grass.

'I have to ask you this question, Mrs Dauntsey. I seem to need a sentence of permanent apology virtually every time I speak in this house. What were you all going to do if the woman became pregnant?' Don't even think of asking the really nasty question today, he said to himself – what happens if it's a girl. 'To put it at its crudest, did you think he was going to divorce you?'

'No,' said Elizabeth Dauntsey firmly, 'I don't believe he was. Alex said the woman's husband wasn't going to live very long.'

'Was the man ill? Did he have some terminal illness?'   ·

'I don't know, Lord Powerscourt, Alex didn't say.'

Christ in heaven, Powerscourt said to himself. Maybe other murders were contemplated, Alexander Dauntsey and his mistress plotting to push an old man down the stairs or shove him under the wheels of a train.

'Did Alex have a time scale, Mrs Dauntsey? Did he think the doctor would have departed in six months, nine months maybe?'

'He didn't say.'

'Let's play make believe, Mrs Dauntsey. Not quite a fairy story, more of a let's suppose. Would you be agreeable to that?'

'Of course, Lord Powerscourt. I'm only trying to help you.'

'I know you are. Now then, let's suppose that in a couple of months' time the young woman becomes pregnant. The husband dies, conveniently, well before the child is due. Then she gives birth, let us say to a son. How, if Alex is still married to you, would he get his hands on the child? The two of them can hardly come and live here. Perhaps the young woman would be happy to give up the child for Alex to bring up here with you. It's all frightfully complicated.'

Elizabeth Dauntsey looked at the ring on her wedding finger. 'Alex said he would work something out, that we had to take one step at a time. He was always an impulsive sort of thinker.'

Powerscourt wondered if it was time for him to go. Mrs Dauntsey was looking tired and drawn all of a sudden, as if these confessions had taken their toll.

She looked at him suddenly, 'It doesn't matter now, Lord Powerscourt, it doesn't matter at all. Alex is dead. Nothing is going to bring him back.'

Powerscourt took her hand. It felt cold, even though she had been close to the fire. 'I will do whatever I can to help you, Mrs Dauntsey. I may have to come back to see you again in a few days. But before I go – forgive me for causing yet more embarrassment but it is important. The name of the young woman with whom your husband was going to spend some time would be most useful to me, if you would be so kind. And the professional address of her husband.'

For the first time since Powerscourt had known her, Elizabeth Dauntsey blushed. 'It might be easier all round,' said Powerscourt, sensing her discomfiture, 'if you wrote them down, the names and addresses, I mean.'

Elizabeth Dauntsey crossed to a small writing table by the window. Powerscourt did not read her piece of paper at once but waited until he was in the train back to London. Rivers Cavendish, he read, 24 Harley Street, W1. A fashionable address. Mrs Catherine Cavendish, 36 Tite Street, Chelsea, SW3. He didn't think it likely, however you looked at it, that Catherine Cavendish was the killer. Excitement and romance were meant to be on the menu as far as she was concerned. But Dr Rivers Cavendish, a man being cuckolded in the last months of his life? At the speed the criminal justice system worked, he would probably have been able to kill Dauntsey and pass away several months later without even being brought to trial. And there was something else. Doctors, Powerscourt said to himself, know all about poison.

Sarah Henderson was thinking about Edward. It was just after nine o'clock in the morning in Queen's Inn but she had been thinking about him for some time already. Sarah spent quite a lot of her waking day thinking about Edward. She had discovered that her fingers could shoot out and turn her shorthand into sheets of typewritten paper on her keyboard while her mind was elsewhere. She wondered when, or maybe if, Edward was going to ask her to marry him. Only the previous evening, encased in the fog, they had spent a passionate forty-five minutes wrapped round a lamp-post together on the Embankment. She had felt then that he might pop the question. After all, 'Will you marry me?' didn't have any of those awkward b's or p's or s's that sometimes gave Edward so much trouble. She wondered if she should suggest that they needed to have a talk about things. But Sarah wasn't sure about this plan of action. Men, according to an old school friend who had been observing two elder brothers at home for years and who had nearly been engaged to half a dozen young men, were always happy to go for walks, to take you to the theatre, to make love to you, but if you suggested serious talks or discussing things like relationships, their eyes would glaze over and suddenly they would have urgent engagements elsewhere. It wasn't their fault really, her friend had explained, it was just the way they were made, rather like they enjoyed watching cricket or playing football. But then there was so much to discuss. If, just supposing, if they were married, where would they live? Ever since she was a small child Sarah had believed that one of the main, if not the principal, reasons for getting married was that she could move furniture about all over her own house whenever the fancy took her. But now, in the real world, there were difficulties. She couldn't leave her mother, but it wouldn't be fair to Edward to ask him to start married life with a sick mother-in-law who took you to her own updated version of the Inquisition about the law courts every time you crossed her threshold. And then there was Edward's future to consider. After his triumph in the Puncknowle case was he going to take up the speaking side of the law, or was he content to go on devilling for ever? Sarah had not detected any eagerness on Edward's part for a change of direction in his career. And then she heard his footstep on the stairs. Edward appeared to have a telepathic knowledge of when her room mate had gone out to deliver some work or to take dictation elsewhere.

'Morning, Sarah,' said Edward, 'you're looking very smart today.' Sarah was wearing a dark skirt, a cream blouse and a dark blue jacket that had a slightly masculine look about it.

'Thank you, Edward,' Sarah replied, thinking suddenly of the two of them wrapped round the lamp-post the evening before.

'I've got some splendid news, Sarah,' said Edward, admiring the way the red hair curled down those pale cheeks. 'Lord Powerscourt has asked us round to Manchester Square any time next weekend. He was going to invite us to their place in the country but Lady Lucy thought that might not suit the twins.'

'And where is the Powerscourt place in the country?'

'It is, in the good lord's words, in the splendidly unfashionable county of Northamptonshire. It's near Oundle. They've got a cricket pitch and a tennis court, though it's a bit early for that. It's frightfully old, Sarah. Powerscourt thinks men went out from it to fight at Crécy and Agincourt.'

'My goodness,' said Sarah, not quite sure how far back in the past those two battles were. It was the kind of thing Edward always knew.

'And there's a ghost, Sarah. Mr Ghost, not Mrs Ghost or Miss Ghost. A real clanking-about-in-the-middle-of-the-night-ghost. But look, I've got to go and look up those wills for Lord Powerscourt. I'm not due in court at all today.'

'Wills, what wills, Edward? What does Lord Powerscourt want with wills?'

Edward lowered his voice. 'It's the benchers' wills, Sarah. He thinks there's a very faint chance they might be connected with the murders. I'll see you later.'

With that Edward clattered off down the stairs. Less than five minutes later Sarah heard an unfamiliar pair of boots tramping up towards her attic fastness. Big man, she thought, quite heavy. That stair near the top only squeaks if you're over fifteen stone. There was a grunt as if the climb up the stairs had taken its toll. Then the door was opened and her visitor was beside her, towering above Sarah at her station by the typewriter.

'Miss Henderson,' said Barton Somerville, 'forgive me for calling on you like this. I was looking for the young man they call Edward. They said I might find him up here.'

Sarah wondered what was going on. Never before had the Treasurer of the Inn been to see her. Nor could she see what he might want with such a humble person as Edward. He might be all the world to her, she knew, but he was a very junior member of these chambers let alone the Inn.

'Edward's not here, sir,' she said.

'I can see that,' said Barton Somerville testily. 'Do you know where he is, by any chance?'

'I think he's gone to look up some benchers' wills for Lord Powerscourt, sir.'

'Benchers' wills?' Somerville suddenly sounded quite extraordinarily angry. 'Working for Powerscourt now, is he? Not for the chambers that pay his wages. We'll see about that, young lady.'

'I'm sure he would have cleared it with Mr Kirk, sir. Edward's always very scrupulous about things like that.'

Barton Somerville snorted. He slammed the door and departed noisily down the stairs. Edward had not told Sarah not to mention where he was going or anything like that. She hoped she hadn't got Edward into trouble. And, once more, as she looked out at the innocent lawns of New Court, a frock-coated porter pushing a mighty pile of documents down the path that led to the law courts, Sarah felt very frightened. And it would be hours before Edward came back.

Two days later Powerscourt was waiting for a visitor in the first-floor drawing room in Manchester Square. Catherine Cavendish was due in ten minutes' time. And he had written to ask for an appointment with Dr Cavendish at his Harley Street consulting rooms for the following day.

Lady Lucy found him pacing up and down the room. She was smiling broadly.

'Francis, my love, you'll like this!' she said happily.

'What news, Lucy?' said Powerscourt.

'It's Catherine Cavendish, Francis. She was born Catherine Chadwick. She was a chorus girl. At the Alhambra and the Duke of York's and the Gentleman's Relish. They say she was the senior dancer at the Alhambra, a sort of Head Prefect.'

Powerscourt tried to get his brain around what would be entailed in being the Head Girl of a chorus line and failed. 'God bless my soul, Lucy, I didn't know you had any relations in what one might call the saucier part of the West End.'

Lady Lucy laughed. 'I don't, Francis. I mean I don't have any relations in that world. Mrs Trumper Smith told me.'

Powerscourt's face registered complete ignorance, if not astonishment, at the mention of Mrs Trumper Smith.

'You know Mrs T, Francis. That's what everyone calls her, behind her back at any rate. She lives three doors down from here. Her son is in the same class at school as Thomas. The husband's a doctor, quite a fashionable one, I think, with a practice in Harley Street or Wimpole Street. He knows the Cavendishes, says the chorus girl is quite delightful.'

'Did the woman say what was wrong with Dr Cavendish, the one who's meant to be leaving this world quite shortly?'

'She did not, Francis.'

There was a ring at the front door bell. A tall, dark-haired woman in a long grey dress was shown in and took her seat in front of the fire. Powerscourt noted that she was very slim, with a tiny waist and a very beautiful face. The eyes, even in the sad circumstances in which Mrs Cavendish presumably found herself, were grey and slightly cheeky and her lips looked as if they wanted nothing better than to be kissed. Powerscourt suddenly remembered the rather vulgar assessment of female beauty carried out by some of his more disreputable fellow officers stationed at Simla, summer residence of the British Raj in India. It was known as the ships test and was based on Marlowe's famous line about Helen of Troy: 'Was this the face that launched a thousand ships/ And burnt the topless towers of Ilium?' The great beauties of Simla were awarded ships by the hundred according to the male estimates of their beauty. Powerscourt thought he remembered one gorgeous creature reaching the dizzy heights of seventy hundred and fifty. That record stood all through that summer, up to and including the Viceroy's Ball. Mrs Cavendish, Powerscourt felt, would have been most eager to play the game. Her score would certainly have approached the record, perhaps even bettered it. An entire chorus line, led by Catherine Cavendish in person, he reckoned, would muster a combined score of many thousands.

'Mrs Cavendish,' he began, 'how kind of you to call.' The eyes, which he had originally thought to be cheeky, had turned cautious as Mrs Cavendish took a lightning appraisal of the room and its furnishings.

'Nice place you've got here, Lord Powerscourt,' she replied.

'I'm afraid I want to ask you some questions about Mr Dauntsey, Mrs Cavendish.'

'Well,' she said, 'I didn't think you'd asked me here to talk about the political situation in the Balkans.'

Powerscourt smiled. 'How long ago did you meet him, Mrs Cavendish?'

'Mr Dauntsey? I met him about nine weeks ago. It was in my husband's waiting room. He was running very late that day, like the doctors often do, and Alex, Mr Dauntsey I mean, was the last patient waiting to go in. I was there waiting for Dr C to come out as we were already late for a reception. We just got talking, the way you do.'

Mrs Cavendish looked rather defiant as she said this.

'And things just went on from there, Mrs Cavendish, regular meetings, that sort of thing?'

'I think he was the most charming man I've ever met, Lord Powerscourt. He used to buy me lunch, lovely lunches, they were, and always with lovely wines. He had a wonderful nose for a wine and a great love for the names, Château La Tour Blanche, that's a Sauterne, Lord Powerscourt, Château Fleur Cardinale, Chambolle Mussigny, Les Amoureuses, Chassagne Montrachet.'

Powerscourt was very impressed that she did not pronounce either of the two t's in Montrachet. Johnny Fitzgerald had been heard describing people who did as little better than Philistines. Powerscourt found himself wondering if Johnny Fitzgerald might replace the late Alex Dauntsey in Mrs Cavendish's affections with their shared love of fine vintages. But however hard he tried he couldn't see Mrs Cavendish in enormous boots, wrapped up to the chin, waiting before dawn for a flight of rare birds over the Suffolk marshes.

Lunch in expensive restaurants with expensive wine lists was one thing, Powerscourt said to himself, weekends away in riverside hotels something rather different.

'Would I be right in saying, Mrs Cavendish, that on the weekend of the feast, you and Mr Dauntsey were planning to go away together?'

Catherine Cavendish looked down at the Powerscourt carpet. 'I'm going to be frank with you, Lord Powerscourt, and I'll thank you to keep what I'm going to say to yourself.' She paused for a moment. 'There's people out there,' she made a vague nod towards the window as if referring to the population of Manchester Square and the wider purlieus of Marylebone, 'who will say that I married Dr C for his money. Well, that's as maybe. He's always been very kind to me. I have no complaints. But there's more to marriage than

174

kindness, Lord Powerscourt, as I'm sure you know. Any girl who heard the sob stories of the sad husbands who used to buy time to talk with the chorus girls could tell you that. Think of what it says in the Good Book. Man and woman created he them, Lord Powerscourt, man and woman. I've always said there was more going on in that Garden of Eden than eating apples, if you follow me. Dr C, well, poor soul, he wasn't up to any of that man and woman created he them business, not up to it at all, I can tell you. It's because of his illness – he's not got very long to live, you know. Alex was, if you follow me, Lord Powerscourt. So, yes, I was going away with him. We were going to a flat that belonged to a friend of his after that feast and going off to Moulsford the next day. That's on the Thames up towards Oxford. I was really looking forward it. You can miss things for too long, know what I mean, Lord P?'

'Of course,' said Powerscourt, wondering how to reach the more delicate ground yet. 'Did you talk about children at all, Mrs Cavendish?'

'What about them, Lord P? I don't know what you mean.'

'I'm quite sure you do,' said Powerscourt, remembering suddenly that nobody had called him Lord P since the lady who came to make his bed at Cambridge. 'Let me be blunt, Mrs Cavendish, did you discuss what might happen if you became pregnant?'

Catherine Cavendish tossed her head back and roared with laughter. 'Is there anything you don't want to know, Lord P? You're the curiousest man I've ever met. Quite what any of this has to do with Alex ended up crocked in a bowl of beetroot I don't know. Yes, we did talk about children once. I said I couldn't stand the little buggers, pardon my French, Lord P, but they've always seemed to me to be an unimaginable amount of work for very little return. It's as if the whole chorus line dances its heart out for one man in the audience and he doesn't even bother to clap. Alex told me he'd been trying to have children with his wife for years and failed so he thought he couldn't have any anyway. Not that that would have got in the way of the man and woman created he them business, I can tell you that for nothing, Lord P.'

'Forgive me for sounding curious, Mrs Cavendish, did Mr Dauntsey ever ask you what you would do if you became pregnant?'

Catherine Cavendish looked at him as if he came from another planet. 'You do ask the strangest things, Lord P. Anyone might think you're one of those perverted blokes who spy on other people from behind a curtain. He did ask me once, as a matter of fact. I said I'd give it up for adoption, that's what I'd do. I've known girls in chorus lines get in the family way, happens all the time. Lots of them open the oven door before the bun is ready and throw it out, if you follow me. Well, I've known girls, perfectly healthy before, ending up with insides like rows of washing lines after that. Not me, Lord P.'

'I've nearly finished, Mrs Cavendish,' said Powerscourt. 'Did Mr Dauntsey ever mention his wife?'

The word wife seemed to trigger some semi-automatic reaction in Catherine Cavendish. Her earlier openness disappeared. She composed her face until it was almost a mask. She blinked rapidly.

'No, he didn't, apart from failing to have the children as I said before.'

Powerscourt was certain she was lying. For a fraction of a second he considered challenging her. Then he thought better of it.

'In the weeks before he died, Mrs Cavendish, did Mr Dauntsey say anything to you about being worried, about any problems he might have had?'

'Not to me, he didn't, Lord P, he was always cheerful with me. And I know he was looking forward to our little weekend away.'

'On the day of the feast, Mrs Cavendish, did you see Mr Dauntsey at all?'

'No, I was going to meet him later,' said Mrs Cavendish.

'You didn't go round to his chambers in the late afternoon by any chance?'

'I've told you,' Catherine Cavendish had turned rather red, 'I was going to see him later.' Powerscourt thought she was lying, but that if she was, she would stick to her story through thick and thin.

Most, if not all, men, Powerscourt felt sure, would have looked forward to a weekend away with Catherine Cavendish. He wondered if they might find it rather exhausting. But most of all, as she departed back to Chelsea, he wondered why she had lied to him. And what had Alex Dauntsey said, or not said, to Catherine Cavendish about his wife? Most men in the circumstances, Powerscourt felt, would have mentioned the existence of a spouse. They might have blackened her name with tales of not being understood, of wives permanently suffering from headaches, wives misbehaving in any number of ways. Such confessions, after all, were how the men justified their infidelity to themselves. But for the man to say nothing at all, which was what Catherine Cavendish implied, must be unusual. And surely, in those circumstances,

Powerscourt thought, the mistress figure would herself inquire about the existence and disposition of a wife.

Then a fresh thought struck him with such force that he was out of his chair and pacing up and down the room. Suppose Alex Dauntsey had told Catherine Cavendish that he was going to leave his wife. Suppose they planned to time his departure to take place after the rather different and more permanent departure of Dr Cavendish. Catherine, as it were, would be lining up the next husband even before the first one was in his grave. Well, it had happened before and would, no doubt, happen again. So far, so good, Powerscourt said to himself. But suppose Catherine discovered that Dauntsey was not going to leave his wife. Naughty weekends in riverside hotels, whole evenings of man and woman created he them, supposedly undertaken with one purpose in view, that Dauntsey should take her if not to the altar, at least to the registry office, would be in vain. She would be giving away her assets for nothing at all, as it were. And suppose she decides to take the ultimate revenge. She takes some poison from her husband's medicine chest. The one flaw in his theory was how she delivered the fatal dose. The answer would, no doubt, present itself. But for the moment Powerscourt was certain that Catherine Cavendish might have as valid a motive for murdering Alexander Dauntsey as anybody else, if not more. During most investigations, Powerscourt said ruefully to himself, the number of suspects decreases as inquiries go on. But in this case, the number of suspects was growing, and he had the feeling that it hadn't stopped growing yet.

13

Mrs Henderson had finally managed to get Edward entirely on his own. This feat, which Edward had asked Sarah to prevent before his first visit to the Henderson household, had been accomplished by the simple ploy of throwing away the milk and the tea. Sarah, when asked to pop down to the shops for replacements, thought her mother must have been consuming tea at an incredibly rapid rate, but had no idea of the deception, or of what was planned in her absence. Edward, his earlier anxieties allayed by the satisfactory nature of his previous visit, had no idea what was coming either. But for Mrs Henderson, this was a duty she owed both to herself and, as she reminded herself sternly, to Sarah's father. Her visit to old Dr Carr that morning had been far worse than she had feared. She, Mrs Henderson, had thought her illness was not getting any worse. True, she found it more difficult to climb the stairs and she now had to lean more heavily on Sarah than she had before. True, even without ascending to the upper floor, she often felt very short of breath. Sometimes even sitting by the fire and reading one of the magazines Sarah bought for her, the quick wheezy breaths told her something was wrong. The doctor had examined her carefully, not speaking as he did so. When he had finished, he put down his instruments and sat down opposite Mrs Henderson. Dr Carr took one of her hands in his and inspected it carefully, as if the lines on the back might help him to foretell her future. Looking at his sad face, she knew things were bad. That was the same expression the doctor had when he told them her husband had not long to live. Now he told her, in the gentlest voice he could, that the illness was progressing faster than he had thought it would. Things seemed to be deteriorating more quickly than he would like. Of course, the process might go into reverse, everything might be arrested and her position stabilized. Part of Mrs Henderson did not want to ask the obvious question at this point. Had she been single, or a widow, she told herself later, she would have walked out without the inquiry.

'How long do you think I have, doctor?' she asked in a very subdued voice.

'I could not say, Mrs Henderson,' said Dr Carr, still holding her hand. 'I can only guess. When you saw me before, I said two or three years, probably. If things continue as they are, I should have to change the figure. Nine months? Twelve months? I could be wrong.'

Mrs Henderson felt, perfectly rationally, that nobody had ever taken away a whole year of her life before, and that it should take more than only fifteen minutes in a doctor's surgery to do it. As she hobbled slowly and painfully out of the surgery, less than a hundred yards from her house, Dr Carr's next patient had to wait some time before being admitted. The doctor was staring out of his window, looking at the distant railway tracks that led to Ealing station and out towards the west of England. When he was younger these encounters upset him, but not for long. Now, after his decades of doctoring, they were heavier and heavier to bear. He felt desperately sad every time he sentenced one of his patients like Mrs Henderson to death and sent them out alone into an unfriendly world. Now he felt there was a part of him under sentence too, that whatever portion of life he had left to him had been diminished. That evening, he said to himself, he would speak to his wife. The practice would be sold. The retirement cottage in Dorset, close to the coast near Lyme Regis, had been bought some time ago. He would spend his last years in contemplation of another of life's great mysteries, not the painful deaths of his patients in this new century, but the ever-changing movements of the sea and the unpredictable movements of the birds above it.

So Mrs Henderson had only one thought left in her mind. Sarah must be settled. Sarah's future must be secure. And soon. Whatever was going to happen to her, Mrs Henderson had to know that her daughter's future was assured. She felt that she would have to approach the matter in a roundabout fashion or Edward might simply bolt, or say he was going to help Sarah carry the shopping. Mrs Henderson had no belief in the ability of young men to last out this particular course. But she knew that she had only a limited time. The shops were not far away, and Sarah moved fast. She and Edward were sitting by the fire in the little sitting room in the house in Acton.

'So, Edward,' she began, with what she hoped was a friendly smile, 'Sarah tells me you had a great triumph in court very recently, when you spoke in the great fraud case.'

Edward found the smile slightly disturbing. Something about it reminded him of the wolf in the nursery story who consumed the grandmother and sat up in her bed waiting for the arrival of Little Red Riding Hood, intending to eat her as well. And he, Edward, was Little Red Riding Hood. 'It was nothing, Mrs Henderson,' he said, 'anybody who had been researching that case could have done it. And I was so glad Sarah was there.'

This admission, although Edward did not know it at the time, gave a slight opening and, it must be said, some hope to Mrs Henderson. The idea that Edward could not have managed his success without Sarah's presence was grist to her mill.

'Are you going to do more work in court, Edward? I know Sarah thinks you should.'

'I'm not sure yet, Mrs Henderson, not sure at all. I want to wait until things have cleared up at Queen's Inn.'

'But if you did more speaking work, Edward, would you be better paid? Would you be able to settle down?'

Edward had a faint suspicion now of where the conversation was going. He supposed that if there were no fathers around to ask a girl's young man his intentions, then it fell to the mother. But he wasn't going to make life easy for the old lady. Sarah should be back soon.

'Settle down?' said Edward, as if this was a custom followed in some remote Patagonian island rather than in Acton, London W3. 'I'm not sure what you mean, Mrs Henderson.'

The old lady was taken slightly taken aback. Surely everybody knew what settling down meant. 'I don't know, Edward,' she said sadly, 'in my young days people meant getting married, finding somewhere to live, that sort of thing, starting a family, all that was settling down.'

Something in the sadness of her voice touched Edward. He was now absolutely sure what she wanted to know. He thought she was looking rather ill. Just then they heard a slamming of the front door and a cry of 'I'm back' from Sarah.

'It'll be all right, Mrs Henderson.' Edward had just time to speak before Sarah came into the room. 'I promise you.'

Edward and Sarah had called round to Manchester Square and

180

Edward had deposited a great pile of documents for Powerscourt to read. These were the remaining wills of the benchers and Edward had promised to come and discuss their contents in the next few days. Powerscourt began to work through them. He was sitting on the sofa in front of the fire in the drawing room on the first floor of the house in Manchester Square. Josiah Beauchamp, died 1861, he read, had left five thousand pounds and two houses in Holborn to the Inn for the relief of poor retired barristers. Horatio Pauncefoot, passed away 1865, had bequeathed seven thousand pounds for the upkeep of poor persons in pupillage. John James Tollard, died 1870, left five thousand pounds for bursaries for poor pupils. The names and the figures were swimming in front of him now. He wondered if he wouldn't be more comfortable lying out on the sofa. Richard Woodleigh Fitzpaine. Peter Stirling Netherbury. Christopher John Knighton. Gradually the names faded from view. He was seeing huge numbers now, dancing across the courts of Queen's Inn, besporting themselves over the Temple Gardens. A giant eight was walking south down Middle Temple Lane towards the river. On the far side of the road a pair of threes who looked as though they might have been hand in hand were dancing their way into the Royal Courts of Justice. A spindly eleven was mincing its way north through the gardens of Gray's Inn. A fat four was wobbling east from the Inns of Court towards the City of Numbers above Ludgate Hill. Then the numbers disappeared. There was a strange distant noise that might come from a funfair. And then he was in the funfair, staring at one of those steam-driven roundabouts where people ride round on wooden horses adorned in bright colours that go up and down in regular patterns. Here was Mrs Dauntsey, still dressed in black, smiling enigmatically at him as she rode sedately around, her position never changing. Behind her on a ridiculously small pony was Porchester Newton, those butcher's hands enormous as they held the reins, glowering at Powerscourt as his horse carried him round and the up-and-down motion rocked him on his way. There was Mrs Catherine Cavendish, riding in chorus girl costume, arm in arm with a friend, their long legs kicking out towards the spectators. Behind them on a black horse Barton Somerville himself, decked for some reason in fool's gaudy, as if he was an aged Fool in attendance on the demented Lear. Round and round his suspects went. Behind the fool he saw another strange figure he did not at first recognize. It was clad in a very long white coat with a knife in its hand. Powerscourt realized it must be Dr Cavendish, come to lighten his last months with a spell on a wooden horse. The only person absent from this funfair of suspects was the missing Maxfield.

Lady Lucy called his name as she was entering the room, unaware that her husband had fallen asleep. 'Francis,' she began, then stopped when she saw that his eyes were closed. She smiled at him.

'Lucy,' he began, 'I've been having a most peculiar dream. All the suspects were going round on wooden horses at a funfair.'

'Did any of them whisper in your ear that they were the murderer?'

'I'm afraid not, my love. If only they had.'

'This has just come for you, Francis.' She held out a letter for him, the writing slightly shaky.

'Half past twelve tomorrow morning, Lucy. My appointment in Harley Street with Dr Rivers Cavendish.' He gave Lady Lucy a firm hug. At the back of his brain those fairground horses were still going round and round.

There were two lions on the left-hand side of the fireplace, their stuffed features looking quizzically at the patients as if nothing would give them greater pleasure than to return to life and make a quick meal of the nearest humans. On the right-hand side was a tiger, a rather weary tiger, who looked as though the long journey from his place of capture to the waiting rooms of Harley Street had exhausted him. On the left-hand wall there were merely a couple of stags' heads, complete with enormous antlers, looking rather mundane and civilized compared with the other wild life. And on the remaining wall Powerscourt saw what he presumed was a cheetah, the fastest of them all. He wondered if his children would like to come and inspect these savage heads. He wondered too if it was Dr Cavendish or his predecessor who had captured this collection on safari in Africa. Maybe he had some more at home to keep Catherine Cavendish in order, though Powerscourt suspected the animals would have had to be alive to have much impact on that young lady.

He was rather disappointed in the reading matter on display. Surely this room warranted magazines for explorers or geographical journals with detailed accounts of the latest expeditions to the lands where tigers roamed. Instead there were the normal daily newspapers and a religious magazine that had no details of any foreign ventures at all, not even to a missionary station. As the last

182

patient before him went into the consulting room, he wondered how Catherine and Rivers Cavendish had actually met. He should have asked her. Lucy had been most indignant, he recalled, when he had been unable to answer her question on that point.

'Lord Powerscourt.' The receptionist was waving him through to the holy of holies. The woman before him in the queue seemed to have disappeared. Perhaps she had been eaten by one of the lions. Dr Cavendish's consulting room had two huge windows looking out into the garden. The decoration on these walls could not have been more different from the waiting room. Here reproductions of the religious masterpieces of the Renaissance held sway. Powerscourt thought he recognized a Filippo Lippi Annunciation from San Lorenzo in Florence, a crucifixion by Tintoretto and the Noli Me Tangere from the Accademia Gallery in Venice.

'Good morning, Lord Powerscourt. How may I be of service?'

Rivers Cavendish was a small thin man, with white hair, a tightly trimmed white beard and a nervous way of looking about him. If you were feeling unkind, Powerscourt said to himself, you could describe him as a frightened rabbit. All he needed was the tail.

'My business is personal rather than professional, Dr Cavendish, but before we get down to details, may I ask if you were responsible for the remarkable collection of wild life in your waiting room? I was most impressed.'

The little man roared with laughter. 'My goodness me, Lord Powerscourt, what a compliment you pay me. I'm afraid that was my predecessor in these rooms. He was always going to Africa and shooting things. It was the death of him in the end, mind you. He went on one final expedition and missed his shot. Rather than his taking the lion, the lion took him instead. Not very much of him left at the end, the native bearers said, certainly not enough to bring home.'

Powerscourt thought the story of his predecessor's unhappy demise seemed to bring great pleasure to the little man. 'My business, Dr Cavendish, concerns the death of a barrister called Alex Dauntsey, poisoned at a feast at Queen's Inn, and the subsequent shooting of his colleague Mr Stewart. Perhaps you are aware of the business, Dr Cavendish?'

The doctor bowed. 'My wife has told me all she knows, Lord Powerscourt. And I believe she has spoken at length to you, is that so?'

'It is indeed, Dr Cavendish. I hope you will forgive me if I begin with a most unusual question. It is not meant to sound rude, I have no wish to pry into your affairs, but it is something which would, if true, colour every other facet of our conversation. Your wife tells me you have but a short time to live. Pardon me, Dr Cavendish, but is that true?'

The doctor's reaction was the last one Powerscourt would have expected. He smiled, no, he beamed with pleasure.

'It is indeed, Lord Powerscourt. Three months left, maybe a bit less. I'm afraid I don't wish to go into the details of my condition in any way, but that is the time I have left, thank God.'

Powerscourt was astonished at the attitude of the little man. 'Dr Cavendish,' he said, with a puzzled frown on his face, 'most people grow fearful, apprehensive, terrified sometimes at the prospect of death. You look delighted. May I ask why?'

'Of course,' the doctor said. 'I believe.'

'You believe?'

'I believe in the Anglican faith. Always have.'

'One God the Father Almighty, Maker of heaven and earth and of all things visible and invisible?'

'Absolutely.'

'And in one Lord Jesus Christ, the only begotten son of God, who for us men and for our salvation came down from heaven and was made man and was crucified also for us under Pontius Pilate?'

'Totally. You left quite a bit out there by the way, or you've forgotten your Creed.'

'And the third day he rose again according to the Scriptures, and ascended into heaven, and sitteth on the right hand of the Father and he shall come again with glory to judge both the quick and the dead?'

'Completely.'

'One Catholic and Apostolic Church?'

'Yes.'

'One Baptism for the remission of sins?'

'Of course.'

'And you look for the Resurrection of the dead?'

'I do,' said Dr Cavendish, 'and the life of the world to come.'

'Christ!' said Powerscourt.

'Him too.'

'God bless my soul,' said Powerscourt, leaning back in his chair. 'No sad cadences from Dover Beach for you then, Dr Cavendish.'

'"Dover Beach". . .' You could see the little man's brain pursuing the poem as if it were some erratic tumour. 'Author Matthew

Arnold, most moving and famous verses about the loss of faith in Victorian England.' He closed his eyes for a second. 'The eternal note of sadness in the movement of the waves, heard by Sophocles long ago, reminding him of the turbid ebb and flow of human misery,

> 'The Sea of Faith
> Was once, too, at the full, and round earth's shore
> Lay like the folds of a bright girdle furled.
> But now I only hear
> Its melancholy, long, withdrawing roar . . .'

'Let me tell you a little story about "Dover Beach", doctor, if I may,' said Powerscourt. 'It concerns a young man reading for the Anglican priesthood at one of those Oxford theological colleges. After a year or two, the young man becomes afflicted by doubt. Did God create man or did man create God? Book of Genesis can't be true if the geologists are right. Creation story can't be true if Darwin is right, can one person be man and God, the usual cocktail of doubt. And he is terribly affected by "Dover Beach". If he can only recite the poem on Dover Beach itself, at the evening time mentioned at the start of the poem, he says to himself, then surely his doubts will be resolved. So, he takes the evening train bound for Maidstone, Ashford, Canterbury, Dover. By Ashford or thereabouts the young man is word perfect on the verses. There he is at last on the beach. He advances to the water's edge and begins his recital in his most powerful voice. I should say that the wind is coming in fairly hard from the Channel at this point so the Matthew Arnold is being carried back towards the town. By the end he is nearly in tears with the beauty of the words and the idea that this world which seems a land of dreams,

> 'Hath really neither joy, nor love, nor light,
> Nor certitude, nor peace, nor help for pain;
> And we are here as on a darkling plain
> Swept with confused alarms of struggle and flight,
> Where ignorant armies clash by night.'

'What happened to him, Lord Powerscourt?' said the doctor eagerly. 'Did his faith come back?'
'I'm afraid his faith didn't come back, doctor. What came instead were two burly members of the Kent Constabulary who were on

patrol looking out for smugglers. They heard these, to them very strange, words and couldn't decide whether the young man was a lunatic or not. They clapped him in the cells for the night – would you believe an explanation like his must have been? – and he was bound over to keep the peace by the magistrate the next morning for a period of thirty days. They say that by the time he got to Maidstone on his return journey, his faith had completely disappeared.'

The doctor smiled. 'Very fine story, Lord Powerscourt. But no Dover Beach for me. I still believe. I believe I shall see God. I believe I shall be reunited with my dead parents and my dead first wife. Now, how can I help you?'

'Could I ask where you were on the evening of Friday, the 28th of February?'

'The evening poor Mr Dauntsey was murdered, you mean? Well, I was here in my consulting rooms until the early evening. I'm sure my secretary could give you the name of the last patient on that day. That would have been about five or half past five. Then I made some notes for an address I had to give at a conference in Oxford the following day. At seven o'clock or thereabouts I took a cab to Paddington station and the train to Oxford. I'm sure Wilfrid Baverstock, the Professor of Medicine who was organizing this conference, will vouch for the time I arrived at his college, Hertford, shortly after nine, I think.'

Powerscourt was doing lightning calculations. If a man walked fast, or if he took a cab and was lucky with the traffic in both directions, he could just about get to Queen's Inn and leave a little something for Alex Dauntsey and be back in time to set out for Oxford.

'In the time you were here, Dr Cavendish, between the departure of the last patient and your own departure for Oxford, was there anybody else about or were you completely alone?'

'Well, there will have been other doctors here in other parts of the building but I didn't see any of them, if that's what you mean.'

Powerscourt took a brief look at the books in a small circular bookcase just to the left of the doctor. His heart started racing very fast.

'I'm afraid I have to ask you about your wife and her relations with the dead man Dauntsey, Dr Cavendish. Could I ask you first of all how you met?'

The little man laughed. 'It's an interesting question as to who picked up whom, Lord Powerscourt. I make no apologies for enjoying the music hall shows. Good enough for the King, then it's good enough for me, that's what I say. I'd been to see this show she was in at the Alhambra, just called *The Gaiety Girls*, if my memory's right, three times. The third time I was fifty yards from the theatre on my way home and Catherine comes up and starts talking to me, bold as brass. Hadn't she seen me in that box before, once or was it twice? Anyway, things went on from there. I may be a believer in the Almighty and all his works, Lord Powerscourt, but I thought I could still enjoy some feminine company in the last months of my life. My first wife is dead. We didn't have any children. I didn't want to leave my money to a collection of medical charities. So there it was. And I told Catherine right from the start that there were certain physical functions relating to marriage that I could not perform because of my illness. I didn't mind if she found outlets for those with other people, as long as she kept coming back to me until I died.'

Once again Powerscourt wondered if the man was telling the truth. Maybe the human capacity for jealousy disappeared when desire faded. Maybe. Maybe not. Maybe you could marry somebody much younger and tolerate them sleeping with other men. But he wasn't sure. And he had noticed a faint flush on the doctor's face as he gave that account of himself. Maybe it had to do with the sensitive nature of the subject matter. Suddenly Powerscourt remembered Catherine Cavendish telling him that she had met Alex Dauntsey when he was the last patient of the day, in her husband's waiting room.

'I think you knew Alex Dauntsey, Dr Cavendish,' he said. 'I believe he was a patient of yours.'

'He was indeed. He had been a patient of mine for some years.'

Powerscourt wondered if length of service would make it more or less likely that you would murder somebody.

'What did you think of him?'

'Dauntsey?' said the doctor reflectively, looking at the Annunciation on his wall as if there might be a message in there for him as well. 'I liked him very much. He had a certain grace about him, a certain style that you don't often see in today's barristers. They're all too concerned with making money.'

Of all the people whose deaths he had investigated, Powerscourt thought, Dauntsey was the one he would have most liked to meet. He thought of the portrait, now presumably lurking in some basement in Queen's Inn, and wondered fancifully if he could buy it off them. He was sure Lady Lucy would have liked Dauntsey too, with those good looks and the charm that had bewitched Catherine Cavendish. He would even have been forgiven the love affair with cricket.

'It's such a pity he's gone,' said Powerscourt. 'One last question, and forgive me if it is personal once again. Did you and Mrs Cavendish ever talk about what would happen after you had died?'

The doctor thought Powerscourt apologized too much. Bloody man's nearly strangling himself with good manners, he said to himself. But then he reflected that while he dealt with the reality of death every day, Powerscourt did not.

'I don't think we have discussed it, actually,' said Dr Cavendish. 'Do you think we should?'

Powerscourt smiled. 'I think that's entirely a matter for yourselves,' he said and rose to take his leave. As he stepped out into the cold air of Harley Street he saw again in his mind's eye those two volumes on Dr Cavendish's revolving bookcases. *Poisons and Their Treatment* was the first one in a brown binding. *The Impact of Poison* was the other, bound, appropriately enough, Powerscourt felt, in black. There was only room for the surname on the spine, not the full details of the writer and his qualifications which would appear inside. On both books the author was the same. His name was Cavendish.

All of the Maxfield replies were now with Powerscourt in Manchester Square with the Army and Calne bringing up the rear. No from Cambridge, he read, no from the Army, no from his old school. Only one reply offered any sort of hope and even that looked pretty slim. It came from the head groundsman at Calne. He himself, he wrote, was unable to be of assistance as he had only been in the post for five years and had no knowledge of Mr Dauntsey growing up. He had, however, discussed it with his predecessor, who believed he might be able to help. If Lord Powerscourt could confirm by return of post, Matthew Jenkins, who had been head groundsman for almost fifty years, would meet him at the Calne cricket pavilion at three o'clock in the afternoon in two days' time.

Johnny Fitzgerald had almost persuaded Powerscourt that Maxfield was a blackmailer, spacing out his demands over the decades to avoid detection. Chief Inspector Beecham's theory was that Maxfield had lent Dauntsey a great sum of money to pay off youthful indiscretions and the cash was now being returned with interest. Lady Lucy believed the bequest was a reward. Maybe Maxfield had saved Dauntsey's life in the past and this was a thank you from beyond the grave. Powerscourt just hoped that this was his last trip to Calne. I should have bought a season ticket when this investigation started, he said to himself, peering anxiously round the estate for armed assassins come to finish him off.

Matthew Jenkins had brought two chairs and a small table on to the verandah of the cricket pavilion. There were a number of note-books lying roughly beside one of the chairs. Jenkins was a small wrinkled old gentleman with a full head of white hair. His hands and his arms were very brown from years in the open air. His face was clean-shaven and looked to Powerscourt like a nut with human features attached. He spoke slowly and seemed to think quite hard before he opened his mouth.

'Good afternoon, Mr Jenkins,' said Powerscourt, opening the batting. 'Thank you very much for seeing me.'

'If there's anything I could do for Mr Dauntsey, sir, I'd walk through hellfire to do it for him, I would.' And with that, Matthew Jenkins nodded his white hair for what seemed to Powerscourt to be almost a minute.

'You told John James, your successor, that you might be able to help me with this missing Maxfield, Mr Jenkins.'

'I can, sir.' The old man stopped there and stared out at the pitch as if remembering matches from long ago. A couple of deer were inspecting them from the far boundary. 'You mentioned nicknames in your letter, sir. Well, that was what set me thinking. You see, we did have a boy and man, contemporary of Mr Dauntsey, with a nickname. Squirrel, he was called. I can't remember, if I ever knew, why he was called Squirrel. Maybe he hoarded things and buried them in secret places. He was born here, his father worked on the estate. He must have been about the same age as Mr Dauntsey. They grew up together, played together, chased the deer together.' This brought another of those long-drawn-out noddings of the Jenkins head. Powerscourt watched it move slowly up and down, the eyes still staring out at the wicket.

'Did everybody call him Squirrel, Mr Jenkins?'

'Somebody told me the other day, sir, that they thought even his own family must have called him Squirrel. But I'm losing my way, Lord Powerscourt. The reason I asked to meet you here was that Mr Dauntsey and Squirrel played cricket together. They opened the batting for the junior team, then the senior team, they even had a trial together for the County. And the scorer for the Calne cricket team was the estate steward, a miserable man who'd been in the Army called Buchanan-Smith. A real stickler for formality, he was, sir. There was no way he would have put just Squirrel in his score book.'

Matthew Jenkins bent down and picked up a faded green volume. 'Here we are, sir, A.M. Dauntsey, caught Pollard, bowled Keyes, thirty-four, Squirrel Maxfield, bowled Hawkins, forty-two.'

Powerscourt picked up another book for another year and found more records of successful partnerships between the two men.

Powerscourt was as interested as the next man in cricket records but he felt he should press on.

'Is he still here, Squirrel Maxfield? Is he still opening the batting for Calne?'

Matthew Jenkins looked so sad, Powerscourt thought he might burst into tears. 'No, my lord, he's not here. He left soon after the catastrophe. You know how they say some people are marked out for disaster, for the vengeance of the gods – well, I think he was one of them.'

The white head was off again. Powerscourt waited. 'He married late, this Squirrel,' Jenkins went on, leafing absent-mindedly through another of the score books, 'must have been about five or six years ago. They had a son, lovely little boy he was, with blond hair and big green eyes. Until he was one and a half, nearly two, everything was fine. Then things began to go wrong with the boy. They took him to a lot of doctors but there was no cure. Epilepsy and mental deficiency, that's what they said it was. Just when they were taking all that in, the wife was pregnant again. Same thing. Another little boy, same problem, same illness. The doctors shook their heads. They needed extra help to look after the little ones. Worst thing was, these children would never get better, they'd need looking after all their lives. People said there were special hospitals and places you could send them. Squirrel Maxfield said nobody ever came out alive from those places. He said if they could just keep them alive long enough somebody would come up with a cure. Squirrel said he didn't believe God could send people out into this world who weren't well without intending to cure them.'

'Did they receive help from anywhere, Mr Jenkins? Financial help?'

'Well, my lord, you know how it is in small communities like ours. Gossip going everywhere, like a weed. People said Mr Dauntsey gave them money, a lot of money, but nobody knew. They all went off to the South of France. Maybe the climate would be better, I don't know. People say it's cheaper to live there, I wouldn't know, I sometimes think I haven't much time left here myself.'

'Nonsense, Mr Jenkins,' said Powerscourt, 'you'll be here for years yet. But tell me, what did you make of the two of them, Dauntsey and Maxfield?'

The old man looked at him carefully and began extracting pipe, tobacco pouch and matches from various pockets.

'Squirrel Maxfield, I didn't know him well. He worked in the town as a carpenter so we did see him here from time to time. Very pleasant gentleman, always polite to me. Mr Dauntsey, mind you, I watched him grow up. I never knew a more considerate man, always happy to help the people on the estate in bad times. He was a real loss, sir.'

'I don't suppose,' said Powerscourt, anxious to remove all possible ambiguity, 'that Mr Maxfield has been back here in the last couple of months or so?' Not on a feast day in Queen's Inn at the end of February, he said to himself.

'No, sir, he's not been back. I'm sure he would have come back for the funeral if he'd heard about it in time. Don't suppose the posts and things work very well over there. And if he'd been back he'd have come down to see his old mother who's still alive in the town and we'd have heard all about it.'

On his train back to London Powerscourt felt relieved that F.L. Maxfield could at last be removed from their inquiries. And he wondered again about the nature of his first murder victim, Alexander Dauntsey, a man whose generosity to his friends extended beyond the grave.

14

Edward found Lord Francis Powerscourt pacing up and down his drawing room with the twins nestling against his chest. Edward could have sworn he was talking to them about Pericles' funeral speech in Book Two of Thucydides' *History of the Peloponnesian War*.

'You've got to talk to them about something,' said Powerscourt cheerfully. 'Johnny Fitzgerald has told them already about all the birds of London and their breeding habits. Would you like one?'

Edward told Sarah later that evening that his host offered him a twin as he might have offered a cucumber sandwich or a slice of cake at afternoon tea. Very gingerly he took a small, well-wrapped bundle in his arms, holding it very delicately.

'They look about quite a bit now,' said Powerscourt happily. 'Sometimes they grab hold of your finger as if they're a monkey. The nurse will be coming to take them away for their bath in a minute, Edward. You won't have to last out for very long.'

'Which one have I got?' asked Edward.

'You've got the boy, Christopher. The other children are calling him Chris already. I'd much rather he had the full name. If we'd wanted to call him Chris, I keep telling Thomas and Olivia, we'd have christened him that. But they don't pay any attention. Do you have a view on this?'

Edward had no wish to tread into some diplomatic imbroglio between parent and children. 'Well,' he said tactfully, 'you don't have to decide yet, do you? Christopher himself might have a view on this?'

At that point a middle-aged nurse, spotless in white, appeared in the doorway. She had two large white towels over one arm.

'Nurse Mary Muriel,' said Powerscourt, 'you have come for the twins, I see. Allow me to introduce Edward, a great friend of the family.'

'How do you do,' Mary Muriel said to Edward, and advanced to claim her charges. 'It's bath time,' she said, as if it were some ritual fixed by Royal Decree or Act of Parliament, and swept out of the room towards the upper floors, her tiny charges firmly under her control.

'Well,' said Powerscourt, parking himself in his favourite armchair to the left of the sofa in front of the fire, 'I sometime want to suggest to Mary Muriel that she postpone bath time for ten minutes so I could have more time with the twins. I am their father, after all. And I pay her wages, come to that. But she is terribly good at her job. She looked after Thomas and Olivia when they were little. But her world runs like clockwork. If you check your watch, Edward, I think you'll find that it is about one minute after six. If bath time does not commence at exactly six o'clock, London will sink below the Thames, there will be a plague of locusts and the waters shall cover the face of the earth.'

Edward smiled. 'I'm glad I've met this titan of the nursery,' he said, 'and it is just coming up to two minutes after six.'

'Now then, young Edward,' said Powerscourt, 'time to be serious for a moment. I've been reading those wills and I'm very confused. There are a number of people supposed to be receiving money from the Inn who aren't. Have you ever come across any poor pupils or students being maintained by the munificence of Queen's and the generosity of its past benchers?'

'I have not,' Edward replied, 'none at all. And I don't think I've ever heard of any money going to retired barristers in straitened circumstances either.'

'I wonder if they could have changed the statutes,' said Powerscourt, cocking an ear to sounds of unhappiness floating down from the higher levels, presumably to do with the total immersion in water, 'but it's very difficult to change people's wills after they've been proved. It's almost unheard of.'

'Do you think there is a connection with the murders, Lord Powerscourt?'

'Not directly, no. But there is certainly something odd going on and I am most curious to find out what it is. Suppose Dauntsey discovers something strange is going on to do with the money. He tells his friend Stewart. Then he tries a bit of blackmail on Barton Somerville. Or maybe it's the other way round I just don't know.'

'So how do we find out what's been happening?'

'I have a proposition to put to you, Edward. I can't say it is particularly glamorous or romantic but it could help a great deal.'

'Anything at all, Lord Powerscourt.'

'Before I outline the task ahead, Edward, let me explain what is going to happen to these wills.' He popped a hand under his chair and brought out a bundle of papers, secured, Edward noticed, with legal string.

'These wills are arranged, first of all, in time order. Then I have tabulated them into categories of payment, help for poor students, help for retired barristers, general discretion of the Inn, that sort of thing. I have put the date of each bequest in brackets before the money. Thank God there weren't any more of these dead benchers, Edward, we'd have suffocated in paper. My brother-in-law, financial equivalent of W.G. Grace as I said before, is coming to collect them this evening and peruse them in his counting house tomorrow. But I know what he will want before he can come to any conclusion.'

Edward lifted a quizzical eyebrow.

'Annual accounts or the equivalent, from last year or some other recent year. Now, listen carefully, Edward, and tell me where I go wrong in this description.' Powerscourt paused. A prolonged wail of great unhappiness shot down the stairs, followed by a second, rather shorter protest.

'I think she's washing their hair,' Powerscourt said, sounding as if he disapproved of the practice. 'Anyway, there is a bencher in the Inn one of whose tasks is to look after the money but only, you might say, in a tactical sense. The strategic direction rests, as you might expect given his title, with the Treasurer. In symbolic recognition of which fact, the box files relating to the annual accounts are held in his outer office, guarded by that gorgonic female with the mousy grey hair and the long fingernails. I forget the bloody woman's name.'

'McKenna,' said Edward, 'Bridget McKenna.'

'She would be called Bridget,' said Powerscourt bitterly, who had a violent dislike of the name since hostile encounters with a very stupid parlourmaid called Bridget in his youth. 'But she has the files all right. They stretch round behind her desk on shelves, two or three levels high, in black boxes with the dates of the accounts written on them. I know that, because I inspected them the first time I went to see Somerville and his gang. How am I doing, Edward?'

'You're doing fine,' Edward smiled, suspecting he knew what was coming. 'What do you want me to do?'

'I want you to steal some of them,' said Powerscourt. 'As many as you can. Preferably tomorrow.'

'I see,' said Edward, and scratched his head.

'Let me give you a suggestion as to the general method I would employ if it was me. I would do it, or Johnny Fitzgerald and I would do it, but I think you would have a better chance if you were caught. You could say you were doing it for a dare or a bet or some other foolish extravagance of youth. I have asked to see them, of course, I asked long ago and was told it was none of my business. I think we may need to involve Sarah, though I leave that to your discretion. There are two ways of approaching the files, what you might call theft or substitution. Theft is self-explanatory, you simply take them off the shelf and walk away. Substitution means that you bring with you a couple of identical files with the same dates as the ones you wish to purloin. You take one out and you pop the other one in. So, at a glance, nobody would know anything had gone. But it all depends on how and when they lock the door.'

There was a faraway look in Edward's eyes as if he had left Manchester Square and had returned on a piratical mission to the courts and walks of Queen's Inn.

'I think it works like this, Lord Powerscourt,' he said, speaking quite slowly as if his plan hadn't finally been settled in his mind. 'If they're both out to lunch, they make sure the door is locked. Any major departures, they close up behind them. But on minor matters there must be times when it's empty, even if only for a few minutes.'

'Does the gorgonic female lock up when she goes to the bathroom, do you suppose?'

'I don't think she would, but that might only leave a very little time. How about this, Lord Powerscourt? Mr Kirk, the head of my chambers, has hurt his leg very badly. It's true. He brought two sticks in with him today. So let's say he appeals to Somerville to come and see him on some important matter, rather than him going through hell to reach the Treasurer's quarters. Once he's arrived, Sarah sets off for the gorgon's lair, with a terribly sad story. Her typewriter has gone funny. The ribbon is wrapped round the cantilever or whatever the thing is called and can't be cleared, so it's now rather like a tangled fishing line. Sarah will know how to do that. The gorgon always prides herself on being Queen Bee or Head Girl to all these stenographers. So if Sarah makes it dramatic enough, wailing away about work that has to be finished by two o'clock that afternoon or whatever it might be, the gorgon will hurry out to help, and she hasn't time to lock the door. Enter the Artful Dodger, me. I depart half a minute later. I like substitution better than theft, Lord Powerscourt. I think they shift about, those files, and throw up a lot of dust if they're all moved three boxes to the left. It wouldn't look right either. I think three is the most you could carry around Queen's Inn. You see people walking about with one or two or three under their arm, very seldom any more.'

Powerscourt supposed Edward must have been exposed for some years now to the inner workings of the criminal mind. 'Do you think Sarah will be able to carry it off, Edward?'

'I'm sure she will, she's female,' said Edward delphically.

'What's that got to do with it?' said Powerscourt.

'I only meant, my lord, that women can always come over melodramatic when it suits them. Even Sarah,' he added darkly.

'When do you think you might be able to effect this piece of criminality, Edward?'

'I shall have to talk to Sarah. I'm on my way to see her now, in fact. I shall let you know. It may be that the opportunity will simply present itself out of the blue. We shall trust in God and keep our powder dry.'

Powerscourt was escorting Edward towards the front door. At the top of the stairs they heard a firm cough behind them. It was Nurse Mary Muriel.

'I know this is very unconventional, Lord Powerscourt, but I wondered if you would like to kiss the twins goodnight, you and your young friend.' She smiled at Edward. 'It's not every day you're here at this time, my lord.'

So Powerscourt and Edward had a double armful each, an armful of perfectly clean, sweet-smelling, sleepy-looking twin.

By half past nine William Burke had still not arrived in Manchester Square. Powerscourt imagined there must have been some frightful financial crisis at his bank in the City. Burke had told him of some of these perils once when they were all on holiday together in Antibes, terrifying stories of books that refused to balance even though the entries had been put in twice, of monies that seemed to be there in the morning, at least on paper, only for them to have disappeared by the evening into some strange hole hidden inside the ledgers. Once, Burke had told him with pride, they seemed to have lost the entire accounts for a whole northern city in the space of one afternoon. They were always found, these missing funds, Burke said, it was always that somebody had made one tiny mistake and never realized it.

Lady Lucy was leafing through the manuscript of Johnny Fitzgerald's book on *The Birds of London*. Powerscourt was running through his strange collection of wills one last time.

'I think this book is going to do jolly well, Francis. There are birds in here that I never knew existed, let alone were flying around London.'

'I shall order fifty copies of the first edition from Hatchard's when it comes out, Lucy. We can give them to people as birthday and Christmas presents.'

Just then they heard low conversation on the stairs. Rhys, the Powerscourt butler, was ushering Burke up to the drawing room and promising to return with a large bottle of beer.

'Good evening, Lucy, good evening. Francis.' The great financier kissed his sister-in-law on both cheeks. 'Sorry I'm late. Bloody money wouldn't add up. I got very thirsty so Rhys is going to bring me a beer. Hope you don't mind.'

He sat down at the end of the sofa and began to revive after his first long gulp of beer.

'Francis, Lucy, can't stay long. Promised to help young Peter with his maths.' Powerscourt remembered that the one thing that pained William Burke above everything else was that his three children could not cope with mathematics. The first two could scarcely add up, let alone remember their tables.

'How would you rate this case, Francis? In comparison with some of the others, I mean.'

'It's proving rather elusive, William. Every time you think you have put a hand on something definite, it disappears. I've got these papers for you, the ones we talked about.'

'You mean those wills? How many were there in the end?'

'Just over a hundred. Look, I've arranged them all in date order. And I've also marked them up in the various categories of expenditure where the dead benchers wanted them to go. And we're hoping to steal a set of accounts tomorrow or the next day.'

'Are you indeed? And how are you proposing to do that?'

'I think you'd be better off not knowing, William. Honestly. We don't want your directors inquiring how you have been concealing criminal intentions and not reporting them to the proper authorities.'

'Very well,' said William Burke. 'Now then, Francis, I have two pieces of information to report, one of them perfectly legal, the other . . . well, not illegal but the bench of bishops might not approve. The first relates to the relative value of money. You remember we talked the last time we met about whether it is possible to translate the money of, let us say, 1761 when Queen's Inn was founded into the equivalent value of today. In the vaults of the Bank of England, Francis – well, not quite that far down, certainly a good way down in the basements – there lurks a very tall man, stooped now with knowledge, called Flanagan. This Flanagan is truly a wizard. You tell him that a bequest was made to the Inn in 1785 of three hundred pounds, he will consult some files and tell you, almost immediately, that it is worth twelve thousand pounds in today's money, or some such figure.'

'How on earth does he do it?' asked Lady Lucy.

'Records, Lucy, he has collected thousands and thousands of records. The man's a human squirrel on a titanic scale. He looks up government records, records of house sales, wills, household accounts, government contracts, military records. They say the happiest moment in his life was when he discovered that some great house, Chatsworth or Longleat, somewhere like that, had continuous records stretching over a period of a hundred and fifty years during which time they noted in great ledgers the cost of everyday purchases like tea, coffee, wine and so on. And they still had the records of the wages paid to every single workman involved in the making of the artificial lake and the creation of the landscape gardens, including the very considerable sums made over to Capability Brown. Flanagan was, apparently, so excited by this discovery that he had to ask the Governor of the Bank of England for a week off for his brain to calm down. Anyway, Francis, the good Flanagan, Thomas Flanagan I believe he's called, will be very happy to make those calculations for you tomorrow on receipt of the wills. He would like to make a copy of them for his own records and I said that would be fine.'

'Does that mean, William, that after this Mr Flanagan has done his sums, as it were, we will have just one figure for the value of all these bequests? One hundred thousand pounds, let us say, in today's money?'

'Exactly, Lucy. Only I suspect it may be a lot more than one hundred thousand pounds.'

'And your other piece of information, William?'

Powerscourt was to tell Johnny Fitzgerald afterwards that William Burke went very conspiratorial at this point. He looked around in a rather shifty fashion. He leant forward in his chair. He lowered his voice till it was almost a whisper.

'Keep it very quiet,' he muttered. 'Bank accounts. Bank statements. I happen to know the fellow who looks after the accounts of Queen's Inn.' Burke looked around him again as if spies might be lurking underneath the sofa or behind the curtains. 'Fact is, the fellow wants to transfer to our bank. Transfer himself, I mean, not some money I let it be known, in a delicate fashion, that his application might be put to advantage if I could, accidentally as it were, have a look at those statements. That should happen tomorrow morning.'

Burke sat back in his chair and breathed deeply as if he'd run a race or just come out from confession.

'You old devil, William. I am most grateful.'

'It's not as bad as it seems,' Burke said finally. 'The chap was going to get the job anyway.'

There was a mild knock on the door and coughing noises on the far side of it. That could only mean one thing. Powerscourt and Lady Lucy looked at each other and smiled. Rhys had come with a message. He had. Rhys always coughed. He did. 'I'm very sorry to interrupt, my lord, my lady, Mr Burke, there's a message from one of Chief Inspector Beecham's young constables.'

The ones Lady Lucy referred to as the crèche, Powerscourt recalled.

'The Chief Inspector thought you would want to know, my lord. He'll be calling in the morning. It's Mr Newton, my lord, Mr Porchester Newton. He's disappeared.'

Edward was relieved to find that his stutter had not returned the following morning. He had an anxious moment about the p of Temple station when he bought his ticket but all seemed to be well. He did, however, feel extremely nervous about the whole operation. What would happen if something went wrong? What if they were caught? Then he remembered something Powerscourt had told him on the way down the stairs the previous evening. 'The thing to remember about any hazardous operation, Edward,' he had said, 'is that everybody feels nervous and a bit wobbly beforehand. No matter how many times a soldier has been in battle, they still feel anxious before it starts.' Well, this was Edward's first engagement and he didn't want to let his general down.

The authorities of Queen's Inn seemed to have moved Chief Inspector Beecham and his men around the place as if he was a piece of old furniture waiting for the rag and bone men. First they had operated from an office very close to the rooms of the late Alexander Dauntsey. The surrounding barristers had complained about the volume of their conversations and the noise of their boots on the stairs. They were then transferred to some empty offices at the top of one of the buildings in Fountain Court. Again, the people who lived underneath complained about the noise. Now the detectives were occupying a former classroom that had seen better days, but was hidden away behind the room with the boilers for the heating so that the policemen themselves were complaining about the racket and had to shout to each other when standing virtually on top of one another.

'Good morning, my lord,' said the Chief Inspector. 'I'm sorry the news about Newton reached you so late last night but I thought you would like to know.'

'I am most grateful to you, Chief Inspector. Do you have any more information about his disappearance? Any leads?'

'We know now that the last time he disappeared he went to stay with a younger sister in Kent. There he went for walks, played with the children, acted out the role of favourite uncle to perfection. But he hasn't gone there this time, not so far.'

Powerscourt remembered his last interview with Porchester Newton, the point blank refusal to answer questions, the veins throbbing in his forehead, those huge hands moving forward into what might have been an attack and strangle position.

'Do you suppose that he had come to learn about your inquiries, that one of them might have really alarmed him? Sorry, Chief Inspector, I'm not expressing myself very well.' Powerscourt found it hard to think and talk in this noisy inferno. 'Is it possible that you were pursuing a line of inquiry which would have revealed to Newton that you now knew him to be the murderer? And that, therefore, he had to disappear?'

'Well, we might have been,' said Beecham morosely, 'but if we were, it was an accident.'

Edward and Sarah had finalized the details of the theft the night before. Sarah had agreed that the typewriter should be successful in drawing the gorgon from her lair, as Edward put it. As it happened, Sarah had in her attic a number of box files that had come from the gorgon's cave, and had labels attached to them in the handwriting of the gorgon herself. Sarah was confident that with a bit of practice she could do a passable imitation of the handwriting to be found on the boxes with the account files.

The first stage of Operation Theft, as Edward liked to call it, was due to take place shortly before nine thirty. Maxwell Kirk, head of the chambers where Edward and Sarah worked, had agreed surprisingly easily to ask for a visit from Barton Somerville on being told that the scheme was really Powerscourt's and might have a minor role to play in the murder investigation. A porter was sent with the request from New Court across to Fountain Court where the Treasurer's rooms were. Edward watched him go, a middle-aged porter with the steady walk of one who had travelled this route many times before. Sarah's room mate was away for the morning so Sarah was contemplating the ruin of her typewriter with some satisfaction. The ribbon had got stuck somewhere in the bowels of the machine, bits of it were wrapped firmly round various keys and would, Sarah thought, take some time to sort out.

Nine forty came and the beginning of the exodus of barristers towards their day in court. There were always a few who departed earlier than they needed to, anxious perhaps to arrange their papers properly before judge and jury. The great mass would go about nine forty-five and it was this throng that Edward hoped Somerville would join. As he watched anxiously at his window, Edward saw the clock move on with agonizing slowness. Ten to ten, five to ten. Maybe Somerville wasn't coming. Maybe he had simply refused as the request threatened his dignity. He was, after all, a man who asked his colleagues to address him as Treasurer. Five past ten. Edward began to feel like a soldier all geared up for battle, bayonet at the ready, who is told by his commanding officer that the battle has been postponed until another day. He wondered if he should go upstairs and tell Sarah. Then he might miss the arrival of Somerville.

Sarah, in the attic floor, leaning out of the window, probably had the best view of the lot.

'It's always seemed to me to be perfectly possible that Porchester Newton was the murderer,' said Powerscourt, 'though I am somewhat confused about the motive. Was it a continuation of the feud that carried on right up to the benchers' election? Was it fury that he would not now enjoy the fruits of being a bencher? Did he know more than we do about how rewarding those fruits might be?'

'It's a great pity we never found out what the row was about,' said Beecham. 'Not one of them would speak to us about it and not one of them would speak to you, Lord Powerscourt.'

'I think I have the better of you there,' said Powerscourt, suddenly animated, 'and I apologize most sincerely for not telling you beforehand. It slipped my mind. I got the information by handing over a considerable sum to the Head Porter. It's amazing how notes can make people talk. Now then, the main bone of contention in the feud was as follows.'

It was ten past ten before the tall, silver-haired figure of Barton Somerville could be seen, marching slowly across his court towards Maxwell Kirk's chambers. Edward watched him come in, just beneath his window. Half an hour was the figure he had given Kirk for the length of time required for the meeting. Sarah was to wait one minute before setting out for the gorgon's lair. Even watching from behind, Edward could tell she was upset. She seemed to have wrenched her hair into a condition of confusion rather than the well-planned order it normally displayed. She was running, if not at full speed, then at a steady pace.

'Miss McKenna,' Sarah panted, 'I'm so pleased you're here. It's my typewriter, it's broken, the ribbon, I can't fix it and I've got this work for Mr Kirk that has to be handed in and I don't know what to do. Will you please come and help me?'

The gorgon inspected Sarah carefully. Her hair was indeed a mousy colour and she was wearing a suit that Sarah did not believe could ever have been fashionable, in a colour once memorably described by Edward as Repugnant Brown.

'Take it more slowly, Sarah. Your typewriter is not functioning?'
Sarah nodded.

'The ribbon is malfunctioning?'

'It's come off,' Sarah said, 'it's wrapped round some other part and I can't undo it. I'm sure you could sort it out for me, Miss McKenna, it would only take you a minute or two.'

By now, in the master plan, the gorgon should have been out of her lair and halfway down the stairs. Edward was rooted to his window. Barton Somerville had been in with Kirk for over ten minutes. It was four minutes since Sarah had set off for the gorgon's cave. The operation was not going according to plan.

'Did you say you had some work that has to be completed for Mr Kirk?'

Sarah nodded. 'Why don't you borrow another machine?' Miss McKenna suggested brightly. 'We could get one of the porters to bring it up for you.'

This possibility hadn't featured in Sarah's conversations with Edward at all, but she rose to the occasion magnificently.

'I thought of that but it wouldn't do. Miss McKenna. Mr Kirk has a special machine which produces slightly bigger type on the page. I think his eyes must be going. It's the only one of its kind in Queen's. And,' here Sarah looked at her watch and groaned, 'it's meant to be handed over by lunchtime and I've got pages and pages to do. I'll get sacked if I don't finish it. It's for that big fraud trial, you see. Please, Miss McKenna, won't you come and help me. You're the only person in the Inn who can save me now! Please! We must be quick!'

'Well,' said the gorgon, 'it's most unusual for myself and the Treasurer to be out of the office at the same time but it can't be helped.'

Sarah half dragged her out of the office and down the stairs, the gorgon pausing only to close the door. Nineteen minutes had elapsed since Barton Somerville entered the Kirk chambers. Twenty had passed before Sarah and Miss McKenna were sighted approaching Sarah's rooms. Twenty-two had elapsed before they had clattered up the stairs and Edward reckoned they were fully engaged with the errant typewriter ribbon. After twenty-three minutes Edward, with three black box files under his arm, set out across the path leading to Fountain Court. He wanted to run but he knew he couldn't. Walking across the court like this was perfectly normal. Running, unless a man was extremely late for court, was most unusual.

'I think the reason the barristers refused to speak to us, Chief Inspector,' said Powerscourt, 'is that they were ashamed of themselves. Even the Head Porter, not a man famous for criticizing his lords and masters, said that their language was often worse than that of Billingsgate Fish Market and the behaviour bad enough to have some of them up in front of the justices for breaches of the peace.'

'I suppose,' said Beecham, 'that if you make a living by being prepared to insult people in a courtroom occasionally, you won't find it too hard when it comes to events back in your own chambers.'

'Exactly so,' said Powerscourt. 'The contest appeared to be going along with little advantage to one side or the other until about ten days before polling day. You must remember, Chief Inspector, that the porters were most intimately involved in the event. They were following the gentlemen's bets on the outcome very closely and they themselves had a variety of wagers at different odds with the unofficial bookmaker, covering bets, bets on the size of the majority, bets on the total number of votes that would be cast, that sort of thing. Anyway, as I say, with ten days to go Newton and his people decide it's time to take the gloves off. They start putting it about that the barristers should not be electing a bencher who would only be able to serve from Monday to Wednesday. This was a clear reference to Dauntsey's nervous depressions, his days off, as it were, the inexplicable occasions when his great talent seemed to desert him.'

'That was a pretty filthy tactic,' said Chief Inspector Beecham. 'Did it work? Surely the barristers knew all that already?'

'It seemed to work for about a week,' said Powerscourt. 'Whether it took Dauntsey's people that long to do their research, or whether they thought Newton's tactics might backfire, I don't know. But they certainly fought back in kind. Newton wasn't a gentleman, they said. His father kept two grocery shops in Wolverhampton. His grandmother had been a junior parlourmaid. They produced a rather vicious but very effective cartoon, apparently. Across the top was the legend "Our New Bencher" with many exclamation marks beside it. Underneath were two drawings, one showing a younger but very recognizable Newton counting out the change in the grocery shop, and the other showing him helping an elderly lady, presumably his grandmother, to fold the ironing in some great airing room. A hundred years ago or less, people fought duels for stuff like this.'

'Have you thought, Lord Powerscourt, that it may be that the people here still haven't stopped fighting duels for this kind of smear?'

'I see what you mean, Sarah,' said the gorgon, inspecting the loops of typewriter ribbon festooned across the top of the machine. She tugged, lightly at first, then harder and harder until the veins on her neck began to stand out. 'Do you have any scissors? And a spare ribbon, I'm sure you must have one or two of those.'

Edward was less than a hundred yards away from the Treasurer's staircase.

Sarah realized to her horror that the gorgon's solution would see her out of the door in a minute or so. Edward might not have enough time. He might be caught by the gorgon in person and confined in some monstrous prison.

'Surely it won't work if we cut it,' she said. 'That bit of ribbon that's stuck around those two keys means that we won't have the letters p and l at all.'

'I think you'll find,' the gorgon said rather sharply, seizing the scissors firmly as if she was going to slit someone's throat, 'that if we cut the ribbon as close as we can to the keys, they will be released as the ribbon falls down into the machine.' She began clipping the ribbon firmly. Edward was now at the entrance to the staircase containing Barton Somerville's quarters. Twenty-five minutes had elapsed. The Treasurer might even now be on his way back to his quarters but Edward did not dare look round.

With a particularly vicious snip the gorgon freed the reluctant keys of p and l. 'There,' she said. 'It wasn't as bad as all that. Do you have a new ribbon, Sarah?'

Edward took the stairs up to the first floor two at a time. The door was closed. Oh, no, he said to himself, peering back down the stairs. Very gingerly, as if the door might explode in his face, Edward turned the handle and pushed. He was in.

'I think I'll be getting back now,' said the gorgon, watching Sarah unwrap another roll of typewriter ribbon. 'We can't leave the Treasurer's office unmanned for too long, can we.'

Sarah was not sure if Edward had had enough time. She wondered desperately if there was some other ruse that might keep the gorgon in her attic a little longer.

Edward had brought down the three files relating to 1899 and the first six months of 1900. He slipped the three dummy files he had brought into the place where the originals had been, checking they were correctly aligned with their fellows.

Miss McKenna waited no longer. With a businesslike 'Goodbye' she was down the stairs, heading rapidly back towards her lair.

'We've checked all those places, of course,' said Beecham. 'Newton's parents in Wolverhampton and the grandmother. No sign of him. My colleague who went to talk to the parents said how proud they were of their son, gone from a Midlands back street to Queen's Inn and maybe even a bencher's chair.'

'Did they have any idea where he was?' asked Powerscourt.

'No, but this is the interesting thing, Lord Powerscourt. My colleague who questioned them said he was sure the parents thought their son was the killer. They looked very rattled when told about the two deaths. And when he asked them if Newton had a temper they both said he did. The father began rubbing his hand round some mark on his forehead as if Porchester had clocked him one in his youth.'

'God bless my soul,' said Powerscourt. 'How very interesting that the parents should think he was the murderer. Not that they'd ever say anything in court.'

There was a knock at the door and another of the Chief Inspector's young policemen came in with a note for Beecham. He read it very fast and looked up at Powerscourt. 'Death calls again, I fear. Not in Queen's Inn but for that former employee you went to see, a Mr Bassett, Mr John Bassett, of Petley Road, Fulham. They only found him today. The sergeant isn't sure if the death is due to natural causes or not. The police surgeon is on his way. I have to stay here for now, Lord Powerscourt, with the various strands of inquiry into Newton still coming in . . . '

'Of course,' said Powerscourt. 'I shall go at once to pay my last respects to Mr Bassett. I rather liked the little man.'

Edward saw the large diary lying open on her desk. Quickly he swung the pages back to the week before the murder of Alex Dauntsey. There it was, six days before the feast, a meeting with Dauntsey and Stewart, at Dauntsey's request, underlined in the gorgon's hand. Edward wondered what other clues might be hiding here. Then he turned and walked as fast as he could down the stairs, his three files under his arm, until he realized he had forgotten to close the door. As he headed back up the stairs, his heart pounding once more, the gorgon was emerging from the main entrance to Edward's chambers in New Court. He came down the steps two at a time, turned right and was out of the back door of the Inn a full thirty seconds before the gorgon came into view. Within a minute Edward and his files were in a cab, heading for Manchester Square. He hoped Lord Powerscourt would be pleased with him.

At first sight Petley Road looked exactly the same as any other Victorian terrace in the capital, most of the front doors clean, a few flowers beginning to come out in the tiny front gardens, one or two ambitious residents trying to grow trees on their section of pavement. But when you looked closely, things were different. There were little groups of women, three at least, Powerscourt thought, conversing quietly on their front porches and casting furtive glances from time to time at the late Mr Bassett's residence at Number 15. Outside that house, looking as though he had been planted there many years before, was a six-foot, fourteen-stone policeman, his task to keep the prying eyes of all and sundry away from what lay within. And then, as Powerscourt was just a few feet away from the front door, he saw a team of four black horses pulling an undertaker's carriage, also draped in black, turning into Petley Road from the other end. They had come, presumably, to take the body away.

Powerscourt found the police surgeon circling the body in the first-floor bedroom. Even here, Powerscourt saw, John Bassett's love of the distant places of the earth had taken hold on the walls. Downstairs in the living room it had been views of Mount Everest and the Sahara desert, the Arctic and the vast steppes of Siberia. Up here there were pictures of a very long train climbing up what Powerscourt presumed to be the Rocky Mountains, a breathtaking illustration of Niagara Falls and a vast panorama of ruins that Powerscourt thought must be the Valley of the Kings in Egypt. He made his introductions to the police surgeon who, he gathered, was called James Wilson.

'Your reputation precedes you, Lord Powerscourt,' said Wilson, when he had been given the briefest of summaries of the Queen's Inn case and Powerscourt's close alliance with Detective Chief Inspector Beecham. 'You and the Chief Inspector must make a formidable team. I presume,' he went on, turning to look once more at the body of John Bassett, 'that you want to know if there was anything untoward about this old man's death. He used to work at Queen's, I gather.'

'That is correct,' said Powerscourt. At first sight it seemed obvious that John Bassett had died in his sleep. He had gone to sleep on his back, something must have happened in the night, and he was gone. A spare pillow was lying halfway down the bed.

'There is every reason to think that Mr Bassett died of natural causes, Lord Powerscourt. None of the examinations I have been able to perform suggest anything else. He was very old. The system decided to shut down. The heart simply stopped beating. He wasn't hit over the head, or shot, or poisoned like your unfortunate legal gentlemen. There is only one thing you could, just possibly, think of as being suspicious if you were that way inclined.'

'And that is?' said Powerscourt.

'It's this pillow,' said the doctor. 'Why do you have a pillow halfway down your bed? The police were the first people into this house so we can be sure nothing has been moved. Do you know anybody, Lord Powerscourt, who sleeps with a pillow halfway down the bed?'

'Not exactly,' replied Powerscourt, thinking of the amazing jumble of pillows, bed clothes, blankets, soft toys, that seemed to surround his eldest children when they woke up. 'But surely you could decide that you had too many pillows and simply move this one away? You could probably do it in your sleep.'

'All of that is true. But,' Dr Wilson bent down and picked up the pillow, 'suppose you were a murderer, Lord Powerscourt. You must have imagined yourself in such a role many times, I should think. You find Mr Bassett asleep. For whatever reason, you have come to kill him. You pull, ever so gently, one of his pillows out from under his head. You press it down over his face. Gradually you hear the breathing stop. You remove the pillow and leave it lying on the bed. There are no marks anywhere. You disappear into the night. I'm not saying that did happen, Lord Powerscourt, I'm saying it could have happened.'

15

Lord Francis Powerscourt was pacing up and down his drawing room in Manchester Square. It was nearly half past seven in the evening and he was waiting for William Burke and his report on the tangled finances of Queen's Inn. Strange memories of the investigation were drifting across his mind. He thought of Alex Dauntsey going to see John Bassett and being poisoned a week later. He thought of his own visit to the Finance Steward of Queen's that was followed by Bassett's own death, whether accidental or not. He thought of the vanished Porchester Newton and those huge hands that could have strangled a man in seconds. He heard, suddenly, the voice of Elizabeth Dauntsey, dressed in black and sitting by her fire in Calne telling him, 'There was something worrying him. It must have been in the weeks after he was elected a bencher, you see. Alex said it more than once, I'm certain of that, Lord Powerscourt. He said he was very worried about the accounts.' He thought about Rivers Cavendish, a man with the mighty motive of the cuckold's horns for murdering Dauntsey, and his two books on poisons. That afternoon Powerscourt had established to his own satisfaction that a man who took a cab to and from Paddington station en route to Oxford, like Dr Rivers Cavendish, could have reached Queen's Inn in time to poison Dauntsey. He thought of Mrs Cavendish, enjoying her lunches and fine wines with Dauntsey, deprived of her nights away. And then he heard the voice of Edward from the very first time they met:

'It was after his election as a bencher, sir. Something changed after that. Not immediately but two weeks or so later, I should say, sir. Mr Dauntsey was very cross about something. I never knew what it was. One afternoon I came into his room when he wasn't expecting me. He was studying some figures on a pad in front of him. He looked at me, Mr Dauntsey sir, almost in despair. "It's not right, Edward," he said, "it's just not right."'

What was it, Powerscourt said to himself, that so troubled Alex Dauntsey in the weeks after his election as a bencher? They should have been among the happiest of his professional life. Where was Porchester Newton? And why had he run away a second time? Was Mrs Cavendish lying? Was Dr Cavendish, the true believer, breaking one of the Commandments he must hold so dear? Was he in breach of the fifth one, Thou shalt not kill? His wife had been on the verge of infringing the sixth, Thou shalt not commit adultery, if she hadn't already broken it. He remembered the portrait painter Nathaniel Stone on Dauntsey: 'Hold on, he did say one thing, but I didn't pay much attention to it at the time. It was something about very strange things going on there' – 'there' being Queen's Inn.

William Burke looked very serious when he walked into the room.

'I think we should go to your study, Francis. We're going to need that big desk of yours.'

And so, for over two hours, William Burke took Powerscourt through the intricacies of the finances of Queen's Inn. There was material in his report from the wills, from the accounts stolen by Edward and Sarah and from the statements provided by the man who wanted a position in Burke's bank. His people had typed out summaries of the main findings. There were brief chapters on what appeared to have happened to particular donations. And Burke kept checking that his friend understood what he was being told. When he rose to return to his wife and the innumerate children, Powerscourt shook him by the hand. 'I am so grateful, William. This is tremendous.'

'Let me know if there is anything more I can do to help,' said Burke. 'I am not available for the next two days but after that I should be only too pleased.'

As his brother-in-law departed Powerscourt remembered a previous occasion when Burke had accompanied him to a fateful meeting with the Private Secretary of the Prince of Wales and had made a dramatic contribution to the meeting.

'William was a very long time, Francis,' said Lady Lucy as he resumed his pacing in the drawing room. 'Have you solved the mystery?'

'I don't think so, Lucy, but I tell you what I'm going to do. Current French military doctrine – God knows where I picked this up, probably down at the Cape – is all for the attack. The French soldier must never retreat. Forwards is the order of the day. Backwards is banned. *L'audace, toujours l'audace*, daring, always daring. Tomorrow morning I am going to spend with my Detective Chief Inspector friend with a brief interlude with Maxwell Kirk. Chief Inspector Beecham and I are going to play at being financiers for a while. And then, *l'audace, toujours l'audace*, I am going to make a preliminary report to our dearly beloved friend Barton Somerville, the Treasurer of Queen's Inn.'

The last note from the chimes of two o'clock was echoing round Fountain Court when Powerscourt and the Chief Inspector took their seats in Somerville's vast office. Powerscourt looked quickly at the full-length portraits of previous benchers and Treasurers on the walls and realized, to his delight, that he had detailed financial information on some of them in his papers. Jack Beecham was in a dark blue suit with a white shirt and a nondescript tie, Powerscourt in what his children referred to as the funeral suit, a very dark grey pinstripe with a pale blue shirt. Somerville radiated his usual combination of arrogance and superiority.

'Tea should be coming in twenty minutes or so, gentlemen,' Somerville began. 'You said you wanted to see me, Powerscourt.'

Powerscourt smiled. 'Yes, Mr Treasurer,' he replied, reckoning that the formality, however ludicrous it might seem, would probably serve his purposes in the end. 'I have come to make a preliminary report.'

'You seem to have a great many preliminary findings,' said Somerville, nodding in the direction of the Powerscourt papers.

'We shall see,' Powerscourt said. 'It is my custom on these occasions to couch my findings in narrative form, commencing not *in medias res*, in the middle of things as the poet says, but at the very beginning.'

Beecham, Powerscourt could see out of the corner of his eye, was taking notes already. The engagement had scarcely begun. 'Let me begin with the murders, Mr Treasurer. On the day of his death, the day of the Whitelock Feast, February 28th this year, Alexander Dauntsey was in his chambers here until shortly after six o'clock. He had been working on forthcoming cases. There were no reports of any visitors to his rooms though there could have been some who were not observed. Shortly after six, as I said, he came to a drinks party here in your chambers, as you know, Mr Treasurer. At the soup course of the feast he collapsed and died almost instantaneously. He had been poisoned. And the medical men believe that the poison was most likely administered here, slipped into the champagne or the sherry he was enjoying with his peers, or taken shortly before he left his own chambers to come here. Twelve days later, a Wednesday, Mr Woodford Stewart disappeared. He was not seen in his rooms after lunch. His body was found on the Monday morning, dumped with some builder's rubble at the side of Temple Church. He had been shot twice in the chest.

'I think I should go back now a couple of months to the time when there was a vacancy for the position of bencher in this Inn. I do not need to tell you, Mr Treasurer, that this is a democratic election with all the barristers who are members of the Inn able to vote. The election is for life, though it was not always so in the past as I understand it. There were two candidates for the position. One was Porchester Newton and the other was Alexander Dauntsey, both distinguished advocates in their own fields. Right at the end the contest degenerated somewhat. Newton's supporters began to put it abroad that Dauntsey would be a three-day-a-week candidate, a reference to Dauntsey's unfortunate affliction which caused him to be superb in court one day and then, for no apparent reason, hopeless the next. I think I would have been pretty cross about that if I had been Dauntsey. But his supporters' club hit back, alleging that Newton was not a gentleman. They produced a rather vicious cartoon which showed Burton performing various menial tasks relating to his upbringing as the son of a grocer and the grandson of a junior parlourmaid. The ballot is secret but I believe Dauntsey won the contest by twenty-two votes, a fair margin.'

'Where did you get that information from, Powerscourt?' said Somerville crossly.

'I'm afraid I cannot tell you my sources at present, Mr Treasurer, I feel it would be inappropriate.'

There was a loud grunt from Somerville. Powerscourt did not wish to reveal that it was the Head Porter who had told him.

'So Porchester Newton had reason to hate Dauntsey. He vanished for a while after the election. He was here at the time of the feast, then he vanished and came back and he has now disappeared again.'

Powerscourt paused while the tea was brought in, the gorgon herself carrying the tray and placing it carefully on the left of

Somerville's desk. Powerscourt wondered if she had checked her records recently. He had been horrified to learn from Edward, when he was asked what he put in the three dummy files, that they had all been filled with back copies of the racing newspapers.

'You will recall, Mr Treasurer,' Powerscourt went on, taking a preliminary sip of his tea, 'Shakespeare's *Macbeth* where there are dramatic instructions about the arrival of the First Murderer, Second Murderer and so on. I propose to adapt the device to my own humbler narrative and label Porchester Newton the First Suspect. He certainly had the motive and I do not believe we can rule him out at this stage.

'I turn now to our Second Suspect. This, I fear, takes us into the complicated waters of the Dauntsey marriage. I do not wish to break any confidences but I feel free to say that the difficulties were caused entirely by the inability of the poor couple to have any children of their own. This was a severe trial to them both. Alex Dauntsey felt it particularly keenly for he was the inheritor of one of the great houses of England. Calne may be covered in dust sheets today, its fabulous galleries preserved from decay but not open to visitors, but it has a great history stretching back to Elizabeth and beyond. For Calne not to have his heir was terrible for Dauntsey. And since he was sure his wife Elizabeth could not conceive, he resolved to try for an heir with another woman. He was indeed, intending to spend the night after the feast and the following weekend with the other woman. Mrs Dauntsey appeared to agree with this decision but it became the subject of a ferocious row between the two of them the day before his death. The Chief Inspector's men, Mr Treasurer, carried out detailed interviews with every member of this Inn who was here for the feast in order to establish, where possible, the times of the movements of the participants. There were a number of reports of a mysterious visitor who came between five and six and was seen leaving shortly after six. Nobody recognized the figure, though one of the porters said later that he originally thought it was Mrs Dauntsey until he realized that was impossible, as the visitor was universally agreed to be male. I am sure, Mr Treasurer, that you attended the three hundredth anniversary performance of *Twelfth Night* in Middle Temple Hall earlier this year. So did Elizabeth Dauntsey, who will have remembered that one of the principal characters, Viola or Cesario, was a girl pretending to be a boy who would have been played in Shakespeare's time by a boy pretending to be a girl, pretending to be a boy. We now know that Mrs Dauntsey was the mysterious visitor, disguised as a man. We know she went to her husband's rooms, according to her account, to apologize for the row and to wish him well for the weekend. She went in disguise, she says, because she feared other members of the Inn would know about the weekend away and would be laughing at her. That is her story. But it is perfectly possible that she was still incensed with her husband and that she came in disguise to the Inn intent, not on reconciliation, but on murder. Her husband, after all, was drinking red wine when she called. It would have been perfectly possible to slip in some poison while her husband went to the bathroom. So she is the Second Suspect.'

Powerscourt paused and looked down at his papers. The Chief Inspector's pen stopped for a moment. Barton Somerville was fiddling with a biscuit. A pair of seagulls settled briefly on the window sill and moved on.

'Suspect Number Three,' he went on, 'is the young woman Alex Dauntsey was going to spend time with in pursuit of a son and heir. Catherine Cavendish is a lively and attractive woman in her early thirties, a former chorus girl who is married to a doctor much older than herself. The doctor is dying of some unknown illness and is unable to perform some of the more intimate functions of the married state. He has, he says, no objections to his wife partaking of these pleasures, forbidden fruit we might almost say, in some mythical Eden, with another man. That man was Dauntsey.'

Powerscourt paused and took another sip of his tea. Barton Somerville was taking notes too. Powerscourt suspected that he might be subjected to a fearful cross-examination at the end.

'I have talked at length with the two ladies involved in this delicate transaction and it seems to me that there was a misunderstanding about Dauntsey's intentions after the first husband had passed on. Mrs Dauntsey was convinced that he would never leave her. Mrs Cavendish, for her part, believed Dauntsey would leave his wife and marry her. If Catherine Cavendish discovered that Dauntsey was taking his pleasure with her, but not, as it were, prepared to pay his bills, then I believe she would have been capable of murdering him. And in a perverse way I think we have to count her husband as Suspect Number Four. For it is one thing to announce that you have no objections to your wife carrying on with another man, quite another when it is about to happen under your very nose and you realize that your objections may be more visceral and more irrational than you had thought. Far from not minding, you suddenly find that you mind very much. And there are two further reasons for placing Dr Cavendish in the suspects' pound. Here was a man with but a few months left to live. The chances are that he would be dead by normal means before his case could come to court. So he wouldn't care about the hangman's noose as others might. And he was an expert on poisons, he had written at least two books on them.'

'Forgive me for interrupting, Powerscourt.' Somerville was peering at him over the top of his spectacles, half a biscuit dangling from his left hand. 'What about Woodford Stewart? You talk as if there was only one murder. There have been two.'

'I am coming to that, Mr Treasurer,' Powerscourt continued. 'There is absolutely nothing in Mr Stewart's private life that either the Chief Inspector or I could discover which might have led to somebody wanting to kill him. His domestic life was beyond reproach. There is, of course, as there is with Alex Dauntsey, the outside chance of some prisoner whose conviction they secured years ago now achieving release and coming to exact revenge. But I do not think that likely. What killed Woodford Stewart had to do with this Inn and it had to do with his friendship with Dauntsey. It may be that he knew who the poisoner was and had to be silenced. It may be that the reasons that led to Dauntsey's murder also led to Stewart's.'

Powerscourt paused again. He could hear footsteps coming up the stairs, rather a lot of footsteps. The Chief Inspector looked across at him. Barton Somerville did not react. Maybe his hearing was not what it was.

'You will know far better than I, Mr Treasurer,' Powerscourt went on, smiling slightly at Somerville 'how sometimes in important cases the defending barrister sets out on what seems to be a completely pointless line of argument, apparently having little to do with the case under trial. The prosecuting counsel objects. The judge quizzes the defence. Eventually, though not always, the judge permits the line of questioning because he believes the defence's assurances that the information is relevant. So it is with me here. Every word I say from now on has, in my judgement and that of my colleague on my left, the greatest relevance to this case, whatever you may think at the time. And, in deference to the surroundings, Mr Treasurer, I am going to call some witnesses. I am sure you will be interested to learn that they are all dead, and, more surprising perhaps, that some of them are here in this very room.'

Powerscourt rose from his chair and walked to the wall farthest away from Somerville's desk.

'This is my first witness,' he said proudly, 'and what a handsome fellow Sir Thomas Lawrence has made him.' Powerscourt waved airily at the full-length portrait which showed the sitter in red judicial robes, looking as much a cardinal as a judge, staring crossly at a long piece of paper which could have been a will or some other legal document. Behind him and slightly to the left was a beautiful room with long Georgian windows and a view over the Thames. 'As you can see, Mr Justice Wallace is a former Treasurer of this Inn, who has presided over this kingdom as Mr Treasurer Somerville does now. He is examining his paper in the very room in which we are now meeting.'

Powerscourt resumed his seat and began to turn over one or two of his papers. 'The good judge,' he went on, 'who came from a respectable family in Dorset, one brother becoming a Cabinet Minister, another an Admiral of the Blue, lived to the ripe old age of eighty-seven. In his will of 1824 he left a lot of money and property to his numerous family.'

Powerscourt now pulled out a will from inside the sheaf of documents in front of him. 'He also left ten thousand pounds to the Queen's Inn for the relief of poverty among the barristers and servants of this Inn and their families. A generous bequest, you might think, and one which is worth, according to the Bank of England, about three hundred thousand pounds in today's money.'

There was a sharp look from Somerville, upset perhaps to learn that the Bank of England were ranged against him. 'We may presume,' Powerscourt continued, 'that the executors made sure the formalities were followed. Thirty years ago, before your time, Mr Treasurer, there were indeed in the accounts of Queen's Inn various payments made according to the Wallace bequest. They are described as such in the documents. But they are not there now. The Wallace legacy has been absorbed into the general accounts of Queen's Inn. When I say the general accounts, I don't quite mean that. The general accounts relate to the running costs, maintenance of property, provision of meals and so on and are all covered, amply covered, by the monthly payments made by the residents of chambers. But there is another account, called the Treasurer's Account, controlled by this office. The Wallace hundreds of thousands have been diverted into there and there they remain to this day.

216

'Consider this other gentleman behind me, Benjamin Rockland, a barrister rather than a judge, a bencher of this Inn rather than a Treasurer, a man famous for his abilities for the defence in capital cases and much sought after by instructing solicitors. He was famous in his day, according to the official Inn history, for his generosity towards the young. He left four thousand pounds in his will in 1785 for the maintenance and upkeep and clothing of poor students attending the Inn. He hoped to ensure that the poorer citizens were not denied the advantages he had enjoyed. Turning once more to the Bank of England reckoning, that figure would amount to two hundred thousand pounds in today's money. You could support a number of poor students on the interest from that sum. How many Rockland students are there in the Inn at present? Not one. Thirty years ago there were a number of these young men gracing the walks and courts of this institution. Once again the monies have been diverted, not into the general accounts where they might benefit everybody, but into the Treasurer's Account, controlled from this office.

'And then consider this. Downstairs in your Hall you have one of the most famous and beautiful paintings in London. People come from far and wide to see *The Judgement of Paris* by Rubens, a glorious and sensuous account of the decision that led to the Trojan War. There is no record, unfortunately, as there might be if it happened today, of either of the two losing ladies going to the Court of Appeal. I am not concerned today with the technique or the overall impression given by the work apart from noting that the three goddesses, as everyone knows who has seen it, are wearing rather less than Catherine Cavendish was in her days as a chorus girl. Rather I am concerned with the way it was purchased twelve years ago. A plaque, as you well know, Mr Treasurer, says that it was paid for by the generosity of past and current benchers and benefactors. I do not believe that to be strictly true. The painting cost twelve thousand five hundred pounds, say fourteen thousand with commissions and taxes and so on. That was the precise total, less one hundred and forty-seven pounds, of a bequest made to the Inn a year before in the will of bencher Josiah Swanton for the relief of barristers rendered unfit for work by injury or illness. There are no records, Mr Treasurer, of any payments going to such people though the chaplain has informed me that there must be four candidates at least who are eligible for such payments today and whose lives would be transformed by them. The sick and the maimed paid for

217

the Rubens. At least its beauty can be enjoyed by all, it has not, like the appropriation of so much other money intended for good causes, ended up in the Treasurer's Account.

'I could go on, Mr Treasurer, with more examples. I have dozens of them here in my papers. All tell the same story. The rich are robbing the poor. Money intended to relieve suffering, to enable poor young men to acquire an education here, has been taken from them and given to old men already wealthy beyond the dreams of most Londoners. They have no voice, the sick barristers fallen on hard times, the young men from the East End who have been denied their proper place by old men's greed. Your greed, Mr Treasurer. Your actions, in fraudulently changing the bequests of generous people who died long ago, are a disgrace to your Inn and to your profession. No wonder the cartoonists so often portray the lawyers of London as greedy fellows only interested in enormous meals and enormous retainers and even more enormous refreshers. I can only make a rough estimate about the amount of money diverted. You, of course, as Treasurer are liable to re-election by your fellow benchers every five years. Maybe you embarked on your criminal career over twenty years ago when you first came up for re-election. A little bribe to the electors never went amiss. The only problem is that they expect a slightly larger bribe next time. Well, you were certainly able to provide it. My calculation, based on the Bank of England figures and some of your own accounts, is that each bencher, who received virtually nothing for being a bencher twenty-five years ago, now enjoys an annual income of between ten and fifteen thousand pounds. Each. For doing precisely nothing. The position is exactly like some of those late eighteenth-century sinecures that paid out thousands and thousands of pounds for doing nothing that so enraged William Pitt the Younger. The value of the principal required to produce such figures is around twenty million pounds, a sum well within the range of the stolen bequests we know of when adjusted to today's values.'

Powerscourt paused again. The Chief Inspector was still scribbling. Somerville looked as though he would like to vault over the desk and hit him.

'Is that all you've got?' the Treasurer sneered. 'A third rate Irish peer and a jumped-up constable from Clerkenwell?' He banged his fist on the desk. Powerscourt looked at him, unmoved by the insult, and untouched by the threat of violence.

'No, Mr Treasurer,' he went on, 'that is certainly not all we've got.

We've got, you'll be delighted to hear, a whole lot more. That last part of my report dealt with finance. It's now time to go back to murder, to the murders of Alexander Dauntsey and Woodford Stewart. Stewart had been elected a bencher some two months before Dauntsey. The two men were very close. They had prosecuted in some of the great financial cases of their times. Dauntsey was one of the few barristers of any Inn who was rated by the sharper minds in the City of London. With his demise they lengthened the odds against a conviction in the Puncknowle fraud trial. So Dauntsey knew about money. It is my belief that he discovered what had been going on in the accounts of Queen's Inn. There are reports of his saying to his wife that he was worried about the accounts, and looking at some figures with a junior member here and saying things weren't right. Shortly before his death Dauntsey had a meeting with the previous Financial Steward in Fulham and asked about bursaries for poor students. He was obviously on the right track. He asked for a meeting with you just days before he died. He brought Woodford Stewart with him. I believe that on that occasion he threatened to go public with the frauds that had been going on. Whatever his weaknesses, lack of courage wasn't one of them. Your blustering and banging of your fists wouldn't have had any impact on Alex Dauntsey. So you killed him. Woodford Stewart was not at the feast. You killed him several days later, probably hiding the body in your private rooms above this one and taking him to Temple Church in the middle of the night. We have heard, Mr Treasurer, about the First, Second, Third and Fourth Suspects. You are the Fifth Suspect. And, I put it to you in conclusion, Mr Treasurer, the other four are innocent. You are guilty.'

Barton Somerville snarled at them. He stopped writing and pointed his pen at them as if it were a spear he could hurl into their hearts.

'What a load of nonsense!' he spat. 'You can't possibly prove any of it. I've never seen such incompetence in a criminal investigation in my life! You!' He turned and glowered at Chief Inspector Beecham. 'I shall report your disgraceful conduct to the Home Secretary!'

'You tried the Commissioner of the Metropolitan Police last time,' said the Chief Inspector, 'and that didn't work. I don't suppose you'll have any better luck this time.' He and Powerscourt had agreed on a policy of initial politeness but that if Somerville turned nasty, they would turn nasty back.

'And you, Powerscourt, you're a disgrace to your class. I shall make sure it's known in society that you're nothing better than a fraud and a charlatan, a man who brings ridiculous charges with no evidence at all.'

'On the contrary, Mr Treasurer,' Powerscourt smiled his broadest smile at Somervillle, certain that this would enrage him even further, 'we can prove lots and lots of things. Figures don't lie. Your own records don't lie. Wills don't lie. Only senior barristers, who ought to know better, lie and they've been lying for years.'

'How dare you?' shouted Somerville, banging his fist so hard on the table that he must have nearly dislocated his wrist. 'That's slander, a bloody slander. I'll take you to court for that!'

'I fear, Mr Treasurer,' said Powerscourt at his silkiest, 'that you're much more likely to be appearing in court conducting your own defence than you are to be prosecuting me. And there's another development you ought to know about.' He looked across at Beecham. 'Ought to know about' was another signal. 'I took the liberty of speaking to Maxwell Kirk this morning. He is, as you know, a bencher, and the head of the chambers where Alex Dauntsey worked. I showed him the figures. Only the figures, we did not talk about the murders but I could see he had his suspicions. Not for nothing is Kirk now prosecuting Jeremiah Puncknowle. He was appalled by what has been happening. He is going to call an extraordinary general meeting of all the members of this Inn tomorrow afternoon. He is going to tell them what you have been doing for the last twenty years. He had no idea that the extra income he received from being a bencher had arrived with a trail of deception and criminality behind it. I believe he is going to put forward a motion calling on you to resign before you are forcibly removed from your office and stripped of your powers. By the time he has finished, you won't have a single friend left in this Inn.'

'He can't do this! You can't do this! I shall forbid the meeting! He can't call it without my approval! You'll pay for this, Powerscourt, mark my words, you'll pay for it. Kirk is a traitor! He can't have this meeting!'

'I'm afraid he can and he will, Mr Treasurer.' It was only the second time Detective Chief Inspector Beecham had spoken in the entire meeting. He had risen to his feet. 'You see, Mr Treasurer, tomorrow afternoon you won't be here.' He went to the door and beckoned in a sergeant and a constable who had been waiting in the outer office. 'Barton Obadiah Somerville, I am arresting you in connection with the murders of Alexander Dauntsey and Woodford Stewart. I must warn you that anything you say may be taken down and used in evidence. Take him away.'

Powerscourt saw that all the files in the gorgon's office had been removed. That must have been the noises they heard in the early stages of the interview. Somerville was still screaming, 'You'll pay for this, Powerscourt!' as they led him down the stairs and out the back door. The gorgon herself seemed to have disappeared too, Powerscourt saw, fled to a different lair.

'You take care, my lord,' said Beecham to Powerscourt as they parted on the bottom of the staircase. 'I don't think it's over yet. And well done, my lord, you were tremendous in there.'

'I just hope I made him cross,' said Powerscourt with a grin. 'The prospect of being voted out in disgrace is going to prey on his mind.'

As the cab bearing Somerville to the cells drew away, Powerscourt heard a final scream. All he could catch was '. . . pay for this'.

There were still a number of Chief Inspector Beecham's men working in and around Queen's Inn, but none of them noticed that Lord Francis Powerscourt was not alone on the journey back to his home. A stocky man with a dark beard slipped out of an alleyway just the far side of the porter's lodge and followed him all the way. The man kept to a distance of about a hundred yards and every now and then he patted his pocket as if to reassure himself he had not left some important object at home.

221

16

Powerscourt walked slowly back to Manchester Square. He was still marvelling at the vicious hatred Somerville had directed his way. All of the vitriol seemed to be targeted at him. Chief Inspector Beecham, object of so much venom at the beginning of the investigation, had escaped scot free.

Perhaps a painting or two will calm my brain, he said to himself as he passed the Wallace Collection, more or less opposite his own house in Manchester Square. It was a quarter to five and there was still an hour and a quarter before the Head Porter closed up for the night, his great bunch of keys jangling on his belt as he patrolled right round the building checking that everything was in order. Powerscourt slipped into the Housekeeper's Room and stared idly at an extraordinary painting by Paul Delaroche showing the State Barge of Cardinal Richelieu on the Rhone. A couple of aristocrats who had conspired to overthrow the mighty Cardinal were being towed in a boat behind, guarded by soldiers with halberds. Richelieu himself was dying at this point but he was still towing his enemies to Lyon for their execution. His barge was luxuriously furnished with red silk drapes and a rich oriental carpet trailed in the water by its side. Delaroche was interested in the reflections in the water, the almost Eastern luxury of his Cardinal. Powerscourt still had lawyers running through his mind, the living and the dead ones he had dealt with earlier that afternoon. He wondered briefly if Richelieu would have been a successful lawyer, Master of the Rolls perhaps, or a hanging judge. He stared briefly at the sister painting on the left which showed Richelieu's successor Cardinal Mazarin literally on his deathbed, playing cards with his friends and surrounded by intriguing courtiers.

For Powerscourt there was something too rich, too decadent about these men of God flaunting their earthly power. It was time to move on. These two Delaroches were in the Housekeeper's Room to the left of the main entrance. And on this particular day Powerscourt had his timings wrong. The Collection was going to close at five, not six. The Head Porter had already completed his circuit of the first floor, ushering the last visitors out of the building. And because Powerscourt was on one side of the building, he was not seen by the Head Porter as he began his Royal Progress on the other side, moving the pilgrims on, seeing to the doors and windows. By the time he did reach the Housekeeper's Room Powerscourt had moved off up the stairs towards his favourite landscape in the Great Gallery, vacated by the Head Porter some ten minutes before. Just as he arrived in front of Rubens' *The Rainbow Landscape* he heard a dull thud coming from downstairs. He checked his watch. It was exactly five o'clock. The Collection must have closed an hour earlier than usual today. He set forth for the front door, fingering the gun in his pocket. Ever since he heard the warnings from the underworld as relayed to Johnny Fitzgerald about threats to his life, he had carried it in his pocket every day. Lady Lucy checked with him every time he left the house. By the time he reached the ground floor he thought that he must be the only person left in the building, certainly the only one inside by mistake. At the front door he realized that no amount of manpower was going to let him out. The locks were huge, dark and forbidding in the shadows by the door. Powerscourt remembered that the nightwatchman came early in the evening, seven or eight o'clock. He would have a couple of hours to enjoy the paintings entirely on his own.

He stopped halfway up the stairs. He thought he heard a noise. Somebody with heavy boots was walking along the Great Gallery. And from the pattern of the steps he thought they were coming in his direction. Powerscourt didn't wait for formal introductions. Something told him that this might be enemy action. His right hand felt once more for the gun in his pocket. Suddenly he remembered being locked in the cathedral with the dead of centuries in his last case in the West Country, when a huge pile of lethal masonry had been poured down, missing him by inches. He tiptoed down the stairs as fast as he could and made his way into the armoury section on the ground floor. Early evening light was falling on the great wood and glass cases that lined the walls, illuminating enormous

223

spears, or ancient sets of body armour. There was a huge collection of weapons of death in here, long lances for horsemen to carry and run through their enemies, heavy pikes for foot soldiers to decapitate their foes, long swords and short swords, swords with pommels and swords without, swords for stabbing people, swords for cutting them in two, straight swords, curved swords, daggers, cuirasses, kris, armour from many centuries. In one of the rooms there was, he remembered, a horse clad in armour, ridden by a man in armour, a general perhaps, his visor slightly open so he could catch a proper sight of the opposition.

Powerscourt listened carefully. He could hear nothing. He suddenly realized that on either the ground or the first floors you could go right round the building in a clockwise or anti-clockwise direction. There was no wall or staircase that would force a man to retrace his steps and go back the way he had come. Here, in this beautiful set of rooms, he was going to play hide and seek round the galleries. The prize might be life or death. Powerscourt thought there was a staircase in the room next to the last of the armoury collections which had once been the Victorian smoking room. He thought he could hear those footsteps again, coming from the upper floors. The noise would continue for about half a minute or so and then stop. Was the man on the floor above waiting for him to appear? Was he looking for a hiding place, inside some great curtain perhaps, where only the barrel of his gun would need to come out of hiding and shoot his enemy in the heart? Very gingerly Powerscourt tiptoed up the stairs into a room full of Dutch landscapes. There was one painting of a ferry boat very early in the morning where the light glittered beautifully on the water and the daily commerce of the Dutch ebbed and flowed across the river. There was that sound again. His opponent certainly wasn't concerned about making a noise. Powerscourt wondered suddenly about Somerville's terrible threats and hoped he had not escaped from the police station to come here and take his revenge in the middle of the masterpieces of Europe and the armour of the East.

If he went round the building anti-clockwise he would be in the Great Gallery, where most of the finest paintings were hung, almost at once. If he went in the other direction he would go right round the first floor before he reached it from the other end. He decided on the long route and glided off through another roomful of Dutch paintings. Dimly on the walls he could just make out a loaf of bread being brought into a house, the interior of a church, a woman making lace, a girl reading a love letter. Any dark paintings, some of the most celebrated Rembrandts, would soon be almost invisible as the daylight began to fade. He checked his watch. A long time to go before the arrival of the nightwatchman. Then it was past the Canalettos, the blue-green water and the blue cloud-speckled skies and the public buildings of Venice rendered immortal under the artist's brush. Powerscourt paused again. The footsteps were still marching up and down in the Great Gallery, almost as if the man was on sentry duty. Perhaps he knew that Powerscourt was bound to arrive there sooner or later. All he had to do was to wait for his prey. He glanced quickly at the Canaletto by his side. For no reason at all he suddenly remembered recently seeing a painting of Eton College done by Canaletto during his years in London. Even that most English of buildings under Canaletto's hand looked as if it really belonged in Venice, somewhere behind San Zaccaria in the sestiere of San Marco, or floating improbably on its very own island like San Giorgio Maggiore. He pressed hard up against the wall by the door and made a rapid inspection of the landing. It was empty.

Powerscourt crossed the landing at a run, bent almost double. He was now trespassing in the improbable world of Boucher, naked gods floating in the skies without visible means of support, pagan heroes living out the myths of ancient Greece in a naked innocence charged with considerable erotic force Still he could hear the footsteps, slightly closer now. He wished he had the same means of upward propulsion as Boucher's characters and could float right through the ceiling and the roof and alight in Number 8 Manchester Square. Then a room full of Greuzes, rather sickly portraits of young girls' faces that looked as if they were designed to appeal to women and middle-aged and elderly men rather than to the young of either sex. He listened for the footsteps again. They seemed to have stopped. He stood absolutely still for two minutes to see if they started again. They did not.

Powerscourt was now in a kind of magic kingdom, the creations of Antoine Watteau making music and love in the open air in some enchanted *fête champêtre*. He remembered reading somewhere that with Watteau, as with Mozart, one could learn that sincerity in art does not have to be uncouth and that perfection of form need not imply poverty of content. Then there was Fragonard, a painter of such sensuous indulgence, such glorious decadence that the French Revolution might have been created in order to abolish him. Why, Powerscourt said to himself, did his brain wander off into artistic thoughts when death might be just a corridor away? He listened again. Still no noise.

When he reached the Great Gallery that ran right across one side of the house he lay down on the floor. He inched his way forward until his head just poked round the corner. At least I'm a smaller target this way, he said to himself. Nothing stirred. On the walls the Van Dycks and the Rembrandts, the Hals and the Gainsboroughs kept to their frames. Powerscourt watched the far door with great care. Maybe his opponent was hiding behind there, biding his time before an exploratory shot down the room. Suddenly Powerscourt wondered if the man might not have taken his boots off and crept round to take him from the rear. He looked behind. Only Watteau on guard there, though Powerscourt doubted if those effete-looking lovers and musicians would have been much good in a fight. He wondered what to do. Charge straight down the Great Gallery? Wait? Go back he way he had come? To his left an austere Spanish lady with a fan and a rosary, painted by Velasquez, was taking the register of his sins. Still there was silence at the far end. Suddenly Powerscourt decided to take the initiative. He rose to his feet, took his pistol in his right hand and ran as fast as he could down the gallery. Fifteen feet from the end he fired two shots just past the door. Then he kicked the door as hard as he could and peered round. There was nobody there. Only some Dutch peasants, too pre-occupied with their own world to have any time for his, lounged about on the walls. Powerscourt stood still and locked the Great Gallery door behind him. He was worried about being outflanked to his rear. So where was the man? Had he given up and gone home? Had the nightwatchman arrived? Powerscourt rather doubted it. He feared he had somehow lost the initiative, that his enemy had the upper hand. Even the views of gloomy Dutch churches, peopled with sombre worshippers dressed in black, would not be enough to save him now. There were only two players left in the Wallace Collection game of hide and seek, and death might be the prize for the loser.

Carefully, cautiously, he made his way along the East Galleries. Powerscourt was concentrating so hard on his opponent's whereabouts that he scarcely looked at the paintings at all. He had his gun ready to fire in his right hand. He feared that if he left it in his pocket he might be wounded before he had time to reach it. Maybe his last stand was to be on the landing above the ornamental staircase that led to the ground floor. Maybe he needed some armour. He checked his watch again. If the nightwatchman came at seven he would be here in less than fifteen minutes. You could, he realized, go round and round the Wallace Collection just as easily as you could go round and round the mulberry bush.

As he rushed out – slow progress affording the enemy too much time and too much target – he saw his opponent at last halfway down the stairs, but facing upwards. He too had his pistol in his right hand. Both men fired at almost exactly the same time. Powerscourt's bullet caught the man at the top of the stomach. He turned round and fell down the stairs, rolling slowly down until he came to rest under an ornate fireplace in the hall. A trail of blood followed him down the steps. Powerscourt was hit in the chest and collapsed on the floor, knocking his head against the marble floor with a mighty crack. Neither man made a sound.

Albert Forrest, nightwatchman to the Wallace Collection, liked to reach work a little early. That way he could feel he was ahead of his timetable. He wouldn't be rushed. He was at an age now, Albert, when he liked to take things at his own pace and in his own time. So it was about five minutes to seven when he opened the great door that led into the Wallace Collection from Manchester Square. The blood had continued to flow from the man by the fireplace. It had now spread all over the floor. Albert Forrest took one look and hurried to his tiny office at the back of the Armouries. He did something he had wanted to do ever since they had installed the thing just before the house was opened to the public in 1900. He pulled the alarm. Then he pulled it again. The noise, meant to warn of fire or flood, of Armageddon or the Second Coming, sounded as if it might wake the dead. Even as Albert was making his way back to the front door – that fellow looked pretty dead to Albert, no point in hurrying – Johnny Fitzgerald was coming down the stairs of Number 8 Manchester Square four at a time. He exchanged alarmed looks with Lady Lucy, who was already concerned that Francis had not come home, and rushed across the square. A small crowd was beginning to form outside the front door. The hotel behind seemed to be emptying all its guests out on to the street. Drinkers from the pub across the road were peering in through the doors, glasses in hand. Johnny took one look at the villain in the hall and shot up the stairs, pausing only to apprehend his pistol.

Johnny sprinted to his friend and knelt by his side. Powerscourt was unconscious and he seemed to Johnny to have a most unhealthy colour. Johnny ripped off his own shirt, the finest silk that Jermyn Street could provide, and did what he could to staunch the flow of blood. He put his jacket over Powerscourt to keep him warm and dashed off to Number 8. Lady Lucy was pacing nervously up and down the hall.

'Lady Lucy,' Johnny Fitzgerald panted, 'Francis has been shot. It looks bad. He's at the top of the staircase on the first floor. Can you get Rhys and the footman to improvise a stretcher? I'm going to get a doctor, man we both knew in South Africa, lives round the corner. He's wonderful with wounded people. Don't move Francis, for God's sake, don't move him at all till I get back with the doctor.'

Lady Lucy felt numb, icy cold on receipt of the news. He had come through so much, her Francis, so many campaigns, so many battles, so many dangerous investigations. Now she might lose him. She could not believe it. She refused to believe it. She tried, briefly, to imagine a future without Francis and she knew she could not bear it. Even with all these children, she thought, she would find it intolerable. She pulled her coat tight around her and waited for the doctor.

Johnny Fitzgerald set off at full speed across Manchester Square, over Marylebone High Street and a hundred yards or so up Marylebone Lane before turning left into Bulstrode Street. In his mind's eye he saw not the great hulk of the side of the Wallace Collection or the fashionable hotel opposite, or the shadowy buildings with the lights being lit in their windows. He saw his greatest friend bleeding to death, surrounded not by his friends but by the Old Masters of centuries long past. Even Francis, he thought, with his great love of art, wouldn't want to go like that. Number 16 had the nameplate. Dr Anthony Fraser, it said, universally known during his time in the Army as Dr Tony.

The scene on the landing now resembled one of those melancholy religious paintings showing Christ being taken down from the Cross that might have lined its walls. A bloodied Powerscourt lying unconscious on the ground. Lady Lucy, representing the weeping women, not actually weeping but gazing at her husband and praying with all her strength for his safe recovery. Rhys the butler and Jones the footman, hovering with the stretcher, might have been Roman soldiers perhaps, come for a last look at the one they had called the King of the Jews.

Dr Fraser knelt down by the side of his new patient. He felt Powerscourt's pulse and grimaced slightly. Then he stood up.

'Let me introduce myself. My name is Fraser, usually known as Dr Tony. I knew Lord Powerscourt in South Africa. You must be his wife,' he bowed to Lady Lucy, 'and you must be his staff. We must get your husband on to the stretcher you have managed to bring. Your house is across the square? That will be best for now. I have sent for some nurses.'

They manoeuvred Powerscourt on to the stretcher and the four men took him, rather like a coffin going to its last resting place, Lady Lucy felt, to the big bedroom on the second floor of Number 8 Manchester Square. There was now a fire in the grate. The sheets on the bed had been changed. Extra chairs had been brought in for those on attendant and nursing duty. The doctor examined Powerscourt very closely.

'There is an exit wound here on his back – the bullet must have gone straight through him. And it has narrowly avoided both his heart and his lungs. I shall wait for the nurses before we clean it all up and put on the dressings. In the meantime I will give your husband an injection against the pain.'

Dr Fraser sat with Powerscourt for over an hour, Lady Lucy on the other side of the bed. The doctor, Lady Lucy observed, was a short slim man in his middle thirties whose hair was beginning to recede. He had a prominent nose and very bright eyes. When the nurses arrived, she left them to it and went to order some tea in the drawing room.

'Lady Powerscourt,' the doctor began about a quarter of an hour later, 'we have done what we can to clean the wound. We could have done more but there is always a slight danger to the patient in carrying out over-vigorous measures at this stage. I shall be going back to keep watch for a little while longer when I have finished my tea.'

Lady Lucy looked at him with pleading eyes. Already, she felt reassured by his presence. 'What is your judgement, doctor? Will Francis...' she paused for a moment to fight back the tears, 'pull through?'

'Your husband has received a most serious wound, Lady Powerscourt,' said the doctor. 'I would not hide that from you for a second. I have seen far too many people with similar wounds to his in South Africa. In the case of your husband it's simple. We must keep the wound clean. In time we can give some assistance for it to

229

heal. The room where he lies must be kept clean. No infection can be allowed to get anywhere near him. But he has also sustained a serious blow to the head. I have no idea when he will wake up from his coma, Lady Powerscourt. So much depends on the will, his will to live. If he despairs, he will die. I have seen men die from wounds that are less serious than his and I have seen men recover from wounds that were worse.'

'What can we do, Dr Tony? Everybody in this house wants Francis alive.' The thought of the twins with no father struck Lady Lucy yet again and she had to turn away for a moment.

'I believe there is a great deal you can do, Lady Powerscourt, believe me. Many of my colleagues would have taken your husband to hospital. I thought of that and rejected it. If he had gone to hospital he would have been placed in a ward full of people as seriously injured as he is, or worse. Death would call every day if not every hour and constantly reduce the numbers. Here your husband is surrounded by love and his loved ones. I think we should keep him quiet tomorrow and the next day but after that your children should go and talk to him, whether he is awake or not. Maybe they could read to him. Other people could read to him, talk to him. The more activity, the better I believe it will be for your husband. If all is quiet people could think they have gone to that eternal silence before their time is due.'

'So there is hope, doctor?' Lady Lucy was looking at him very closely.

'Oh yes, Lady Powerscourt. Of course there's hope. Let us not forget that. Let us never forget that. There is always hope.'

Lady Lucy felt a small, but definite, onset not of hope but of resolve, of determination. Maybe it was courage. She thought of her love for Francis, she thought of all her ancestors who had marched and sailed and fought and died for their country across the centuries. Maybe some small portion of their bravery would come to help her in her ordeal. If she was not brave, she knew, Francis would surely die.

Those first two days seemed to most of the inhabitants of 8 Manchester Square to be like a dream. Thomas and Olivia refused to believe their father was seriously ill until Lady Lucy took them in to see him. Thomas turned white and stared at his father for a very long time. Olivia rushed off to her room to pray for her Papa's recovery. Dr Tony came at regular intervals. The nurses changed over every eight hours, keeping endless watch over their patient, making him comfortable, washing his face, taking his pulse, entering their findings into a large black notebook. Lady Lucy kept vigil when she could. She had made a private arrangement with Johnny that one of them should be awake when the other was asleep and vice versa. The staff tiptoed about, popping in every now and then to look at Powerscourt. The flowers began arriving late the first morning. William Burke sent an enormous bunch. Lady Lucy thought how amused Francis would have been as the bouquets began arriving from her relations, dozens and dozens of them, enough to open a bloody flower shop, she could hear him saying. Soon a whole wall in the Powerscourt bedroom was lined with flowers. Only the twins were immune to the change of lifestyle, Lady Lucy convinced that it would take the Second Coming to make the slightest dent in Nurse Mary Muriel's routine.

On the third day the atmosphere in the sick room was very different. Gone was the silence that had held the sick bay in its grip, broken only by the whispered conclaves between the nurses and Dr Tony. For a good section of the morning the twins were now placed on chairs close to the bed in their Moses baskets. Occasional wails punctuated the morning conversations between Dr Tony and the nurses. They took great interest in the twins, the nurses, peering into their faces and talking a great variety of nonsense to them. Thomas came in his most grown-up mode and read to Powerscourt from the sports section of the newspapers. Olivia tried to make up stories of her own for him. As these were largely based on stories her father had invented for her, it was, as Lady Lucy said, rather like hearing the brain of Francis come back in the voice of Olivia. When they got tired of stories, the children would talk to him, saying whatever came into their heads usually, and the nurses found that even more captivating than looking into the faces of the twins.

Just before lunch Detective Chief Inspector Beecham arrived. He had felt he would be intruding if he called on the Powerscourt household. Only after he had met Edward and Sarah in front of Queen's Inn and learned that they were going to call at 8 Manchester Square very soon, did he change his mind.

'Lady Powerscourt, Johnny Fitzgerald, how is Lord Powerscourt? Is he making good progress?'

Johnny Fitzgerald and Lady Lucy looked at each other.

'He's not getting any better, Chief Inspector,' said Lady Lucy, 'but he's not getting any worse.'

'I would like to see him and pay my respects, before I leave, if I may, Lady Powerscourt. This has been truly terrible for you all. I do have some fresh intelligence which fills in some of the final details of the case your husband so ably solved, Lady Powerscourt. But I would not want to keep you from your duties here.'

Lady Lucy smiled. 'It sounds to me, Chief Inspector, as though Francis would want to hear your news at some point quite soon after he recovers consciousness.' Beecham thought he could hear a repressed 'if' in that last sentence.

'I shall be brief,' he said. 'Let me begin with the villain who shot your husband.'

'The fellow at the bottom of the stairs?' asked Johnny.

'The same, Johnny. Lord Powerscourt is an excellent shot but his bullet landed a couple of inches too low. Had it been a fraction higher, the bullet would have killed him. It nearly did for him, the rogue is still in hospital. But he is alive.'

'Has he spoken?' said Johnny. 'Has he told you what was going on, Chief Inspector?'

'He certainly has. I regret to say I tricked him into making a confession he might not have made otherwise.'

'How was that?' asked Johnny.

'I didn't get to see him until early this morning. The man was unconscious in the Marylebone Hospital round the corner from here. The Hippocratic oath is a wonderful thing but I don't think you receive the fastest treatment in the world if you're brought in as an attempted murderer. Anyway, I told him he had half an hour left to live and that he should speak up at once. It wasn't true, of course, but he wasn't to know that. It seems he had a very religious education from his mother when he was little. He began muttering bits of prayers and hymns at me. I thought, in for a penny, in for a pound, so I told him St Peter would be pleased with him if he told the truth before his departure from this vale of tears. So he did, or I think he did.'

The Chief Inspector pulled a notebook out of his pocket and checked a couple of entries halfway through.

'It seems Somerville defended him some years ago on a charge of grievous bodily harm. Tompkins, Dennis Tompkins, that's the fellow's name, admitted the other man had been beaten almost to a pulp. Sentence likely to be ten years minimum, probably more. But Somerville gets him off, Tompkins is pathetically grateful, says he would do anything for Somerville as a result. Three weeks ago he gets a note from Somerville asking Tompkins to meet him in the gardens of Hampton Court. Bloody enormous grounds they are, as you know, my lady, you could plot anything in there without anybody being the wiser. Anyway, Somerville gives him an envelope with five hundred pounds in Treasury notes. Says there's another five hundred when the job's done. The job is to kill Lord Powerscourt, description and address to be supplied. Somerville told Tompkins Lord Powerscourt was coming to see him at the Inn three days ago. He followed him from there to the Wallace Collection. Tompkins said it was pure chance they both got locked in there together. He had no idea what the building was, he was only planning to see where Powerscourt lived and make his attempt later.'

'That would explain the funny looks and the whispers I was getting about Francis when I went to check out the underworld,' said Johnny. 'Did he say why Somerville wanted Francis dead?'

'Somerville had explained some of it, but brother Tompkins didn't remember it very well. And, by this time, on my own timetable, I'd only six minutes left before he was due to pop off. Brother Tompkins was probably thinking his time was nearly up too. He kept looking at his watch. I've thought about it since and this is what I think Tompkins meant. Somerville was forced to invite Lord Powerscourt in to investigate the murders by the other benchers. But I think he was also the man who opposed appointing Lord Powerscourt at that first meeting. I imagine he felt he might be caught out. But what really rattled him was when no suspects were hauled off to jail. He thought Newton would be arrested. Then he thought somebody else must be picked up. When they weren't he felt he must have been rumbled so the man who was about to expose him had to go.'

'So what's going to happen to this Tompkins person?' asked Lady Lucy. 'Will he have to stand trial? And that horrible Somerville, will he be put in the dock as well?'

'When Tompkins is recovered, he will have to stand trial,' replied the Chief Inspector. 'Mr Somerville, well, he may be on trial somewhere else, but he won't be attending any trials down here. This is the other piece of information I am sure your husband would wish to know. We had to let Somerville out on the most enormous bail after twenty-four hours. You will recall that Maxwell Kirk, the barrister at the head of Dauntsey's chambers, was going to address a meeting of protest of all the barristers in Queen's Inn. Somerville tried to prevent it but failed. The barristers were incandescent with rage at what had been happening about the money. Edward said I was to mention this point in particular, Lady Powerscourt. He said your husband would have enjoyed it hugely. They decide, these lawyers, to pass a vote of no confidence in Somerville. Just one sentence was all they needed. According to Edward, a roomful of monkeys with typewriters would have produced it quicker. It took them fifty-five minutes to agree the wording and even then there were six different caveats on the final version. So the Petition of Right, as one wag called it, is sent off to Somerville. It must have been terrible for him, total public humiliation at the hands of his peers. At any rate, when the servant goes into his rooms yesterday morning, there was Somerville slumped at his desk. The vote of censure was in front of him. The pistol was by his side. He'd blown his brains out.'

There was a brief silence. 'There are just two other things I'm sure your husband would like to know, Lady Powerscourt. The man Porchester Newton has turned up again. He came back about three o'clock in the afternoon on the day of the shooting. Said he'd been fishing in South Wales. We asked the local police to check it out and it was all true. And John Bassett, the old Financial Steward – it's been confirmed that he died of natural causes.'

'I'm sure my husband will be most interested to hear all this news, Chief Inspector,' said Lady Lucy, upset far more than she could have imagined by this new death. 'And now perhaps you would like to come and see him and talk to him before you have to leave. The doctor is very keen people should talk to him.'

On this day too, other visitors began to arrive. There were relations, always too sombre in their appearance and too gloomy in their assessments. 'They look,' Johnny Fitzgerald observed sourly to Lady Lucy, 'as if they've decided he's dead already and are trying to work out what to wear for the funeral.' But some of them had been involved in earlier Powerscourt investigations. Patrick Butler, the young editor of the local newspaper in the cathedral city of Compton in the West Country, called late in the afternoon. He had been very closely involved in the Powerscourt investigation into the mysterious deaths in the cathedral the year before. He gave Lady Lucy an enormous kiss and a huge bunch of flowers. She took him straight in to see her husband and told him the details of the shooting. Compton Saviour Shot in Legal Feud was the headline that flashed through his newspaper brain. Patrick Butler thought in headlines just as farmers think of the seasons and the weather. He always had. The young Patrick sensed that beneath the surface optimism, the good cheer and the impeccable manners reserved for visitors in this politest of households, despair was probably not very far away.

'I saw him, Lady Lucy,' he began with a smile, 'the morning after those bastards tried to kill him with all that falling masonry in the cathedral. Do you remember? Of course you do. Well, he looks to me very like he did then. He pulled round on that occasion and I'm sure he will this time.'

He stopped talking suddenly. Lady Lucy remembered that this was a fairly rare occurrence and waited for what was coming next. They were sitting side by side by the edge of Powerscourt's bed. Patrick Butler reached out to take her hand.

'I'll tell you what we'll do, Lady Powerscourt, with your permission.' A whole front page of his paper, the *Grafton Mercury*, was flashing through his brain as fast as the paper would come off the presses. A long article on Powerscourt's role in the salvation of Compton the previous year. A brief description of his present difficulties. A prayer for his recovery from the Dean, maybe even the Bishop. 'We'll give the whole front page of the next edition of the *Grafton Mercury* over to Lord Powerscourt! An account of his role as the Saviour of Compton. A brief summary of his current predicament. And a prayer from the Dean or the Bishop! I'm great pals now with the new Dean, Lady Powerscourt. He says I'm the only person in the city of Compton who can tell him the whole truth about what went on before. Tell you what, even better, I'll get the Dean to organize a service of prayer for Lord Powerscourt's recovery. The whole of Compton will turn up and pray he gets better. That's bound to help!'

Lady Lucy remembered Patrick's wife's description of him as being rather like a puppy. He hadn't changed.

'That would be very kind, Patrick,' she said, smiling at her editor. 'Francis and I were very fond of Compton. But tell me, how is Anne and what brings you to London at this time?'

Patrick Butler blushed. 'Anne is well, Lady Powerscourt. She is expecting our first child in August.' He made a close inspection of the nearer twin at this point as if intent on getting some practice in child care early on. 'And I,' he was going rather red at this point, 'I have been asked to London for an interview about a position on

235

The Times. I should know in three or four days if I have been accepted.'

'That's wonderful news, Patrick,' said Lady Lucy, feeling, as she often did with Patrick, like an elderly aunt with her favourite nephew. 'It would be splendid to have you and Anne in London.'

'I must flee, Lady Powerscourt,' said Patrick, pulling a reporter's notebook from his pocket, 'or I shall miss my train. Please give my very best love and wishes to your husband. I shall write part of the front page on the train!' He took a last sad look at Powerscourt as he left the room. Patrick Butler had tried his best to be cheerful, to keep up the spirits of the little band on the second floor of 8 Manchester Square. But anybody watching him set off up Marylebone High Street towards Baker Street station would have seen that his eyes were filled with tears.

On the next day Dr Tony came early in the morning. He went through the usual routines with his patient and had a long conference with the nurse on duty. Then he went downstairs to talk to Lady Lucy.

'What news, Dr Tony?' she asked him with a smile.

'Some of the time, Lady Powerscourt, we doctors swing between very different emotions. At eleven we may have to tell some unfortunate person that there is no hope, their time is almost gone. At twelve we may be in the fortunate position of having to tell some other luckier soul that the treatment has worked, that they are cured and may well live for another thirty years.' He watched Lady Lucy's face swing between hope and despair as he spoke. The lights were going on and off in her eyes. Perhaps that was a mistake, he said to himself, and hurried on.

'Lord Powerscourt is much the same as he has been since he was shot, more or less. I can detect little change in him today from yesterday, Lady Powerscourt. I shall return after lunch to see him again.'

'Hope?' said Lady Lucy, very quietly.

'As I said before,' briefly he took her hand, 'there is always hope. You must not give up. You must not let your household give up. I can only guess how difficult it must be for you all. But, please, please, hope, hope for your husband, hope for your children, hope for yourself.'

Thomas and Olivia had decided on a different tactic for their papa on this day. They were going to read to him together, they told Lady

236

Lucy over breakfast, well, not exactly together because Olivia wasn't a great reader yet while Thomas was quite proficient by now. But they were going to read *Treasure Island*, a work their father had often read to them. Thomas was to do most of the reading. Olivia had a number of tasks to perform. She had some paper and a pair of scissors and pens of different colours as she had to make a black spot for Blind Pew to press into the palms of his victims as he did in the story. She had to join in the reading every time the book said 'Fifteen Men on a Dead Man's Chest, Yo ho ho and a bottle of rum' or the longer version with the two extra lines 'Drink and the Devil Had Done for the Rest, Yo ho ho and a bottle of rum.' The children had agreed upstairs that they should be able to make enough noise with this chorus to wake their father, if not the persons at rest in the nearest graveyard.

In the end the nurse put them off. Nurse Winifred was one of the kindest people alive and loved children of every age. But her appearance, what Olivia privately thought of as that sea of starched white at the front of her, put you off if you were only six years old.

There was one very important visitor late that afternoon. Shortly after five o'clock a beautifully dressed man of about forty years presented himself at the door. He had an enormous bunch of flowers. 'They're from Lord Salisbury's Hatfield greenhouses, Lady Powerscourt. The Prime Minister was most insistent I should deliver them in person.'

The impeccable suit bowed. Inside it was Schomberg McDonnell, Private Secretary to Prime Minister Salisbury, now, so the gossip said, nearing the end of his tenure at Number 10 Downing Street. Powerscourt had taken his orders twice before, once in saving the City of London from a terrible plot, and on the second occasion taking up, at Salisbury's request, the position of Head of Army Intelligence in the war in South Africa. Truly, the great world had come to pay its respects to Francis Powerscourt in his hour of need in Manchester Square.

McDonnell listened gravely to Lady Lucy's account of her husband's situation. 'I would stay longer if I could but I have to return to the Prime Minister, Lady Powerscourt. I have often brought your husband messages from Lord Salisbury in the past. I have another one for him today. Lord Salisbury says that he is weary of office, and, between ourselves, expects to leave it soon. He does not expect to live very long in retirement. But his message to Lord Powerscourt is very clear. He is damned if he is going to have to

237

attend Powerscourt's funeral. He expects, nay, he orders that Powerscourt should attend his, whenever that may be. Your husband, Lady Powerscourt, in the Prime Minister's words, is under government orders to recover.'

Johnny Fitzgerald took the last watch that day. The children were asleep. He hoped Lady Lucy was too. He walked up and down the room for a long time, lost in the memories of his and Powerscourt's lives together. They had been to so many places after leaving Ireland and had shared so many adventures. He thought of Lady Lucy and the enormous strain she must be under. Johnny had seen how, more than ever now, all the threads of this house and of Francis's life ran through her hands. Lady Lucy had to determine the altered routines of the house with the cook and the domestic staff. She had to liaise with the nurses and with the frequent presence of Dr Tony, who demanded total attention when he came. She had to look after the two oldest children who stitched on, at her instructions, he suspected, a mask of cheer and optimism about their father's chances of recovery during the day. At night, he knew, the hope deserted them and Thomas and Olivia fled to weep in their mother's bed. Johnny had heard them crying from two floors further up the night before. And all the time, reassuring her children, organizing her household, welcoming the visitors and ordering yet more tea, Lady Lucy must, Johnny felt sure, have her own private nightmares. Would Francis pull through? Could she imagine life without him? How would the children cope? And this worry above all, he was sure, how would the twins, so tiny and so young, cope with life without their father?

At about half past eleven Johnny sat down by the side of the bed. He began telling his friend stories about the officers and men they had known in India, the eccentric, the mad, the brave, the cowards, the ones who liked the Indians, the ones who despised Indians, the very occasional ones who went completely native. Most of these stories contained jokes, some of them very good jokes. But the laughter Johnny hoped for did not come. As the church clock rang the midnight hour Lord Francis Powerscourt was still in a coma, drifting uncertainly between life and death.

17

Edward and Sarah came round to Manchester Square in the middle of the fifth afternoon. They brought fresh news of the Inn. There had been little sadness over the suicide of Barton Somerville, Edward reported. The remaining benchers, on the instigation of Maxwell Kirk, had all resigned to mark their failure to rein in the previous Treasurer. There had, Edward and Sarah quickly realized, been considerable progress in the story of *Treasure Island* in the sick room. Olivia had quickly mastered the production of Black Spots, supposed to bring bad luck to those holding them, and had pressed one into the palm of virtually every member of the household. Edward himself had collected two already and the unfortunate butler was marked with four of the things. Edward was able to bring another dimension to the story. While Sarah took over the job of reading *Treasure Island*, Edward, with the aid of some elastic, some very long socks and some string, taught the children how to tie one leg up so the foot was attached to the thigh. Two retired broom handles were discovered in the pantry and cut to the appropriate sizes for Thomas and Olivia. With the leg tied up and the broom acting as a crutch they could each pretend to be Long John Silver thumping his way across the boards of their parents' bedroom that was really the upper deck of the *Hispaniola* sailing across the oceans to the fabulous island of treasure. Edward regretted that there were no parrots available but he suggested they ask Johnny Fitzgerald to say 'Pieces of eight' in his best parrot voice when he next appeared. The only problem in acting out the role of a handicapped pirate in quest of treasure was that it was much more difficult to walk with the broomstick than you might have imagined, even if you were small and supple. The two children kept falling over and giggled helplessly on the floor until some kind person helped them up. If there hadn't been anybody else around to assist them, Thomas told the assembled company, he and Olivia would be left there until the end of time. Edward assured the children that there was a section of the book, he couldn't remember exactly which chapter, where the author says it took Long John Silver himself over a year to learn how to walk properly with his crutch. For a brief quarter of an hour the children forgot about their sick father. Then the doctor came in for his afternoon visit, accompanied by Lady Lucy. The children disappeared upstairs. Edward took Sarah by the hand and led her out into Manchester Square.

'Where are we going, Edward? Are we going to the Wallace Collection to see where Lord Powerscourt was shot?'

'We are going to the Wallace Collection, Sarah,' said Edward, as he led her up the drive, 'but we are not going to the scene of the shooting. I want to take you to look at a painting on the second floor, if I may.'

They walked up the grand staircase where Powerscourt had been shot. They came to one of the smaller rooms on the first floor. High up on the wall by a window was a mythological painting about three feet square. In front of an Arcadian landscape with a brooding sky of dark clouds, it showed the Four Seasons, facing outwards, hand in hand in a stately dance. Autumn, at the rear of the painting, had dry leaves in her hair and represented Bacchus, the God of wine. To the right of Bacchus was Winter with her hair in a cloth to keep out the cold, then Spring, her hair braided like ears of corn, and Summer, linked to Spring on her left and Autumn on her right. The picture was framed on the right by a block of stone that might mark the site of someone's grave and on the left by a statue showing the youthful and mature Bacchus with a garland. At the bottom edges of the painting two putti played with an hourglass each. The musical accompaniment was provided by Saturn, the god of time, playing on his lyre, and in the clouds above, Apollo, the sun god, drove his chariot across the sky to create the day.

'It's called *A Dance to the Music of Time,*' said Edward, looking closely at Apollo's companions in the clouds. 'It's by a Frenchman called Nicolas Poussin. He was always doing stuff like this,' Edward went on airily, 'mythological scenes, idealized landscapes, philosophical messages tied up with the poetry of Ovid or somebody like that. I think he painted some of them for a cardinal or some other grand fellow in Rome.'

Sarah was wondering why Edward had brought her here to see it. It was certainly beautiful but there must be a reason. 'What does it mean?' she said.

'Well,' said Edward, 'originally it had to do with the myth of Jupiter's gift of Bacchus, god of wine, to the world after the Seasons complained about the harshness of human life. It could mean lots of things. It could mean we should all be thankful not just for the gift of wine but for the stately order of the seasons which hold our lives in the pattern of their dance. I don't think these Seasons are dancing very fast, you see. Time is going round at a fairly steady rate. The infants with the hourglasses, of course, represent the passing of time, the vanity of human aspirations, the fact that everything is going to end.'

'You sound as if you think it's a sad painting, Edward,' said Sarah, taking his hand.

'No, I don't think it's sad,' he said, his eyes locked now on Saturn with his lyre. 'These Seasons in a way are all trapped in their dance, like the characters in Keats' 'Ode to a Grecian Urn' whose happy melodist, like Saturn here, unwearied, is forever piping songs forever new. They could go faster but the painter won't allow it. They could change places but Poussin won't allow that either. If you were inside the circle, you wouldn't be able to get out. Maybe, for the moments we look at the painting, we're trapped too, trapped in the contemplation of our own mortality.'

'You're sounding very philosophical today, Edward. Do you think it's the influence of *Treasure Island*?'

'No,' said Edward laughing. 'It just made me think about time and time passing, Sarah. What's happening over there in the square also makes you think of time passing. You can't help it.' You can't put it off much longer, Edward said to himself. 'You think time doesn't affect you. People talk about having all the time in the world. They don't. We don't. It's going away from us constantly, like the sand in those hourglasses. Eventually time, our time, quite literally, is going to run out.'

Suddenly Sarah thought she understood what was going on, the visit to the painting, the philosophical musings, the digressions into the history of art.

'So, you see, Sarah,' Edward went on, unaware that he had been rumbled, 'I have been thinking that sometimes we must seize time in the way people talk about seizing the day. We can't put things off till another day or week or month. Delay is futile. We must grasp the moment. Sarah, will you marry me?'

241

The question came on Sarah very unexpectedly. She knew it was coming but she hadn't expected it to pop out so suddenly. Maybe Edward hadn't intended it either. Maybe Time had seized Edward rather than the other way round. She squeezed his hand very tight.

'Of course I'll marry you, Edward,' she said. 'What took you so long? I thought you'd never ask.'

Lady Lucy was keeping watch in the hour before midnight. The nurse had tiptoed out of the room, saying she would be waiting outside on the stairs. This, Lady Lucy realized, was the first time she had been alone with Francis since he was shot. All day she had been seeing the same scene. She was at a funeral. She was burying another husband. Like the first one, this funeral had an honour guard of military colleagues, jackets pressed, trousers immaculate, clouds and sky visible in the burnished toecaps of their boots, polished swords raised in unison to give the last salute. By the graveside she had a child holding each of her hands as if their hearts would break. The Dead March from Handel's *Saul* echoed round her head to accompany these pictures. She remembered the military bands playing it as Victoria's funeral cortège had made its melancholy way through the streets of a mourning London.

She was sitting on the edge of the bed, holding her husband's hand. She remembered him suddenly at the National Gallery where he had taken her on their first outing and she had talked about Turner's *The Fighting Temeraire*. She remembered him talking to the twins only the week before, walking them in his arms up and down the drawing room, that soft voice telling the latest of his children about the house he came from in Ireland, and the blue colour of the mountains and the great fountain at the bottom of the steps. She started to cry. She hadn't let herself cry very much in case it upset the children but now there was nobody here, only Francis, and he couldn't hear and he couldn't see and she might never hear his voice again. She was racked by sobs, wondering if he knew how much she loved him, how happy he had made her, how her whole life with him had been illuminated by the power of his love for her.

'Oh Francis,' she whispered to him, 'my poor darling. I love you so much. Please come back. I can't bear it when you're not here.' Suddenly she remembered saying 'Please come back' to him before, at that terrible early morning parting at the railway station when he went off to the Boer War. Day after day, she remembered, there had been notices of the fallen in the newspapers, columns of names of the dead that seemed to grow longer every month. But Francis had survived all that. He had come home without a scratch. Now this investigation into an Inn of Court had left him virtually dead. She made a resolution there at a quarter to midnight on the fourth day of her husband's illness. When he was better she was going to take him away somewhere warm, Amalfi perhaps or Positano, where they could look at the spectacular views and the deep blue sea. She would give him a beaker full of the warm south, with beaded bubbles winking at the brim. And when he was better, not before, she was going to ask him to give up investigating for ever. No more heaps of masonry falling on him in cathedral naves. No more maniacs tracking him through the elegant galleries of the Wallace Collection. No more desperate races down the mountain roads of Corsica with the bullets whining off the rocks. No more butchered bodies dumped in the fountains of Perugia. Nobody could be expected to put up with all that any more. She certainly couldn't. Then, as she looked at that beloved face, which seemed now to be turning slightly grey, she started weeping uncontrollably again. For she might never have the chance to take Francis off to the Italian sunshine and the winding streets of Positano. He might be dead before she had the chance to take him there. He might die tomorrow. He might die tonight.

Somewhere above her she heard a child weeping. It's Olivia, she thought, come for her midnight cry. She began to compose herself. As she trudged slowly off to comfort her weeping daughter, she tried to steady herself with the words of Dr Tony: 'Of course there's hope. Let us not forget that. Let us never forget that. There is always hope.'

Next morning the children continued their progress through *Treasure Island*, Olivia, possibly because she wasn't reading, becoming much better at hopping round the room on her crutch broomstick. If she were allowed outside with it, Johnny Fitzgerald felt sure, she would begin hurling it at her enemies like Long John Silver himself. Just after lunch Edward and Sarah arrived and their engagement was toasted in champagne. Edward apologized for daring to bring any glimmer of happiness into such a tragic household and was immediately told to shut up by Johnny Fitzgerald. Olivia wanted to know what an engagement was. She thought gauges had something to do with trains. She remembered a long story her father had told her

243

once which involved, for some reason, train gauges. Were Edward and Sarah going on a train? If so, could she come too? Like her father, she was very fond of trains. When all was explained to her Olivia decided that she had better not ask any more questions. She thought now it would be like the twins' christening all over again but with Edward and Sarah having to put their heads in the font.

After lunch Johnny Fitzgerald ordered a change in the reading matter for Francis. Lady Lucy and he, Johnny informed the company, were going to read Tennyson. Tennyson, after all, had been one of Francis's favourite poets. Johnny did not think it wise to mention it, but he remembered Francis saying years ago in India that he would like someone to read the last section of the poem he, Johnny, was going to read at his, Powerscourt's, graveside after his funeral. And, Johnny remembered, it was a poem Francis knew off by heart.

Lady Lucy gave a spirited rendering of 'The Lady of Shalott', the children and the nurse enchanted by the rhythm and the romance of the story. Then Johnny began 'Ulysses', a poem about the Greek warrior hero who finally comes home to his island of Ithaca after twenty years of war and wandering. Soon he is bored, he cannot rest from travel.

> 'Much have I seen and known; cities of men
> And manners, climates, councils, governments,
> Myself not least, but honoured of them all;
> And drunk delight of battle with my peers,
> Far on the ringing plains of windy Troy.'

The twins were asleep beside the bed. Edward and Sarah were sitting beside the flowers. Lady Lucy was by her husband's side and Thomas and Olivia were on the opposite side of the bed. Thomas remembered his father telling him stories about Troy, about Achilles sulking in his tent, about the body of Hector being dragged round the city walls, about the wooden horse that finally ended the war. He looked at his father's face and began to cry silently. Only the nurse noticed the tears running slowly down his cheeks and slipped him an enormous handkerchief when nobody else was looking. Johnny was thinking as he read of the various Indian councils and the even stranger Indian governments he and Francis had seen. He went on.

> 'I am a part of all that I have met;
> Yet all experience is an arch wherethrough

244

Gleams that untravell'd world, whose margin fades
For ever and for ever when I move.
How dull it is to pause, to make an end,
To rust unburnished, not to shine in use!'

Lady Lucy suddenly wondered if her question to Francis in
Positano would be fair. How dull he would find it to make an end
to detection, to give up what had become his career since he left the
Army for what he might call a woman's whim. No, she corrected
herself, casting a guilty glance at her husband, he would never say
that to her. But he might think it. He would hate it, Francis, rusting
unburnished. Had she the right to ask him? Johnny Fitzgerald
remembered that there was a tricky passage coming up about the
passing of Ulysses' life: 'of life to me little remains; but every hour
is saved from that eternal silence.' That, he felt sure, would not seem
appropriate in these circumstances. Nor would the lines about
handing control over Ithaca to his son Telemachus. That might set
Thomas off. So he moved on, hoping nobody would notice.

'There lies the port; the vessel puffs her sail:
There gloom the dark broad seas.'

It was at this point that they heard a low muttering noise from the
bed, like thunder far away. There was a faint stirring of the
bedclothes as if Powerscourt was wriggling about in his sleep.
Johnny Fitzgerald read on. Edward and Sarah left their chairs and
tiptoed over to take a closer look. Olivia had grabbed hold of
Thomas's arm and wasn't going to let go.

'My mariners,
Souls that have toiled, and wrought, and thought with me –
That ever with a welcome frolic took
The thunder and the sunshine, and opposed
Free hearts, free foreheads –'

During this passage the murmuring turned into a recognizable
voice. The voice was weak but it was definitely Powerscourt's and
he was speaking the words of Tennyson's poem in unison with
Johnny Fitzgerald. Lady Lucy began to cry. Thomas was squeezing
the bedclothes in disbelief. Olivia stared at her father as if she had
never seen a male person before. On they went, the two friends,

Powerscourt and Fitzgerald, that had ever with a welcome frolic taken the thunder and the sunshine so many times together in so many different parts of the world in days gone by.

> '. . . you and I are old,
> Old age hath yet his honour and his toil;
> Death closes all: but something ere the end,
> Some work of noble note, may yet be done,
> Not unbecoming men that strove with Gods.'

We're not finished yet, Francis and I, Johnny Fitzgerald said to himself. He paused as if Powerscourt's return from the dead should be properly celebrated.

'Don't stop, Johnny, please don't stop.' Lady Lucy felt the thread, the skein of her husband's life was tied up with the poem, that they had to continue together, she was certain of it. Powerscourt's voice was almost normal now. The nurse and Lady Lucy had raised him to a semi-sitting position. He smiled weakly at the people around him as if he had just come back from an afternoon nap.

> 'The lights begin to twinkle from the rocks:
> The long day wanes: the slow moon climbs: the deep
> Moans round with many voices. Come, my friends,
> 'Tis not too late to seek a newer world.'

If the return of Powerscourt's voice was the first miracle of this extraordinary afternoon, the second was just about to begin. Master Christopher Powerscourt, youngest of all the Powerscourts, was waking up in his Moses basket.

> 'Push off, and sitting well in order smite
> The sounding furrows; for my purpose holds
> To sail beyond the sunset, and the baths
> Of all the western stars, until I die.'

Christopher knew that voice. He had been listening to it nearly every day of his life, except for the last four or five. He liked the voice. He raised a small hand. Then he smiled at his father. It was a beautiful smile. It lasted a long time. It was the first time Christopher had smiled at anyone in his life. Lady Lucy and Thomas and Olivia all saw it, those deep blue eyes lit up, the great beam going right

246

across his tiny face, his look of intense happiness. Powerscourt began to cry. Tears of joy were running down his face until he saw that his twin son might follow his example and start crying too.

The poem went on. There was now a ring of hands, Edward to Sarah to Johnny Fitzgerald across to the nurse, weeping uncontrollably, to Lady Lucy, to Powerscourt, to Olivia and Thomas and a last link to Christopher in his basket. A circle of love, with words by Alfred Lord Tennyson.

'It may that the gulfs will wash us down:
It may be we shall touch the Happy Isles,
And see the great Achilles, whom we knew.'

Christopher smiled once more, this time at his mother. He seemed to like smiling. Maybe he was going to be a happy child. Everybody round the bed felt certain that Powerscourt had turned the corner, that he wasn't going to die. A very faint colour was beginning to return to his cheeks. Lady Lucy felt incredibly tired suddenly as she looked at her Francis. She wondered if she would have the courage to ask him to give up investigating for ever when they went to Positano. Edward was thinking of the terrible ordeal Powerscourt had gone through in solving a couple of murders in an Inn of Court. Sarah supposed she would have to describe this extraordinary scene to her mother, the return of Lazarus Powerscourt, Powerscourt Redux, helped on his journey back to life by a beautiful first smile from his baby boy. Casting his eyes down to the end of the poem, Johnny Fitzgerald knew how right Lady Lucy had been to insist on his reading to the very end of 'Ulysses'. For these last lines could be Powerscourt's epitaph, not an epitaph for him now, but one that would serve so well when his life had run its natural course. Johnny let his oldest and closest friend say the final words on his own, Lord Francis Powerscourt's voice firm now, his two sons holding hands, his own hands locked with those of his wife and his daughter.

'Though much is taken, much abides; and though
We are not now that strength which in old days
Moved earth and heaven; that which we are, we are;
One equal temper of heroic hearts,
Made weak by time and fate, but strong in will
To strive, to seek, to find, and not to yield.'